Forgotten Places

A Short Story Collection

Forgotten Places

Volume One:
The Void & Beyond

Short Stories
By
Colin Walker

For Rachel and Julian

Table of Contents

Introduction

As far back as I can remember, I've been fascinated with monsters and the macabre. I don't know what triggered this mania, but it's sort of always been there. Even on those nights when I cowered under my sheets, dreading an alien abduction or squeezing my eyes shut to avoid the jumping ghosts on the Haunted Mansion, I still gravitated towards these things — these creatures of the night.

An older kid I went to school with and who lived down the block from me always had me over for sessions of *Crossfire*, *The Legend of Zelda: A Link to the Past*, or watching the Simpsons *Treehouse of Horror* episodes on VHS. A visit to this friend's house for me was not complete unless I got to lie on the living room floor for a time, flipping through a big book his family had on movie monsters. I was obsessed with the tome, drinking in the dark and moody German Expressionist look of the Gollum and dazzling at the rich, vibrant hues of the Hammer Horror creatures and the accompanying buckets of blood. For little me, Ray Harryhausen was more than a special effect guru; he was a freakin' God, bringing such incredible creations to life on the screen.

That being said, Halloween was never just a holiday; it was a holy day. I spent the months leading up to October 31st planning my grisly and horrific costumes, picking out the right makeup, prosthetics, teeth, masks, and such. While many have their Sunday best for church, I had my All Hallows Eve best and I loved it. With every mask I bought, I had to create an elaborate story about the monster. Monsters were never just something to fear. For me, they were complex, searching, wanting, looking for as much meaning and purpose in this world as the tiny child obsessed with them.

As I grew older, I grew into an avid reader, gobbling up the Goosebumps and Fear Street books as quickly as they were turned out. I found my happy place between the volumes of *Scary Stories to Tell in the Dark* and countless books filled with ghost stories and goblins. This was a wonderful time, ripe with literary fruit for me to pick and devour and savor. This was also around the time my parents, normally not ones to let me indulge in horror movies, did indulge me by renting *Alien*. We watched that film as a family and it thrilled me, not only the movie, but that my parents were participating in something I immediately adored. As obsessed as I was with Star Wars (both then and now), I suddenly had new films to hold up as some of my all-time favorites: *Alien, Psycho, Evil Dead 2: Dead by Dawn.*

In high school, I was surprised and excited to meet other kids, my age, with the same love of horror. In my film class, we would critique and guide each other on our film projects — mostly slasher films in the vein (pun intended) of *Halloween, Scream,* or *Friday the 13th.* While slasher flicks never grabbed me in the same way, I still gravitated towards the tales of monsters and the fantastical and paranormal. The ideas of madness brought on by those trying to ascertain the impossible to comprehend or understand fascinated me. Problematic authors such as H.P. Lovecraft (let's not beat about the bush: the man was an open fan of White Supremacy) added another layer to my love of monsters — now they could be beyond imagination and as such, so utterly terrifying that they attacked with their mere presence before letting loose with their claws or fangs.

All of this is just to prepare you for the collection of tales you now hold in your hands, gentle reader. These stories have been compiled over the last few years into a collection divided into two parts: The Void and The Beyond. While none of these stories are connected, I began to see patterns emerging within some of my writings. The first five tales all deal with the Lovecraftian terror and unknown depths of the void — something beyond the emptiness and endlessness of outer space — something intangible but terrifying to behold, nonetheless.

The rest of the collection is more or less a sort of grab-bag of stories, which, while some may deal with similar themes, are all tales of monsters, murder, and more. These stories deal with fears and anxieties that I carry with me daily, but in a form more palatable and enticing for you all to read and hopefully enjoy.

If this first volume of tales is successful, I do hope to continue with a second volume in the near future. There may also be plans around the digital front as well. But don't fret, my gentle readers; those plans don't hinge on you and your support so much as they hinge on me and my ability to deliver the best possible tale that I can to you.

INTRODUCTION

A final warning: these tales are not for the squeamish — these tales contain blood (buckets in some instances), violence, and gore. Why sugar-coat something that was never meant to be sugar-coated in the first place? This isn't a box of Nerds candy; it's a bag of Atomic Fireballs.

If this warning hasn't turned you away yet, then I suggest that you turn down the lights, fire up your favorite playlist of spooky Halloween sounds, and prepare to explore some frightening and fascinating Forgotten Places.

Thank you,
-Colin Walker

Part One: The Void

Pomogi Mne

Danbury, Nebraska — 2022

The sound of the crash carried for miles, spreading out in an ever-widening bubble; a sonic snapshot of one terrible moment. Upon impact, leaves rained down slowly from the tree like orange and brown snowflakes. The sky above filled with a hundred black forms as the crows that had been roosting in the tree's many branches took flight in a panicked flurry. Heading northeast, they dared not look back. The small white sedan sat underneath the tree. Its front bumper and most of the hood hugged the tree, forming a tight horseshoe of destruction around the thick trunk. Airbags had deployed and the driver, unconscious, lay across the steering wheel. The sound of the car horn was pinched, a muffled cry against the trunk of the tree.

By the time Lee Sullivan pulled up to the wreck in his old, battered, gray-and-red Ford tractor, the afternoon sunlight had turned golden — hauntingly picturesque. Quiggly, Lee's basset hound, sat in the farmer's lap with his tail swishing back and forth in unbridled excitement. A trip on the tractor was something special, and the hound knew it. The dog, happy as always, was oblivious to the chaos he was approaching.

Coming to a stop beside the wreck, Lee pulled on the brake, then cut the engine. "Stay put, ya mutt," Lee muttered as he slid out of the seat and eased himself to the ground with the help of one of the large, mud-caked rear tires. Quiggly barked a short response, his tail wagging now in a near-constant blur. Lee stopped a moment and dabbed his faded, rust-red handkerchief across his brow to soak up the sweat that had gathered there during the hot drive down the road from his farm. Slipping the damp cloth into his back jean pocket, he replaced his beat-up Husker's cap atop his bald head. "Hello? Can you hear me?" he called out to the driver inside the wreck.

The hiss of steam escaping from the front of the car was a steady, unnerving sound. Lee looked into the car through the rolled down passenger window. Inside he found only the scent of the small yellow tree air freshener. It was still swinging back and forth from the rearview mirror like a condemned man hanging from the gallows. Lee discovered the steering wheel was unattended. Aside from some hastily packed trash bags full of old clothes on the back seat, there was nothing else of any note — most glaringly, the driver. From the other side of the car, someone coughed, long and low.

Lee strolled around the back of the car and found a young man, dressed in a business suit, lying in the ditch beside the wreck. Blood from a gash on his forehead trickled down the front of his face and onto his lime-green dress shirt. Every time the man tried to get up, he groaned before his legs buckled, and he collapsed back to where he had been lying in the dirt. Fluids of light, unnatural colors oozed from the car engine and wove a sticky web in the hard, packed dirt, mingling with the man's hands as he struggled for a perch.

"Son, you all right?" Lee inquired of the young man. Surprised at Lee's question, the young man jumped where he sat, then turned to see who had addressed him. Pure, primal panic filled the young man's eyes. His face contorted and his mouth tried to work but instead looked more like an unlatched door banging open and shut in a storm. Lee drew closer, getting on his knees. As he approached, the young man tried to scramble in the opposite direction.

"Where you off to? You're in no condition to run. Let me help you," Lee said in a soothing, kind tone. "I got my tractor; let me help tow your car and get you all situated. There ain't much of a cell signal out here in the valley, but you can use the landline back at my place to make any calls you might need to."

The young man's mouth continued to work open and closed, open and closed; the motion now reminded Lee of a gasping trout pulled up on the deck of his fishing boat. Slowly, the man turned to face Lee. Gazing into the young man's eyes, Lee saw something he had never seen before, not even in all his years as a combat vet — a kind of fear, pure and basic. It went deeper than that. Lee recognized the trauma and terror commingling behind the young man's pale eyes. He'd seen something like it in Iraq, but that was a distant cousin to what he was witnessing here. This was fear that, no matter how hard or how far down one buried it, would always remain just under the surface — a trauma to end all traumas. Looking the man over, Lee noticed the dark stain that had set in around the crotch of his trousers. The man shook spasmodically; adrenaline pumped through his veins, searching for that fight or flight decision in the reptilian portion of his brain. The young man's mouth stopped its open and close looping and instead remained closed. The pity Lee felt for the young man snapped him back into the moment.

"Why don't you come with me, and we'll see about getting someone out here to tow your car into town," Lee said. The young man shook his head slowly.

The fiery afternoon sun continued to set. Lee turned off the car and pocketed the keys. The strained horn cut off, abruptly returning the world to her natural melodies and chords. Coming back around, Lee smiled down at the young man.

"Quiggly here is gonna keep a close eye on you while I run back to the field and fetch my pickup. No sense in dragging you to the house on my tractor." Quiggly rounded the side of the car and plopped down next to the shaken young man. With a quick and polite tip of his cap, Lee was off and driving back down the road from where he had come.

When Lee pulled his truck up to the spot his tractor had been occupying not ten minutes earlier, he found the young man still badly shaken and still sitting in the dirt, but this time his shaky, stained hand rubbed the bowser's exposed belly.

"Well, he sure took to you mighty fast, didn't he?" Lee said. The young man nodded and tried to throw a smile Lee's way but came up with only a modest grin.

A few moments later, the farmer had the young man sitting shotgun in his beaten, old pickup while Quiggly paced back in forth in the truck bed.

"You feeling any better?" Lee asked as he got situated behind the steering wheel. The young man nodded. Lee looked into his eyes. They were still wide with terror, but with each passing second, he could see some semblance of normalcy trickling back in.

"I've been better," the young man whispered.

"I bet you have, son. I bet you have."

Tires squealed and dirt flew as the pickup bounded away from the wreck and straight down the road. Within moments, the pair and the pooch were pulling up in front of a modest two-story farmhouse. A barn stood nearby. All around the house grew the fruits of Lee's labors: corn, nearly as high as an elephant's eye. In the oncoming darkness of night, the house and farm appeared downright cozy, an immaculate picture of pure, unapologetic Americana.

As the truck pulled up to the end of the gravel driveway, Quiggly hopped out the back and bounded up the porch steps to take his place — tail wagging, barking encouragingly — beside the front door. Lee helped the young man out of the truck, and together they made the short journey to the house. The young man's limp slowed them down, but Lee was pleased to see that his guest was looking less flushed and more alive. They navigated the stairs one at a time. When they reached the stoop, Lee guided the young man into the porch swing and rummaged about in his pockets for his house key.

"Used to sit out here with my wife nearly every night," Lee said, making the kind of small talk he knew was good at directing the young man's attention away from the day's traumatic events.

"Is she out of town?" the young man asked, nodding toward the house key Lee produced from his pocket like a rabbit out of a hat.

"You might say that," Lee replied. He eased the key into the lock. "Lizzy and I have been divorced now, going on twenty-eight years."

"I'm sorry," the young man said.

Lee fiddled with the lock before opening the door. Without saying another word, the farmer popped inside his house. Light spilled out onto the porch. Lee reappeared.

"Don't be," Lee said with a chuckle. "She and I get along far better separated than together."

"Twenty-eight years. You must be, what? Fifty, fifty-five? Did you get married young?"

"Right outta high school. And no, I'm neither fifty nor fifty-five. I'm forty-eight, but close." Lee chuckled at his comment before helping the young man up and inside of his home. Quiggly, excited as always, made a mad dash inside, barking as he rushed down the long entrance hallway and all around the first-floor rooms. Lee steered his young guest into the living room and helped him ease onto the dusty, old sofa. He flipped on the light switch and the darkened room sprang to life. The wallpaper was old, an original print that had come with the house when Lee and his wife had bought it decades earlier. Patterns of faded yellow and white flowers ran in strips from the ceiling to halfway down the wall where they met the deep red wood of the wainscoting. A roll top desk sat closed next to a large window that overlooked the cornfields outside. A series of bookshelves ran along the opposite wall of the sofa. Framed family photos lined the walls. A small fireplace sat in the corner of the room, its mantel displaying a folded-up American flag and several display cases filled with various military medals.

"Were you in the army?" the young man asked, pointing toward the mantel.

"Air Force. I was in Desert Storm. I was just a stupid kid back then. Did my tour of duty, came back home, and eventually got an honorable discharge. Came back here and took up the old family business. Typical American story. Nothing fancy, just the facts," Lee said, hooking his thumbs into his jean belt loops. "Say, let me get you a glass of water, uh — "

"Lewis. Lewis Pelter. And thanks, I'd love a glass of water right now."

Lee left the room and was back moments later with two glasses brimming with cool, clear tap water. The farmer handed Lewis a glass, and together they drank in silence for a few moments. Quiggly followed Lee over to a patched-up armchair near the couch and curled up at his master's feet.

"How are you feeling?" Lee asked.

"I'm feeling better. Thanks again for your help."

"Do you recall what happened?"

Lewis looked miles away. Lee had seen that look on many a face over the years. Here was a man trying to organize his thoughts. Trying and failing.

"Honestly, I can't. I think there was something...someone in the road. I swerved to avoid them and hit the tree, and then you showed up. I can't seem to picture the rest," Lewis responded. His face was a fluid landscape of confusion and thoughtfulness. "The rest is all a kind of a blur. But hey, thank God you were in the area.

I can't imagine what would have happened to me if you hadn't come by and if you hadn't found me."

"Well," Lee said, raising his glass, "here's to being found."

"Cheers," Lewis replied with his own glass raised in toast. The dark malaise that had momentarily settled over the young man seemed to lift. The pair gulped down their liquid bounty. Lee stood, leaving Quiggly behind to doze.

"Let me see if I can't phone the sheriff or a tow truck. You stay here. Kick off your shoes and stretch out on the sofa."

Lee crossed the living room quickly and made a beeline for the landline telephone at the back of his kitchen. Through the large windows overlooking the farmland, the darkness of a Midwest plains night had fallen. The phone in the kitchen was at least three decades too old; its cord was a jigsaw puzzle of loops, curls, and knots all passing effortlessly through one another. Taking the phone off of the wall mount, Lee dialed the sheriff's office. The phone rang. With each ring, a static sound began to rise. It reminded Lee of the time he had visited Lake Eerie and spent the afternoon alone, watching the waves come in slowly with the tide. The static intensified until it was all Lee could hear. It was impossible to tell if anyone on the other line had picked up.

"Hello?" Lee called out. "Anyone there?" Static and nothing more. After a few moments of intense crackling and garbled clicks, Lee hung up the phone. He tried three more times, and each time the ringing faded to pure chaotic static. Finally, Lee gave up, collected his glass off the kitchen table where he'd deposited it before attempting the call, and headed back into the living room.

Quiggly continued to snooze beside the armchair and, without batting an eye, allowed his tail to happily thump the floor upon his master's return to the room. On the sofa, Lewis dozed, softly snoring as he slept. Lee accepted that he was as far from a doctor as anyone could get, but he still knew to keep any eye on the young man as he slept. Knowing there could be a concussion or something worse, he resolved to watch out for any signs of something troubling. As for the phone, he figured the lines were being worked on and he'd try again shortly. Returning to his armchair beside Quiggly, Lee picked up the mystery novel he'd been reading all week and dove in. Within minutes, he, too, was snoring.

* * *

Lee woke with a start, inadvertently tossing his paperback novel across the room. Quiggly flipped over in a flash, teeth bared, growling long and low. On the sofa, Lewis was thrashing about with what Lee felt was an unsettling intensity. Tears were streaming down the young man's face. His eyes were tightly shut.

"Spaceman!" Lewis cried out as though in pain. "Where the fuck did he come from! Go away, spaceman!"

Lee hesitated. While he wanted to help his guest, he also didn't want to come away with a bruised lip, or a black eye, or the possibility of a cracked rib or two. Quiggly continued to growl. Soon the growling intensified into frightened, defensive barks. Lee had never seen the bowser react in such a manner. As his mind reeled at the situation, he couldn't tell which disturbed him more, his dog's raised hackles and bared teeth, or the young man still violently tossing and turning on the sofa across from him.

Quiggly barked and barked and barked. At last, the young man's eyes flew open as he managed to roll himself off the sofa and onto the hard floor. Lee ran a soothing hand across Quiggly's back, stroking the animal from head to tail. Slowly, the dog began to back down, his back losing its rigidness.

"You okay?" Lee asked as Lewis curled into a ball and began to sob heavily.

"He's going to kill me. He's coming to kill me…"

With Quiggly's unrest quelled, Lee got up from his chair and approached the young man, still unsure exactly what to do.

"Who's coming to kill you?" Lee asked.

"The spaceman. He's in my head. I can see him. I saw him in the road. I swerved and missed him, but he was still coming for me."

"Spaceman? Well, I can tell you, fella, with all the confidence in the world that there ain't a single spaceman around here."

"You're wrong. You're going to die, too, if he catches you."

Lee bent down and shook Lewis's shoulders. "What are you saying?"

Lewis looked up at Lee, his eyes wide and unblinking, terror now replaced by confusion. "Wh-what happened? How did I end up on the floor?"

"What do you mean? You fell there a moment ago," Lee said, confused. "You were tossing around, screaming and crying about a spaceman come to kill you."

"Spaceman? Kill me?" Lewis asked more to himself than the farmer. Quiggly sauntered over and began to lick his face. "Man, that crash must've messed me up more than I thought."

Lee nodded. "That's a possibility," he replied. "Here, let me help you back up."

Lewis scrambled back onto the sofa with Lee's help. "Well, I'll tell ya one thing," Lewis replied after adjusting himself amongst the throw pillows. "I'm not going to fall asleep again anytime soon, that's for sure."

Lee nodded knowingly but still cast a skeptical eye at the young man. "I'll go see if I can phone the sheriff again."

"You didn't get a hold of him earlier?" Lewis asked as Lee began to head for the kitchen.

"Nope. Something wrong with the phones." A worried look passed across Lewis's face. "Be right back. Let me try again."

Lee picked up the phone and placed his ear to the receiver — nothing. No dial tone, nothing. He dialed the sheriff. No ring, no static, nothing. As he fiddled with the phone, Lee spotted something outside his kitchen window. A figure, staring in, bathed in an eerie, purple glow that seemed to gather the darkness of the night about them. Lee hung up the phone and stepped out the kitchen side door onto the back porch — there was no one there. *Funny*, Lee thought. *Could have sworn...*

"Hello? Anyone out here?" Lee called out.

No response and no more purple glow; just the wind and the buzz of night insects.

A strange and sickening realization began to dawn on Lee that the figure he had seen in the kitchen window wasn't outside — they were reflected in the window itself. Whoever it was had been standing right behind him. From within the house, Quiggly howled a bloodcurdling cry. Lee shot back inside, through the kitchen, and into the living room. What his eyes beheld was something nature had failed to mentally equip him to comprehend.

Lewis was still on the sofa, sitting up, tears once more streaming down his cheeks. His gaze was locked upon the stranger, dressed head to toe in a badly damaged spacesuit. The spaceman appeared to float just a few inches above the floor. The air around both Lewis and the hovering stranger wavered and shimmered like heat rising from asphalt on a hot day. A deep and twisted wheezing issued forth from behind the spaceman's dark and impenetrable faceplate. Burn marks dotted his silver suit like the brown furry patches on Quiggly's cream-colored fur. The tubes that hung from various sockets on the suit dangled limply, the ends charred. Looking past the wheezing spaceman, with his rattling breath as deep as the ocean and beyond, Lee spotted Quiggly scratching furiously at the front door, whining to be let out of the house and away from the strange new arrival.

Lewis's face, distorted in the convex blackness of the spaceman's helmet visor, stared unblinking — transfixed. Slowly, a gloved hand reached up to the bottom of the faceplate, unclasped the base, and, slower still, pulled the darkened shield up. From where Lee stood, he could not see very far into the helmet. The spaceman's face remained obscured by the deepest of shadows. Still, as the face appeared before Lewis, a strange, otherworldly glow began to emanate from the helmet, enveloping Lewis's face as well. Arcs of purple lightning crawled off the spaceman's body, reaching out toward Lewis, ensnaring him in an electric octopus's tender embrace. With each pop and arc of a bolt, the lights in the room dimmed and flickered. Static electricity filled the air, along with the scent of burning ozone. Lewis's tears continued to stream down his face, but the look of confusion was slowly replaced by one of unhinged and unending terror. It was the same look Lee had seen on the young man's face when he had found him at the crash site. Lewis opened his mouth to scream, but no sound came out. Blood, thick and dark, began to ooze from his nose, ears, eyes, and the corners of his mouth.

In that moment, the world became nothing more than a series of vibrations, each one helping to shape the chaotic world Lee was now disconnected from. A cacophony of sounds and feelings — an orchestra warming up for infinity — filled Lee's very being. He felt as though he was glimpsing the merest sliver of the very fabric of reality. The curtain was slightly pulled back, and what lay beyond was too much for any human to comprehend. Through the noise and chaos, a phrase, unrecognizable, struck Lee in the back of his mind. *Pomogi mne.* For a fleeting moment, images passed by — images of Lewis turning to dust from the face down, and slowly being vacuumed into the spaceman's helmet like stardust into the heart of a black hole.

Lightning flashed behind his eyes, and Lee realized that he had shut them tight. How long he had stood there, his eyelids locked, he could not say. In a snap, the vibrations vanished, and the world seemed at peace. Lee's eyes fluttered open. Still standing over the sofa stood the spaceman, his faceplate sliding closed on its own. Lewis was nowhere to be seen. Quiggly, defeated by the closed front door, cowered in the corner between the hallway and the door itself, tail tucked between his legs and whimpering. The silence was broken once the helmet sealed, and the terrible wheezing breaths started to rattle once more.

The spaceman turned to face Lee with a slowness that told his mind that this thing, this creature, was moving faster than it appeared. Lee noticed the writing above the helmet, burned letters bubbled over by an intense heat — C.C.C.P. The spaceman's arms extended before it, making it look less like a cosmic traveler and more like a shambling mummy straight out of an old horror film. In the moment between heartbeats, Lee knew what he had to do. His mind, still trying to figure out just what was going on, shoved comprehension aside and kicked deftly into fight or flight mode, giving in easily to that ancient reptilian part of his brain. Ducking the oncoming spaceman's arms, Lee hit the floor, rolled past, and shot up toward Quiggly and the front door.

As he threw open the door, Lee glanced back over his shoulder — the spaceman was gone, vanished into the ether. Lee turned back to his dog and snatched up the cowering pooch. Quiggly whimpered, his tail locked between his shaking legs. Closing the door behind him, Lee was unsure what to make of the situation.

"Calm down, Buck-o," Lee said soothingly to his dog. "Shhh…it's alright." Carrying Quiggly back into the living room with him, Lee looked at the sofa where Lewis had been sitting not moments before. Save for a few sparkling particles of dust still clinging to the sofa's surface, there was no sign of the young man. The logical part of Lee's brain tried to kick in but failed to engage.

As his mind shuffled through his years of combat experience, Lee began to notice the literal writing on the wall; burned into the wallpaper and wainscoting in large letters was the phrase he'd heard during the spaceman's attack, not in his ears but in his very being. *Pomogi mne.*

Growing up in the 60s, Lee had become intimately aware of the U.S. and Soviet's endless bickering and buildup of arms. Hell, the space race alone had been the deciding factor in pushing the now farmer into a career of flying at and past the speed of sound. He pondered why a damn Cosmonaut was floating around his living room, and how he was capable of doing what he had done to that poor young man.

For a pained moment, with Quiggly slowly calming down in his arms, Lee's eyes locked on to the still smoldering words in front of him. He felt a pang of regret for stopping to help the young man. Selfishly, he reasoned that if he'd just left the young man out there, alone, he wouldn't be in this strange and frightening situation. Reason began to break through, though. Casting his self-doubt aside, Lee began to think more logically. What happened to Lewis was far outside of his control. He had done the right thing to help the young man and to open his home to him. How was he to know about this terror? Besides, not helping the poor soul would have contradicted his Air Force training and his own strong moral compass.

Lee began to calm down. Like Quiggly in his arms, he could feel his adrenaline draining away. His head started to clear. Another rational thought struck his mind like a bolt of lightning out of the blue; Lee desperately wished he had a Russian dictionary on hand. He also wished he had a computer in that moment. Lee was no Luddite — in fact he was far from it — but his computer was in town being repaired after he accidentally opened a suspicious attachment in an email a few days prior.

Lee's breathing slowed, as did Quiggly's. For the moment, they still seemed to be in sync. Placing the dog on the floor beside him, Lee headed for the kitchen, his pooch in tow. Lifting the receiver to his phone, Lee once more found only the coming and going of static. He hoped that it was all over, but something nagging at the back of his thoughts told him it was just beginning. In that moment, the universe decided to answer his concerns — a long, loud screech erupted from the cornfields outside. In Lee's ears, it sounded angry and unearthly. Quiggly howled before running out of the room and upstairs, presumably into Lee's room where the dog usually slept under the bed. The hair all over Lee's body stood on end. The adrenaline coursed through his veins once more.

A thought struck the farmer: he needed to defend himself and his dog; he needed to get to the barn where he kept his gun safe. Lee ran back through the living room and made a bullseye for the front door. Throwing it open, he was greeted by the now familiar shimmering wall of heat distortion and the vein-like bolts of purple lightning. Lee stepped back not a moment too soon — the spaceman popped into existence where he had been standing seconds before. Arms outstretched, purple bolts reaching out and feeling, the spaceman unleashed its bloodcurdling, otherworldly howl. Lee turned and ran back into the living room, cutting back through the kitchen. Glancing over his shoulder, he noticed that the spaceman did not pursue him on foot. Instead, it vanished, only to reappear a split second later, still floating but just a little closer to where Lee was in time and space.

Lee tossed open the back door in the kitchen and rushed outside, hoping that the spaceman would follow him and leave Quiggly alone. Another quick glance over his shoulder told him that the strange entity was closing in on him. Each time the creature moved, it popped out of existence before popping back into existence, causing the area around it (presumably reality itself) to snap back into place. Lee took pride in his education paid for by the Air Force. He had taken a fair number of college courses back in the day that had fueled his interest in physics and some of the other mysteries of the cosmos.

Ahead of Lee the cornfield beckoned, a maze he knew he could easily vanish into and navigate deftly. Ducking into the first row of stalks, Lee felt like a man trying to outrun a barreling train on a narrow bridge. Before him lay a long, tight path of green stalks and protruding leaves; an alley that reeked of earth and scratched at his bare skin. Into the field he dove, the unearthly cries of his pursuer coming and going like the static sounds on the phone.

Slowing down, Lee took a moment to catch his breath, throwing his arms behind the back of his head to open his chest. His lungs ached, his head throbbed, and his side burned with a searing stitch;

all the while he could hear the intake and release of the night air nearby as the spaceman followed him into the cornfield, disappearing and reappearing at will. The moon was out now, painting the dark night an eerie shade of blue. The stars twinkled above, uncaring of the world below and indifferent to Lee's plight. The air around Lee began to grow cold. Purple bolts lanced out, feeling their way through the rows of corn. Lee watched in awe as deer fled up ahead, bounding through the forest of human engineered crops.

Out of the corner of his eye, Lee kept a close watch on the top of the two-story farmhouse, now to his right. This was his north star, guiding him straight and true toward the barn; toward salvation, he hoped. In the half-light of the moon, the barn loomed like the dorsal fin of a fantastical whale patrolling the rippling currents of corn, hungry for scarecrows. The howl of the spaceman erupted in his skull, and with a quick intake of atmosphere it was there, hovering before him, *right there* between himself and the path to the barn. Lee could feel the world around him begin to melt away. Once again, it was as though he was standing on the very precipice of reality, inches from the edge and struggling for a perch to gain balance and not fall in. The darkness within the spaceman's helmet was deeper than anything imaginable — it swirled and undulated like a creature at the bottom of the ocean waiting to uncoil and snatch its prey.

One moment the spaceman had arms outstretched, purple lightning glancing off every green stock around him; the next, the lure of the creature was severed. Lee hesitated, unsure of what had happened. The spaceman was still there, floating, but it seemed almost distracted. That was when Lee noticed the doe and her fawn dashing off and away from where he stood.

"Damn corn eatin' sons of guns just saved my bacon," Lee said to himself, caught up in the moment. The movement of the floating figure out of the corner of his eye reminded the farmer just where he was and the imminent danger he was in. Using the distraction to his advantage, Lee managed to side-step the floating form and make a mad dash for the barn dead ahead. The sound that issued from the spaceman behind him sounded more like sorrow than anger, but still he ran. The stitch in his side was searing now — a stab wound without a knife.

The air behind Lee filled once more with the static *pop-hiss* of the creature pursuing him. Bursting from the corn, Lee could see in the moonlight that the strange phrase from his living room — the one that had seeped into his thoughts — was scored into the wooden doors of his barn. Just like in the living room, embers still burned within the black handwriting. *Pomogi mne.*

Lee tossed one of the barn doors open, threw himself inside, and closed and barred the door behind him. In the back of his mind, he knew his actions were futile, but he also knew he had to take the chance, no matter the outcome. Flipping on the light switch near him, Lee took stock of his surroundings. The barn housed his workshop and most of his farming equipment. It had once held animals, but those days were long gone. Lee spotted a wheelbarrow full of bags of seed; that was a start. Within seconds he had the wheelbarrow, his air compressor, his blowtorch tanks, and three crates full of Quiggly's dog food braced against the doors. Outside, Lee could hear the spaceman howl.

Turning to the workshop, Lee made for the gun safe. He was halfway across the room when he realized the keys were back in the house. "Goddamn it. You are one damn fool, you know that?" Lee chastised himself. In that moment, the lights flickered and dimmed. All at once the bulbs shattered, sending a twinkling rain of glass and sparks to the ground. The air filled with purple bolts as the oxygen seemed to vanish. Reality bent, then snapped back, and suddenly there was the spaceman floating right in the middle of the barn, its helmet open once more, the blackness inside still swirling, waiting to lash out.

Lee spotted the pitchfork near the workshop door. He lunged for it, ducking and rolling, and scooped up his prize before jumping up to face the threat, pitchfork at the ready. The spaceman was gone. Lee looked about the darkened room, trying to discern shape from shadow in the moonlight shining in from the high windows.

"Son of a —"

Nothing. His pursuer was gone. Lee's pulse raced. Spots danced in front of his vision, an artifact of the bulbs bursting and the lightning crackling. He breathed a sigh of relief. He turned around the room once, then turned and looked about again. As Lee turned that second time, the spaceman appeared before him, inches from his face and still inches above the ground. Lee looked down at the pitchfork buried deep in the spaceman's torso. The spaceman wavered, flickering like the ghost image after a tube television has been shut off. The creature gurgled, and then — like that — it was gone, the pitchfork with it.

Half an hour later, Lee felt convinced his ordeal was finally over. His mind kept tumbling back and forth as he headed to the house. He could still hardly believe that what had happened had been real. His mind wandered, wanting answers to questions he didn't even have or know how to begin asking. At the same time, he knew he needed to figure out who to contact regarding Lewis. This wasn't the kind of story, as odd and bewildering as it was, that needed to be reported. Lee found Quiggly just where he suspected he might, curled up under his bed, whimpering. Not knowing what else to do, the farmer slid under the bed, hugged his dog, and curled up and whimpered himself.

* * *

Southern Kazakhstan — 1963

The launch had been a complete success — the booster rockets had pushed the capsule up through the atmosphere faster than a bullet from the chamber of a gun. On the ground, there had been much cheering and shaking of hands. The Premiere smiled from cheek to cheek as the heads of the space program accepted his thanks on behalf of the people. From down there, everything had gone according to plan for once.

High above the Earth, the Cosmonaut watched as the blue-green planet below slipped by silently before his very eyes. Oceans, clouds, land masses — they all seemed so fragile, so delicate from that high up. Looking out beyond the horizon, the Cosmonaut thought about answers; answers to the questions he would be asked by the state-run newspapers.

What did you see? they might ask.

The majesty of it all, pure and simple.

What did it feel like? a follow-up to the first question.

Disconcerting at first, then after a time it felt like going home.

When your children and your children's children ask what struck you while you were up there looking down upon all of us, what will you tell them? someone would undoubtedly broach.

I realized that the cartographers and rulers were wrong. There are no dividing lines, no borders, no boundaries — only the endless horizon and the stars.

Slowly the craft, with its spherical capsule at the head, rotated, the image shifting in time to music unheard — the music of the spheres. The Cosmonaut watched as the Earth's curved horizon gave way to darkness as the impossibly tiny craft crossed the terminator. There were no stars embedded within that darkness. All the Cosmonaut could see was the void. And beyond that void, another. And another. And so on and on. The void crept ever closer. It surrounded him, smothering him with infinity itself. The Cosmonaut could not move. He was no longer floating, and yet he felt himself pinned in place. The void was neither cold nor warm. It simply was. With a shaking hand, the Cosmonaut reached for the communication controls.

"Pomogi mne," he whispered, in a voice filled equally with terror and awe. "Pomogi mne!" he managed to call into the microphone once more. There was no response, simply the silence of eternity. As the void enveloped the Cosmonaut and drew him into its unfeeling embrace among the alien stars, he continued to cry out, as if it was a mantra to undo what was happening to him, "Pomogi mne!"

The void took him.

When the capsule was recovered several hours later, there was no sign of the ejector chair or the Cosmonaut. For miles, the recovery team searched. When the chair and parachute were finally recovered, the Cosmonaut was nothing more than a smoldering skeleton. The skull was found with its jaw fused open, forever in a rictus-scream. The ground crew puzzled over this find, but they puzzled even more over the pitchfork that had apparently pinned the Cosmonaut to his capsule seat. The chair, chute, and body were brought back to the scene of the capsule. Everyone was told to keep this incident under their hats. No one spoke as an unmarked black van pulled up to the recovery scene, took the body, and left — no doubt scientists from the State. An official story would be released by the government and, as far as everyone was concerned, that would be the only story. The recovery crew agreed to this. Sometime later that day, as a team of soldiers sent out to assist with the recovery hoisted the remnants of the spacecraft onto the back of a transport, they made the final, disturbing discovery. Scratched as if by fingernails into the inside glass of the capsule's viewport was a single phrase. *Pomogi mne.*

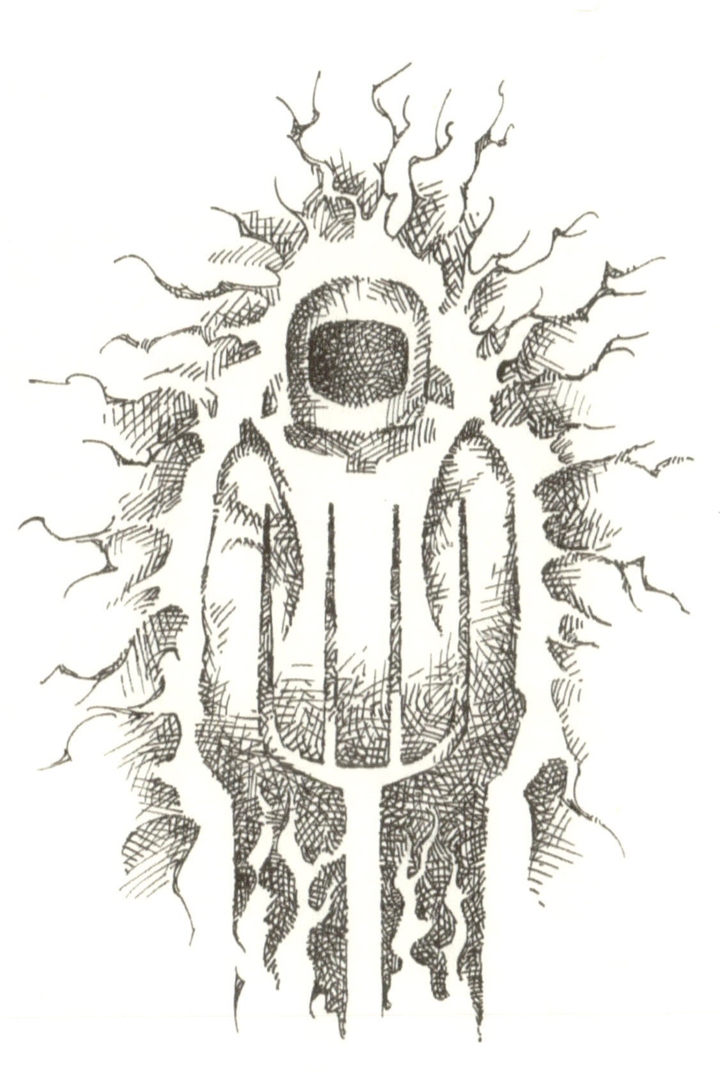

A Blackened Mirror

The toilet in the next stall flushed, giving James the opportunity provided by the cacophony to mask the sound as he snorted another line of blow. Sitting on the toilet, his slacks crumpled around his ankles in an effort to complete the illusion of taking a shit, James leaned back against the tiled wall behind him. The plumbing and his back met like puzzle pieces from two completely different puzzles. James didn't care; he could barely feel the cold, hard pipes as they dug into his spine. Breathing deeply, he waited for his teeth to stop buzzing as he simply relished the rush, living in the moment as the blow coursed through him.

The next stall over creaked open, followed by the echoing slap of receding footsteps as his former stall-mate left the restroom in a rush. *And all without washing his hands, to boot*, James mused with a screwed-up smile pasted under his glazed eyes. As if on autopilot, he slipped the small mirror — still streaked with a few fine powder lines — atop the metal toilet paper dispenser. James closed his eyes tight against the dull humming of the fluorescent lights in the office's third floor restroom. His head swam, and a song floated to the surface of his hazy thoughts, from mental recesses unknown. With his teeth still buzzing, he began to hear the voice of The Monkees' Micky Dolenz, haunting and far away.

Something, something about clocks and dolphins and something and such...

Sitting there on the john — eyes shut tight, letting the blow do its job — James tried to remember where he'd last heard "Porpoise Song." Moments slipped away as he concentrated on the tune. Like a third-rate birthday party magician, he began to conjure memories like silk scarves and doves from a top hat. He recalled watching the movie *Head*, a strange film starring The Monkees that used the song for the opening number. Olivia had insisted on watching it a couple of nights before. He'd taken a couple of hits of ecstasy in her bathroom before starting the film. It was his only choice: Olivia loved The Monkees, but to him the 1960s and everything about the era was depressing. *How the fuck did people live without smartphones and the internet in the heyday of the Civil*

Rights Movement? he sometimes wondered when his girlfriend went on about mid-century tangents. He spent the whole of the film tripping balls, wishing he was back in his apartment getting slowly baked and beating snot-nosed little shits in *Fortnight*.

Slowly, his teeth began to settle. He could feel his nerves tingling. He needed this. More lyrics came to him.

Something, something about giraffes and clocks and something and such...

James wondered how much dope The Monkees must have consumed to come up with their bizarre attempt at cinema. He thought about how much blow it took him now just to get through one stinking day at the office. *Besides*, he thought, his mind wandering back to the movie, *any flick that didn't have at least a few exposed titties just isn't worth my time.*

James opened his eyes to find his arm hovering before him, as though being held aloft on a marionette string, the sleeve unbuttoned and his watch ticking slowly at him, face to face. His lunch hour was nearly over. When he had first started at Prometheus Industries, he had gone to lunch with his team on a semi-regular basis. But, as the pressure from his higher paid coworkers mounted, and as he slowly started to plot his way up the company's metaphorical ladder, James had taken to saving his scratch for something more effective than a burger and fries. Energy drinks and snake-oil energy boosters be damned, Phil in accounting had the answer to all of James's problems. Phil still dressed like someone from the 1980s, so it was no surprise that he supplied the office with enough booger-sugar to send even the heartiest employee careening back in time to the era of Crockett and Tubbs.

With seemingly endless meetings and impossible deadlines, James saw no other way to get so much done without burning out. A few lines of white, and he could power through even the worst PowerPoint presentation. After "lunch," all his spreadsheets and numbers danced their waltz, effortless and elegant. His head lolling to one side, James spotted the rolled-up dollar bill in his other hand. Someday, he figured, he would be doing this shit with a hundred-dollar bill, and no longer in the goddamn bathroom but in his own plush office. He just needed to get through this quarter, make the big boys upstairs notice his name and numbers, and he would be in like fucking Flynn.

The door to the restroom creaked open. Footsteps, heavy and slow — almost shuffling — came echoing into the room. The owner of those awkward steps breathed heavily with a marked wheeze. In James's humble opinion, the man put Darth Vader to shame. James reached over for his pocket mirror. He had to act fast. As the asthmatic arrival settled into the vacant stall next to him, James waited for the signature crinkle of his new neighbor's useless wax paper seat cover. James saw his window and dove right through, snorting up another line, but not before spotting his reflection — his face locked behind three white, powdery bars in the palm of his hands. Darth Vader took his seat. The new arrival's groans of protest were loud enough for James to steal yet another quick snort of his second-to-last line. Seconds later, the stench hit him like a slap in the face. Realization quickly dawned on James: he was sitting next to the Destroyer. That was the nickname James and the rest of the team came up with one day when his chair broke beneath him in the middle of a business call. The Destroyer's reputation had been sealed in that very moment. His real name was Austin, and he worked in Analytics. He was good at his job, but James didn't care about that. All James cared about was laughing at a man who was over 300 pounds, sweated profusely, and — half the office seemed to agree — had a rank odor akin to a dead fish. *Now*, James thought through the cocaine haze, *here he is destroying the peace and quiet of the restroom*. Hopefully he wouldn't destroy the plumbing. James stifled a chuckle. He would have to tell the team that one; more fodder to fling at the modest giant.

As unpleasant sounds emanated from the stall next door, James split his last line between both nostrils before rubbing a moistened finger across the mirror and then across his gums, doing his part to waste not, want not. Slipping the mirror back into his pocket, he pulled out his wallet and tucked away the dollar bill. James forced himself not to laugh at the thought of how his old friend Georgie Washington must be as blissfully high as him — every ounce of the good stuff flowing through his green, paper honker. That was the one that did it. Holding a hand over his mouth, James unleashed an audible snicker and snort. Something wet and warm began to trickle down the front of his face.

"Shit," James grumbled under his breath as he looked down at the sight of two dark spots of blood blossoming on his white briefs. Like a madman, he pulled away a bundle of toilet paper. Half was applied directly to his nose, while the rest went toward his underwear. With any luck, the droplets had not soaked through to his pants. His mind began to reel at the prospect of being found with blood between his legs. What would happen then? Would his coworkers, the same chums who had helped him name the Destroyer, comment that he was on the rag? His head still swimming and the lyrics to The Monkees' song still buzzing around his brain, James inspected his tan slacks.

Something, something about castles and kings and something and such ...

A heavy sigh of relief came from the stall next door. A groan rose from deep within James's throat upon spotting the two red eyes, gazing up at him angrily from his slacks. "Fuck me," he grumbled.

Dabbing at his underwear and inseam, James ignored the thickening odors still coalescing around him. His mind was focused like a laser on what his coworkers would say about him and his tragically placed stains. If anyone from the team caught wind of this, he was a dead man — doomed to remain on the slow track to nowhere. James pulled a wad of toilet paper from the dispenser and soaked it in the unused toilet beneath him. With the paper dripping in his hand, he slowly dabbed at the red stains on his clothing, watching the water stains envelop the blood stains. Eons seemed to pass as he patted at the spots, hoping and praying that this act would be enough to save his reputation. All the while, Austin the Destroyer continued to groan and strain in the next stall over. As James worked at his pants and underwear, he failed to notice that blood, warm and crimson as the dawn, was still tracking down the side of his face.

James looked his handiwork over and, the toilet filled to the brim with bloody toilet paper, felt cautiously satisfied with his obviously damp underwear and pants. Shivering against the cold wetness of his situation, James pulled up his slacks, buttoned and belted them, then left the stall. *Let some other asshole deal with my unflushed mess*, he reasoned while glancing back at the steadily swelling mound of bloody paper still floating at the top of the toilet bowl. He tossed the door to his stall open with a slightly dramatic flourish and strolled briskly through the restroom, his head swimming. His stiff polished shoes clacked all the way to the sink.

Unfazed now by the strong odor and sounds of the Destroyer and living primarily off the cocaine high and his own sense of accomplishment and superiority, James turned the faucet knob so quickly he sprayed himself and the counter with warm water. The basin gurgled as the water flowed down into the drain's unseen depths. As the water's temperature climbed ever higher, tendrils of steam rose to greet James's face. The large mirror in front of him fogged. Any other time, the hot water in the sink would have made him flinch, but he hardly noticed as he cupped his hands into the burning stream. Before plunging his face into the small puddle in his palms, he took a moment to glance at himself in the mirror of water — distorted and stretched, over and over again like taffy in a pull. Finally, he allowed the water to meet his face. He jumped back with a jolt, splashing water everywhere. Fumbling, James reached out and turned off the faucet. His hands shook ever so slightly.

Needing to feel, if this is for real; living life as a lie...

James gawked as water dripped down his face. Eventually he found the paper towel dispenser. He waved his still-shaking hands as if flagging down a taxi. The machine birthed its pulpy contents for him to snatch away. With one quick tug, the towel was loosed from its paper umbilicus — brought forth into the world only to be slapped to James's face without any sense of ceremony. Seconds later, soaked through, it met its end in the wastebasket directly below its mother dispenser, left to rot with its crumpled-up brothers and sisters. Another frantic wave, and another towel was spat out for James.

Looking at the fogged mirror, James grumbled at the collected moisture that prevented him from seeing himself. This time he slammed his new paper towel heedlessly into the large mirror above the twin sinks, wiping away most of the fog to reveal a circle of glass surrounded by condensation. Water droplets streaked the smooth surface of the mirror; James looked past them to the unrecognizable specter gazing back at him.

Tiny rivulets of blood mingled with water ran down the figure's gaunt, sallow face from the nose to the chin. The shirt was spotted with water and maroon flecks. The tie, prominently hung about the figure's neck like a loose noose before the drop, was streaked with red. Eyes, sunken and sleep-deprived, peered back at James. The hair was unkempt, the face covered in mossy patches of five o'clock shadow. *Who the fuck is that?* he wondered. James felt his hands traveling up the sides of his face. He felt the stubble, the dampness. He watched silently as the figure across from him copied his every move.

Something else in the mirror, just beyond his haggard reflection, caught his eye.

A dark spot was floating above his reflection's head, slightly to the left. It wasn't much, barely there, no larger than a thumbprint. To James it looked like a stain on the other side of the glass, some kind of flaw or tarnish. His mind still on cocaine auto-pilot, James reached up with the paper towel and began to wipe at the spot — nothing — still there. His hands fell at his side. James swore that he could see the spot slowly begin to grow. He watched with a child-like fascination as small veins of black began to unfurl and spread in all directions, like roots searching for water. He shook his head. He rubbed his eyes. He even began to slap himself. After each attempt to gain control of his faculties, James looked back at the mirror in the hopes that what he saw would be gone — just some trick of the light or, more likely, a trick of his blow-drenched mind. It was still there, increasing in size and growing darker and more pronounced by the second.

That fucker, James thought. *Phil must've sold me some tainted shit.* James had done coke dozens of times and never once had he hallucinated. Either the stuff was bad, or he'd finally done enough for his brain to start shorting out. As he watched the dark spot grow, he began to hear whispers. There were voices, dozens — no, hundreds — of voices, all whispering over each other. Nothing they said made sense, but their gibberish began to fill the room. James's eyes widened with terror as the black spot began to overtake the mirror itself — its darkness deeper than the blackest of blacks.

The door to the restroom flew open. James could feel his heart leap into his chest, while his stomach backflipped to parts unknown. A tall man, older, a ginger mop of hair upon his head, walked into the room with the cavalier step of someone in charge of many people. In that instant, recognition went out the window as James's brain tried and failed to register the man as his boss's boss, Thomas Anderson. Mr. Anderson eyed James the way an exterminator might eye a wasp's nest before spraying it.

"Everything all right, Mr. Joyner?" Mr. Anderson asked, more out of politeness than actual concern.

James tried to meet Mr. Anderson's steely blue eyes but found his own gaze snapping back to the still-darkening mirror. James nodded, more out of politeness than actual acknowledgement of the other man's question.

Mr. Anderson turned from James; the sneer he wore seemed to linger in the air right where he had left it. Mr. Anderson washed his hands, then checked himself in the mostly fog-free mirror. James could not see the other man's reflection, just the whispering darkness.

"How do you not see that?" James asked in a pathetic, strained voice. "How do you not *hear* that?"

Mr. Anderson turned slowly, shaking his hands dry. He squinted at James. "Mr. Joyner, if you insist on acting like a paranoid nincompoop, I'm afraid I must put off that little meeting we were scheduled to have in my office in a few minutes." As he spoke, Mr. Anderson's flesh split open with a sound like the crack of a whip. Yellow pus began to ooze out of the fissures that now ran the length and breadth of his face. "You are scum, Mr. Joyner."

James found himself frozen with fear, his skin crawling, his pulse quickening.

Soon the flesh on the man's face started to peel and slough off like dead petals on a rotten flower, falling to the bathroom tile with a sickening, stomach-churning plop. The maggot-infested skull that stared back at James flashed its toothy, bloody grin and screamed in James's face, "You are the worst kind of shit, Mr. Joyner! Useless and fucked!"

James tried to scream. He could feel it burning in his lungs, clawing at his throat. It never came. Instead, he watched as the corpse before him began to melt, coalescing into a puddle of festering, bubbling bile.

James, paralyzed by terror and awe, gaped as the puddle slowly crawled up the side of the sink, over the counter, and up into the deep, unending darkness of the void in the bathroom mirror. *This must be what staring into the event horizon of a black hole must be like*, James reasoned. *Losing one's sanity gazing into the void, knowing that the void also gazes into you.* Something told James that Mr. Anderson had never actually entered the room; that he was back in his office, waiting for James to show up for their meeting.

The whispering rose to a near shout — unintelligible, guttural sounds not unlike Gregorian chanting. Dark forms began to ooze out of the void, small and scurrying. They filled the sink basin and crawled across the counter. Over the bathroom floor tiles, they flew and spun, leaping into the air one moment and crashing into the walls the next. James watched as they lapped against his shoes like waves on a beach. Before he knew it, the shadowy forms with their many legs and arms, and various other appendages, had made their way up his legs. He could feel their pinprick claws as they quickly ascended toward his upper body. They, like the void in the mirror, made a noise — a horrible, unending clicking sound. James could not decide which sound was worse, the clicking or the whispering.

As quickly as the scurrying forms had come, they were gone, along with their clicks. In their absence, James gazed helplessly at eyes — hundreds upon hundreds of eyes of varying sizes and colors — all of them regarding him coldly from beyond the void. They studied him the way a predator observes its prey just before the kill. Tendrils of darkness poured from the mirror and reached out for James, who stood transfixed by what he was witnessing. The eyes all focused on him while the tendrils found his legs and arms. As their cold, biting touch stole through his skin, he could see the horrors — unending, maddeningly inconceivable creatures and realms, and so much more! — as he found himself dragged slowly toward the waiting darkness of the void. No, it wasn't just a dark, unending void; it was the million-toothed maw of a great and mighty beast. He would have screamed, but in that moment James's mind had popped its final circuit, and the man found himself unable to comprehend what he was seeing, what he was facing.

The whispers rose in a cacophony of unintelligible shouts, and screams, and wailing, just as James found himself halfway out of the mirror. His hand flailed and failed to find purchase on the slick, chrome faucets of the sink. The voices began to resolve into one booming crescendo.

The dolphin is waiting. So long, farewell…

The tendrils wrapped around James's face and hands, covering his vision as they managed to wrest him and his loose grip from the edge of the sink. They pulled him wholly into the void itself — taking him far beyond the mirror and far beyond comprehension. The last thing he saw before the darkness enveloped him entirely was the corpulent figure of Austin the Destroyer on the other side of the bathroom mirror, shuffling up to wash his hands at the sink.

* * *

Austin left the stall. He hated coming in here, but he had no choice. His doctor had put him on medication to help ease his gastric troubles, but it would still be a while before they kicked in. Until then, he would still have bowel issues and that embarrassing smell. Austin cast his gaze downward as he made his way to the sink. He dreaded going back out into the office. He knew what others called him, but what choice did he have? His job was all he had.

It was only after running his hands through the warm stream from the faucet that Austin noticed the blood flecks all over the counter. Sickened by the sight, he stepped back away from the counter. Austin plucked his paper towel from the automatic dispenser, wiped his hands, then looked himself over in the mirror. He tucked his shirt in below his protruding belly and straightened his tie. A smudge in the top left corner of the mirror caught his attention. Reaching over with his damp paper towel, Austin wiped the dark spot away with ease before balling the paper towel up and placing it into the trash on his way out.

With his hand pressed against the door, Austin stopped to heave a deep and pained sigh before stepping through and back into the office. He only hoped that Mr. Anderson had some good news. Rumor was, there was a manager opening and he and James Joyner from the Development team were up for it. As he left, Austin told himself to buck up; that things could be worse. After all, he reasoned, he was a dedicated and hard worker. Why shouldn't he get that promotion? As Austin headed for Mr. Anderson's office door, he began to hum a tune to himself. He couldn't quite place where he had heard it before, and yet as he strolled confidently through the rows of cubicles illuminated by the dull fluorescent lights of the office, the lyrics came to him slowly, like a flower blossoming. He sang under his breath, "Hmm, hmmm, dolphins and something and such…"

The Hole Out Back

No one in the family knew where the hole out back had come from — it just appeared behind the toolshed one day. Micah and I found it one afternoon while playing with our GI Joe toys. It wasn't a very big hole back then. When we first found it, it was no larger around than my skinny, little arm. Micah and I had been waging all-out war against my brother Deon's Star Wars action figures for the better part of the day when Cobra Commander slipped from Micah's grip and rolled down the dirt mound we had built the day before. Both of us were too slow to stop the evil head of COBRA from falling into the inky blackness of the hole.

Micah and I debated for a few minutes about who had dug the hole; it turned out to be neither of us. Once we agreed the hole was not any of our doing, we started to ponder if it could have been built by a snake or gopher. After all, the hole was no larger than one dug by either of those animals. However, unlike a gopher hole, this one went straight down into darkness and just seemed to keep going. We looked into that earthen tunnel but could see nothing — nothing but deep darkness leading down into unseen depths.

Scrambling for a better view, since the back of our family's toolshed was under perpetual shade thanks to the avocado tree next to it, we dashed into the shed and rummaged about, frantically searching for my dad's flashlight. After tossing aside some girlie magazines my dad kept hidden out there, we found the flashlight, tested it, and headed back out around the shed to the hole.

I had seen my fair share of snake holes in Scouts, and this, Micah and I quickly realized, was no such construct. While most animal holes weren't very deep and quickly veered off to join the underground network of similarly built tunnels, this hole appeared to just keep going down. The beam from the Maglite carried on for what looked like a few feet before darkness swallowed the rest of the beam.

Micah and I exchanged knowing glances — we knew just the man to rescue our beloved, villainous figure from the abyss far below. Minutes later, Snake Eyes (tied to the end of a freshly opened spool of twine) was slowly lowered into the hole — our brave ninja traversing regions unknown as he descended into the depths unseen. Micah and I watched with mouths agape as the string remained taut after several long minutes. Our soldier had not yet hit the bottom. We came to the end of the spool, and it seemed that we still had depths to go. After rescuing Snake Eyes from suffering a similar uncertain fate as Cobra Commander, we re-spooled the twine and decided to play in the house for the rest of the day.

Something about that hole made both of us feel ill at ease.

It would be years before Micah, and I discussed the uneasy feelings the hole left us with that afternoon. I don't know if Micah had the same disquieting dreams as I did after that, but my nightmares were always filled with that hole. I never fell into the hole completely, but every night I would be inches from the edge, toppling over by accident, only to awaken in a sweat just before actually falling into the abyss.

Of course, I told my folks about the hole. "Probably belongs to a garden snake," my mother would say distractedly.

"I bet it's gophers," my dad would lazily reply while looking over his morning newspaper.

A few days after the discovery of the hole, I began to formulate a plan. I had intended to ask Micah for his help, but when we hung out, he never wanted to discuss the hole (and I, for one, did not blame him). While my idea was simple, the thought of going near that hole scared me something fierce. Since my folks and Micah were not a viable option, I instead told my brother about the strange hole. He agreed to help, but I could tell that my plan left him feeling shaken too.

The day after I talked to Deon about the hole, he and I headed out to the shed. Inside, we moved boxes from one end of the shed to the other, like ants carrying crumbs of food back to their colony. We found what we were looking after a few minutes. Dragging out the old, wooden pallet that lay against the back wall, we brought it around behind the shed. Deon and I measured the pallet. It was just barely big enough to lay flat between the back of the shed and the garden wall. Together, with me pulling and him pushing, we managed to slowly move the pallet closer to the hole. As I backed nearer and nearer to the small circular pit, the feeling of dread continued to mount — I was beginning to feel like a thermometer in a slowly boiling cup of water. I kept my gaze over my shoulder at all times as I pulled and strained to bring the pallet ever closer. From what little of the hole I could see in my periphery, it now looked a little larger, about the size of the opening of a can of coffee.

Eventually, Deon and I managed to get the pallet directly over the hole. Deon hopped up on top of the pallet and began to do a little jig. My heart caught in my throat as the pallet creaked and groaned under his feet. I knew the pallet was far wider than the hole, but still terror rose in me, washing over and washing away all other feelings in that moment. I begged and pleaded with Deon to stop what he was doing. Deon kept at it, laughing and giggling. Then we heard the sound of dirt moving. Deon blanched. In one brazen leap, he jumped from atop the pallet and landed on his knees in the dirt beside me. Stricken with fear, we both turned to look at the pallet as it sat there, the faint sound of dirt still crumbling underneath the wooden structure.

Deon and I backed away from behind the shed and returned to the house. I quietly thanked my older brother for his help, and he quietly told me, "You're welcome."

Just as with Micah, it would be many years before Deon, and I talked again about the hole.

* * *

By the end of our junior year in high school, Micah and I had been dating for several months. He was on the track team, and I was in tennis; between the two of us, we had a full regiment of exercise and training. Every other day, Micah would come over and we would do jumping jacks, or jump rope out back, or shoot some hoops in front of the garage. The days had grown longer, and with that came extended shoot-outs in the driveway. One afternoon, the two of us played a game of Horse to pass the time until my dad finished making dinner. I leapt, the ball in my hands, the pre-summer sweat covering every inch of my body, when Micah, leaping up like a damn jackrabbit, slapped the ball out of my hands. As I came back down to the earth, my ass hitting the pavement hard, I watched the ball soar away from where Micah had slapped it, up over the backboard, over the garage roof, and deep into our back yard.

"Shit, I'm sorry," he said, pulling me up from where I landed on the hot driveway.

"Go get the ball, you moron," I said playfully. I couldn't blame my boyfriend or his excitement. After all, I was often guilty of the same tactics, so I certainly wasn't one to judge. Micah flashed me that winning grin of his, melting my heart as he dashed around the side of the garage and into the back yard. Several minutes passed and Micah did not return. "Did you get lost?" I called out from the driveway, my hands cupped around my mouth in a crude megaphone.

For a long time, I did not hear a reply. Then Micah called out weakly from the far end of the back yard, "You need to get back here."

I jogged around the side of the house, opened the backyard gate, and walked slowly across the hilly lawn my parents kept behind the house. Walking past the rows of ferns and flowers and the shitty cement fountain built by the house's original owners in the 1950s, I headed toward the far end of the yard. I did not see Micah anywhere. As I cast my gaze around, my eyes fell on the avocado tree and the old toolshed. My heart sank. A creeping feeling of dread, something palpable I had not felt in a long time, began to envelop me.

"Micah?" I heard myself ask.

"Behind the shed," Micah replied, my worst fears realized. He had found the hole.

When I came around the corner, I was immensely relieved to see Micah standing there, the ball tucked under his arm. Fear left me for a split second, but then I spotted what Micah was pointing at. The pallet Deon and I had pulled over the small hole so many years ago was rotted and crumbling under its own weight. The wood was green with growth and porous from being eaten inside-out by termites. Underneath the bent and broken wood, I could see what Micah was pointing at. The hole, the thing that had been no bigger around than a child's arm when we were little, was now nearly as wide as the pallet.

"I had convinced myself it was all a dream," Micah said in a somber tone. "It wasn't a dream, was it? We weren't just playing make-believe that day, were we?"

I shook my head. I don't know if Micah could see the gesture in his periphery. His gaze was locked on the pallet and the absolute darkness of the hole peeking out from below it. I stood there transfixed, unable to move or speak, just barely able to comprehend what we were both gawking at. A snapping and crackling sound made me jump. It took my brain a moment to recognize what was happening. Micah, still in a daze, had kicked the pallet. We both watched in silent horror as the wooden platform succumbed to gravity and time and split apart into the gaping maw below. We could see the splintered remains tumble down into the inky, absolute darkness for a few seconds, and then it was gone. Even the earthen walls of the hole's circumference vanished into oblivion just a few feet below the surface.

The idea of falling into the literal unknown made my mind feel as though it had unceremoniously dropped from my skull straight into my bowels. Before I knew what was happening, I began to retch where I stood. My body shook and my skin was cool and clammy like plastic. Micah led me into the house. I could tell he was shaking too, as he helped me along. I could see just how unsteady his hands were when he fetched a glass of water from the kitchen, spilling the contents down the sides of the cup. I took the glass from him and gulped down as much water as I could. I looked at him for some kind of comfort, a dash of reassurance in a peculiar situation. Micah, I could tell, was gone. He had a faraway look that told me he was beyond being merely lost in thought. That look worried me.

Drinking too fast, I began to cough and sputter. Micah snapped to attention, returning to the moment. He saw what a mess I was and helped me clean up, but as he wiped me down, I could see him casting curious glances out the back window and toward the shed.

Later that day, when I showed my parents the hole, they simply laughed and said it was nothing, probably something a raccoon dug up. "Does that look like the kind of hole a raccoon would dig up?" I demanded. "Honestly, does it? Because it looks like something else entirely to me." My words seemed to fall on deaf ears.

Over the next couple of years, my parents never once brought up the hole. I would watch them from my bedroom window as they tended to their garden in the back yard and was stricken by horror whenever one of them headed behind the shed to dump whatever refuse they carried with them into the hole. Anything and everything seemed to get tossed down the hole, and my parents didn't think anything of it. I watched them toss grass clippings, leaves, weeds, dirt, garbage, and even broken furniture down there. Our garbage bill with the city became next to nil as a result. But I kept my eye on the hole, seeing it get slightly bigger with each load my parents tossed down. At the time I didn't know which frightened me more, the hole itself or my folks' apparent lack of acknowledging the thing.

* * *

Micah and I had been married for almost a decade and a half when my folks announced their retirement plans. In addition to no longer working, they were going to sell us the house and move back to Oklahoma. Micah and I were thrilled — we would finally have a home where our kids could have separate rooms, and the dog could run around in the back yard.

Three months into my parents' retirement, we signed the documents that transferred the mortgage to us and moved in. The four of us, Micah, myself, and the twins, had our first dinner alone in the house. It was bliss. I couldn't think of a more perfect place to raise our children than the home where I had been raised. But all throughout that dinner, something kept gnawing at the back of my thoughts. We had the house, both a front and a back yard, a detached garage, and the old toolshed — everything was perfect. Wasn't it?

That night, I sat up in bed while Micah snored next to me. It felt as though something was missing, or that I'd forgotten about something. Something terrible. Maybe, I began to reason, it wasn't that something was missing but that I was afraid to find something.

I couldn't quite explain it, but over the years the hole had left my thoughts. I couldn't think of the hole that night as I sat awake. Gazing at the far wall of what had once been my parents' bedroom,

I could see something forming in my memories of the place —
something terrible — something I did not want to face. A cavity, a
deep, dark abyss into the unknown, sat perched in the back of my
thoughts. After a few hours of staring at the wall, I attempted to go
back to sleep; but sleep did not come.

The next day, Micah and I set to work making the house a home
for us. I wanted to be more thrilled than I felt. I wanted to shout
my excitement from the rooftops, but I couldn't. That afternoon,
the kids and I pulled weeds in the back yard, a dark cloud hanging
over my every thought.

At some point I encountered a root from a long dead tree that
needed to be exhumed to make way for new plants. My trowel
wasn't cutting it. Standing up and wiping the dirt from my jeans, I
headed to the old toolshed to see what my dad had left behind for
us. I hoped that the old shovel might still be in there. As I reached
for the handle to the shed, a thought struck me.

"Kids, have you seen your father?"

The twins shrugged before returning to their pile of dirt, playing
with dirt clods rather than actually helping with any gardening.

"Back here," I eventually heard a small voice respond.

Walking around the shed, searching for what sounded like my
husband's voice from miles away, I found Micah. He stood there,
transfixed, his eyes cast to the ground in the shade of the avocado
tree. I thought he was gazing at the tree's shadow. Then it all hit
me like a train running at full speed. Every memory of the hole,
every feeling, every fear, all came flooding back. The hole was
larger now, reaching from the edge of the fence to the back of the
shed, easily big enough for someone to fall into.

"Do you remember this?" Micah asked as I stood beside him,
fear pulsing through my body with every beat of my heart.

"Micah, I think you need to step away from it," I said as
soothingly as I could. Micah would not look at me. He only had
eyes for the hole. The gaze in those eyes scared me more than the
hole did. I looked from my husband's face, possessed by some
unknowable desire, to the endless darkness of the earthen pit.

Without saying another word, I stepped away from my husband,
bundled the kids into the car, and made straight for the home
improvement store. I grabbed several feet of chicken wire, five-
foot-tall wooden posts, and lots of nails. When I got back home, I

unloaded the van by myself and dragged my tools and purchases to the shed. Micah was still out there, gazing into the hole, the dog whimpering beside him on the ground at his feet.

I was not going to let one of my babies or the dog fall into that fucking thing.

I silently set to work. First, I covered the hole with a few layers of chicken wire, which I pinned to the ground using small stakes I fashioned from one of the big stakes. After that, I made a fence from the back of the shed to the walls on either side of the hole. I did all of this quickly and without Micah's help. Panic threatened to flood my thoughts as I worked. While I scurried about, doing what I could to fence off the nightmare in the earth behind my new home, I kept an eye on Micah — still unwilling to help — frozen in place. Finally, with the hole cut off from the rest of the yard, I threw a tarp over the fenced pit to hide it from view. This act alone seemed to pull my husband out of his trance and back into the moment.

That night, we all ate in silence. I tucked the twins into bed and let the dog out in spite of my trepidation about doing so. Thankfully, the pooch returned quickly after doing his business, and I was able to get into bed. In all the years I had known my husband, I had never seen him look so possessed by anything. It was a feeling beyond disturbing. It wasn't a lust or a desire — it wasn't even an obsession — it was something else, something unnatural. But then again, so too was the hole. That porthole cut into the living earth behind our house was unlike anything I had ever seen or known.

I eventually fell asleep. If Micah fell asleep, I could not say. It was sometime later when I woke up from my restless dreams — I could hear the dog whining to be let out again. Groggily, I dragged myself out of bed and into the kitchen where I found the dog scratching and whimpering at the back door. The dog shot out of the house and into the back yard like a bullet. Patiently, I waited for the dog to finish his business and indicate that he wanted back in the house. I began to doze off as I sat at the kitchen counter, waiting. At some point, my hands holding my head slipped, and I was woken by the motion.

There was still no sign of the dog. Grumbling, I opened the back door and stepped out into the early morning darkness. I called the dog's name a few times, but no response. *Great*, I thought, *he probably caught an opossum and is playing with it.* At that early hour, the back yard was an intricate tapestry of shadows, some quite still and some moving in the light breeze. Searching about for the dog, I gave a few small whistles. Eventually, I heard the pooch. He was out near the shed. An uneasy feeling began to swallow my thoughts whole. As I came around the side of the shed, I could see the dog sitting by the fence I had erected earlier, his ears pulled back in fear, his body low to the ground. Squinting in the half-light, I could see that something was wrong, not with the dog, but with my handiwork.

The fence had been cut cleanly down the middle and was now peeled back on either side like a patient's chest during open-heart surgery. Cautiously, I stepped forward and looked into the shadows. The stakes were pulled up. The tarp and wiring I had run across the hole were both gone. The deep, unending darkness of the pit against the deep, unending darkness of the night looked ready to consume. I stood there on the edge of the precipice, daring not to look directly into the maw of eternity. Slowly, I began to back away. The dog barked. I jumped and turned around. Micah was standing there behind me. I could feel his hot breath on my face, his chest heaving.

"Micah?" I said.

Micah did not reply. Looking into his eyes, I could see that something terrible was wrong; he still had that look of a man possessed, only now it was worse. They say that the eyes are the window to the soul, but whatever soul was gazing out of my husband's eyes in that moment was not his own. The next thing I felt were Micah's hands as his strong arms pushed me in the chest. There was a moment of stepping backwards and, in that moment, I could feel not only the empty air beneath my feet, but I could feel whatever was possessing my husband leave him as the deed was done. I tumbled in the air for a moment, my world turning end over end until all I could see was the look of sadness in Micah's eyes and then nothing more. I suppose I expected to see anguish or shock but deep down, I think he knew that it was always going to end this way.

I don't know how long I've been falling. I still have that sickening feeling in my stomach. The wind is strong and stings my eyes. I've been trying to reach out in the darkness to feel for the earthen walls of the hole, but I cannot feel anything. Even if I could, I know that at this speed I would never be able to grab hold of a perch or find the strength to pull myself up out of this thing, whatever it truly is. Nearest I can figure, I've been falling for hours now. I wonder what will kill me first, hunger or the fall. If this hole truly has no end, I can only assume that I will be falling forever. There's no point in pondering where this thing came from, what it is, or even where it leads. I know that this is my fate, to fall forever in darkness, the wind rushing by.

Sometimes, I think I can see stars in that darkness — far-off galaxies — infinite worlds. In those moments, I blink away the tears and allow the void to continue endlessly swallowing me.

At least I can take some small comfort in the fact that the sensation of falling, the sensation I now recognize as the one that has been plaguing me all these years, has passed. All I can do now is just embrace the fall and feel no more.

The Waiting Room

The waiting room was long and empty, save for the small boy sitting attentively on a couch in the back corner; his expression was placid, but he gave off an air of bundled nervousness. Aside from the child's slow, steady breathing, his eyes were the only part of him that moved. The gleaming white parquet floor glistened underneath a row of starburst Sputnikesque lights that ran down the middle of the ceiling from one end of the room to the other. In the center of the room sat a mid-century space-age table and chairs made of white curved plastic and deep orange cushions. Egg-like seats, also adorned with orange cushions, were arrayed against one wall. The couch the small boy occupied by himself was long and also a deep burgundy orange.

Nothing about the waiting room was unusual save for the far wall. The boy looked at the wall, his eyes struggling to focus. The wall was composed of several honeycomb alcoves that reached from floor to ceiling and ran from one end of the room to the other. Despite the warm and rather intense light from the fixtures above, the alcoves remained nearly pitch black — no sense of depth to be discerned. One might mistakenly think they were painted in a matte finish, but the boy knew deep down that this was not the case.

While there was no music in the waiting room, no flipping of magazines, and certainly no chattering people about, there was the whispering. It was impossible for the child to discern what was being said, but the whispering was constant — low in volume and unending.

The small boy was dressed in overalls, sneakers, a t-shirt, and a red hoodie. He did not move. No one, as far as he knew, was supposed to do anything else in the waiting room except wait. What he was waiting for, the boy could not say, but he knew that he had to wait, and so wait he did.

A colorful, spoked clock on the far wall ticked away each second, and yet neither of the hands moved even the slightest across the painted face — both the hour and minute hands hung limp and dead like a pair of dangling corpses from a gallows. The boy had no idea what time it was or how long he had been sitting there, but he knew that he must wait. Occasionally, his eyes would dart from the doorway to the black, hexagonal alcoves, and then back to the door.

The whispers continued to coalesce and reverberate around the room. Still the small boy could not understand what was being said. The boy wanted to get up and look around. He wanted to stretch, and speak, and play with something or someone — but still he sat, doing as the waiting room dictated. He waited on and on.

Eventually, the door at the far end of the long room opened. The room beyond the waiting room was blindingly bright. The small boy could not make out any details before a man stepped into the waiting room and closed the door silently behind him, latching it shut with the softest of clicks. The whispers continued their unending chorus, unabated as the man stood there in front of the door just below the clock that ticked but did not move. The man stepped away from the door and took a seat at the table in the center of the room, not paying the small boy on the sofa any heed. Like the small boy, he, too, sat perfectly still, waiting.

The man was portly and stout and wore a Hawaiian shirt, resplendent with tropical birds and palm fronds. His head was balding, a laurel crown of hair around his head and a pair of dark glasses over his face. The man did not say a word. He just gazed at the wall of alcoves and did nothing more. The small boy stopped looking from the door to the alcoves and instead watched the man. The man sat bolt upright in his chair, his twiddling thumbs the only betrayal of movement. The small boy had an urge to twiddle his thumbs too, but still he did as he knew he must. He waited.

The child was so intently focused on the man that he nearly missed the door opening again. This time a young woman stepped into the room, and once again the door closed softly behind her. She stood tall, her hair shoulder-length and her blue flower-print dress cut to ankle height. She wore high heels and deep scarlet lipstick. Her dress swished as she walked and took a seat at the round, plastic table across from the man in the Hawaiian shirt.

The whispering continued and the small boy remained in his seat. Something about the pair in the room felt familiar to the small boy, but the feeling was fleeting. The boy was good and obedient and continued to wait. The man and woman sat across from each other but did not look at each other. Instead, like the small boy had been doing, they cast their gaze at the alcoves in the wall.

The door opened a third time. The boy spotted the handle turning and watched as an older couple, stooped and bent of back, shuffled into the room. Their faces were a web of wrinkles. The couple both wore expressions similar to the younger man and woman who still sat across from one another — eyes still locked upon the alcoves. The man held a wooden cane in one hand and the old woman's hand in the other. He wore a smart suit and jacket while she wore a skirt and blouse underneath a long, warm-looking coat.

Slowly — accompanied by the shuffle of their feet, and scrape of the cane, and the chorus of whispers — the couple made their way across the room to the couch and sat down with great effort next to the small boy. Like the man and woman who had entered before them, they turned to gaze in silence upon the wall of alcoves.

No one else entered the waiting room for some time.

Finally, the door opened one last time and a young man dressed in a beat-up pair of jeans and a black t-shirt entered the room. His face also wore no expression, save for the blank one all the others in the waiting room shared. Without saying a word, the young man, his hair slicked back and his cheeks rosy, found a seat in one of the egg-shaped chairs along the far wall. Like every other soul in the room, he gazed at the alcove wall and remained stone-still and silent.

The small boy noticed that, while he had watched the newcomers step into the room with great curiosity, none of the room's other occupants had moved their eyes from the alcoves as the others entered. The whispering continued, filling the room like an invisible smoke that danced unseen but felt.

Time did not seem to exist — the small boy sat perfectly still, as did the middle-aged man, and the young woman, and the elderly couple, and the young man. Watching the room, the small boy's jaw clenched tight as he swept his gaze from visitor to visitor. The whispers slowly began to grow louder. While the droning never formed into coherent words, the hissing tone grew in pitch and volume.

Across the room, the young woman in the flower-print dress pushed back her chair, stood, and turned to face the wall of honeycomb-shaped alcoves. The darkness within each one appeared to grow darker still — less a lack of light and more a lack of existence. The woman, without saying a word or acknowledging anyone else in the room, stepped forward and walked to the nearest waist-high alcove. Stooping down, she pulled herself in, hands and arms first. After a few moments of adjusting, the small boy could see her sitting sideways in the alcove, her form, a lonely profile fixed in time and space. The darkness seemed to envelop her slowly, swallowing her whole — all of this happened in complete silence.

Moments later she was gone, replaced only by that deep, impenetrable darkness of the alcove. The whispering continued on, still undulating in the small boy's ears like waves on a beach rushing and receding with the tide.

Time passed. How much time, the small boy could not tell, but it passed all the same.

The whispers continued.

Out of the corner of his eye, the small boy watched the older couple help each other up from the couch without a word. They slowly shuffled their way to the wall of blackened alcoves. Dropping to their hands and knees, joints creaking and popping audibly, the old man and old woman crawled like babies into floor-level alcoves next to one another. They, too, vanished into the thick, oppressive darkness.

Sometime later, the young man who had entered the room last stood from his egg-like chair and crossed the room in a few long strides. He selected an alcove higher up than the old couple's and the woman's alcoves. He climbed up to the alcove of his choice, one that sat midway up the wall. Once he reached it, the young man hoisted himself up and slid into the alcove on his back, headfirst. The small boy watched, expressionless and emotionless, as the young man's feet were swallowed by the darkness that slowly pulled him inside itself.

There were only two left now: the small boy and the middle-aged man in the Hawaiian shirt. The man continued to stare at the wall from his seat at the table. The small boy continued to stare at the man. The clock on the wall persisted in waging its war against entropy and sat unchanged. The whispering continued to echo and reverberate throughout the room. The man did not move; he was statue-still with only the slight, almost indiscernible rise and fall of his chest to betray that he was made of flesh and bone and not stone.

Slowly — slower than any of the other occupants, including the elderly couple — the man rose from his seat. His chair glided silently across the floor as he pushed it back. Stepping forward, he reached out toward the wall as if he was about to grope in the dark. One step, then another, and then another, carrying on until he reached the wall. The alcove the man selected was at knee-high level. Ducking down, he sidled into the hole in the wall and sat waiting in the alcove. Like a thick mist, darkness enveloped the man, and within seconds, the alcove appeared to be empty.

Alone once more, the small boy remained unmoving. He had to wait — everyone had to wait until their time came, he knew. He was a good boy, after all, and wanted to remain so. The room seemed instantly bigger than it had a moment before; with no one left, the furniture came off as a pale substitute for a warm, waiting body. For a while the small boy kept his gaze locked on the door on the other end of the room, but no one entered. He dared not look at the alcove wall. With everyone else gone, something about it did not sit right with him.

In that moment, the whispering vanished, and the small boy knew what he had to do. Sliding off the couch, he walked slowly across the room, past the egg-like chairs and the table, passing silently underneath the starburst ceiling lights, and stopping at the wall. The darkness in each alcove was deeper than he could comprehend — it hurt his eyes and brain to gaze into it. There were no shapes to make out, only the purity of darkness. It was both the absolute lack of light and, at the same time, all colors mixed together.

The darkness in the alcoves gave off no heat or cold. There were no sounds or sensations. There was simply the darkness. Knowing what was expected of him, the small boy crawled into the nearest alcove, sat with his back against the wall and his shoulder facing the room. He sat there for what felt like an eternity without moving, without speaking, just waiting. The darkness came and enveloped him. The darkness passed. The waiting room sat empty and waiting.

Northern Lights

The forest primeval was dark and frozen but it was very much alive. An owl, wings unfurled, eyes keenly searching the Earth below, a silent sentinel on its nightly patrol. Through brush and bramble stripped of their leaves and blossoms, a pair of snow foxes dashed and weaved; their small, furry forms elegantly and effortlessly adjusting to every contour of the snowy terrain.

The Snow glistened that night, almost phosphorescent, covering the world like a cold, indifferent blanket of winking fireflies. In the distance, the sound of a twig snapping, and the crunch of snow underfoot echoed throughout the skeletal trees, breaking the primordial silence. A light bobbed and weaved with each step as it cut through the forest, shattering the darkness within the circle of illumination emanating from the young woman's flashlight.

Ingrid's breath escaped her mouth like smoke from a powerful steam locomotive. Her eyes peeked out from deep underneath the brim of her cap. Ahead in the darkness, something moved from branch to branch in the trees above. Ingrid knew it was an owl. She had seen a few watching her, their large, cat-like eyes following her with every movement in rapt concentration as she passed through their domain so late in the night.

Her eyes set upon the small circular window of illuminated forest in front of her and she found herself taken back to her childhood — how many times had she sat on Papa's knee, listening to his fantastical tales of trolls and fairies and monsters of the woods? How many nights had his stories kept her up with fear and excitement? In those days she would listen attentively and in pure awe, always wondering what sort of creature or beastie Papa would pour into her head, and the subsequent dreams and nightmares once she found herself tucked in and falling to sleep.

As Ingrid got older, her thoughts left the woods of the goblins and trolls and instead found their way to boys and parties, makeup and gossip. Eventually, she came to reject the makeup and found her thoughts lingered less on boys and more and more on women. Inevitably, Ingrid grew older, as did her friends — small lives growing toward adulthood in a small town. With the last vestiges of her childhood fading into adolescence, she and her friends spent their time working after school, smoking after work, and drinking and cavorting the nights away whenever, wherever, and however possible.

In such a small town, drinking was the only escape. Ingrid had watched as her friends dropped out of school, one by one, and taken up work logging, or working in their parents' shops, or joining the fishing fleets. The perpetual winters and long nights only helped fuel the isolation Ingrid and her friends felt growing within them day by agonizingly long day. She could think of no one in town who had ever gone off to college and returned. The joke among the teenagers was that their town was the kind of place you either returned to when you were ready to die, or that you never escaped in the first place.

Ingrid wanted to escape more than anything else in the world. Filling her days with hunting and stripping reindeer carcasses for market was not even close to the life she had imagined for herself. Amongst all the drinking and partying, Ingrid and her small circle of friends had found joy in music and movies. Through these mediums, they all began to plot their escape. Someday, they all promised each other, they would flee their frozen hell and find solace amongst the glitz and glamor of Hollywood or New York.

Taking a step through a deep patch of snow, Ingrid felt the tip of her boot catch on a root. Gravity took hold, and the young woman felt the earth rushing to meet her. Hitting the snow face first, her eyes burned with tears while her face flushed red as unfounded embarrassment seized her in spite of the lack of anyone being around to witness her stumble. She stifled a cry and as a result felt her body convulse, wracked by sobs. She was so close to where she wanted to be — she had to keep going. The mantra of pressing on played in her head like a tape on loop; each time she told herself to keep moving forward, she could feel a little more strength take hold and fill her with the adrenaline she so desperately needed.

After what seemed like an eternity, Ingrid found herself standing in the snow, surrounded by the darkness, the woods, and her need to move on. Wiping frost from her cheeks, Ingrid spotted a small smear of blood on the back of her gloved hand. A twig must've caught her face on the way down, she reasoned. Tightening her grip on the flashlight, the young woman brushed herself off, wiped at her tears and bloody nose, and continued on her way.

Setting off once more, Ingrid allowed her thoughts to resume their wandering nature. She thought about her friends and about their escape plans and their pact. One by one they had started to flee from the drudgery of it all. First Lars, then Sven, followed closely by Gertrude, and the most recent departure of Amelie. It had surprised Ingrid to find out that many others before her had escaped at one time or another. No one in town talked about it willingly despite it happening. Now, here she was making her own escape, fighting the bitter cold and trudging through the woods and snow toward her destination.

The night dragged on, and eventually the woods began to thin out before her. The sky above was a panoply of stars — the moon, a curved sliver of ice. Ingrid came to a clearing, the place where the others had come. Casting the beam from her flashlight about, expelling the darkness, she spotted the rock, the one all those who had come before her had made the pilgrimage to. In the middle of the clearing sat a dark hunk of ancient volcanic rock, like a splinter in a fingertip. Ingrid trudged the last few feet from the tree line to the rocky outcropping that jutted toward the dark void of the heavens above.

She found a relatively flat spot upon the rough stone, dusted off the freshly fallen snow, and sat. Switching the flashlight off, the young woman allowed the darkness to envelop and embrace her like a mother's hug. From inside her coat, she produced a small bottle of whisky. Tossing off the cap and putting the bottle to her lips, Ingrid welcomed the warm flow as she poured the whole thing down her throat in one go. Warmth washed over her as the blood vessels constricted from the sudden rush of alcohol in her system.

Without a second thought, Ingrid tossed the bottle out into the snow, followed closely by the flashlight. Leaning back against the frozen stone, she gazed at the endless starry void before her. With the trees no longer in her field of view and with only the heavens above in their seemingly endless depths, Ingrid swore that she could feel the pull of all the Earth's gravity upon her. She clung to the surface of the planet as though being strapped in and riding a rollercoaster. Here she was, a tiny speck of dust clinging to a slightly larger speck of dust, careening through the void at speeds she could scarcely begin to comprehend.

The night passed on. The light from the moon began to fade as the sliver set beneath the tree line. For a time, the young woman had the sky and darkness to herself. The backbone of the night spread from one end of her view to the other, as though Mother Earth had let loose her precious breast milk. Seconds turned to minutes that eventually turned to hours. Slowly, almost imperceptibly at first, a new light began to grow all around Ingrid. Her eyes wide open, still gazing at the stars, she began to see the dancing ribbons of light that frequented the night skies of her hemisphere at this time of year. The aurora began to unfurl its sheer, undulating curtains in reds and greens and blues — a cosmic display just for her and her alone. Like a child growing up next to the sea whose whole life experience came from their environment, Ingrid was keenly aware of the phenomena now playing out high above her but had been nonplused by the very experience — this time, however, something was different.

Along with all the monster tales and fairy stories of her youth, Ingrid had been told that if she listened closely, she could hear the crackle and hiss of the aurora. Never in her young life had she heard this, but now her ears were filling with the mysterious voice of the aurora itself. As she listened, Ingrid could hear what sounded like whispers as the bands of light rippled and shuddered above her. Was this what the others had seen when they, too, escaped, Ingrid wondered? Closing her eyes tightly, she simply let go and listened.

A voice began to speak all around in hushed, haunted tones. "I am here." It sounded as neither man nor woman — genderless and as ancient as the cosmos. "I am here, Ingrid."

Ingrid's eyes flew open, and she gazed back up at the cosmic fireworks display.

"Ingrid, I am here for you," it whispered seductively. "Are you ready, Ingrid?"

Ingrid nodded.

"You know what to do, child. You know what the others did to escape. You must do the same."

Ingrid reached back inside her coat and pulled out the cold, glinting form of a small revolver.

"Ingrid, join the others. Join with me. See me for what I truly am, Ingrid."

Ingrid held the pistol firmly above her face — a cold, steel reality floating between the stars and her. Ingrid allowed her focus to move casually, almost in time with the unheard tempo of the aurora, from the gun back to the night sky. Without awe or surprise or any discernible emotion, Ingrid watched as the curtains of the aurora spread wide, revealing the darkness of the void beyond. No stars dwelt within that void. Ingrid could see a landscape carved of dark mountains and valleys, and black as pitch oceans filled with dark smoke and dark beings. She could not make out the beings' exact shapes, as her mind was unable to comprehend their true forms. She could feel the beings gazing at her and knew that her friends had been looked upon by these denizens of the void as she was now. The void, she could tell, was pure and endless darkness. Suddenly she no longer felt the gravity of the Earth holding her in place against the rock she lay upon. Now she felt weightless as though the planet had stopped in its orbit and allowed the revolving of eons to switch off with a halt. Reaching out with one hand, Ingrid sought to touch the void while pulling back the hammer on the revolver with her other hand. Mechanically, her arm moved to her head and pressed the cold end of the barrel to her throbbing temple.

"Ingrid, join us," the voice growled, no longer the seductive whisper. "Ingrid, join us!" the voice now demanded.

Ingrid's finger squeezed the trigger.

There was a click.

There was a chemical reaction.

There was a moment of momentum.

There was a bullet leaving its casing.

There was a momentary feeling as the bullet moved from the machine to the flesh and bone and then back out through bone and flesh and into the night.

The gun fell to the rocks, clattered, then lay silent. Ingrid's body fell to the snow with a soft thud. At the same moment, Ingrid found herself screaming without noise and kicking as she flew with the speed of the bullet into the starless void above her. She saw her friends briefly as they pulled her with arms no longer human.

Ingrid wanted to turn back once realization dawned, but it was too late.

Tumbling into the all-consuming nothingness, Ingrid finally found her escape as the denizens of the void feasted once more.

59

Part Two: Beyond

COLIN WALKER

IV

The Bad Door

Massachusetts — Spring, 1955

To Rose, the house was perfect.

2312 Brookstone Avenue was a modest turn-of-the-century house. The two-story abode had a wraparound porch, stonework around the outside, and sat on a lovely plot of land sprinkled with trees, a large lawn, and a sturdy gate and fence. While many of the other houses on the street were larger and more modern, 2312 was a little slice of the past — it was exactly what Rose and Sam had been looking for. Although the couple was still childless, the promise of multiple bedrooms in the house gave the pair visions of rug-rats in every room. They had been so thrilled to find out that even with Sam's modest earnings from the factory job he had landed after the war, and with Rose as a dedicated homemaker, they could afford the house of their dreams right out the gate. The realtor had been blunt during their first meeting, telling the young newlywed couple that no one ever found their dream house the first time they set out to purchase a home. Rose and Sam had bristled with excitement at the notion that, despite their realtor's reality check, they had done the seemingly impossible.

Moving day came quicker than Rose expected. The day was a whirlwind of boxes and furniture and strangers — men from the moving company taking orders on where to place what, and what to place next, and so on and so forth.

"Oh, Sam." Rose beamed, her face flushed from excitement. "It's really happening, isn't it?"

"It sure is," Sam said with a broad grin. "It sure is. By this time next week, you'll have your kitchen and sewing rooms all set up the way you want them." Sam looked around and watched as two young men came in through the oak front door, a loveseat between them as they contorted their bodies and wriggled the small couch into the house. The air was thick with dust as the movers went about their tasks. Through the windows, the shutters thrown wide open, and curtains pulled back, soft, late morning light poured in, warming the rooms in a welcoming way.

It had been some time since Rose last felt this much excitement and anticipation. Sam usually had a temper on him, especially when drinking, but to Rose's knowledge, he had not touched a drop in the last few weeks. As a result, his spirits were up, and she had not had to cower from his anger and the back of his hand. Rose told herself that boys will be boys, and on those angry occasions she figured he was right to put her in her place. Still, she did hold out some hope that his drinking days were behind him, if only for the extra attention — this loving attention he now paid her. Not since their days of dating, before Sam was unceremoniously shipped off to Korea, had she felt so good about their relationship. Rose contentedly slipped out of her reverie as the movers stepped away from where Sam had directed them to place the loveseat.

"Sam?" Rose asked. "What time did Mr. Diabold say he was coming over?"

"Anytime now," Sam replied.

As if on cue, the front door opened and in stepped a small, mustached man in a tweed suit and clipboard.

"Hello, Sam!" the small man shouted across the room before skittering toward the couple. The two men shook hands.

"How ya doing, Mr. Diabold?" Sam asked, beaming. Sam's father and Mr. Diabold had been close college chums. So, naturally, the real estate agent leapt at the chance to help his old fraternity pal's young son and his blushing bride settle into a new home.

"I'm doing splendid, my friend. How are you and the missus getting on?" Mr. Diabold asked, nodding politely at Rose but addressing his questions about her at Sam.

"Oh, she's getting on fine. I know she's itching to get to know that kitchen," Sam said.

Rose nodded coquettishly, as she knew she should, throwing in a little blush for good measure.

"Good, good," Mr. Diabold replied, clearly not interested in the actual answer to his question. Placing his arm around Sam's shoulder, he continued, "Say, why don't I give you the grand tour of this fine home of yours? Show you the best place for a workbench for your tools. All the technical ins and outs of the place. You can show the little woman around later."

"Sounds like a swell plan," Sam said, grinning from ear to ear. "Say, Rose honey, why don't you go check on the kitchen, see how the movers are getting on in there with your boxes."

"Of course," she replied. "It was wonderful to see you again, Mr. Diabold," she added as the men turned to leave the living room for their boys-only tour of the place. Heaving a contented sigh, Rose turned to take in her new kitchen from where she stood in the living room. The pair had only seen the house once, on the day of their walkthrough when it was still on the market. Once the place had been confirmed for purchase and put into escrow, the couple had gone down to Mr. Diabold's office where Sam signed all the paperwork. Taking a big, excited breath, she stepped over the threshold and into her new kitchen — while Sam had the garage and the car and his tools, she had her realm of baking and cooking and luncheons.

Rose stood admiring her new stove as the movers hung her pots and pans on the rack above the range. There came a soft but steady knock at the back door. The back door in the kitchen led to the back of the yard. Since the house sat in the middle of the property, there were no fences separating the back yard from the front yard, just the fence and gate that surrounded the property itself. With a kick in her step, Rose shot across the room and made for the back door. In the door's stained-glass inlay, Rose could see the dark, shifting form of the visitor on the other side. Rose threw open the door, a smile on her face. "Hello?"

The woman who stood before Rose was old, her hair held in an Aqua Net bubble. She wore pearls around her neck, a simple blue dress, and a dour, disapproving expression.

"You the new owner?" the woman asked, her eyes squinting from behind her large cat-eye frames.

"Yes. I'm Rose," Rose replied. "My husband and I are moving in today."

"Well, I can see that," the woman said in a curt, no-nonsense tone.

"How can I help you, Missus...?"

"Miss, thank you very much," the old woman snapped. "It's Miss June Bleaker. I used to be a caretaker here."

"Oh, how wonderful," Rose replied.

June snorted. "Well, are you going to invite me in?"

Not wanting to be rude, and happy to make the acquaintance of someone new, Rose beckoned the old woman inside. Stepping into the kitchen, June gave another snort as she removed her glasses and began to rub the lenses intensely with a small floral-patterned cloth she had produced from her handbag. "It's too dusty in here," she grumbled before giving an obviously fake sneeze.

"God bless you," Rose said.

"Oh, it's my allergies. This dust is going to give me such a sore throat and headache," June grumbled, slipping her glasses back on and covering her mouth and nose with the floral cloth.

"I'm afraid the moving has kicked up all the settled dust. Once the movers have left for the day, I planned on dusting a bit. If I can find my duster, that is," Rose replied courteously.

"Have you had a proper tour of the grounds and house?" June asked, clearly interested in changing the subject from domesticity to something else.

"Not an extensive tour, no," Rose replied. "Sam, my husband, and I took a quick tour when we first saw the house, but that was about it." Rose turned to see Sam and Mr. Diabold, thick as thieves, deep in conversation as they passed through the living room. "Maybe you could give me a tour since you used to work here." Rose noted how June watched the two chummy men, daggers in her eyes. Rose gave a small, polite cough, hoping to regain the older woman's attention.

June squinted at Rose, then nodded approvingly. "This house," the old woman began, "was built in 1892 by the Lomwell family. You'll know them — the grandson Tobias runs the pharmacy in town. Considering that this place is some sixty-five years old, it's in very good shape, if I do say so myself." Rose nodded along as June continued breathlessly, "Tobias sold the house a few months back — 'house is too old for my taste,' he told me. It worked out fine, though, as I was getting set to retire, and without a Lomwell to *lord* over this place, staying on just seemed pointless."

June led Rose out of the kitchen, continuing to discuss the history of the house and its relation to nearly everyone in town. Wordlessly, Rose followed June from room to room and from story to story. Every brick, and stone, and crack, and corner of the house was laid out in a level of detail Rose had never imagined possible for such a modest and well-preserved piece of local history. Back in the living room, June went on at some length about not only where the Lomwell family had come from (Arkham, Massachusetts) but where their relatives had come from (Hessian mercenaries employed by the British to fight against the colonists). In each bedroom, June had discussed the finer points of raising the Lomwell children, all of whom had moved away, save for Tobias. June followed up the inside of the house by continuing the tour in the garage (once a stable) and around the grounds. In the wooded back yard and gardens, June, between exaggerated bouts of sneezing and coughing, went on at great length about what plants caused her allergies to flare up.

Rose took all this in stride. She indulged the woman, even if she suspected that half of what she claimed to know was a complete and utter fabrication. Rose had been raised to be polite. As the child of a life-long schoolteacher, she had grown up with a strong sense of patience that even her husband admired. Rose let June yammer on about this and that, allowing the woman's obvious sense of self-importance continue to feed her desire to impress the new owner of the house she had once called home. After an hour and a half of strolling around the property, the tour came to its natural conclusion where it had begun, back in the kitchen. In the time the two women had been out and about, the movers had unpacked nearly all of the pots, pans, dishes, and other such culinary and dining odds and ends.

In the living room, the movers were trying to figure out how to get the bed frame upstairs and into the master bedroom. Rose had hoped that Sam and Mr. Diabold would have finished their own tour so that Sam could go back to directing them. Instead, she spotted her husband and the realtor slinging back beers outside of the garage, laughing. June's icy gaze lingered on the two men outside of the kitchen window, while Rose politely stood nearby, inwardly saddened to see alcohol once again in her husband's hand but helpless to do anything about it.

"Well now, that about does it. If you have any questions or need anything, please don't hesitate to call," June said, turning from the view to the excited new homeowner standing across from her.

After rummaging in her dress pocket a moment, June produced a folded piece of paper and handed it to Rose.

Taking the paper and unfolding it, Rose took note of June's phone number.

"Call me if you have any questions about the place or need a friendly ear," June said with her apparently permanent scowl.

"Once the phone company comes out and hooks up our line, I'll give you a ring to test it out," Rose replied with a convincing smile.

"That's fine. Maybe you could have me and some of my gals over for afternoon tea," June replied. Rose nodded her approval of the idea. "You'll have a far better time with my gals than if you call the party line once your phone is set up. Trust me, the gossip and gab in person far outweighs what those clucking hens on the phone will go on about."

"Thanks for the advice," Rose replied politely.

"You're welcome, young lady," June said. "I'll see you soon, dear. Don't forget to call once your phone is up and running."

"I will," Rose said.

June turned to leave, took a single step toward the back door, and stopped dead in her tracks. She turned back to face Rose once more. The younger woman noted the look of grave concern on the older woman's face.

"I..." June started. "I think there is something else you should know." June extended her hand for Rose to take.

Tucking the piece of paper with the phone number away in her pocket, Rose took June's hand and allowed the older woman to guide her. June pulled with a strength she had not expected. Rose followed June through the back of the kitchen, through the basement door, and down the basement steps. This had been the one part of the house June had not discussed at all throughout the tour.

The air, Rose noticed as the pair descended into the darkness of the cellar, grew cold quickly. The scent of rotting vegetation and the taste of earthy moisture assaulted the senses; and yet June did not cough or sneeze once. At the base of the creaking, wooden steps, June flicked on the light switch, parting the darkness as the dim bulb's filament began to steadily glow from a single hanging socket in the middle of the room. Rose's eyes adjusted quickly as she looked around at the basement. It wasn't much to write home about: a pile of logs along one wall, caked in webs and sawdust; cans of paint; empty shelves ready for pickling jars, and a single, small window set high — its light practically absent due to the thick layer of grime that clung to the glass. Rose noticed that what little bits of light had managed to find their way inside through cracks in the dirty window fell across the modest room and landed on a small door.

The door was no more than a few feet tall, rounded at the top, and made of dark, stained wood. It was held together with metal brackets and bolts painted black. There was a small handle and a keyhole. June walked Rose over to the door and stopped several feet away, as if she dared not go any farther.

"This," June said, letting go of Rose's hand and pointing with a trembling finger at the small door, "this is the bad door. I don't have the key for it. No one has the key for it. Whatever you do, do not try to unlock it. Leave this door be. I suggest you stack some boxes in front of it or move some shelving to block it."

Rose nodded. "Okay," she said, regarding the door with the same kind of curiosity a baby has for their hands upon first discovering their digits. What, she wondered, was behind the door? And why, why was it called the "bad door"?

"Promise me you won't go opening it, child," June snapped. "At least not until the time is right."

"I promise," Rose replied, returning to the present. June nodded her approval, turned, and dashed up the stairs, leaving Rose alone with the door and her thoughts. Looking at the small thing chilled the young woman to her core. She did not know why this was the case, but it left her feeling uneasy in a most nagging way.

✳ ✳ ✳

"Are you certain that's what she said?" Sam asked as he and Rose sat at the kitchen table, surrounded by stacks of empty moving boxes ready for discarding. "You know that you're slightly deaf in your right ear, and you did say that the woman's allergies were acting up," he added in a slightly annoyed tone. Regardless of

Sam's condescending comment, there was some truth to it — ever since a childhood fever had damaged her hearing, Rose had been a bit hard of hearing in her one ear. But still, something in the way June had talked about the door left Rose feeling a little unsettled, and no matter how hard she pushed herself to agree with her husband, her doubts lingered.

"I'm pretty sure that's what she called it," Rose said, looking down and poking dejectedly at her dinner. This had not been the first time she had misheard someone. The shame Rose felt at the possibility of having heard the wrong thing began to take hold. Across from her, engulfed in his own bubble of thought, Sam took another swig from his bottle of beer before forking another mouthful of Chinese food into his mouth. It had been so long since Sam had indulged in alcohol, and now here he was, not even a full day in their new home and he'd already downed several bottles.

"Maybe she said bat door," Sam replied, his mouth partially full.

Rose shrugged. "I suppose," she replied.

"Makes about as much sense as bad door, that's for sure." Sam took another long drought of beer, finishing the bottle in one last go. "Why don't you show me this door," Sam said, wiping his mouth with his sleeve. Rose cringed at the action. Her husband had a habit of carelessly ruining his clothes. Thankfully it was a white shirt and she had plenty of bleach on hand.

"Right now?" Rose asked.

"Sure. Let's go take a look." Sam rose from the table, offering a hand to his wife as though he were asking for a dance. Rose accepted his hand and stood. Together, the pair took the old, wooden steps one at a time, making sure to watch their footing as much as they could in the dark. When they reached the bottom of the stairs, Rose felt out along the wall for the light switch. A moment later the small light hanging in the middle of the room began to hum softly as the bulb steadily glowed to life, casting long, twisting shadows along the walls.

"So, where is this bad or bat door then?"

Rose walked across the small room, past the dormant furnace and piles of wood, past the shelves waiting for their bounty of canned and pickled goods, and right up to the back wall where the small, rounded, wooden door resided.

Sam regarded the door with a genuine curiosity. "That's a strange place to put a door," he said.

"Could it be an old coal shoot or something like that?" Rose inquired.

"Possibly," Sam said in thought. A moment passed. "I have an idea." Without another word, he turned and dashed up the stairs, leaving Rose alone in the basement. "Wait down there, will you, honey?" Sam called down from the top of the stairs.

"Okay," Rose said. She heard the back door in the kitchen open and close upstairs. A few moments passed. Rose gazed at the door, her mind lost in thought as to what the door could be for, when she heard something. Straining with her left ear, her good one, Rose thought she heard whispers coming from the other side of the door. It was faint, almost impossible to make out over the soft buzz of the bulb above her. She squinted in concentration as she strained her good ear to listen. *It almost sounds like breathing*; she thought after a few moments.

A tapping at the basement window made Rose jump. Turning around, she found her husband gazing down into the cellar. Sam waved with a dopey grin on his face. His words were muffled by the glass when he spoke. "I don't see anything up here. I'm coming back down."

Rose nodded, then watched as Sam vanished from the grimy window above. Several seconds passed. In that time, Rose was unable to hear the whispering again. Upstairs, Sam opened and closed the back door, then came bounding down the basement steps two at a time. "Nothing?" Rose asked as Sam stepped up to her.

"No, nothing," he replied. "I don't see any evidence of a coal shoot or an outside access door. Nothing. I guess it's just a peculiar old door."

"I guess so," Rose replied. As she and Sam headed back up the stairs, she turned off the light. Turning back around, she could now see that soft moonlight was cascading in through the filthy window, wreathing the small, strange door in a ghostly pale light.

That night, Rose had trouble falling asleep. Every time she closed her eyes, she could see the door drenched in moonlight, whispers emanating from it like steam from a kettle. In her dreams, she found herself helpless, gazing in awe and frozen in place by terror as the door slowly began to open to reveal a blinding light surrounded by an all-consuming darkness.

The next morning, Rose settled on the notion of simply forgetting about the door. How, she wondered, was she ever going to get any sleep if her nightmares were so vivid and frightening? She resolved to let the door just be some funny little door down in the basement and nothing more. But still, just to be sure, she decided to do as June had suggested and move one of the shelves in front of the thing.

* * *

Over the next few weeks, life moved on, and the door was all but forgotten. The weekend after the move, Sam and a coworker friend of his managed to heave one of the basement shelves in front of the small door. With that act completed, the door remained out of sight and, thus, out of mind.

As the days grew steadily hotter and longer with the onset of summer, Rose found herself settling into her domestic life quite easily. In the late mornings, June and her friends, a group of older women, chatty as all get-out and all in their fifties or sixties and who all shared a penchant for card games such as gin rummy and bridge, would flock to the house and take over the living room. Rose enjoyed the company and quickly became adept at the art of cards and conversation. Tall glasses of lemonade were often passed around but were not consumed before copious amounts of liquor were added, usually by Miss Kay, an ex-librarian who had a hollow leg and the mouth of a sailor.

Occasionally the women would stop their games and sit out on the porch, watching people passing on the street, gossiping and gabbing, and enjoying the pleasant weather. Rose, never fond of rumors, did her best to try to change the subject to something more mundane, but since she wanted to be seen as a good host, someone who could willingly roll with the punches, she usually found herself caving and listening to the women chit chat about this and that, and who was who, and who had a grudge against whom. It took her a while to realize it, but Rose was surprised to find that all the women in June's group were unmarried. They never spoke of husbands and seemed to spend more time avoiding conversations about the opposite sex as much as Rose tried to steer them away from gossip about the townsfolk.

On days when the Hen House (the name the group had affectionately given themselves long ago) did not convene, Rose usually found herself wandering the house, noting all the unique little details in every nook and cranny — the patterns in the upstairs hallway wainscoting, the way the light refracted off of the crystal-like glass ornaments that hung from the living room lamps, and other such discoveries of one living primarily in a single place day in and day out. Other days, Rose would wander into town, usually riding her bike or walking since Sam took their car to his job at the factory. On those days, she would either shop or head to the library and do some research on the house and area, bolstering her local knowledge and giving her something to occupy her mind.

In all the time that passed, the subject of the bad door never came up. Sam never mentioned it, nor did June or any of her ilk. Rose used the shelf downstairs for storing the empty jars she had found in a couple of crates down in the basement. What better way to prepare for pickling season, Rose reasoned, than to clean and sort the jars she had found — her glass vessels, gleaming and glinting as the sunlight poured in from the small and thoroughly washed basement window, warming the otherwise cold room.

Rose was happy and couldn't be any happier if she tried. There was talk of a promotion for Sam in the near future if work at the factory kept at its current pace, which, if true, meant more income and hopefully the chance of Sam's mood improving. Work had been hard and long, Rose reasoned, and as such, Sam usually came home late at night, smelling of oil and grit, wanting nothing more than a beer, some dinner, and a couple of hours with the television and the ball game. With the talk of promotion, there had also been talk of bringing a child into the world. While Sam went on and on about how great it would be to have a tough boy to raise, Rose just looked forward to having more company in the house. The pair did not set about trying so quickly, though. As much as Rose tried to entice Sam, he was usually too tired at the end of the day, and when he did feel in the mood, he was rough and controlling. It scared Rose, but she also knew that as his wife, it was not her place to say or do anything about her husband's moods and desires save for being there for him. She took her wifely duties seriously, even if June and her friends did not seem either able to relate or did not care enough to relate.

Life continued in this way for some time. It was life as Rose had known it, and all things considered, she hoped that life would remain this way. Then, one day, it all changed.

The day that things changed was just like any other day — Sam had left for work and Rose had just gotten off the phone with June, ready to receive her friend and the rest of the clucking collective for an afternoon session of cards, tea, and finger foods. June had offered to bring some pickles for brining. Rose, excited by the prospect of finally getting to pickle something, pulled the vinegar out of the pantry before heading down to the basement to grab a couple of empty jars. Taking the creaking steps two at a time, Rose flew down into the basement. Outside, the sun had failed to make an appearance; instead, it was gray and wet. The light eking its way into the basement was dull and dreary. Rose flipped the light switch and watched as the bulb grew steadily brighter.

With her way now lit, Rose crossed the room and made straight for her jar shelf. As she selected a couple of squat jars, something perked her ear. It sounded as though someone was whispering, long and low. Then came the sound of chittering, unintelligible but disconcerting nonetheless as though a hundred conversations were occurring far off and all at once. Rose looked around the room for the source of the sound. At first, she thought that it might be coming from all around, but as she stood still, chilled to the bone, her gooseflesh rising, she began to realize where the sound was actually coming from. For the first time in weeks, the small door entered Rose's thoughts, sending a shiver down her spine. The whispering began to grow in intensity. Panicked, Rose clutched the jars to her chest, backing slowly away from the shelf. The bottom in her stomach dropped out and she scarcely felt herself bump into the far wall; her eyes locked on the shelf. She watched in abject terror as the whole shelving unit began to wobble, its jars clinking and clattering as though they were in an earthquake. Rose hoped that it might be an earthquake but deep down knew better. Once she realized that the ground was solid and unmoving and that the shelf was the only thing shaking on its own, her fears were founded. She watched in horror as the chittering and whispering grew louder and the shelf continued to sway. Suddenly, the whole of the piece of furniture scraped along the ground an inch or two away from the wall. There was a loud banging, like that of someone hitting something wooden very hard over and over again.

Rose watched, frozen to the spot as several jars toppled forward, shattering on the ground at the base of the shelf. Upstairs, the doorbell rang. Rose looked up the stairs, then back to the shelf. While some of the jars were still rattling back and forth, the shelf was no longer moving, and the sounds of angry whispering and chittering had vanished. In a flash, she bolted up the stairs, slammed the basement door behind her, then crumpled against the shut cellar door. Her hair had been pulled back into a bun earlier but was now falling in front of her face. Rose could feel the beating of her heart in the pulsing of her hands as they clutched the jars with such fierceness. Rose closed her eyes, letting the adrenaline slowly fade away into oblivion. The doorbell rang once more and Rose jumped, dropping her jars, shattering them on the kitchen floor beside her. Before she realized it, her hands were clutching bits of broken glass on the floor around her. The soft flow of fresh, warm blood began to cover her palms. A cry of pain and shock escaped from Rose's mouth as she held her hands up to assess the damage. Deep crimson streaks of blood ran like rivers down from her palms and fingers, collecting at her wrists and dripping to the sticky tiled floor below.

In the living room, the front door opened, followed by a cacophony of voices as June and the gals saw themselves into the house. Rose was more than familiar with the term "blinded by pain," but never in her life had she experienced such trauma. Now, here she was, blood everywhere, shards of glass jammed into her hands, and every alarm in her brain and body blaring about something being terribly wrong and terribly painful.

When June found Rose a few moments later, she rushed to help her. "Rose! Rose, honey. What happened?"

"I dropped the jars," Rose said through strained tears.

"I can see that," June replied with a smirk. "Agatha, go get your kit. Sybil, fetch the broom, a mop, and whatever cleaning chemicals you can find. Sarah, get Rose something hard to drink." The three women nodded in compliance before rushing off to complete their assigned tasks. June helped Rose to her feet and took her to the kitchen sink. With warm water flowing, the older woman helped Rose to clean her hands. Rose winced as the stream of warm water cascaded over her sliced palms and fingers. Streams of red water ran down into the basin as June fussed over her host's condition.

A few minutes later, Agatha returned, her medical kit in hand. The kit had not been what Rose would have expected — there was nothing familiar in the first aid sense within the small pouch the older woman had returned with. While Agatha used a pair of tweezers to remove the shards of glass still embedded in her palms and fingers, she also rubbed a thick, creamy salve that stung like hell as it seeped into every cut. Rose expected stitches next, but after the oily black goop had been applied, Agatha went about wrapping her hands in thin sheets of fabric. June and the other women of the group passed a small charm from one to the other while Agatha worked. Rose could not see what the tiny, black object on the end of some string was, but each of the women took it for a few moments, muttered under their breath, and then passed it on to the next in the group. "There, all set," Agatha replied, wiping her bloody and greasy hands on a kitchen towel.

"Do I need stitches or anything like that?" Rose asked, looking her bandaged hands over.

"Of course not!" Agatha said, almost sounding offended. "You should be right as rain in a few days' time. I stand by my work, dearie. There is nothing more you need to do. There is no need for a *doctor* and his butcher ways," Agatha added, acid in her words.

Rose nodded solemnly. Part of her felt guilty at having her card and gossip friends fuss over her so, and part of her felt embarrassed by the whole situation. And yet, another part of her was scared, scared of the basement, and scared of the fantastic possibilities of what could possibly exist on the other side of that odd little door. Not to mention scared by what she had just been through — Rose did not want to offend Agatha or June or the others, but she still felt it best to see a professional. She had no doubt that Sam would demand it of her when he got home from work. No need to tell the others, she reasoned. Once they all left, she would phone up the family physician and make an appointment.

With her hands bandaged up, the women decided that cards might not be the best of distractions, so instead, they set about chatting about this and that — discussing their television stories and who in town was seen with whom — the usual gossip. And as usual, all of it went in one ear and out the other for Rose. This time, though, it wasn't due to her aversion to other people's lives; instead, her mind was on the door in the basement. That afternoon, as the other women left, June hung back.

"You want to talk about it?" she asked. Rose shook her head.

"It's nothing. I just got scared by the doorbell is all."

"Honey, that wasn't a reaction to the doorbell, was it?" Rose shook her head, looking less like an adult and more like a guilty child. "What was it that scared you?" Rose looked up, meeting June's eyes.

"I...I think there's something in the basement. Something behind that door." The expression on June's face hardened like clay in a kiln. Gone was the warm smile. Instead, her eyes bore into Rose's gaze; a dentist's drill ready to strike. The warmth that had so slowly and steadily filled the woman's expression drained away to reveal the cold, judgmental woman who had invited herself in to give Rose a tour of the house all those months ago.

"I told you to leave that door alone; leave it be, I said. The time is not right."

"I did," Rose pleaded. "Sam and I put some shelving in front of it, but something was trying to get out. It scared me."

"As it should," June growled. Rose's world was now painted by confusion. Why, she wondered, was her friend so upset about that door, and why was she so upset at her? Fresh tears began to flow down Rose's cheeks as she stood there, facing June Bleaker's withering stare. Like a cloud passing before the sun and then moving slowly away, June's cold expression warmed and melted away after a moment. "I'm sorry, dear," she went on. "That door is dangerous, and I would simply hate to see something terrible happen to you." Rose nodded. "Tell you what, if what happened today happens again, give me a ring as soon as possible, alright?" Rose nodded again, the ghost of a smile pulling subtly at the corners of her mouth. With the matter settled, June hugged Rose goodbye and left her standing on the front stoop, alone.

* * *

In spite of Agatha's suggestion of not visiting a doctor and giving in to the tiny, nagging voice in the back of her mind that told her otherwise, a few days after her accident, Rose slipped out of the house and into town after Sam had left for work. When Sam had come home to find Rose's bandaged hands, he grumbled and chastised her for being so careless. She did not tell him the whole truth about the door in the basement or the medicinal help Agatha had offered and instead claimed that hearing June ring the doorbell as she stepped out of the basement caused her to jump and drop the jars. It was as she was cleaning up the mess, she claimed, that she cut her hands.

Sam was not having it — this news, along with a bad day at the factory and further bolstered by three beers after dinner, had him slamming doors, screaming at Rose for being so incompetent, and giving her a slap to her face that left a bruise now covered by a thick application of foundation. Poor Sam, she thought as she covered her face that morning. Work was tough on him, and she was not making it any easier.

As she expected, Doctor Bernstein scolded her for not calling him immediately after cutting her hands. Rose shrank back at his chastising after she had told him the same half-truth story she had told Sam the day of the accident. Doctor Bernstein was a tall, balding man with a permanently hawkish look — he always appeared to be examining anything and everything from over the rim of his glasses that sat low on his nose.

When Rose told him that she had just bandaged her hands with no stitches, the doctor summoned his nurse to come in with a needle and thread. Rose did not want to look down at her hands as the doctor slowly and carefully uncovered them, but upon hearing his expression, she had no choice.

"Is this some kind of joke?" he snapped. Rose looked down to see both of her hands completely healed without so much as a scratch or scar, let alone open wounds.

"No," Rose pleaded. "There was blood everywhere and glass in both palms."

"Well, more than likely what happened was that whatever was in those jars got all over the place and the glass stuck to the liquid and then your hands. You look just fine to me." Rose knew the jars were empty — the whole point was to use them to pickle the cucumbers June had brought for her. Still, it seemed as likely an explanation as any. "Listen, don't bother me with these petty housewife fantasies in the future. Unless you are really in some kind of distress, I don't want to hear about it."

Rose lowered her head in shame. Was he right, she wondered? For the first time she could remember, Rose began to feel a small amount of anger. She pushed it down, far, far down. Part of her wanted to scream at this man telling her she was wrong, but a bigger part told her that he was correct, and she was wrong and that it wasn't her place to question the judgement of a man.

Rose left Doctor Bernstein's office that morning feeling worse than before she had arrived. She was just thankful that no one seemed to notice that her tears had begun to wash away the makeup covering her bruised cheek.

* * *

Rose wanted nothing more than to forget about the door under the house. As the weeks rolled on and the house began to feel more like a home, the basement still felt like alien territory. Rose had stopped going down into the basement, and lofty notions of pickling were tossed out the window. Sam ventured down the steps into the dank underside of the house without question, but even he seemed to return to the kitchen with a far-off look as though he couldn't believe what he was experiencing down in the basement.

80

Rose did not press him for answers, as she wanted nothing to do with that place or the door.

The seasons came and went and soon winter was knocking at the front door of 2312 Brookstone Avenue. With the days coming to an end quicker, Rose's games of cards with the gals ran only half as long as usual so that everyone had enough time to make it back home before it got too dark. Soon the snows came, lightly at first and then heavier as the days dragged on. Sam had chopped plenty of wood out back and brought it down to the basement before the storms got worse. There was plenty of firewood for both the fireplace and the furnace.

More than the cold and the shortened visits with the gaggle, the thing Rose hated more than anything else was the hour or two between her girlfriends leaving and Sam coming home. She found little comfort in the living room or their bedroom, reading Agatha Christie novels or drawing a warm bath and masturbating, her deep moans filling the house for a few minutes almost every evening. These distractions were just that, distractions. It was during these times that she felt more alone than ever. Her mind would often reel at fantastical visions of June and the gals getting lost and snow-blind, freezing to death at the foot of their own porches or Sam spinning out on the road home after hitting a patch of black ice. Rose hated herself for thinking such dark and macabre thoughts, but no matter how hard she tried to dispel these notions, they always came back, stronger than ever.

It was on one of these nights, while waiting for Sam to come home, Rose found herself lounging on the sofa, reading a dog-eared copy of *The Bell Jar* when an icy, cold shiver struck. As the late afternoon wore on, and with June and company long since headed home, Rose had put the roast in the oven with the veggies to marinate and curled up in her sweater with a warm cup of coffee. With the coffee drunk, the cold slowly but surely had begun to creep into her bones. A shiver ran a marathon down the young woman's spine. Rose put her book down and, in the half-light of her reading lamp, struggled to read the face of the ticking grandfather clock across from her in the living room. Quarter until six, it read. Sam, she knew, should have been home by now.

As if it had read her mind, the phone on the table by the stairs began to ring. Rose leapt to her feet, placed her open book face down on the arm of the couch to save her spot, and made straight for the ringing Bakelite receiver. "Hello?" she answered cautiously.

"Rose? It's Sam," came the crackled voice on the other end of the line. A feeling of relief swelled up inside of her, similar to the warm, welcoming feeling of those bathtub orgasms.

"Sam. Where are you, Sam? I can barely hear you?"

"I'm still at work," Sam said, "Don needs us all to stay a little longer — one of the smelters is acting up and with the big storm coming in this weekend, we don't want to take any chances." Rose nodded solemnly and looked out the living room window at the swirling flakes of snow in the dim light outside.

"When will you be back?"

"Hard to say. Tell ya what, I'll call you when I'm leaving work. Sound good to you?"

"Yes. Thank you, Sam," Rose replied with a small, coy smile. "The house is getting chilly, dear," Rose added.

"Dammit, I was worried about that," Sam said through the crackling phone line, "You might need to head down into the basement and check on the pilot light in the furnace. If it's out, you'll have to turn the gas back on and light the pilot. I've got the matches in a box on the wall nearby." A lump began to form in the back of Rose's throat.

"Okay then," she replied weakly. "I love you, dear."

Rose heard Sam hang up on the other end of the line, all the way across town. Things at work must have been stressful, she thought. He didn't even say "I love you too" before hanging up. Rose began to shiver, not just from the cold but from the grim task that lay before her.

Hanging up the phone on her end, Rose took a deep breath, walked over to the umbrella holder by the front door, pushed aside the umbrellas, and found what she was looking for. Sliding the old, wooden baseball bat out of the holder, Rose hefted what Sam referred to as "Slugger" and choked up on the handle. Sam wasn't a fan of owning guns, but he was a fan of swinging for the fences if he and his family were in danger. Thankfully he had never had to use Slugger, but he kept it ready by the door at all times, just in case.

Cautiously, Rose made her way through the house to the kitchen. Approaching with all the potential energy of a compressed spring, she approached the basement door, reached out for the handle, took hold, and began to turn. The door slowly swung outward, over the staircase that descended into nearly pitch-black darkness. Reaching out, she flipped the switch Sam had installed at the top of the steps. A moment passed and then the hum of electricity being fed through wires could be heard. Rose watched silently as the newly installed bulbs above the stairs lit up, a trail of luminous breadcrumbs, ending in the depths of the basement.

Taking another deep breath and ignoring the flickering of the overhead lights, Rose stepped into the basement for the first time in months. Each step she took down into the abyss left her feeling more and more alone. Finally, after what seemed like a lifetime and a half, Rose's feet made contact with the stone floor of the basement proper. The air was warmer than she had anticipated. With the furnace off, she had not expected it to be so stiflingly hot. Moving through the heat, the skin under her sweater began to prickle with anticipated sweat. Keeping her eyes away from the shelving Sam had moved in front of the door once more, Rose made a beeline for the furnace in the corner of the room. With its pilot light out and despite the odd amount of residual heat in the room, the metal was groaning and making tapping noises as it began to cool and condense.

Looking to the side of the furnace, she saw that Sam had piled the logs on one end and had hung a box of long matches on the wall opposite. Throwing on a pair of mittens Sam had also left down there, Rose managed to open the door to the furnace. Using a nearby flashlight, she gazed about inside the belly of the metal beast. With the pilot spotted, Rose took a long match, struck it against the box, and reached back into the furnace's open mouth, all while her other hand still held tightly to the baseball bat. Checking the gas valve, she slammed shut the furnace door and jumped back as the flames roared to life, casting long, odd shadows around the room in the places where the overhead lights failed to reach.

Her task completed, Rose turned to leave, to flee up the stairs and away from the creeping sense of dread that still tugged at her. She felt her heart leap into her throat as she spotted the door peeking out from behind the wall of shelving. Bewilderment and terror took hold of the young woman's senses. The shelves that Sam had moved in front of the small, wooden door were now haphazardly perched against the shelves on the adjacent wall. Rose wanted to scream. She wanted to flee, but once again, primal fear kept her rooted in place and locked her joints. Above the hiss of free-flowing gas and the crackle of the flames behind her, she could hear the whispers rising in intensity. They sounded angry and only seemed to be growing angrier. Her eyes fixed on the door; Rose watched in horror as the small iron handle began to jiggle. Something or someone was trying to come through, Rose reasoned. The whispers began to grow louder still, drowning out the sounds of the furnace. She could not tell if the whispering was really all that loud or if her mind was making it seem louder. Regardless, the door handle moved again. A thought struck Rose in that moment — the first time she had met June, her neighbor had informed her that there was no key. *Could whatever it was on the other side of the door have the key*, she pondered amid the panic?

The handle continued to jiggle, moving faster and more intensely as the seconds crawled by. Rose watched, wide-eyed and with bated breath as the handle finally stopped jittering and instead began to slowly turn in one, smooth motion. Before she knew what was happening, Rose realized that she had managed to grab hold of a log near the furnace, which she promptly jammed against the door and just underneath the handle.

Breathing heavily now, sweat dripping out of every pore, she watched as the handle, now unable to turn any farther, beat uselessly against the log before falling silent. The whispers began to die away. Rose stood all alone, the hissing of the furnace and the occasional flickering of the overhead lighting pulling her back to the moment. Rose looked down at her hands and the smudges of grease and oil from the furnace all over her palms. She looked at the door, her dread temporarily replaced with a sense of victory.

Rose cast one last look at the stopped door before snatching up the baseball bat and heading back up the stairs and out of the basement. With the lights turned off, she closed the door behind her and headed into the living room. The roast would be done soon, she knew, but in that moment, she needed a bath and some serious relief.

Sam came home a couple of hours later. As Rose dished out Sam's portion of his meal onto the plate before him, Rose locked eyes with her husband. "Did you move the shelves downstairs?" she asked.

"Did I move the shelves?" Sam echoed back, seeming to search his thoughts as Rose ladled beef sauce over his diced potatoes and carrots. "No. I haven't touched them since you asked me to cover that weird little door down there," he replied. Rose stood still, the ladle hovering between the serving dish and Sam's plate.

"Well, they've been moved," Rose said, her voice tinged with a hint of the worry that was now beginning to course through her veins once more.

"I didn't touch the damn things," Sam snapped, not so much at his wife but at the universe around him. "Stay here." Before Rose could answer, Sam was on his feet, his chair forcefully pushed back. Stomping across the room, Sam vanished into the kitchen. Rose heard the creaking of the basement door and the click of the light switch. A minute or two passed before she heard those sounds again, this time in reverse order. Sam walked in a daze back into the living room, his expression impossible to read. "I moved your shelves back."

Sam took the moment to open a fresh bottle of beer that he had no doubt snatched from the icebox on his way back to dinner.

Rose nodded, and the two ate in silence. The rest of that evening and the rest of that week, the subject of the door and the shelves never came up again. Rose had her suspicions, but like her own fears, she had a feeling that Sam was not entirely comfortable talking about the bad door in the basement. No, Rose knew how his mind worked, and denial was the name of the game.

* * *

The remainder of the winter season passed without incident. Christmas came, as bright and cheery as the newly fallen snow, and Sam had surprised Rose with news of a promotion. Quickly, the pair's discussions soon turned to starting that family. Sam's mood improved as the winter thinned out — he drank far less and seemed to keep his temper in check. Rose was thankful for this on many levels. While she had felt it was her duty as a wife to be there for Sam, the thought of him hitting her again filled the back of her mind with a fiery rage she had to smother with distractions around the house and by meeting with the gals as often as she could.

As the first signs of spring began to make themselves known — a patch of green here and there, poking out of the snow-caked lawn — the mood around the house continued to lighten. While the thoughts of the door and the unknowable that seemed to reside behind it occasionally popped up in the back of Rose's mind like the last, lingering bubbles in a glass of champagne, she was overall very pleased to not have to worry about the door.

The night Sam had come home so late and the furnace had gone out, he had gone down into the basement and checked the work Rose had done in wedging the log between the handle and the floor. Sam had complimented her ingenuity, but he still did not seem to believe her about the door trying to open. Instead, he humored her, boarding up the door with wooden planks and many, many nails. Rose held no illusions about her husband; she knew he could hear the occasional whispering down there, behind the closed door, and she knew that he was doing his best to not hear what he heard — at least, she hoped that was the case and not simply him dismissing her as a woman caught in the grips of hysteria.

Early one spring morning, the door a distant but still disturbing memory, and her and Sam trying daily for a little one, Rose took the bus into town to see Doctor Bernstein. For several months now, the couple had been trying — sometimes multiple times a day and in various positions and places around the house, and yet still, Rose's period flowed freely and right on schedule. While her mother and mother-in-law had often colluded in saying that she would get pregnant in no time once the couple started to try, Rose wasn't so sure about their rather unscientific assessment based on their own child-bearing experiences.

With the winter storms mostly a thing of the past, there were still patches of snow, defiant against the seasonal rains that seemed to come and go throughout the gloomy days. Her raincoat snapped to the top and her head wrapped tightly in a scarf, her feet snug in rubber rain boots, Rose dashed down the road that led from their place, down the neighborhood and out onto the main road into town. A tall rusty sign for the bus stop greeted her from out of the gloom. Rose stood shivering under her umbrella for some time before the bus, its headlights glowing in the distance like the eyes of a predatory cat on the hunt, pulled up and admitted her.

By the time the bus pulled into town, the worst of the rains had stopped, giving way to a light drizzle. Rose stepped off the bus near the city center and walked the three blocks down Main Street to Doctor Bernstein's office. The nurse, who happened to be married to the good doctor, took Rose's vitals before admitting her into a room. Minutes later, Doctor Bernstein came in. "Hello, Rose," he said, smoke billowing from his pipe as he stepped into the examination room.

"Hello, Doctor," Rose replied with a courteous smile.

"So, Stella out there tells me that you and Sam have started to try to grow your little family," he said, consulting the notepad his wife Stella had passed to him, showing Rose's medical history.

"That's right," Rose said with a confident nod. "We've been trying for a couple of months now and I'm still getting my period." Doctor Bernstein took a moment to thumb through the pages of personal medical information before him.

"Well," he said with the hint of a sigh, "it could be you or it could be Sam. I highly doubt it's Sam, so I want to run a few tests if you don't mind."

In no time at all, Rose found herself dressed down in a hospital gown and her legs spread wide before the doctor. With his glasses perched on the end of his nose as always, Doctor Bernstein started his exam. Rose had never felt more uncomfortable in all her life. She pulled herself back mentally, taking refuge in her thoughts of having a baby as the doctor poked and prodded at her nether regions.

"Tell me, Rose, have you started to take any kind of vitamins?"

"No. Should I?"

"It might not hurt. I can give you a list," Doctor Bernstein said, poking his head out from between her legs. "It might not hurt to also put you on something for your nerves."

"My nerves?" Rose asked, taken aback.

"Oh yes," he said in a matter-of-fact tone. "I have a sneaky suspicion that the problem may indeed lie with you. You're clearly under some kind of stress. Your female parts are tense, and it's difficult for me to open them up. This could be the cause. Tell me, do you experience much pain while engaging in intercourse?"

"A little, yes," she said. The truth was it was a lot of pain.

"I thought so," Doctor Bernstein went on, standing up, removing his gloves, and then proceeding to refill and re-light his pipe. "I think once we get you on some vitamins and something to soothe and calm your nerves, you should get pregnant in no time. If you're this tense all the time, it could be affecting how your body is taking in your husband's seed. If you're in any sort of pain or discomfort, just grin and get through it. I can tell you in full confidence, it will be worth it in the end. Children are such wonderful things."

Rose felt sick. Taking her legs out of the stirrups, she looked crestfallen as Doctor Bernstein puffed away across from her. Rose had never enjoyed the pain, but who was she to complain, she thought — her husband had every right to put his seed in her, and after all, wasn't that exactly what she wanted? But still, something about the whole assessment did not sit well in Rose's mind. As she gathered her clothing, the doctor, his pipe still glowing and puffing away, wrote out Rose's prescription in his unintelligible scribble.

"Take this to the pharmacy downtown and take the vitamins daily and the nerve tonic nightly," Doctor Bernstein said, tucking his pen and notepad away. "You take care of yourself, Rose, and we'll see you again in a few weeks to check up on your progress."

Rose nodded in silence as the doctor turned and left her by herself in the room — left her feeling alone, humiliated, and violated. Before getting dressed, Rose vomited into the sink basin in the exam room. Shakily, she dressed and hurried out of the office, Stella the nurse calling after her, asking about a follow-up appointment. Rose kept on walking.

Rose felt violated in a way she had never felt before. Even on the nights when sex with Sam had hurt or been slightly uncomfortable, she had never felt this way. She wanted to feel angry — she wanted to scream, but who, she thought, who could she talk to? Prior to the move, Rose had seen another doctor, one who handled her with the utmost respect. What Doctor Bernstein had done, his manner and attitude had left her feeling hollow and dirty. As she walked down the street and to the pharmacist on instinct alone, her hands clenched and unclenched, crumpling the handwritten prescription in her hand.

The door to the pharmacy jingled as Rose stepped in, her thoughts still lingering on the exam while her feet automatically shuffled her toward the back of the building where the pharmacist's counter resided. Rose came to the counter and slid the note across to the small, balding man on the other side. He had given Rose a cordial greeting, but she had not heard it and so did not respond in kind. The small, mouse-like man took the note, squinted at it from behind his thick lenses, then scuttled off to fetch the pills and tonic. Rose stood at the counter, her jaw clenched, her fingers tapping a steady beat on the polished countertop.

A few minutes later, the small man returned with a bottle in each hand. Rose looked at the little man and then spotted the name plaque beside him on the countertop: Tobias Lomwell. Something about the name rang familiar in the back of Rose's mind. As he slipped her bottles into a small paper bag, her memory made the connection. "Are you Tobias Lomwell?" Tobias nodded as he rolled up the top of the paper bag before sliding it across to Rose.

"I am," he said with a grin. "Your total today is two-fifty." Rose nodded and began to rummage about in her purse for the money.

"Did your family used to live in the old house at twenty-three twelve Brookstone Avenue?"

"We did," Tobias said, taking the money Rose slid across the counter. Tobias walked over to the till and began to ring her up. "Do I know you?"

"I don't believe so," Rose said, "but my husband and I live in that house now."

"Oh, do you?" he asked.

"We do. June told me about your family history. Honestly, as far back as it goes with that house, I'm surprised you don't still live there." A strange look came to his face as she said this.

"We moved out when I was little," Tobias said. "My parents never gave me a good explanation as to why, but I think that after my brother passed away, they didn't feel right living there anymore."

"Your brother?"

"Yes, my older brother Charlie," Tobias said, handing Rose her change and a small, printed receipt.

"What happened to him, if you don't mind me asking," Rose said, taking the change and receipt but never letting her eyes stray from Tobias's gaze.

"He was found in the basement. They said he had died of smoke inhalation from the furnace down there."

"Oh, I'm so sorry to hear that," Rose said as she pocketed her medicine and change into her purse.

"It is what it is, I suppose," Tobias said with a sad, faraway look.

"Tell me," Rose probed after a moment of uncomfortable silence passed between the two of them, "what can you tell me about the bad door in the basement?" What little color there was in Tobias's face flushed out, leaving him pale and sickly looking as though he had been struck by a sudden pox.

"I had forgotten about the bad door," he said in a whisper. "Is it still down there then?" Rose nodded. "I just remember Mother and Father telling us to leave it alone. June, who was our caretaker then, also told us to leave it be. June had been around a long time when she used to babysit us as children, and the stories she told about the door filled our heads with the most terrible nightmares. She used to tell us about the legends of the door and how some believed that it was a gateway to Hell or that it was the entrance to a cave with no bottom. She often spoke about a woman at the birth of the nation, who was murdered and placed behind the door, accused of being a witch."

"My god," Rose said, her mouth agape.

"As for me, I only ever heard whispering on the other side, but I never dared to open it, not like Charlie. He was always testing the limits of his elders," Tobias said with a weak grin. "Well now, June must be getting on in years if you saw her recently. Honestly, I thought she was long dead." This comment gave Rose pause — were they talking about the same woman? Rose's June was no more than in her early sixties, but Tobias looked older than that.

Thanking the little man, Rose wrote down his instructions for the medication and then headed home, her head swimming with confusion as she recalled her first meeting with the old woman and how she described her time taking care of the Lomwell family in their youth in the house she now called home. All the while, in the back of her mind, Rose's thoughts drifted from June to the door and the whispering both she and Tobias had heard.

* * *

For weeks after the doctor's visit, Rose stewed. Sam's constant reminders to take her pills did nothing to improve her mood. Since the visit, she had been unable to touch herself or masturbate as she often enjoyed engaging in before Sam came home. While Sam kept pushing for sex, Rose denied. Even when he got rough and demanded that she give herself to him to suit his mood or for the excuse of trying again for the sake of starting a family, Rose would leave the room and lock herself in the bathroom where she would sob herself to sleep as she sat against the door or in the empty bathtub. Each morning after Sam had left for work, Rose took her pills for the day and flushed them down the toilet, and each night she would present Sam with the bottle for his inspection. Satisfied with what he saw, he left her alone about the pills until his not-so-gentle reminder the next morning as the cycle would begin again.

Sam hit the bottle harder than ever, and the results left Rose feeling terrified. Not only had his beatings become a regular, nightly occurrence, but his attitude toward her turned from the familiar to the cold. The way he described their marriage, he owned her, and she had to do what he demanded or else. Rose was never without her makeup each morning, especially when the gaggle gathered for cards, drinks, and gossip.

During this time, Rose found herself confiding more in the gaggle than ever before. Each of the women would put in their two cents about the situation. No matter what kind of advice the old hens gave, the one thing that did remain consistent was how adamant they were in not letting Rose give in to Sam's unchecked sexual demands. Rose's frustration with her marriage was enough to distract her from approaching June about the conversation she and Tobias had at the pharmacy. Even the thought of the door down in the basement, the thing that until recently had been her biggest concern, was now nothing more than a fleeting afterthought. A pall had settled over 2312 Brookstone Avenue and did not seem ready to pass any time soon even with the sun shining and the flowers blooming.

One afternoon, after a particularly violent morning outburst from Sam that had left its mark under her left eye and gave Rose a nasty split lip, she found herself hosting the gaggle, her face, as usual now, caked in foundation and lipstick. None of the women had said anything, so Rose assumed that none of them had noticed. Bringing a tray of lemonade into the parlor from the kitchen, June, the scowl on her face seemingly set in stone, stood at the entrance to the room as Rose stepped inside. June's arms were crossed, and her foot tapped to an invisible beat. "What are you hiding?"

"Nothing?" Rose said, trying to sound more confident than she suspected she sounded.

"You never wear this much makeup, and you tend to wear a lot of makeup these days," June said, stepping up to her host and placing a finger under Rose's chin. Rose looked up at the slightly taller woman's face before averting her gaze and casting her head down to the tray with its pitcher of sun-gold drink and empty glasses.

"I thought I would try something new," Rose said, maneuvering around the older woman and sliding the tray onto the table the rest of the women sat around. No one else spoke; they just watched, their hands clutching their cards like the talons of a hawk clutching a small rabbit.

"What has he done to you?" June demanded.

"I...I don't know what you're talking about," Rose managed to stammer, her hands shakily filling but mostly spilling around the glass on the table in front of her.

"Don't lie to me," June said. "Rose, you are a terrible liar for one thing, but for another, if there is one thing I cannot abide by, it's lies." Rose felt like a child, scolded for losing her homework in front of the entire class. Without another word, June picked up a nearby napkin, spat in it, and began to rub away the layers of thick makeup on Rose's face. After a few seconds of hard scrubbing, the yellowing-purple bruise under her left eye was revealed, followed closely by the split lip hiding under thick lipstick. Tears began to stream down Rose's face, now reddened by June's vigorous scrubbing. June stepped back while Rose continued to weep.

"He didn't mean it," Rose sobbed. "He was frustrated. I've...I've...I've been so difficult with him lately. He's my husband and..." In that moment, Rose broke down, spilling everything out of her like a burst dam — she told them about the realtor, and Doctor Bernstein, and the painful sex and humiliation with both the doctor and Sam. She told them about the drinking and about how she hated the men in her life at that moment. By the end, Rose felt deflated and drained of every ounce of strength within her.

"He's your husband, but that does not make you his property to do with as he pleases," June hissed. "That *man* may think you are part of his family, but that *man* deserves no family. Consider us more of a family, love." The women around the table placed their cards down and exchanged excited looks. "Rose, why don't you go into the kitchen, clean yourself up, dear — the rest of us have something to discuss, as a family." Rose nodded solemnly as she dragged herself out of the parlor.

Taking a kitchen towel out of a nearby drawer, Rose wet the end and then proceeded to clean up the rest of her face. Her eyes were becoming puffy and tender from the crying and the bruise on the one side. Rose jumped as the kitchen phone began to ring. Without a moment's hesitation, she rushed to answer.

"Hello?" Rose asked into the receiver.

"Rose? It's Sam." She heard the voice on the other end of the line crackle and hiss.

"Sam?" Rose said.

"Babe, I've got a terrible headache; it's almost blinding. The foreman is sending me home. Please have a cold compress and some soup ready for me." Rose glanced up at the clock; it was half past noon, which meant Sam would be home within the hour.

"What about the ladies? We were in the middle of a game," Rose asked.

"They can stay. I'll just need to sleep upstairs in the bed," Sam responded. "See you soon." Rose heard the click of the phone on the other end of the line hanging up. It took her a moment to find herself and to hang up the phone on her end.

"Everything alright, dear?" June asked, her head poking into the kitchen.

"It's the damndest thing. Sam is coming home sick. He never gets sick."

"What is it? A cold?"

"No, a migraine or a headache, it seems," Rose said.

"Well, those things can happen," June replied, the fading ghost of a smile leaving her face.

"I suppose they do," Rose said, lost in the thought of her husband coming home early and not feeling well. In all the years they had known each other, Rose had never heard Sam complain once about the sniffles, let alone a headache. The notion puzzled her as she walked from the kitchen and followed June back out to the parlor and the card game. Rose took her seat, her mind in a fog. One of the other women handed her a freshly poured glass of lemonade. Rose took the drink in one hand and continued to stare past the gathered women and instead focus on the front door. A kind of fear began to well up in her. It was funny, she thought, how the fear she had for that damn door downstairs had transferred completely to Sam.

Rose sat in a semi-catatonic state, occasionally sipping her drink while the rest of the gals continued their game of gin rummy; all the while, the faint scent of herbs and incense seemed to hang in the air around the girls and their card game. At some point, the front door opened with a loud creak and Rose jumped. The ladies paused their game again, their cards fanned out before them. Rose watched as Sam dragged himself in through the front door, his back slumped and his head held low. With a backwards kick, the front door swung closed and latched while Sam made his way up the stairs. Rose and the rest of the gaggle sat in their seats, listening to the slow creak of each step as Sam made his way upstairs. Rose stood after a few moments and excused herself.

She found her husband splayed out atop their bed. One of his boots remained on his foot while the other lay at the end of the bed. His lunchbox lay on the bed beside him while Sam lay face down. "Sam, honey, is everything okay?" Rose asked cautiously while peeking into the bedroom. Sam mumbled a reply. "What was that?" Rose asked, straining to hear his words through the bed sheets.

"I said," Sam grumbled, "my head feels like it's on fucking fire."

"I'll fetch you some aspirin," Rose said helpfully. "Do you want me to call Doctor Bernstein?" she asked, a slight chill running up her spine at the mention of the man and the thought of his probing fingers and casual disregard for her feelings.

"No doctor, just aspirin," Sam snapped. Rose rushed back down to the kitchen, filled a glass from the tap, then swung by the upstairs bathroom where she snatched the bottle of medicine from the cabinet above the sink. Sam sat up against the headboard, taking several more pills than was recommended while Rose removed his other boot. Sam gulped down his glass of water and demanded another. Rose dashed downstairs to find June at the foot of the staircase, a freshly filled glass in her hands. Rose shot her a quizzical look.

"I don't mean to pry, dear, but I overheard your husband's request." Rose nodded and exchanged the empty glass for the full one. Back upstairs, she handed her husband the new glass of water, and he downed it in one swift motion.

"You can go back to your goddamned cards and gossip," Sam sneered. "I'm going to try to sleep this thing off." Sam shoved the empty glass into his wife's hand.

Closing the bedroom door behind her and leaning against the closed door, Rose let the tears stream from her eyes. Needing something to drink, she looked at the glass still in her hand and found it entirely drained. Through the trickling tears, something caught her attention. Holding the glass up in the early afternoon light coming in through the upstairs hallway windows, Rose noticed a strange film around the bottom of the glass. Wiping her eyes, she pulled herself away from the door and slowly made her way downstairs once again.

June was once more at the foot of the stairs, this time a glass of scotch in her hand. "Here, drink this," June said, shoving the scotch into Rose's empty hand and snatching the empty glass she had given her earlier from her other hand. Rose regarded the drink the way a professional florist might regard the same bouquet of a dozen long-stem roses day after day. Lazily and in a daze, Rose took her medicine, downing the whole glass in one gulp. She plopped down on the nearest sofa and continued to look over her now empty glass with an appraising eye.

"June?" Rose asked as the woman in question came out of the kitchen and took her seat between Gale and Pearl, two of June's oldest and dearest friends and the quietest of the gaggle. Agatha, Sybil, and Sarah sat across from the other three, sipping slowly at their lemonade and casting worried glances at Rose.

"Yes, dear heart?"

"Did you put something into Sam's glass of water?" Rose asked, the tears on her stained cheeks quickly drying into salty streaks upon her makeup.

"It was nothing," June replied half-heartedly as she began to shuffle and reshuffle the playing cards. "I merely gave that oaf a little something to help his head is all. Something to help prepare the way," June continued, passing out cards slowly to the other women at the table.

"Do you have any of what you gave Sam left? I think I'm gonna need some," Rose said, sitting up hopefully.

"I'm afraid not, "June said. "Besides, you wouldn't want that sort of thing." Rose stood and walked over to join the others at the table for another game of cards. As June handed out the last card and placed the rest of the deck before her, a loud banging noise from under the floor caused Rose to jump. None of the other women moved. They remained sitting, concentrating on the fanned-out cards in front of their faces.

"What was that?" Rose asked.

"What was what?" Agatha asked.

"I didn't hear a thing," Sarah added.

"Are you sure you're feeling alright?" Gale said. Rose nodded. From upstairs, she could hear the sound of the bedroom door opening, followed closely by Sam's heavy footfalls as he shot down the staircase and into the parlor.

"What in the world was that noise?" Sam asked, a worried look pinned to his face while sweat dotted his brow.

"Sounds like it came from the basement," June said as she casually dropped an Ace of Spades on the table in front of her.

"The basement?" Sam asked, looking at his wife with a pained expression.

"Should we check it out?" Rose asked.

"A great idea," June said. "We'll keep the game on hold until you come back." Rose pushed her chair back, stood, took Sam's arm, and led the pair of them out of the parlor and into the kitchen.

"Do you think that noise came from the door down there?" Rose asked.

The couple stood before the closed basement door, neither one willing to take the first step forward. Rose began to wonder if Sam was starting to believe her about the door down there. After a few seconds, he lunged forward, opening the door with reckless abandon. "The hell with this," he grumbled as he pulled Rose along after him. "I don't know what made that noise, but it certainly wasn't that fucking door and I'm going to prove it."

Rose followed Sam clumsily down the steps, blinded by the darkness. At the foot of the stairs, Sam flipped on the light switch. The pair were greeted by the sight of the small door banging back and forth as something on the other side pushed and pulled at the handle. Rose's breath caught in her throat, and she could tell Sam was struck by the sight too as his hands had gone cold and clammy and seized up at once.

The door shook and rattled violently, its iron hinges straining while the wooden panels of the door itself groaned and creaked. Sam stood there, slack-jawed and unblinking. "What on Earth?" he asked more to himself than Rose.

"I told you there was something behind the door," Rose said. The door continued to shake and bang.

"There has to be a key for this thing," Sam shouted over the din.

"There isn't," Rose replied, her hands now over her ears as the door continued to cause its seemingly unending cacophony. "When we moved in, June said that no one had the key."

"Well, no one but me," a voice from behind the couple rebounded through the room, almost drowning out the sound of the door. Rose and Sam turned to see June and the other women of the gaggle, standing one behind the other on the staircase, their expressions unreadable. June stood at the head of the group; a large black skeleton key held out in her hand.

"But you said no one had the key," Rose interjected. "You told me to never open the door."

"I told *you* not to open the door until the right time. Well, today is the right time," June said with a slight smirk as Sam brushed past his wife and, like a man possessed, went straight for the key. Snatching the key away from June's hand like a greedy older child taking candy from a younger child, Sam looked the object over for a moment before dashing back across the room. With the key held out, Sam pushed the end of it into the lock, but before he could turn it, he began to sway like a human metronome before finally collapsing at Rose's feet.

"Looks like your tincture worked just fine, Agatha," June said to her friend above her on the basement steps. Agatha nodded and smiled — a look of the cat that caught the canary painted upon her face.

"Sam?" Rose cried out. Her husband lay, unmoving, his breathing shallow. Rose felt June's hand upon her shoulder.

"This is your story, my dear," the older woman said kindly.

"My story?" Rose asked, looking up from Sam's crumpled form and into the fiery eyes of her now closest and dearest friend.

"Yes. You see, we," June said, motioning to herself and the gaggle behind her, "have all played and continue to play our own parts in our own stories. We relish in our agency and gleefully do as we see fit, as should you. But this is your story, so I leave such things to you. These are your choices to make, your tale to unfold how you see fit. Your destiny is in your hands, my dear, not the hands of any man."

Rose looked down at Sam and allowed a kind of resolve she had never in her life felt before take hold. Her story. Her choice. Agency. It all made perfect sense.

She had had it with the beatings and the drinking and the control. She loved reveling in her body and not letting those she could feel nothing for do the same. All the men in her life who had spit upon her, ignored her, told her what to do and who to be, all marched across her thoughts, casting withering gazes and rude whistles. Fuck them, she thought.

Turning from June and stepping over her husband where he lay unconscious on the basement floor, Rose took hold of the key still sticking out of the bad door where Sam had left it a moment before.

Taking a deep breath, Rose knew what she had to do. She knew what she wanted to do. This was her choice and she made it willingly.

The lock mechanism was rusty and stiff from years of neglect, but eventually, squealing and grinding, the tumblers shifted and Rose slowly pulled upon the small door.

A mighty rush of wind burst into the room as the door flew open, causing Rose to shoot back toward June and the others on the stairs, tumbling over Sam. A steady and thick darkness billowed out from the doors and filled the basement. Rose's hair whipped back and forth in the flurry, and her view of the basement around her came and went. Above the din of the wind and what sounded like countless pieces of flapping leather, Rose heard Sam's maniacal laughter.

Slowly, the darkness began to shift upwards to the ceiling. It was in that moment that Rose realized what she was staring at — a thousand tiny, dark eyes peered curiously down at her from above. "Ahahahahaha," Sam laughed, where he lay on the ground. He was awake, groggy but aware once more. "You heard that bitch all wrong; it isn't a bad door, it's a bat door." Sam began to laugh again. Rage, embarrassment, and fury all swelled in Rose in a way she had never known to exist. "It's a bat door, you fucking clod," Sam continued to chide his wife as he lay splayed out on the dusty ground. Rose could feel her fists clench and her teeth do the same.

With the door open, the stony shaft of a cave was barely visible in the dim light of the basement. As the anger in Rose became stronger, she could feel her temples pulsing with every heartbeat. From their place on the staircase, the gaggle slowly moved down and across the room. June reached down and helped Rose to her feet as the rest of the ladies gathered behind the pair, all of them casting a malevolent gaze upon Rose's husband as he continued to laugh on the ground. Above, the bats hung silent, as if waiting for something to happen — and then it did.

Through the small doorway, a thin fog began to creep out and into the room, slowly covering the floor of the basement. Sam continued to laugh at what he perceived to be his wife's ineptitude, unaware of the cold fog filing into the room. A sound from deep within the small cave entrance beyond the open door cut Sam off. Sam's laughter was replaced by a sinister cackle, high-pitched and full of glee.

Rose watched all of this, unafraid and unaware that the women behind her now rested their hands upon her shoulders in solidarity and sisterhood. From the darkness beyond the door, a shape that seemed to be made up of an even darker substance than the mere absence of light began to coalesce, slowly taking on the form of a tall, slender woman.

She was a shimmering, pale specter, willowy hair, and hauntingly beautiful eyes. She wore both sadness and rage upon her face. She was a being of pure light now, hovering in a blackness of pure nothing. She was both beautiful and frightening all at once, and in that instant, Rose both knew her and loved her.

"Mother of darkness, take this *man* and consider him an offering so that Rose may be a part of our covenant," Rose heard June say from behind her, noting the acid in her voice at the pronunciation of the word "man."

"What say you, Rose?" the spectral woman asked. Rose nodded, smiling.

"So be it," the woman's voice echoed all around the room, and the swirling form of pure darkness reached out with black tendrils that weaved through the fog like writhing serpents, quickly wrapping and binding Sam. "Come, join me behind the bad door! The bad door for bad men…" The voice reveled. The women watched as Sam, fear in his eyes and tears streaming down his cheeks, unable to speak as the dark tendrils covered his mouth, was pulled into the cave beyond the door. In one instant, Rose's husband was there, and then he was gone.

The door slammed shut behind Sam and the echoing cackle began to fade with the fog. Up above, the bats hung nearly motionless, occasionally stretching their wings or yawning. Rose stood stunned, unable to truly comprehend what she had just seen, what had just happened, but pleased all the same. She had no words and yet she felt no remorse at seeing Sam dragged off. Now, she only felt her own growing sense of true freedom, and its taste was one she instantly enjoyed. Something deep down inside of her gradually rose to the surface. It was a smile, a simple smile that reflected the newfound freedom. Her fear of the door was replaced by adoration, and her fear of Sam was nothing more than a distant memory.

Rose turned to look at her friends, the small, crooked smile still pinned to her face. "Welcome, sister Rose, to the fold," June said. "Welcome to a world of agency. You are free to make your own choices. As your moon-blood flows, so will grow your burgeoning powers. For the age of man is coming to its last days, and someday soon shall be the age of the Miss over the Mr." The other women congratulated Rose with hugs and encouraging words, and all the while, the smile on Rose's face grew bigger and broader. Reaching into her pocket, Rose produced the bottle of medicine Doctor Bernstein had prescribed for her nerves. Unscrewing the cap, she poured out the bottle's contents upon the dusty basement floor while the rest of the Covenant looked on with pride at their newest member. "Welcome to your true family," June said proudly.

What Does It Want?

It's Thursday night, and Mom and Dad are at it again — their screaming and shouting is so loud I'm genuinely shocked the whole house isn't crumbling to its foundation. Dad's boots clomp loudly upstairs as he parries each verbal jab and accusatory swipe Mom lobs his way. Mom is slamming her fists on the dresser now; she has to hold herself back from wringing Dad's neck like a chicken. This is hardly their first spat they've had, and God knows it won't be the last.

I turn away from the darkened staircase and face the glowing television. It's late, way past my bedtime. The house is dark, the only light downstairs coming from the dancing black and white images of Jackie Gleason and Audrey Meadows as they move across the screen. Jackie addresses Audrey, chest pushed out like a gorilla — his body language and tone are pompous, commanding. The audience laughs.

Upstairs, Mom lets off a string of obscenities like bullets from a machine gun. Dad takes the barrage; he always does.

Leaning forward, I crank the volume on the television up, way up. The laugh track just barely drowns out Dad's deep, bellowing yells. Meanwhile, Jackie Gleason threatens to hit his television wife so hard she'll enter the moon's orbit. While Gleason gripes and grumbles away on the television, I realize that I can't make out what either Mom or Dad are screaming at one another behind their bedroom door — their words are now more or less a tangled jumble of harsh sounds mixing in with the rise and fall of the canned, television laughter.

I sit on the floor in front of the television, my legs crossed, my back straight as a board, hovering just above the back of the couch. My cup of milk is already too warm to enjoy. I pick up a Hydrox and begin to absentmindedly dunk it in my warm milk. Eating the cookie, my eyes fixed on the television, I feel neither joy nor fulfillment from either my treat or the soft glow of the vacuum-tube box before me as I chew the moistened cookie methodically. I sit like this for a while — all sense of time leaves me. *The*

Honeymooners ends. I watch the news with the volume lower; they're still fighting upstairs, but now it's Mom crying and Dad pleading.

Steve Allen comes on around the time the two of them go to bed. I can only assume they either made up or came to a stalemate since Dad doesn't seem to be making his way downstairs to camp out on the couch for the night. Kim Novak is on, talking about her latest film. Sleep begins to tug at my eyelids. I watch as the images on the television slowly fade in and out — my focus shifting quickly — sleep finally winning out against my desires to keep awake.

How long I am asleep, I cannot say.

Something pulls me out of Orpheus's grasp and into the moment. I hear a noise. The television is still on, but the image of the static Indian in profile in the tall headdress proclaims the end of the broadcast day. Someone is coming down the stairs. I turn, pull myself into a sitting position on the couch, and squint at the darkness of the stairwell behind me. I guess Dad must've figured that the couch was the place for him after all. The sound I hear, though, isn't footsteps. It sounds like hissing static coming slowly down the stairs — chattering and gibbering, not my dad's usual grumbling.

I watch in awe, my eyes finally adjusting to the dim light as something, not someone, comes down the stairs. All I can see is a dark figure, seemingly devoid of substance and definition — a stalking shadow. Their hands and feet appear to ooze viscous, oily pitch wherever they touch. The slim, bent figure has no real features to speak of, just that black sticky pitch-skin. The head, a round protrusion, lolls back and forth with each wet step it takes. Slowly, the bulbous, rounded mass that I can only assume is a head, begins to turn my way. No nose, no eyes, nothing.

I'm frozen where I sit, there on the couch. All I can do is watch. My breathing comes in shallow fits, and I feel like I will pass out unless I can take bigger gulps of air. Whatever it is, it stops at the foot of the stairs. It continues to stand there, oozing all around and looking straight at me — at least I assume it's looking at me. Slowly, a horizontal slit begins to appear along the lower portion of the head that grows wider and longer. It's smiling at me.

The teeth, as white as they are, are all wrong. One moment the smile is perfect, a picket fence of pearly white perfection — the next moment, the teeth are a jumbled mess. Suddenly the teeth are jagged, serrated like those of a shark. The teeth continue to change as the smile slowly widens. An unintelligible sound comes out of its dark and repulsive mouth — part radio static, part howl, part wild animal, and all unearthly and terrifying.

We both stare at one another for what seems like eternity. Is this eternity? Am I asleep? If I'm awake, then what is this thing? What does it want?

Slowly, the mouth with its dynamic teeth begins to close. The sounds fade as the mouth slit vanishes into that tar-like surface. From the foot of the stairs, it begins to move across the foyer and toward the front door. Passing into the entrance hallway, I don't see it leave, but I hear the front door open with a bout of creaking and then close quietly — almost politely.

My breathing deepens once more. I cannot even begin to comprehend what I have just seen. Slumping back onto the couch, I let sleep come and then the dreams.

* * *

Dad picks me up at the curb. It's raining pretty hard. The air is muggy, and I feel sticky. The passenger door to Dad's pickup groans and squeals in rusty, oil-denied resistance. Crawling into the worn seat beside my old man, I toss my school pack between us. The door closes with some effort and we're off. The windshield wiper blades move back and forth hypnotically across the spiderweb cracks — I often wonder when the old girl will finally give out and the whole windshield will shatter in on itself.

Pulling a pack of Camels out of my breast pocket, I offer one to Dad. Predictably, he turns it down and gives me that sad, disapproving but ultimately defeated look. Popping the lighter out of the dashboard console, I touch the glowing tip to my cigarette and take a long, glorious intake of tobacco and nicotine.

Dad doesn't ask how school is going. Dad doesn't ask how my social life is going. Dad doesn't know about the tattoo or the abortion or how my professors are all useless twits. He doesn't even talk about overseas — everyone is talking about overseas, about Saigon. He just sits and glowers. The rain is falling harder and heavier. I crack my window to let the smoke out.

There are so many things, unspoken, that we can talk about, but Dad doesn't want to. Dad just wants to not look me in the eyes. I think Dad is scared of me. Is he scared of me as a whole or is he scared of who I have become? The fuck if I know.

I should ask about Mom. I should ask about Melinda, his new girlfriend. I should, but I'm not going to. Do I even give a shit?

At the stoplight, I flick the remains of my cigarette out the window and onto the soaked asphalt far below. The rain pelts the smoldering butt like cannonade. The cherry slowly fades to black — the smoke slowly fades with it.

The light turns green, and we move faster than I thought we would. I hit the seat's back hard. I don't think Dad has noticed. Looking at the rain falling on the pickup's cracked and pitted windshield reminds me of TV static. Shit, when was the last time I watched television? My hand absentmindedly goes to my backpack. I can feel the heavy, solid forms of my schoolbooks.

We hit a bump in the road and something in the truck bed makes a heavy sound. Turning around, there is nothing to see back there, just the rain and a couple of old leaves. Leaves can't make a sound like that. What was that noise?

Another stop. Dad's hands grip the steering wheel so tightly they're turning white at the knuckles. What the hell does he want to tell me? I don't want to talk to him, but obviously, something is pissing him off — he has something to say and, like me, he won't say it — like father, like child.

Something in the truck bed makes a loud thump again. We're still stopped. Maybe it's hailing. Maybe this is the day Dad's windshield finally shatters. I watch in awe as a hand, black as pitch and slick and slimy, grabs hold of the back of the truck. Slowly, I see it pull itself up and over as it slithers into the truck bed. It hasn't changed — I certainly have, but it hasn't. I recognize my old friend. How long has it been?

The smile is there, rictus and full of that ever-shifting array of teeth. Despite the pelting rain, I can hear that voice issuing from its mouth. I still don't know what it's saying, but it sounds familiar. Buried there among all the static, howling, guttural noises, I can hear something. My spine begins to shudder. Dad pulls into the intersection. Does he see what I see? The engine roars — Dad is driving faster than I expected him to in this rain. Unfazed, it is moving from the back of the truck bed, creeping its way to the pickup's cab.

I wish I could feel something; anything. Should I be afraid? Anxious? Sick? Angry? What? Why is it here again? What is it? What does it want?

Whatever it is, it drags its wet, molasses body and smiling maw closer. There are no eyes to peer into — no expressions to interpret save for that stupid, fucking grin it always wears. There is only that round dripping head, that skinny, dripping body, and those thin, black, dripping limbs.

Dad stops the truck and rolls down the window at his side. Dad orders a burger from the McDonald's drive-through. When the hell did we arrive here? I can see that his knuckles are loose on the wheel again. I don't think we're gonna talk, but he doesn't look as upset as he had moments before.

Dad asks me if I want anything to eat. He tosses a weak smile in my direction. I tell him what I want. Dad orders for me. I turn back to see what it is doing in the back of Dad's truck, but whatever it is, it is gone.

* * *

Mom is pissed. Mom is almost always pissed, but right now she is extra pissed with a side of fuck-off. I always thought that drugs made you more mellow. Whatever Mom is on is making her a fire-spitting, fist-pounding, shithead right now. Of course, a lot of it could be the booze.

From what I've been able to piece together, Mom hasn't seen Dad in a while — they stopped speaking to each other after I got out of college. I don't even know if the divorce was ever finalized — something to look into sometime, I suppose. Mom's apartment is cramped — there's hardly enough room for her shitty furniture, let alone my modest luggage.

Sam and I had another fight. This time I left the house. Dad has been nigh impossible to reach — even his new family seems hard-pressed to answer the phone these days. Mom was my only familial option — either that or the sketchy Motel Six a couple miles away from my house. I opted for my sketchy mom.

I can tell she's lonely. She's never been outgoing, not like Dad. We sit and watch *Wheel of Fortune*. I hate this show. I think Mom does too, but she also just likes to have something on the television; something she can rage at when no one is around. Mom used to read day and night when I was little. We used to have three bookshelves in the living room, filled to the brim with all manner of books. Now all she wants to do is sit in front of the goddamn boob tube. I don't see a single book or magazine in the house — catalogues, yes, but those hardly count as decent reading material. The most stimulating pieces of literature I come across is the pile of Chinese take-out menus she has stacked on the end table next to her front door.

Part of me wants to get Mom a cat, let her fall into that archetype, but that would be cruel for the cat. The woman can hardly take care of herself, let alone a small animal.

The contestant on the show misses the clue, and Mom curses at him for nearly fifteen minutes. She hasn't even broached the subject of me being these — I doubt it will come up — after all, missed puzzles are far more important to discuss than my life. I can only take so much of this bullshit tonight. I need a smoke.

I leave Mom screaming at her TV between swigs of Jim Beam. Sliding the patio door closed behind me, Mom's ranting is nothing more than a small buzzing fly, miles away. My watch tells me that it's after midnight. The courtyard down below is drenched in darkness, broken only by the occasional walkway lamp.

I light up. I take a drag. I let the smoke fill me up. I exhale — I can feel the bullshit passing like water through a filter. I close my eyes. I think about Sam. I try to remember what we were arguing about. Was it the fucking car payment again or was it the utility bill? I cannot for the life of me remember, and I'm willing to bet that Sam can't recall right now either.

I should call Sam.

I open my eyes, watch the smoke from my mouth and nose distort my vision. I watch through the haze and let the sparkling waters of the community pool far below, still lit up, hypnotize me. It takes me a few moments to register that someone is breaking curfew and crawling, dripping out of the pool. I can't see who it is, but they are backlit by the pool lights.

Another satisfying drag — more smoke in my eyes. The smoke clears and the figure is gone. The light in the pool has been switched off. I hear something. I hear someone walking around down in the courtyard. It sounds like someone is dragging something heavy, laundry, perhaps.

One of the walkway lights next to the pool goes out with a sputter, then the next light, and the next. The lights along the path that lead to my mom's apartment are slowly going out, one after the other. The dragging shuffling is getting closer. I smoother my cigarette on the banister while I strain to see who is out there in the dark.

All the lights along the path are out now. I can hear whoever it is below Mom's balcony. I toss my cigarette butt aside and look down. I can't see anything below me, just darkness. I watch. I wait. How long have I been watching? How long have I been holding my breath? The light pouring out of Mom's apartment isn't very strong — I think I can see something climbing the wall just below the bathroom window. Fuck, Mom didn't close it.

A shadow on the wall. God, I hope that's all it is. Was it there earlier? That smile — those fucking teeth shifting and those animal sounds chittering. My flesh is cold to the touch. My heart races. I'm helpless. I can't for the life of me move. Why can't I move? What the hell is that thing? What does it want? It's looking my way. One second it's there smiling — white teeth on a black, oily form, and the next moment the thing is pouring itself into the bathroom from the open window.

I've lost track of my cigarette butt. I've lost track of time. I hear another muted string of Mom's obscenities and jump at just how loud she now sounds. Even with the sliding door still closed, she sounds as though she's just on the other side. Shaking, I think I need to go back inside. I need to pee, but that thing might still be in the bathroom. God damn, I feel like I'm seven years old again — scared of the dark.

I slip inside. Mom's just where I left her, ranting and raving. On TV a contestant buys a vowel. Mom tosses her ashtray at the wall behind the television. There is no longer a need for me to use the bathroom.

* * *

Where is Sam? He should be here right now. I need him to be here right now. My fingers feel fat — I can barely manage to open my pack of nicotine gum. Quitting sucks. Knowing that the fuck-faces who hooked you are also selling you their cure cuts deep. I've run all out of tissues. I've run out of patience. I've run out of fucking everything. Where's my energy? Why do I ache all over?

The phone rings. I hear Mom on the other end of the line; she's so calm. How can she be so calm right now — so nonchalant? I'm here crying my eyes out, and she is acting like she doesn't have a god-damned care in the world. Fuck her.

Mom babbles. Mom rambles. Mom just doesn't know when the fuck to shut up. Her cough is loud, wet, and nasty; and the woman wonders why I am trying to kick the habit. I'm her kid and she's the freakin' child. I wonder if she'd even notice if I just hang the phone up right now. I let her talk. I let her go on and on. I stopped listening a while ago.

All I can think about is Dad, Dad and the family he let me be a part of — I can understand why he had to get away. I can understand why it took him so long to bring me back into his fold. What I cannot for the life of me understand is how he can be gone. How can he be there one moment, then gone the next? Brain, do your thing; make this all make sense.

Part of me wishes I had been there. Part of me wanted to see it happen. A lot of me, most of me, is glad I didn't. It was hard enough to see him in the morgue. I don't envy Tina and Junior. One minute you're walking down the street with your family, and the next, you're pinned under the front tire of a drunk's Oldsmobile.

Fuck, life is strange.

I don't want to be sad. I'm sick and fucking tired of being sad. I want to be pissed. I want to raise hell. I want to make someone suffer.

Mom needs to shut up. You know what, fuck it. Hanging up the phone feels good. I'll let Mom chew on the dial tone for a while. I need a cigarette. I know Sam has thrown them all out. Dammit,

Sam. Maybe if I work at it a bit more, I can get the gum open. I need scissors.

The kitchen is dark. The whole house is dark. The living room is my island of light right now. I've been in this kitchen a million times in the middle of the night. I know where the drawer is with the scissors. The fridge begins to hum. Fuck, that shit scares me. The scissors are on the counter where I was clipping coupons earlier.

Something brushes past me. Cobwebs are the worst. Something brushes behind me. The kitchen is dark still. Something is chittering. Oh god…

Scissors out, the pointy end is ready to stab whatever comes out of the dark. The time on the microwave dims. In the corner between the fridge and the pantry, I can just make out a shape. I want to ask if it's Sam, but I know it isn't. A half-moon smile. The teeth — always those teeth. The animal sounds are getting louder. I can feel them vibrating in my own teeth. It is moving slowly. I've never seen it move fast.

It's been a long time coming. How long has it been since I saw it last? I back slowly out of the dark kitchen and into the living room. It's following. It's dripping pure dark syrup all across the linoleum floor. The smile is just as I remember it, always changing. Yellow teeth, jagged teeth, blunt teeth, missing teeth, rounded teeth — the cycle never ends.

The scissors fly from my hand and straight at it. The damn things pass through it and land with a clatter on the floor behind it. I try to scream. I've never seen it move so fast, ever.

It's pinning me down to the floor. The teeth and that endless exaggerated smile are just above my face. I scream. Black bile pours from its open mouth and straight into my open mouth. I try to cough. I try to spit. Nothing works. Whatever it is, it's growing smaller, but the bile keeps coming.

I black out.

I'm shaken awake. My vision is blurry. My vision is focusing. Sam? When did Sam finally get here? He helps me to sit up. He rushes to the kitchen. A glass of water. Fuck, I'm thirsty. Sam takes the empty cup from me. He asks if I'm okay. Do I look like I'm fucking okay? I don't feel okay. A small smile for Sam — something to deflect.

He goes to unpack the groceries in the kitchen. My hands automatically go to my face. Why am I still smiling? What did that thing do? Where did it go? I think about Dad. I think about Mom. I think about Sam. I think about that thing. Everything clicks.

Finally, I know what it wants.

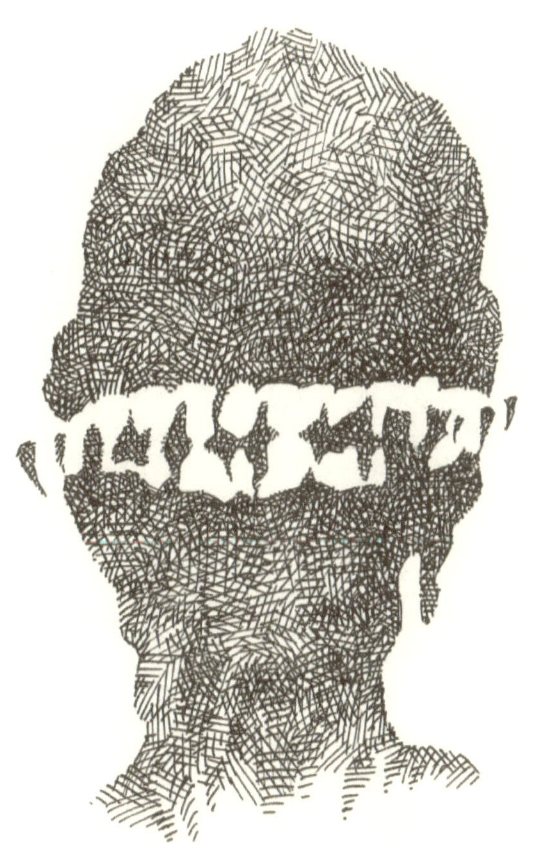

Just Desserts

Sitting patiently, Melody listened to the droning march of time as the grandfather clock across from her in the long, lonely hallway ticked and tocked the seconds away.

Tick — Melody's legs swung under the bench beneath her.

Tock — her legs swung up and out in front of her.

With each metronome upswing of her legs, Melody studied the shiny silver buckles of her pretty, new shoes. The shoes had been a recent gift from her father and a constant source of irritation for her mother, who insisted that Melody kept them shiny and free of mud and scuff at all times. It had been Melody's mother's wish that the child laid her new shoes and togs tucked away safely in the wardrobe, but today was a special day and a special day, Melody knew, meant a chance to dress in her finest.

While she relished the opportunity to dress as fancy as she imagined adults to dress, Melody hated visiting The Manor. The Manor, as the old house at the end of Cottonwood Lane had been dubbed by the locals, was a large and intimidating abode. The place had a full staff, chefs, maids, gardeners, and the like, and yet from the outside, the villa looked rotten, like a moldy apple left in the sun. Vines, green and thick, snaked their way up every available surface outside of the house, threatening to either constrict the old brick and mortar structure or crush it like a hand squeezing a beetle. Like most people in town, Melody feared and loathed The Manor, but unlike most people in town, she had no choice in her visit. Since the end of the war, before Melody had been born, her mother and father had worked in The Manor.

Melody's mother was a fussy woman but loving, nonetheless. At home she chided Melody's father whenever he doted on their only child. Melody often noticed the way others in town regarded her parents — cold and distant, as though they carried some sort of illness. Sometimes she wondered if it was because they were rather well off and so many others in the village were not so "financially independent," as her father had called it once. When Melody had broached the subject to her father one evening, he had told her simply that the looks they got in the streets and shops were not so much due to their station in life but due to where they worked. The Manor, her father had told her, was loathed by nearly everyone.

Melody's mother, never one to shy away from her opinion on any number of topics, was the head of the cleaning staff within The Manor. Melody's father kept the books for The Manor's owner, a whisper of a man: Justice Brackish, the village's sole judge and magistrate. To say that Justice Brackish was a thin man was an understatement of a most egregious nature — Justice Brackish was easily the thinnest man in the county if not the country. When seen in person, he had a tendency to make one's skin crawl — while his frame was thin and skeletal, his skin looked as though it had been draped over his bones, left to hang in odd ways about his form. When Justice Brackish spoke, his jowls shook with each word — dancing like a marionette, legs all akimbo on the end of its strings. For such a waif of a man, he was known for his deep and commanding voice. The man's clothing was custom made; it had to be. Before Melody's uncle had been appointed his official tailor, three others had taken up the task only to leave as the man lost more and more weight in less time between fittings. Melody had never understood why such a lucrative position as the tailor to a man of immense wealth and need did not stay on, but she reasoned it was the ways of adults, not to be understood by a child such as her.

Melody withdrew her legs quickly on an upswing as three men in matching chef's hats and smocks roared down the hallway and past her in a flurry of anger, alcohol, and French. To Melody's knowledge, no one else in town spoke French and yet Justice Brackish was fluent and surrounded himself with chefs who only spoke the strange, foreign tongue. None of the chefs regarded her with so much as a nod — as quickly as they had come, they were gone.

Her rhythm with the clock now thrown off, the young girl began to fuss at the ribbon her mother had used to tie back her long, straight, blond hair. As she tugged and tightened the bow at the back of her head, a door down the hall opened, spilling warm lamplight into the hallway. The exposed flames in the wall sconces that ran the length of the hallway flickered, the hiss of gas rising in pitch for just a moment. Someone stepped out of the room. Melody leaned forward in her seat and watched as a woman, her dress wide and heavy, made her way down the hallway, toward her. In the half-light of the weak lanterns and dark oaken paneling, it took Melody a moment to realize who was approaching. Mother's scent — vanilla and loganberry — was rich and creamy, and it proceeded her like a calm before a storm.

"Melody," her mother snapped, "what have you done to your hair?"

Melody reached up to touch her bow once more but found her hand slapped away as her mother busied herself with the piece of velveteen ribbon. Looking up at her mother's face as the woman fretted, Melody took in every detail of her mother's swan-like neck. Years later, she would adorn her own long, elegant neck with the same set of black pearls her mother now wore. The pearls matched her dress, black as night and lovely. It had no frills, no lace, nothing to exaggerate the female form, and yet it was simple and pretty.

"Mama?" Melody asked, her feet beginning to arc in small circles in the space below the bench as the magic of the clock's beat cast its spell once more.

"Yes, my songbird?" This was the pet name her father had bestowed upon her when she was small; a holdover from when Melody had sung little babbling tunes to herself as she played with her dolly.

"Why must we have supper with the justice tonight?"

"We must because he asked it of us," her mother replied, putting on the final flourish to the bow in her hair.

"But why? You spend all day here in this place. Why must we dine with him?"

Melody's mother stopped and lowered herself to look her child in the eyes. Melody now took in every detail of her mother's eyes — the deep blue-green of the seas after a storm, the darkness below them from lack of sleep, and the hint of sadness, something her mother could not bear to expose, hidden in those eyes. They were the eyes of a woman who had lived too many lives, a woman with too many secrets, a woman with too much pain and anguish in her heart.

"Sometimes," her mother said in a calm, soothing voice, holding her daughter's gaze, "sometimes we are meant to do things whether we want to do them or not. The Justice has asked you and me and your father to dine with him this evening, and we must oblige."

"Does he own us?" Melody asked. The sadness behind her mother's eyes deepened. Tears would not come — her mother never shed tears for anyone or anything, no matter the occasion or circumstances.

"No, of course he does not. But he does own the house we live in, and as our employer, it is expected of us. It is simply one more duty we must perform." Her mother, rising up, reached out a hand. Melody took hold of her mother's offered hand and slid off the bench. "Come with me, my songbird."

In the pale, flickering light of the gas flames, the hallway seemed an endlessly stretching tunnel — Melody imagined herself being swallowed by a long, oaken worm. Shadows crept and crawled out of every corner, dancing along the walls as the flames commanded them to. Moving down the hall at a brisk pace, the child's footfalls began to fall in line with the tick-tock of the old hallway clock.

Tick — right foot.

Tock — left foot.

The irony was lost on Melody in that moment, but as an adult, thinking back to that night, she found it chilling how much she felt like a condemned prisoner walking the long walk to the gallows.

A stuffed owl, its eyes glittering and surreal, regarded Melody and her mother from its perch on the wall with the cold ambivalence of a hunter studying its prey. In the back of her mind, Melody thought she heard the screech of the big brown bird. While The Manor felt like a lonely place, Melody could have sworn that countless sets of eyes from countless, restless souls were watching her, willing her on and into the grand unknown. Ahead of Melody and her mother stood the door her mother had entered from earlier; a door that appeared as black as pitch at first but slowly revealed itself to be so deeply red it might as well have been painted black. At first the door's hue reminded Melody of the color of the fur on her Irish Setter back home. Soon, though, it began to remind her more of blood on a wound, long since dried-up. A shiver shook the child like a branch in a storm. Melody's mother looked down at her daughter, slowing her pace in that moment.

"Are you well, my dear?" her mother asked. Melody nodded; her eyes still fixed on the door ahead.

"I am fine. A little chilled but fine," she said in a tiny voice.

Melody's mother gave her a weak smile. Her face carried a sadness Melody had not expected to be there. It was a new sadness, the sadness of a mother who must come to the realization that her child was about to grow up far too early.

In silence, the pair reached the dark door. Melody's mother reached out for the handle, took a deep, calming breath, and pushed. Bright, golden light flooded Melody's vision as her eyes struggled to adjust. Slowly, the flickering, dancing sprites began to coalesce into the shuddering flames of candelabras and a gilded chandelier. Melody took it all in like the first gulp of a glass of water after a long, dry night. The walls were adorned with gold plates and gilded portraits of men and women dating back through the ages. Along the far wall, windows gazed out upon the darkened grounds of The Manor. Frost had begun to collect around the base of the windowpanes. Gas flames blazed like the fires of hell, casting a golden light made even more golden as they reflected off the gilded surfaces from floor to ceiling. In the center of the room stood a table of rich, blond cedar. Upon its surface danced the flames of at least a hundred candles in dozens of candelabras. Beautifully ornate goblets and plates, covered in vortices of swirls and intricate and detailed patterns, were placed before every seat at the table.

Melody's attention, now drawn to the table, noticed the dinner guests. Nearly every seat was occupied, save for three — her seat, her mother's, and at the head of the table what she could only assume was Judge Brackish's seat. Brackish's seat was practically a throne — tall, ornate, and intimidating. As she took her own seat, Melody looked at the dozen or so guests around her, some she recognized — her father, Miss Beachwood, the local apothecary, Mayor Daniels, Doctor Reinhardt, and Mr. and Mrs. Crest. In the seat closest to Judge Brackish's sat a young man, impeccably dressed and wearing a look of absolute dread upon his face.

Everyone else, Melody noticed, appeared worried and determined not to look at the scared young man at the head of the table. Slowly, as she studied the faces around her, fraught with concern, it began to dawn on the child that no one was speaking. The silence that hung over the room cast a melancholy spell.

As time dragged on amid the silence, a side door to the chamber opened, and out stepped the three French chefs, each taking a place behind the throne at the head of the table, each as silent as the grave. Next came servants, men and women Melody knew very well — her mother's charges. The six servants took up places around the table and reached for the bottles of champagne that lined the middle of the table, making it look less like a place of eating and conversing and more like the ridged spine of a terrible beast. Turning to her mother, Melody noted the slight nod her mother gave the servants before they began to pour out the golden liquid into each and every glass, save for Melody's. While her father fidgeted with his glasses, cleaning them with his cloth napkin over and over, the rest of the guests began to quickly drink their champagne.

The last glass to be filled was that of Judge Brackish. Melody was curious to see the servants bring out a delicate teacup, which one filled from a teeming teapot while the other added carefully measured out amounts of cream and sugar. The task completed, the servants placed the coupon upon a matching saucer and the pot on the table before the cup. Melody had known few to take tea with a meal, especially one so fancy. With the drinks now served, the servants all stood back and took their respective places along the walls of the dining room. Moments later, the double doors at the head of the table, the same ones the chefs and servants had entered through, parted, and without fanfare, Judge Brackish was pushed into the chamber in a wheeled chair, a heavy blanket upon his lap. The man looked pale, lighter than humanly possible, it seemed to the small child. The man's eyes were two black specks, surrounded by the drooping flesh that clung to his face like a series of stalactites. His face was a patchwork of stubble in places a razor could not easily navigate. While the judge's suit was tailor-made to account for such a tiny frame, the buttons on the front appeared to bulge ever so slightly, as if his skin had been crammed into the suit along with his skeleton. As she watched him being pushed into place in front of the throne that she now came to realize was a backing for the wheeled chair, Melody wondered why the man did not simply use a cane to walk, or was he too proud to do so, or too feeble to move under his own power?

A sickly cough, deep and phlegmy, rattled the man's chest. After considerable effort, Judge Brackish, huffing and wheezing, slowly raised a shaking hand. Moments seemed to turn to hours as the man caught his breath. Each winded rattle and wracking cough from his hallow chest sent a chill down Melody's spine. Around the room, no one dared to speak — the fear contained within the chamber was palpable. While Melody herself felt no such fear of the cartoonishly deflated man at the head of the table, she could practically taste the tension on her tongue.

The young man at the head of the table, closest to Judge Brackish, began to shiver violently. Finally, after catching his breath and audibly clearing his throat, the judge spoke slowly, as though each word were a savory morsel.

"Ladies and gentlemen of the Village Council and distinguished guests," Brackish stated in a heavily slurred voice while motioning to his guests. "I want to extend a heartfelt thank you for heeding my invitation and joining me here tonight for this special occasion." No one spoke, no one coughed, no one seemed to breathe as their host spoke/ "As many of you have no doubt ascertained, I have invited you all here on behalf of young Mr. Wagstaff." Brackish gestured to the young man, still quaking in his fancy suit and seat. "Mr. Wagstaff was recently found guilty in my court of bribery and extortion. The cabal he formed with many on the Village Council is now known, and as you all can attest, I am a strict man, lenient when necessary but strict to the letter otherwise."

The air in the room seemed to vanish at these words.

"While those on the Village Council, graciously pointed out by our esteemed guest, were charged and punished, it now falls to Mr. Wagstaff to receive his due punishment in turn. Tonight, we will give this upstanding young and very wealthy man — a man who has given so much to our town over the years, even if he took quite a bit in turn — a lovely send-off before he is to serve his punishment. For your dining pleasure, I will be serving to you all a fine sea bass simmered with garlic and herbs served with a side of roasted red potatoes and a medley of winter vegetables. For dessert, we have a wonderful custard pudding. Tonight's vintage is a lovely Chateau Le Blanc from seventy-six, I believe. As for myself, I will be indulging in something prepared specially for me. As for Mr. Wagstaff, as a convicted man, he will be accompanied by my kitchen staff and given the opportunity to choose his last meal as a free man."

At these words, three large and thuggish Officers of the Law entered the room from the servant's entrance. One held a pair of dull, worn handcuffs while the other two brandished wooden cudgels and stern, sweeping looks from beneath their caps. Their pressed blue uniforms were immaculate, and their loyalty to Justice Brackish was plain to see.

No one spoke — no one dared move. In his seat, Mr. Wagstaff was having fits the likes of which Melody had never imagined a human being capable of having. With Judge Brackish's words spoken, the servants returned to their task of preparing the guests' places for their entrees and offering fresh wine. Melody watched as the three French chefs and three brutish officers flanked Mr. Wagstaff. Melody watched in awe as they cuffed the young man before escorting him through the double doors to the kitchen. A few moments passed before one of the chefs returned to Brackish's side. Bending over, the chef lowered one ear to the judge's mouth. Melody watched as a web of spittle slowly formed from the end of the man's mouth and began to work its way down many rippling chins. "Je le veux préparé de la manière habituelle," Brackish whispered into the chef's ear. The chef nodded, turned to take his leave, and headed back into the kitchen to see to his duties.

With Wagstaff gone, conversation began to spread as the tension from moments before slowly seemed to dissipate. At the head of the table, Judge Brackish smiled, his thin, purplish lips undulating like a pair of night crawlers — the man wore the look of a cat that caught the canary. Judge Brackish made a joke, something Melody did not understand, about the difference between sheep and women. The room erupted into a stifled, forced laughter as the skeletal man delivered the punchline. Melody looked to her parents, hoping they might see the confusion pinned to her face. Her mother shook her head somberly while her father held her mother's hand from under the table and flashed Melody a strained smile.

Soon enough, though, the tension in the room began to recede, and honest conversation began to take hold. Brackish said nothing at this point — the man sat in his seat, his chest heaving with labored breathing, his tiny teacup touching his lips now and again as he gulped long and loud. Before she knew what was happening, the servants were removing the plates their small salads had been served on and were bringing forth the main course. The tension in the room snapped back, like a rubber band under too much tension. While the guests' meals were placed before them, Melody noticed that Brackish's meal had yet to arrive. As the last of the meals was placed before the guests, the servants withdrew to the perimeter of the room once more. Brackish did not stand but instead raised his glass high.

"Tonight, I should like to raise a toast. I raise my glass high to you all. I raise it to you in hopes of good health and many years of good crops. I raise it high in honor of the young," — Judge Brackish nodded in Melody's direction, the youngest guest at the table — "and the old. I raise my glass high in the name of justice and peace."

A chorus of "Cheers" echoed throughout the room. As Judge Brackish lowered his glass, the doors to the kitchen burst open and two of the French chefs entered the room, a platter at least three feet across between them. They placed the platter delicately before Judge Brackish. The platter was piled high, a foot or more, with the most delectable-looking sausages Melody had ever seen. Around the room, someone stifled a cry of surprise. The judge did not seem to notice this as he took in the sight of a meal that seemed too much for someone of such a frail and withered form.

"Tuck in," Judge Brackish commanded, his words garbled, thick with saliva. No one moved to touch their plates. Cutlery and napkins remained as they were. Everyone watched in silence as Judge Brackish began to eat his sausages. A woman near Melody swooned as though she might pass out. The mayor stood, excused himself, and stepped out of the room. When he returned a few moments later, he dabbed at his mouth with his napkin, his flesh as white as a sheet. Brackish ate, pleased with himself and his meal, while no one else dared to move.

A pall spread through the room — an unseen fire consuming all. Brackish leering down at his guests from his throne on high and his fork in hand gave his guests a commanding eye. Slowly, very slowly, the guests continuing to shift in their seats, cutlery began to ever so lightly scrape, and food and drink was consumed. Unsure whether or not to eat, Melody sank deeper into her seat, her hands falling to her side. She allowed her fingers to dance across the cushion frame of the chair, feeling her way across the intricate carvings, her fingers exploring like those of the blind reading Braille. Something caught on the tips of her fingers, something that stayed her hands. On either side of the chair, her fingers found and felt their way, probing and exploring what felt like gouges. Instantly, she could tell that they were not part of the chair's original design. No, these were made by someone — someone clinging to the chair for dear life.

Glacially, as the guests moved to reluctantly eat their meals, the gears in Melody's head began to turn. As long as she had remembered, the people in town had whispered and murmured amongst themselves about Justice Brackish. Even the children in the village feared the man. It was not uncommon for young children to dare and tease each other into throwing rocks at The Manor or slamming the gate. There were rhymes and limericks about Brackish — many involved him gobbling children up whole. Melody had always brushed these tall tales aside. After all, she reasoned, her parents worked in his household. Such upstanding people as her mother and father, she knew deep down, would never stand for such inhuman behavior. And yet the rumors persisted and grew with each passing year. Some people, the children whispered amongst themselves, claimed that the justice would eat those whom he judged as guilty, especially those of the town's higher ranks. Poppycock and flimflam, Melody thought — and yet the fear in the room was real, as real as the look of terror on young Mr. Wagstaff's face as he was escorted out of the room. Where was Mr. Wagstaff? He had yet to return with his specially selected meal.

The pit in Melody's stomach dropped out like one of the old mineshafts the children in town were constantly warned not to play nearby.

"My child, you do not look well. Are you feeling poorly?" Melody's mother asked, the back of her hand pressed firmly against her child's forehead. Melody gave a weak nod. Her stomach tightened — she needed to get out. Melody nodded at her mother's question. "Well, why don't you go to the washroom, see if that does not help you some."

Melody began to slide from her chair. Seeing that she wanted to leave, one of the servants rushed up and moved the chair away for the child. "Where is the washroom?" Melody asked her mother.

"Go back into the hallway and it is the second door on your right. Do not leave the hallway, though. Head straight to the washroom and straight back. Do you hear?" Melody nodded. Without saying another word and knowing that nearly every eye in the room was on her, Melody walked across the dining room and back out the door her mother had escorted her through earlier.

The hallway, already a place of long shadows and strange sounds, began to take on a much grislier presence. Shadows cast by the gas lanterns slowly turned into black bile and blood, oozing out of every corner and crevice in the long hall. Moving down the hallway, as if in a daze, Melody eventually made it to the washroom door. Inside, she filled the small basin with water from the pitcher nearby and proceeded to wash her hands and splash her face. Chills wracked her body through and through. Drying herself off with one of the hand towels on the rack near the basin, Melody began to feel better as logic took hold.

How silly, she thought. The notion of Justice Brackish and his rumored *exotic tastes* were no more real than the snipe hunts some of the older village boys would send the younger ones on in the summer months. The stories, she reasoned, were just that, stories. It was so obvious: the people in the dining room, the local council, and magistrates were simply in fear and awe of such a powerful man. Perhaps, she reasoned, young Mr. Wagstaff had been returned to the dinner table by now.

Her head now filled with thoughts that made sense, Melody made her way down the hall and through the door. The room

Melody entered had an unfamiliar air — this, she quickly realized, was not the dining room. Rounding a corner, the young girl found herself in the kitchens, the walls lined with skillets, pots, and pans and stoves spewing red and orange licking flames. In the middle of the room, on a raised table, sat the most delicious and extravagant custard pudding Melody had ever seen. Her mouth began to water at the very thought of tucking into such a magnificent-looking dessert. Approaching slowly, so as not to startle any of the chefs who might be lurking about, Melody scanned the room. From what she could tell, she was all alone. As she drew nearer to the tall, golden, frosted delicacy, something caught the child's eye.

On a counter along the far wall, streaks of wine red ran across and down the other side of the surface. A trail of congealing blood on the floor led the way from the counter and around the corner. Cautiously, minding her footfalls, Melody quietly followed the trail. The trail, she noticed, ended (or began) at the far end of the room at the foot of a tall door. Melody crept closer to the door. Wispy tendrils of vapor leaked out from below the door — a freezer and one left unlocked. Reaching her hand out, Melody gripped the handle and slowly pulled the freezer door open.

Stifling a scream as she opened the door, she was greeted by a cold blast of air and a familiar face. Like a spider creeping toward its prey, realization slowly dawned on the shivering child. The face, as familiar as it was, was frozen solid, lips blue and icicles of blood running down from the nose. As Melody took in the sight before her, her mind began to reel — the frozen face was attached to nothing more than a mangled torso, which hung lazily on a meat hook, swaying gently in the air currents within the freezer. The arms and legs had been hacked off. Melody had never seen a man's genitals before, but what she saw was shriveled from the cold. Shock overtook the child. No one had seen young Dudley Myers, the pharmacist's assistant, after he had been arrested weeks ago for drunkenly disturbing the peace after a bad break-up. But here he was, a look of rictus shock permanently frozen to his pale, blue face. As she stepped back and away from the freezer, she began to make out other faces and torsos. There were more meat hooks and racks upon racks of severed limbs. The faces gradually came to her in that moment — Mr. Devonshire, found guilty by Justice

Brackish for swindling several in town of their life savings. There was Mrs. Pritchett, who had been found guilty months ago of selling meats at the market without a proper license, and there, in the back, slumped over as though he was napping, Mr. Wagstaff, his face bloody and beaten and a still oozing gash across his throat — his arms missing.

Melody quickly turned around, the bile building up in her throat — a geyser about to blow. Across from the freezer, along another wall, sat a meat grinder, the remains of a hand, pale and bloody, poking out from the top as if ready to wave at her. In that moment, Melody retched. The contents of her stomach spent upon the black and white honeycomb tiled floor; the child ran. Running blindly out of the kitchen and back into the hall, she burst through the doorway back into the dining room. All eyes fell on her.

Seeing her daughter, Melody's mother flew to her child's side. "My sweet songbird, you look worse than earlier." She fawned over her brood. Melody looked past her mother at Judge Brackish. The man was gesticulating wildly as he told a story to the couple closest to him — his plate of sausages empty — picked clean. With her mother's help, Melody somehow found her way back to her seat. Sitting down, everyone in the room began to look at one another, a sense of knowing passing between them.

Melody fought to comprehend what she had just seen. Her mind refused to work as abstract images flickered in and out of existence. She wanted to scream, to cry, to do anything to rid herself of the memory and feelings, but she knew that in that moment she would find little sympathy for what she had witnessed.

After some time, the French chefs wheeled out the pudding from the kitchen and allowed the servants to begin dishing out yellow globs of sweetness to each guest. Melody stared blankly at the dessert in front of her, unable to eat. The guests all around her began to cautiously enjoy their treat. A loud guffaw caught the child's attention. Turning very slowly to face Judge Brackish, Melody gazed at the ghoul of a man in a whole new light.

"What's the matter, my dear? No taste for pudding?" Brackish asked, a seemingly knowing grin splitting his gaunt and sallow face. "Well, don't fret, little one, it won't hurt you. After all, it's only just desserts..."

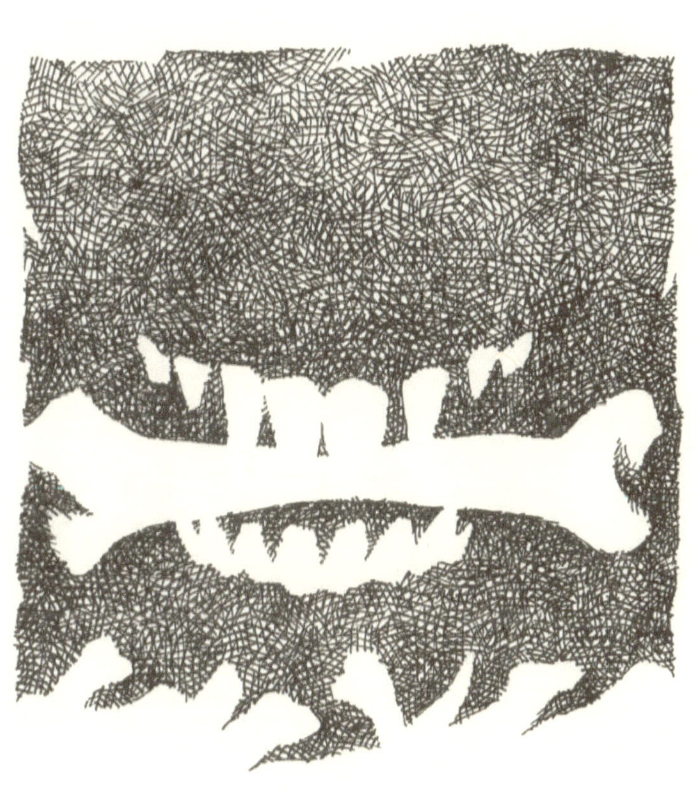

Twilight Time

Harry's leg bounced up and down in agitation — the scent of antiseptic hung in the air like a pall, seeping into every corner of the waiting room and seeming to cling to every surface. Harry could feel a sense of nausea, partially from nerves and partially from the deep, permeating scent of disinfectant mingling with ozone. The sterile, white waiting room with its hypoallergenic plants, stacks of half-a-decade-old magazines, and the droning blare of cable news on the television in the corner of the room upset Harry more than the scent of the overly clean hospital. Paintings on the white-on-white walls depicted Saint Bartholomew, the namesake of the hospital, as he fed hungry children and nursed wounded animals. Behind the patron in the painting stood a pair of nuns clad in black and white, and behind them, what appeared to be a distant streak of blood-red paint; was that supposed to be a person farther back in the image, he wondered? Harry turned his attention away from the oil on canvas, distracted by a pair of nurses in their minty green uniforms walking by in the hallway, chatting excitedly about something Harry could not hear, for at that moment the intercom crackled to life, calling for a "Doctor Bradshaw" to "come to the pharmacy."

Just like his grumbling bowels, he was somewhere far beyond irritation — he was deep in Pestilent County and he was Lord-High Mayor. He had been up all night, sipping the thick, chemical-tasting bowel prep medication laced with white cherry sports drink between bouts of liquid shits as he cleared out his system in preparation for his appointment. At sixty, this was Harry's third colonoscopy and his second endoscopy, and he was having none of it. Harry hated hospitals; always had. Something about a place filled with death and sickness never sat right with him. Sure, he often reasoned when he stopped and thought about it, people were also born in places like this, but there was still so much blood, and mucus, and screaming. A hospital, he had long ago decided, was a place of extremes — birth and death, blood and cleansing, and all that came with such opposites. It had been nearly two days since he had eaten solid food, and his stomach groaned in protest of his medically required fasting. In a flash, the twisting and grinding of an empty stomach shifted his train of thought to his guts with all the reckless speed of a semi barreling down an incline, its brakes cut and its horn blaring.

"Shit," Harry mumbled to himself, slicking back his shock-white hair in frustration.

"The toilet is around the corner, dear," Edith, his wife of forty-seven years, said nonchalantly as she licked her finger before turning the next page in her dime-store romance novel with its early 90s Fabio cover art. Edith usually read more academically interesting and engaging fare or more thematically crafted tales, but this was her cheat week — the week between good books when she would dive head first into whatever trash she found in the big box in the attic that had belonged to her late sister.

Harry stopped gazing at the cleavage showing on the young, scantily clad woman in the torn dress on the cover, being held aloft by two of the most primed and oiled arms he had ever seen on a man and dashed out of the lobby and into the head. In that moment, the toilet seemed a mile away. In a sudden urge of speed, he managed to make it to the door and plant his ass firmly on the rim of the bowl just in time — he hadn't even locked the stall door behind him before everything came crashing out. The clear, piss-yellow liquid that filled the bowl had all the scent and charm of the thick sludge he had been forced to drink the night before, and it took another force of will just to keep himself from vomiting at the sight and smell.

His business concluded for what he hoped was the last time before his procedure, Harry washed his hands and headed back to the waiting room and Edith and her masturbation material. Passing a pair of nuns in their white and blue dresses and habits, Harry noticed Edith, no longer sitting, her book tucked away in her purse, was talking with a young male nurse in the waiting room.

"Here he is," Edith said, turning from the young man in the same soothingly mint duds as the nurses that had passed by in the hallway earlier.

"Morning, Mr. Prescott. Thanks for coming in early today for your procedure," the young nurse said.

"Harry. You can call me Harry," Harry replied, taking the nurse's hand and, much to the young man's surprise, shaking it. "And what's your name?"

"Daniel. I'll be helping with the prep this morning." Harry grimaced upon hearing the "p" word. All week he had been forced to eat a low-fiber diet and to avoid anything with fun red or blue colors, and it had been excruciating to down the whole bottle of laundry detergent-smelling crap all for a measly thirty-minute visit to Saint Bartholomew's — the word prep had been a steady part of his diet, his vocabulary, and his life for the last seven days — he was over that word. Daniel handed Harry a clipboard and a blue inked pen. "If you could please fill this out real quickly, Mr...." Daniel blanched. "Sorry. If you could fill this out, Harry, we'll get you all squared away."

Harry nodded as he looked down at the questionnaire before him. Pen in hand, he filled out the requisite information; his emergency contact, his ride home, his family and history with cancer, and just how clear his stool looked this morning. Edith all the while was busy talking in a low voice with Daniel the nurse about some such political nonsense being discussed on the television. Daniel, spotting that Harry appeared to be done, took the clipboard and pen, quickly scanned what Harry had filled out in his chicken scratch, and then motioned for the couple to follow him to the other end of the waiting room where a set of double doors awaited them, framed by portraits of Saint Bartholomew, deep in prayer, his face lit by candlelight in the portrait on the left and lit by holy glow in the portrait on the right — the same smudge of red hovering in the background of both paintings, standing perfectly still, hands folded — Harry could see the little details and knew it was meant to be a person in prayer.

"Come with me, please," Daniel said while Harry and Edith followed dutifully behind the young man as he slapped an ID card against a panel next to the doors, waited for a low buzz, and opened them. The hallway before the trio was long, well-lit in the sickly amber tint of stained fluorescent lighting and reeked of the same unending stench of cleaning chemicals and soap. Harry's fingers began to twitch and dance at his side as he and Edith followed the young nurse down the hall to another set of double doors. These doors opened without the security measures of the ones they had entered from.

The prep/recovery room was painted in a glossy eggshell white that reminded Harry of the froth at the top of an egg cream. Three of the four walls were comprised of curtained stations while the fourth wall was taken up by the nurses' station — overseeing the room like a medical panopticon. Many of the beds in the curtained stations were occupied either by patients waiting for their procedures or those recovering. Some curtains were drawn while those behind them changed either into or out of their clothes and hospital gowns. The steady beeping of heart-rate monitors mixed with the dull buzz of electronic equipment, low voices as nurses and doctors and patients talked amongst themselves, and the shuffle of feet and the squeak of gurney wheels as people were passed to-and-fro into and out of the room all came together in a strange, discordant cacophony.

"Here we are, station number twelve," David said with a grin as he led Harry and Edith into a curtained-off area with a bed, a chair, and a bevy of equipment for monitoring one's vitals. Edith sat down and watched Harry with a hawkish gaze. "Alright, so if you could just undress," David said, handing Harry a clear plastic bag, "everything can go in here, and feel free to leave your socks on. I'll be back in a few." Harry took the bag from David and watched as the young man left, closing the curtain behind him.

"How's your stomach?" Edith asked, pulling a roll of mints from her purse.

"It's okay, I suppose," Harry replied, wincing a little at the sight of his wife popping a round mint into her mouth while his empty stomach groaned. Pushing the thought of eating out of his mind, he began to undress. As each piece of clothing came off, it went right into the bag Edith held out for him — shoes, shirt, pants, underwear — everything but the socks. Harry sat down on the edge of the bed and heaved a heavy sigh. It had been a long night without food, and sitting on the toilet from sundown to sunup, he was tired and irritated, and ready to go home and sleep and eat. As important as the procedure was, and knowing how crucial something like it could be for his health, Harry still felt like most doctors had to be a little insane — after all, they kept demanding that you do the same thing again and again and always expected the same results. While Harry would be the first to admit that the idea of something being found scared him, it did present something new, and it certainly would make him feel as though all the agony and annoyance he had been forced to go through might actually be worth it.

"Your watch," Edith said, pulling Harry out of his reverie.

"Hmm?" he asked, his focus returning to his wife, smiling at him from the chair next to bed.

"Your watch and wedding ring."

"Oh, right," Harry replied, looking down at his hands. Harry removed both and handed them to his wife, who promptly slipped them into her purse. Harry grinned back before lying on the bed and closing his eyes.

"Don't fall asleep, not yet anyway," Edith mumbled. Even with his eyes closed, Harry could tell she was going back into her purse for the book. Once he heard the light sound of pages being turned, Harry allowed his mind to wander, to drift — his mind cleared, he simply took in the mixture of sounds filling the room while trying not to notice the scent of over-cleanliness that still made his stomach twist. He felt like a cloud, small and light, able to move from here and there, passing by and through things as he pleased. He was miles away from the hospital now, no longer waiting to be poked and prodded. Now, he was a hummingbird, lithe and quick, flitting about in his pursuit of something new and unknown to him.

"Mr. Prescott?" Harry opened his eyes and saw Daniel, his hands filled with tubes, an IV bag, and monitoring devices.

"I'm up. I'm awake," Harry grumbled. Daniel set about busying himself, hooking up the heart rate monitor and IV drip. Harry sat up in the bed. Seeing that Harry's head was near the top of the gurney, Daniel adjusted it accordingly, placing his patient in a more comfortable position. Daniel then proceeded to take Harry's blood pressure while sticking monitor pads to either side of his temple and his chest.

"Let me see your right hand, please," Daniel asked. Dutifully, Harry held it out for the nurse to take. He watched, chewing the inside of his cheek, as the young man swabbed the top of his hand with alcohol before sticking the IV needle into a vein and taping it down. Harry wasn't afraid of needles per se, but he loathed the stinging they caused when going in due to the residual alcohol on the tip of the needle. Daniel released Harry's hand and then began to flip switches on the monitor next to the bed. "Alright," he said as he turned from the display, satisfied by what he was seeing. Reaching over, he quickly removed the blood pressure band from around Harry's arm. "I have to go check with the doctor, but I'll be back in a few moments to take you in for the procedure."

"Do what ya gotta do," Harry replied with a false grin.

"He shouldn't be more than thirty or forty minutes," David said, turning to Edith.

"I'll wait out in the lobby then," she replied, slipping her dime-store novella back into her purse and standing. Bending over, Edith gave Harry a soft and sweet kiss on his forehead. "Have fun and play nice with the other patients," Edith chided with a smirk.

"Oh, you know it," Harry replied, grinning back. Edith turned and headed out of the curtained area and down the hall and out the double doors they had come in from.

"So, we'll be putting you into a twilight state once we get into the room," Daniel said. "I'm sure you remember this information from the last couple of procedures, but you're gonna have a Swiss cheese memory once this is all done. The doctor will need you to be conscious so that you can swallow once they put the scope down your throat." Harry nodded, his silent agreement to getting everything over with. "Once you're done and coming out of twilight time, we'll let you go. Recovery should be pretty quick."

A thought nagged at the back of Harry's mind, something about the requested procedure — something he not done in a decade — the endoscopy.

"Tell me," Harry ventured, "does my file say why Doctor Price recommended the endoscopy? She never mentioned anything being wrong with my throat or stomach when I saw her last and she set this appointment up."

Daniel shrugged.

"Your guess is as good as mine. Odds are she found something out of sorts and just wants to take a look at it while you're in for your scheduled colonoscopy."

The answer in no way satisfied Harry. He and Edith had been with Doctor Price for nearly two decades, and in all that time, she had been very open and honest with the both of them about their health. She did not sugar-coat it when Harry was diagnosed with type two diabetes, nor did she gloss over any details about Edith's ruined lymph nodes. This time, though, something felt off. Ten years ago, they had ordered a look at his throat during his colonoscopy to check on any damage from the bouts of acid reflux he had suffered at the time. But this time, she had not given any indication if and/or why his throat needed to be checked again.

"Alright, Harry," Daniel said, raising the gurney bed and slipping the bag with his clothing underneath, "I'll be back in a minute." Harry lay back, closed his eyes, and tried not to think about how much his hand with the needle jammed into it and awkwardly placed tape bugged him. While he could not feel the tube feeding him nutrients and sugars, the tape that held it in place was not set right and pulled at his skin. *Well*, he thought, trying not to scratch or touch the top of his right hand, *hopefully this is the worst thing I'll have to deal with today.*

Harry's stomach began to grumble again — his bowels seized, wanting to release. The moment passed and his body relaxed. *Soon*, he continued to think, *it will all be over and done with soon.* Harry could no longer detect the overpowering scent of the hospital or the constant murmur of the room echoing about in his head. Instead, he poured all his concentration into that one, blissful word: *soon*. The seizing of his bowels returned, this time with an angry force. Harry grumbled, his hands rubbing his belly.

"Everything all right?" Harry heard Daniel ask. Harry looked down at the foot of the gurney and spotted the nurse, a clipboard in hand, which he slipped onto the railing by Harry's feet.

"I think I've gotta shit again," Harry said, sounding more like a child's plea than he had intended.

"Well, if you can hold it just a few more moments, the technicians will be sucking up the remainder of what is in your system before they proceed with everything." Harry nodded his understanding of the situation, then felt his muscles relax once again. "Alright," Daniel said from the head of the gurney, "hold on. Here we go."

Harry watched the ceiling panels and fluorescent lights fly by as he was being pushed through the prep and recovery room and through another set of double doors and into a long, lonely hallway. From what he could see where he lay, Harry noticed that one side of the hallway was lined with sets of double doors while the other wall was adorned with more paintings of Saint Bartholomew, looking saintly as always, feeding the poor, sheltering the sick, and washing the unclean. The paintings all looked like the standard, Renaissance-style of art — bright, vivid colors, creepy adult-like children, and strange angles that looked more like an ancient Egyptian Hieroglyph than something that came hundreds of years later. As before, Harry noticed that smudge of red in each of the paintings. What had started as a simple little background detail now began to stand out more and more to him. A nun, it was a nun dressed in red.

Daniel navigated the gurney to the end of the hall and turned toward the last set of double doors. As the bed swung around to face the doors, Harry caught sight of the image on the wall across from his procedure room — the painting was a different style than all the others he had seen so far — this picture looked more like a Salvador Dali painting than something from the so-called "Enlightened Era." The eponymous saint looked distorted, like a wax figure melting in the hot sun. The colors were muted, more red and brown and black than what was in the medieval pieces of art, and they ran, drizzling lazily down the canvas. But there, perfect and in no way abstract, stood the nun in red once more — the chaos of the post-modern nightmare of shapes and shadows all around her, framing and focusing her. Something began to gnaw at Harry's gut, and it wasn't a need to relieve himself.

In that moment, the doors swung open and an older nurse stepped out into the hallway. She took hold of the railing at the foot of the gurney and began to pull the bed into the room beyond. "Thank you, Daniel," the woman said as she pulled the gurney up to a series of monitors and then stopped. "Make sure you close the doors securely behind you," the woman called out.

"Can do," Daniel said to the woman. "I'll be back soon to fetch you, Harry."

Harry heard Daniel leave and close the doors behind him. While he could hear several other people in the room with him, Harry had never felt more alone in all his life. Slowly, the word *soon* began to contort in his mind just as his insides felt — twisting and turning into the grotesque image in the hall outside.

The room was modest in size, no bigger than an average master bedroom. Harry's gurney was brought to the center of the room by two technicians dressed from head to foot in teal scrubs. Along one wall sat an array of monitoring equipment, tables with various medical instruments, and a bank of monitors. As he looked at the equipment, that something that had begun to gnaw at the back of Harry's thoughts upon seeing the eerie painting tightened his already twisted gut even more — nothing was turned on, not a single piece of equipment or medical machinery. The two masked technicians began to turn Harry onto his side, bracing and bolstering his back and belly with cushions. The woman who had spoken with Daniel approached the gurney; her mask lowered.

"Hello, Harry," Doctor Price said with a friendly smile. Doctor Price was younger than Harry and Edith, somewhere in her early forties, freckled, and always smiling.

"Hello, Doctor Price," Harry replied weakly.

"And how are you feeling this morning? How did the prep go last night?"

"I'm feeling okay, I suppose," Harry lied. "The prep went as well as could be expected, foul-tasting and uncomfortable." Doctor Price humored Harry with a polite chuckle.

The two technicians began to hook Harry's IV up before pulling open the back of his robe, exposing his naked rear. "Now then, we're going to be doing both procedures at the same time," Doctor Price said as one of the two technicians came around and placed something over Harry's mouth. It took him a moment to realize what was going on. The technician ran a strap around the back of his head and snapped it in place on the other end of what was in his mouth. Harry had seen *Pulp Fiction* long ago and had been introduced to the idea of a "gimp" — now, with this thing in his mouth, he felt like that strange ball-gagged creature in that film. Harry found that whatever the device was, it forced his mouth open. He could breathe through it, so he figured there must be a hole in it. An instinct, a deep-seated fight or flight, kicked in, and Harry tried to move his hand to remove what was in his mouth.

Instead, he found himself unable to move. Doctor Price watched him, her smile no longer friendly. "Now, now, now, Harry," she said as the two technicians moved back behind him and out of view. Harry wanted to turn and follow them with his gaze but found that he was utterly incapable of moving on his own. Sweat began to bead down his brow and cheeks as the tension in his gut twisted to a new and excruciating level. "Just relax, Harry," Doctor Price went on. "We put a mouthguard in so that you don't choke on the probe or bite down on your tongue." Harry began to feel something cold and wet as a mist-like sensation touched the hand with the IV in it that now rested on top of his side. "Don't worry, you won't remember any of this."

One of the two nurses hooked up a new tube to the IV in his hand, and as the new liquid flowed into his veins, he could feel a cloudiness start to form in his vision and thoughts. Suddenly, there was a sensation in Harry's lower back, the misting was continuing, and something behind him was purring loudly. Harry tried to speak but only garbled, muted sounds escaped from the bite-guard. "How is it going?" Doctor Price asked the technicians working behind Harry.

"Suction is good. I can see them now. Beginning the harvest," one of the technicians, a young man from the sound of it, said from behind Harry.

"Good. Keep at it, Ezekiel. Mary, I want you to call down to the chapel and send for Sister Graves," Doctor Price said.

"As you wish, Doctor," the other technician replied.

Nothing made any sense — Harry's mind was reeling at what he was hearing. Harvest? Chapel? Sister Graves? Harry was no fool; he knew what Last Rights were, but he'd never heard of them being performed by a nun and never for a colonoscopy. Moments passed and the strange feeling in Harry's rear continued. The sweat also continued to pool below his face and onto the gurney's pillow. *Don't be stupid*, Harry thought, trying his best to quell the panic still rising. *You're not dying. You're not in any real trouble*. Oh, how Harry wished he could believe in those thoughts. No matter how hard he tried to push such ridiculous and sensational notions out of his foggy mind, nothing changed — he was still terrified and very, very confused.

After what felt like an eternity, the sensation in Harry's lower back subsided and the loud purring quieted. Harry looked to Doctor Price but found her back to him as she busied herself at one of the small tables she had wheeled over, next to the gurney. The technician, Ezekiel, stepped into Harry's view, a clear container the size of a football and filled with an amber liquid with about a dozen or more glowing spheres floating and sloshing about as the medical tech placed the vessel on the table.

"Thank you," Doctor Price said. Stepping aside from the table, Harry could see the strange, glowing container next to lit candles, a small array of crucifixes, and a tiny portrait of Saint Bartholomew, the now terrifying figure in red also visible just over the Saint's shoulder like in all the other portraits. A door opened into the room. Harry could tell that it was not the door he had been wheeled in through. Mary stood beside Ezekiel on one side of the table while Doctor Price stood on the other. "Thank you, Sister Graves, for gracing us with your presence this day. The vessel is ready to receive the light once again," she said, her voice sounding miles away. The strange foggy feeling came once more; it felt like waves breaking on a distant beach, and each time his thoughts grew more and more hazy.

"Oh, Holy Father, we beseech you this day," an unfamiliar voice said over Harry's shoulder. "We ask that you guide us and our hands as we go about your most holy and sacred task this day."

"Amen," Doctor Price and the two technicians said in unison.

"We have gathered the Harvest of Light from your vessel, and we see that your children are well and healthy and will soon be joining you in the sacred place." Harry watched as the owner of that voice stepped into view. A lump formed in Harry's throat, and his gut tightened so much he thought it might burst through his rectum — the woman before him, standing next to Doctor Price, was a young nun, her face unblemished by age and her cornflower-blue eyes piercing and observant — holding a wisdom deeper and more ancient than her age. The woman herself did not shock Harry; it was her clothes. She was a nun, dressed in a blood-red frock and habit with deep black trim. Harry watched, unable to move or scream, as she picked up the glowing jar and held it aloft above her head. "Oh holy saint of saints, your children have come home!"

The nun in red lowered the container and handed it to one of the technicians, who took it, held it to their chest, and lowered themselves in reverent prayer. Harry wanted more than anything to get up and move away from there. Harry began to wonder if the glowing contents of that jar had been taken from him, and if so, what the fuck were they, and more importantly, what the fuck was going on? A moan, deep and pained and Harry's only means of communication, escaped from his now chapped and sore lips. The nun approached Harry, stopped mere inches from the gurney, and began to unbutton her frock. Harry's eyes bulged in their sockets as the young woman allowed her frock to slip, revealing a lithe, naked body with something clinging tenaciously to it.

Harry fought back the intense desire to vomit as he looked upon the nun's body and the strange thing slinging to her side. The growth was the size of a toddler, its skin was the color of butcher paper but slightly translucent. Legs, at least a dozen or so, clung to the nun's body, the ends digging deep into her flesh. Where the legs anchored, her skin was red and irritated like an untreated and severely infected staph infection. It took Harry a long while to realize that the thing on the nun's body was a wholly separate being from the woman herself. The creature's body undulated and bulged as it breathed. Under that thin skin, Harry could see twisted organs and strange shifting tubes and fluids.

The nun, her hands raised to the sky, her eyes rolled back in her head, and her mouth working wordlessly, allowed Doctor Price and the other technician to approach. Harry watched in frozen horror as the two reached out to the creature on the nun's body and, speaking together in Latin, coaxed its head to appear. As the head rose from near the nun's hips, Harry could see that where the head was buried in her body, there was nothing more than a rotting, empty cavity.

The creature's eyes were large, lidless, and the deepest of amber — they were compound eyes like those of a housefly. Something unfurled from the creature's head, a long tube-like probus that dripped a pink, bloody slime as it splattered onto the floor. Harry began to dry heave as Doctor Price and the technician picked up the creature's appendage and walked it up to where Harry lay paralyzed and utterly helpless. Harry's eyes grew wider. His heaving grew more intense, and his body began to convulse involuntarily.

"Oh Saint Bartholomew, the sacred saint of fire and life, we give this vessel to you on this sacred day," the nun invoked, her head still thrown back and her arms still open wide in prostration to the heavens above. Harry could do nothing as Doctor Price and the technician began to feed the creature's tube into the mouthpiece and slowly, painfully down his throat. Tears streamed down his cheeks as he began to feel the tube inching down his throat, farther and deeper with each passing moment.

"Swallow, sinner," Doctor Price whispered into Harry's ear as she and the tech continued to feed the tube farther down his gullet. Dutifully, he swallowed at her coaxing. After what felt like an eternity, the creature began to convulse and undulate. Without warning, a strange, burning sensation began to travel down Harry's throat and into his stomach. The sensation lasted for a few seconds and then ended as quickly as it had begun. With great care, Doctor Price and the technician pulled the creature's tube from Harry's mouth, inch by agonizingly burning inch.

"As we did before, we do again, bless this sinner's body and make him a vessel for our Lord's offspring for the next decade until the next harvest!" Sister Graves bellowed. As the end of the ovipositor was removed from the mouthguard, Harry's mind completely shut down, and the fog that had been swirling around, threatening to take over all his thoughts, won out.

The next thing Harry knew, he was sitting in the edge of the gurney, his shoes half on. Edith sat next to him on the edge of the mobile bed.

"Do you need any help getting your shoes on?" she asked, rubbing his back. Harry blinked a few times before noticing that he was dressed back in the clothing he had worn upon his arrival. Looking around, he also realized that he was back in the prep and recovery room.

"Is it over?" Harry asked.

"Is it over?" Edith asked back. "Oh, Harry, that's at least the fifth time you've asked that in the last few minutes. Of course it's over. Now let's finish getting you dressed so we can get you something to eat and then get you into bed."

Harry nodded, then returned to the task at hand of putting his shoes back on. Daniel and Doctor Price stepped into the room.

"Hello, Harry," Doctor Price said with her usual, cheery smile. "And how are you feeling?"

"Funky. I don't remember a thing."

"That's twilight time for ya," Daniel said as he helped Edith get Harry's shoes on.

"Well, you can rest easy; we didn't find anything unusual. No polyps or anything like that. The endoscopy went well too. It looks like you're all good to go, and we'll see you back here in another few years."

Harry smiled weakly. He was tired. He was hungry. His throat was sore. Harry was ready for a nap — a real one this time. "Sounds good," he said. Doctor Price shook his hand and Edith's before turning to leave the room.

With his shoes on, Daniel helped Harry into a wheelchair and began to push him out of the confusing cacophony of the prep and recovery room. Harry's mind still went in and out of the fog, but he was feeling more and more lucid with each passing moment. As the trio headed out of the hospital wing and down into the main lobby, they passed one of the many paintings of Saint Bartholomew. Harry looked at the one across from the lobby elevators as the three of them waited to go down to the carpark.

He looked at the saint's painting, his hands offering food to the poor — an image, primal and unusual, flashed in the back of his mind and then faded from existence. The painting, for a fleeting moment, had felt terrifying, but now it felt like nothing more than a work of art. As Harry felt himself being pushed into the elevator by the handles of his wheelchair, he caught sight of something peculiar in the corner of the painting — it was a woman, a nun, dressed all in red. The sight of her left Harry with a strange, unexplainable numbness in the back of his very being for a day or two and then, like a whisper on the wind, it passed, and life went on.

Medium

Michelle Whitehall's parlor room looked less like a place to receive guests for tea and more like a chamber for meeting the Pharaohs of old. The four men and two women who sat around the small table in the dim light all wore the same expressions of wonder, concern, and giddiness — each face cycling through the three emotions, picking up on and mimicking the unspoken social cues of those facing them. The room was dimly lit by candles of varying sizes, their flames dancing and flickering lightly in the thick, still air. Strange shadows stretched and contracted around the guests as the men fidgeted with their cufflinks and the women spun their wedding bands about on their smooth fingers. In the half-light, peculiar shapes and figures could barely be discerned along the walls while embers and incense burned in small braziers atop plaster pedestals around the circumference of the room.

The power to the electrically lighted chandelier was cut low, causing the dim bulbs to drone — a soft buzzing that agitated the nerves and danced at the back of one's teeth. A white tablecloth with small, immaculately kept tassels, was draped over the large, round table in the center of the room. The table was clear of all flatware, cups, saucers, plates, and the like, and in the center where one would usually keep a centerpiece of a vase of seasonal flowers, there was instead a small, raised wooden ring, a few inches in diameter.

"Tell me, Albert," one of the men said, pointing at the wall behind the man he was addressing, "you studied some of this Egyptian nonsense. Can you make out what any of this means?" Albert turned, pulling out a pair of wire-rimmed glasses from a pocket within his coat and putting them on before gazing past his high-backed chair.

"It's hard to say," Albert replied, squinting at the small painted black figures and images that adorned the walls made to look like something from King Tut's tomb. "It might be something, but it also looks like it might be gibberish. In this light, I can't tell if I'm looking at an ibis, a crane, or a feather."

"Chester, do you think we'll be able to see Mum?" the younger of the two women asked the young man sitting beside her.

"Hard to say," Chester replied. "I suppose anything is possible, but we shall have to wait and see." The other woman, older and dressed more conservatively, with a collar up to her chin, gazed down at the young woman across from her like a scientist gazing at a new form of life drifting across the lens of a microscope.

"Hush now," the tall, frumpy, older woman said as she lowered her glasses and coughed politely. "The Madam is coming." No one spoke, no one breathed. Somewhere in the house, soft footsteps could be heard approaching the parlor doors. The footsteps stopped, and a door at one end of the room opened slowly, creaking loudly. In the doorway, framed by a soft light from the hallway beyond, stood a middle-aged woman with short strawberry blond hair, dressed in the attire of an old Gypsy witch. In her hands she held aloft a cloth hiding something rounded underneath.

No one spoke — no one moved — save for their eyes as they followed Michelle Whitehall as she glided into the room and around the guests like a shark circling and closing in for the kill. The air in the room grew thicker — heavier — hotter. Beads of sweat began to form on the upper lips of the women and enmeshed in the mustaches of the men. After making a few rounds, Michelle took her place in the only empty chair in the room. Her chair had the highest back, carved with intricate images of roses and entwined vines covered in thorns. Michelle placed the covered mass in the middle of the table, then moved her hands quickly to her armrests.

"You have all come here to see something *extra ordinary*," she intoned, with a thick, poorly performed Eastern European accent. To most in the room, it sounded convincing and as authentic as could be. "You have all been drawn here to witness the unusual and to gaze into realms beyond, no?" No one spoke. Michelle swept her piercing blue-eyed gaze across the room as if she was reading the contents of each guest's very soul. Finally, a small voice squeaked.

"Yes," the younger of the two women said, "yes indeed, madame." Michelle gave a thin smile and nodded slowly in the direction of the young woman.

"Very good," Michelle replied with all the charm of a hungry snake. The candles flickered all at once, causing the shadows to lurch and lunge before withdrawing. "I want you all to hold hands, if you would be so kind," she asked, leaning forward in her chair. Everyone in the room complied, their hands either open palm up to receive or palm down to give. "This," Michelle went on, "will be the conduit that will not only lend power to what we will see and experience tonight, but that will dictate who or what we speak to."

Everyone around the room began to murmur amongst themselves.

"Silence!" Michelle demanded in her paper-thin accent. "I will have absolute silence from you all." The room grew quiet once more. Pleased with her request, she reached out toward the cloth-covered bulge in the middle of the table, took hold with one hand, and pulled away the off-white silk cloth to reveal a darkened crystal ball. The glass was perfectly spherical and, from what could be observed from around the table, clean and untouched. The darkness within was complete while the candlelight buffed and rebounded on the glazed, slightly pearlescent surface. "My crystal ball was gifted to me many years ago by the self-proclaimed King of the Gypsies!" Michelle said dramatically. "He gave it to me along with the secrets of how to contact the other side so that I could make it my mission to help others in understanding what lies beyond the very veil of mortality."

In that instant, the ball lit up, a brilliant, electric white and blue — the colors undulating seductively. The air began to fill with the very real sensation of flowing power. The sound of a furious gale could be heard, and yet no wind blew inside of the room. Michelle reached out her hands, waiting for those on either side of her at the table to take hold. As both men's hands touched hers, everyone in the room's hands and wrists began to convulse and spasm. The women shrieked and the men cried out.

"Hold tight!" Michelle demanded, her eyes reflecting the undulating lights contained within the sphere of glass before her. "I will attempt to see the past, the present, and the future all in one," she cried out over the windy din that could still not be felt, only heard. The hairs on the guest's arms and heads began to stand on end while those on Michelle Whitehall remained perfectly still atop her head. "I see...I see..." Michelle's voice began to deepen. The sound of it echoed around the room as though it was coming not from her but from everywhere else. "I see someone coming," her voice boomed. "I see the past racing toward the present."

As quickly as the cacophony had arisen, it ceased — cries of the howling gale faded as did the dancing lights in the crystal ball. As the hairs on the guests' heads began to settle back into place, an eerie sense of dread fell upon the room. In the flickering candlelight, the guests could see the form of Michelle Whitehall, collapsed in a crumpled heap in her tall-backed seat. The four men and two women disengaged their hands and began to massage their wrists.

"Is she dead?" Albert asked, stroking down his thick mustache.

"Should we help her?" the younger of the two women said, nudging Chester in his side with her elbow.

"I suppose we should," her husband responded. Before he or any of the other men could move from their chairs, the candles in the room snuffed out one by one. Suddenly, the buzzing of the bulbs overhead died to silence as darkness completely overtook the room.

"I say," Albert said in a matter-of-fact tone.

"Who dares to disturb the great Amun Ra?" a raspy voice inquired from where Michelle Whitehall sat. The question was followed by a low moaning. Slowly, a light from an unseen source began to shine dimly where Michelle sat. The woman's small frame was balled up in her chair — her legs pulled up under her gown. No one said a word as a deep, scratchy breathing came from the limp form of the medium. Michelle's eyes remained closed, and her breathing began to deepen.

While none of the guests spoke, their panic and excitement could be felt all throughout the room. They watched in horror and awe as Michelle lifted her head ever so slightly. Her mouth fell open and the group watched as thick, stringy tendrils of ectoplasm began to slither down her chin. A collective gasp of shock drew the guests closer together as the tendrils of glowing material snaked their way from Michelle's gaping maw and began to wriggle their way up her shoulder. The moans continued until the last of the phantasmagorical material was free of her mouth. Michelle heaved a deep sigh and lowered her head to her chest. From over the woman's shoulder, the end of the ectoplasm trail began to form into a face, blank of expression and hollow of eye.

"Who has summoned me?" the same raspy voice asked as the head floated over Michelle's shoulder, still trailing an ectoplasmic tail along the length of her torso. The women screamed, shrill and terrified. The men sucked in a collective breath. No one dared to speak. "You are tampering in domains you know nothing about," the voice of Amun Ra continued. "You have summoned me here and yet none of you will dare to address the great Pharaoh? You pitiful, foolish mortals must know by now the great powers I wield."

The younger of the two women fainted, her husband in the seat next to her diving in and scooping her up. At the same time, a polite cough came from the seat opposite the medium. All the guests, save for the unconscious young woman, all turned to the two men gazing intently at the hovering spirit.

Both men were older. Both wore thick, wire-rimmed glasses. One, the gentleman who had coughed, sported an impressive set of muttonchops while the other man's thick and immaculately trimmed beard was something not to be scoffed at. The two men had an air of old money about them but were the only two in the room not acquainted with the younger or the older couples.

"Tell me, great Amun Ra," the gentleman with the polite cough and muttonchops asked in a proper English accent, "I am wondering, as I'm sure we all are, what the other side is like?" The Englishman's question was direct and full of confidence.

In her husband's arms, the young woman slowly came to. Spotting the still floating face of Amun Ra, she immediately shrank back into her husband's embrace.

"The other side," Amun Ra rasped, "is a place of strange colors and unusual sights. You will see those long gone and know those still living. We can see your world and follow those of our kin, but without the abilities of one such as Madame Whitehall, we cannot make direct contact with your plane of existence."

"I see," the English gentleman said, stroking his chin in contemplation.

"What are you making at?" the Englishman's bearded companion asked in a flat Bostonian accent.

"Well," the Englishman said, more to the room at large than the man he had arrived with, "I suppose a spirit as powerful and well-traveled beyond the veil might be able to summon any number of other lost souls from the great hereafter." The murmuring in the room started once again.

"Silence!" Amun Ra demanded. "I shall do as you have requested. I shall use the medium to act as an intermediary between the spirit world and your own. Now then, before I depart, do you have any specific questions for me and for me alone?"

"Oh, I should say," the older woman said, finding a little courage to face the hovering specter, "do you happen to know when we might go? Or should I say, when we might shed this mortal coil and depart for realms unknown?"

"I do," Amun Ra said with a slight nod at the older woman. "I see all that has been and all that shall one day come to pass. I see death printed upon your faces, each and every last one of you — a grandfather clock ticking toward midnight."

"My word!" the older woman replied, her hand to her chest in deep concern.

"Shall I indulge you with an answer to your query?" Amun Ra hissed.

"I think not. That will do. Please carry on," the older woman stammered, trying her best to hide how flustered she was at the spirit's response and utterly failing. Amun Ra gazed from face to face, his hollow, eyeless sockets boring into the soul of each of the assembled.

"I shall be departing you now, but I will leave you in the capable hands of another wayward soul from the great beyond." At these words, Amun Ra began to sink, his spectral trail pulling into Michelle's chest. Within seconds, the ghostly head was gone, leaving the six guests alone, in the dark with their host. No one spoke a word as they watched in the half-light as Michelle rose from her chair, her head lolling from side to side like that of a rag doll. She seemingly glided from her chair to a cabinet in the back of the room, nestled between two plywood columns adorned in gaily painted hieroglyphics. The cabinet itself was tall, at least seven or eight feet from its base to its top. Two large doors slowly opened as the cabinet admitted Michelle before closing behind her with a light click of the door's clasp.

For a long time, nothing happened — no sounds, no movement — nothing in the room's darkness save for the nervous shuffling of the guests' feet and the tapping of their fingers on the tabletop. The guests waited patiently with bated breath for the next phantasmagoric episode to transpire. After what felt to the six in the room to be a small slice of eternity, the cabinet door clicked and slowly creaked open. In the darkness, they watched as a hand seemingly crawled out of the interior of the large piece of furniture, followed closely by an arm, and then a body.

The figure that emerged from the cabinet was small; she wore what appeared to be a silk kimono. Her hair was black and rolled up in a manner befitting of a Japanese Geisha. Her face was pale as were her hands. Her lips were painted red and her cheeks rosy. Gliding, the figure moved around the circumference of the room, behind the assembled guests.

"Greetings, round-eyes," the figure said in Pidgin English. "I am the venerable Soo Tran Hamoto, dearly departed Oriental Princess of the Ming Dynasty. I have come bearing messages for each of you from the great beyond."

As the spirit continued to circle the table and guests, soft murmurs of excitement began to fill the room.

"Doctor Peaks," the spirit said as she passed by the young couple, "I have word from your mother…"

"My mother?" Chester said, relatively shocked. "I just saw my mother not more than a few hours ago."

"I mean the mother of your mother," the spirit said, sounding almost a little taken by surprise.

"Granny?" the young doctor replied. "What does she say?"

"She brings you tidings of good health and good fortune. She says that you may need to consult a spiritual advisor more regularly as dark times will be drawing neigh." The doctor found that he was speechless.

"Thank you, great spirit," his young wife replied. "We shall do as his grandmother instructs."

"See that you do," the spirit intoned as she continued her rounds. The spirit pointed across the table to the English gentleman. "I have a message for you too."

"Oh, really? Who is it from, my wife?"

"Yes. This message comes directly from your wife."

"Do tell me, spirit, what are her words? What were the last words my dearly, departed love spoke to me before her untimely passing?"

"Your wife," the spirit said, "she says that she does not blame you for her sickness. She says that the pox that took her was unavoidable. She says that her last words to you were that she loved you and that you were the love of her life…"

"I say," the Englishman said in an overly astonished way. "Does she now?"

"She does…" At these words, the Englishman produced a small, metal tube, placed it to his lips, and gave three short but high-pitched blows. At the sound of the Englishman's whistle, the spirit seemed to lose her balance as she tripped and fell over her feet, tumbling to the ground in front of the cabinet in a heap. The other guests looked shocked and dismayed at what had just happened. The Englishman and the Bostonian beside him stood up from their chairs and stood back against the wall as the door to the parlor burst open and half a dozen police officers and a dozen reporters swarmed in.

"What the bloody, fuckin' 'ell is going on?" the spirit said in a very thick, cockney accent as she struggled to her feet.

Light from outside poured in as two of the officers pulled back the room's closed curtains. Several reporters stood in the hallway, eagerly trying to peek into the inner sanctum of Michelle Whitehall's home. The Englishman pocketed his whistle and stood. The rest of the guests with exception of the Bostonian, looked at the Englishman in complete and utter shock.

"I say," the young man said, his brow knitted in fury, "what is going on?"

"Yes," the older woman across the table said, slamming her fist upon the tabletop, "I, too, demand a good, straight answer." There was no confusion or frustration in those words, simply anger and lots of it.

The spirit rose from where she had crumpled and now looked more disheveled than ethereal. Long blond hair poked out from beneath a crushed wig, and her makeup, which had practically glowed in the darkness of the room moments before, was now smudged and streaked — red lips, black eyeliner, and white all mixed together in an awkward mosaic.

"Who the bloody 'ell do you think you are?" Michelle Whitehall demanded, tossing off her twisted kimono and revealing her slip and shoes attached to roller skates. As the woman stood, her legs went akimbo, and she further struggled to regain her composure and stature.

"Ah, yes," the Englishman said with a wicked grin, "I am Sir Reginald Collier — world famous magician and exposer of mediums, psychics, astrologists, and other such frauds." At these words, photographers' bulbs began to flash, and the Englishman reached up to his face and peeled off a thin layer of fake skin, taking away with it his false mustache and heavy-set eyebrows. What remained was a set of graying muttonchops, piercing blue eyes, and a long, equine nose.

"Excuse me, Sir Collier," the older gentleman, Albert, said with a polite cough, which caused the reporters and their photographers to turn their attention from the tall, lanky, gentleman in his early fifties and instead focus on the much older man with the fuming wife.

"Yes, my good sir?"

"How can you accuse Miss Whitehall of such fakery? My wife and I have been seeing her for years, and I can say with utmost confidence that most of her predictions have been spot on as well as her communications with the other side."

"Yes, my husband is right," the older woman said sternly, jabbing a finger in Sir Collier's direction. "She has been able to speak with my ancestors with great success as well as steer my husband's assets in the right direction. We've made a tidy profit from her visions." The young couple sat there, unspeaking and confused.

"Captain Keller," Sir Collier said, turning to the nearest bobby.

"Yes sir?" the officer asked, saluting the older magician.

"Please escort Miss Whitehall and guests and all our reporting friends outside where I wish to address everyone about what has been going on here for the last five years."

"Right," Captain Keller said as he and his other officers began to help the four other guests up out of their seats and out of the room. Two officers walked over to Michelle Whitehall, still struggling to stand up on her own two feet, then took her, one grabbing each arm, and helped propel her out of the room. The reporters and photographers followed, snapping photos and chatting away as they exchanged notes and jotted down on their notepads.

The Bostonian and Sir Collier were the last to remain. The Bostonian removed his cap and pulled off his false beard, wincing as the spirit gum refused to let them go so easily. The man was smaller, shorter, and rounder then the much taller, lankier Sir Collier.

"Well, that went about as well as we could have hoped," the man said, still retaining his American accent.

"And did you doubt me, my friend?" Sir Collier asked.

"No, not at all, but honestly, it all went smoother than some of the other busts."

"True," Sir Collier said, balling up his false face and stuffing it into his coat pocket, "but remember, Roger, we had time on our side. If you had not attended so many of these dreadful performances and looked into so many of Whitehall's connections, then yes, this would have gone less smoothly, as you said, than it did."

"I suppose we should head outside and meet with your adoring public then," Roger said with a playful grin.

"I suppose we should, old friend."

With the house cleared, the two walked briskly from the parlor, through the main hallway, and into the foyer where the front doors were thrown wide open and the reporters and guests stood behind a line of blue and buttoned bobbies.

Outside, the pair had to shield their eyes from the afternoon sunshine pouring down across all of London. Despite the harsh light, the flash of photographers' bulbs assaulted their eyes. The frenzy was maddening as men in brown coats and fedoras with notebooks in hand struggled to push past the barricade of policemen. With his companion in tow, Sir Collier made his way to the edge of the steps where the police line stood fast against the inquiring throng of reporters.

At the side of the mass stood the other seance guests along with the Mr. and Missus Whitehall in handcuffs, their faces both crestfallen and filled with unbridled rage as they watched the two men step out to address the crowd. The house behind them was a modest estate, larger than most London flats but smaller than anything owned by a lord or lady. The house stood on the outskirts of London, where the roads led to the countryside.

Sir Collier raised his hands and, like the magician he had once been, wordlessly commanded the attention and respect of the crowd as they grew silent, in complete awe of his stature and presence. His features were handsome, more so, some would argue, than when he had been dazzling the West End with his feats of prestidigitation and mastery of the illusionary arts. Now, some thirty years later, he still looked just a regal as he did in those days of black, smartly cut tuxedoes and slicked back hair. Roger Applegate stood behind him, allowing his business partner to do what he did so well these days. Applegate had been Collier's manager for nearly half a century — he had even introduced Collier to his late wife, a dancer in a number of productions, who became the Collier's fresh-faced, smiling assistant — one usually expects the magician to marry his assistant, and Lord Collier did not disappoint his public.

"Ladies and gentlemen of the press, I thank you all for coming out this morning," Sir Collier said in his best stage voice. Even out in the open air, he had a way with tone and pitch that allowed his words to carry far and wide. "I asked you all here this morning to witness the culmination of nearly half a decade of research, study, investigation, blood, sweat, and tears. For going on ten years now, my business partner, Mr. Roger Applegate," — Applegate nodded politely from where he stood — "and myself have been investigating and debunking any and all who would seek to make their fortunes off of others in the name of spiritualism and the like."

The silence of the reports broke as an assault of questions flew at the old, retired magician.

"Lord Collier! Bert Falsting of the *London Times*. What makes you so certain that the people you have been investigating are indeed frauds?"

"A good question, Mr. Falsting," Sir Collier replied. The dozens of reporters, as if working off an electrical circuit, began to jot notes quickly on their paper pads while the photographers continued to snap away. "It is nineteen twenty-five — we live in a world where man has conquered electricity and the radio — a world just a few precious steps away from understanding the majesty of the atom. This is a new and strange world, but it is a world built on science and facts; a world built on evidence and truth! This is not a world for the ghosts and goblins men once believed in. When we can send someone's voice from one end of the Atlantic to the other in a heartbeat, can you really believe in a world where the dead can come back to haunt the living?"

"What proof do you have?" another reporter asked.

"My good fellow, I was once a renowned stage magician. I know all the simple parlor tricks each and every one of these charlatans has employed."

"Can you give us some examples?" another reporter asked.

"I certainly can," Sir Collier said, his chest puffing out in pride. Sir Collier turned toward the entrance to the house and gave a sharp whistle. A beat later, half a dozen officers emerged, their arms laden with all manner of items from the seance.

"That's my fuckin' property!" Michelle Whitehall screeched. "Get your bloody mitts off of me livelihood!" The bobbies stood fast while Michelle fought against her cuffs and the officers holding her shoulders. Her husband simply sat down on the end on the last step of the staircase leading up to the entrance of the house. The other guests, none of whom had been detained in cuffs, just detained for questioning, watched, their mouths twisted in confused expressions.

"The objects you see before you, ladies and gentlemen, are but a mere example of Michelle Whitehall's trickery," Sir Collier said, seeming to stand even taller than the rail-thin man already stood. The retired magician stood next to one officer, struggling to hold a small metal box with a two-foot-long metal tube jutting straight up and ending in a mushroom-like donut of wound copper wire. Various lengths of insulated wiring hung from the base of the box. The officer groaned, sweat beading on his forehead, as he held the device up for all the crowd to see. "This, my friends, is a rather brilliant contraption known simply as a Tesla Coil — named so after Mr. Nikolai Tesla. The device, when plugged in, is capable of generating arcs of alternating current — many times frightening and dazzling. I, myself used this sort of device in some of my last shows before I left the stage. They are perfect for creating lightning effects and, in the case of Michelle Whitehall, phantasmagorical images contained within a crystal ball."

Sir Collier nodded, and the officer placed the device on the ground beside the aged magician. Roger took up the wires and vanished into the house. A moment later, there was a spark from the tip of the copper wire donut and then a sound not unlike rushing wind as the generator burst to life. The press jumped back as the three-foot-tall device shot arcs of blue lightning all along the front porch. Without missing a beat, Sir Collier picked up a smooth, crystal ball and held it up before the bolts. The audience oohed and ahhed at the sight of such fantastical images dancing and undulating in the magnified and distorted world of the crystal ball. Even in the harsh afternoon sun, the sight was something to behold.

Sir Collier nodded and Roger, who had been poking his head out of the front doorway, nodded back before vanishing. Moments later, the last of the sparks died away and the terrible rushing sounds of the machine faded, leaving everyone's ears buzzing.

"Michelle Whitehall has a table in her parlor with a circular hole cut into the middle, which allows for the Tesla Coil underneath to provide its convincing illusion. The sound, as you can hear, from the device is masked to give the effect of a strong wind and not the machinations of a fanciful bit of scientific curiosity."

Sir Collier stepped past where the now quiet Tesla Coil stood on the porch, along with the officer who had been holding it, and approached the next officer. In the man's outstretched arms hung a long skein of cheesecloth.

"This," Sir Collier explained as he picked up the cheesecloth, "is what is meant to be ectoplasm or the essence of a spirit. During the seance, this cloth is quickly shoved into the medium's mouth and then slowly spit out to give the illusion of a specter leaving the body of the host. In this instance, Whitehall here has attached a rather silly-looking mask, the kind children use in the States on Halloween. This one, though, has been painted in a fine layer of radium to give it an otherworldly glow."

Sir Collier held aloft the face of Amun Ra in all its crudely painted glory. The cheesecloth was sewn to the back of the mask and dangled limply and rather silly-looking while Sir Collier showed the prop off to the press. After a few moments for the photographers, he placed the mask back in the officer's hands and then moved to the next item, a pair of roller skates.

Holding up the metal frames with their small black wheels and leather straps, the magician smirked at Michelle.

"This, my friends, is how the ghost of Soo Tran Hamoto, a character of Whitehall's own concoction, appeared to float about the room. After changing from one of the many layers of clothing she wears, Michelle Whitehall emerges from a large cabinet lined with hidden compartments made to conceal all manner of costumes and makeup. She then proceeds to float around the room."

"This all may be true, but how is it that she is able to be so accurate with her information when communicating with the dead?" the older woman from the seance asked. The reporters turned to face the woman and jot down her question before turning back to Sir Collier.

"Simple, my dear," he said, stepping down from the porch and stepping up to the woman. Holding one hand to his temple and holding out his other hand before him as if to read the very air, Sir Collier took in a deep breath. "I...I...I see that you will be taking a trip soon."

"Yes."

"I see that you will be traveling someplace warm. A resort?"

"Yes!"

Sir Collier lowered his hands and gave the older woman an impish grin. "In the industry, we call this a cold reading. I could just have easily asked if you had just been on a vacation. You see, the technique works by probing just around the edges of your questions or life and then finds a way in through the familiar. In this instance, knowing that you are a woman of means, and with the cold season soon approaching, I could deduce that you would be going on a vacation to a resort, somewhere warm."

The woman began to stammer, her facing turning a deep red. A beat passed and she turned to face Michelle Whitehall, striking the so-called medium hard across the woman's face with her open palm.

"How dare you, Michelle! How dare you take advantage of me!"

The crowd gasped at this display. The flashbulbs snapped, and the reporters scribbled their notes at a feverish pace. Michelle's mouth worked, open and closed, open and closed — she looked less like a shocked woman and more like a fish gulping its last breath.

"My husband and I have sunk so much money into your lies and manipulations," the older woman screamed. "We took your so-called financial advice and life advice — we let you in, we trusted you."

"Tell us," a reporter asked, pushing against the throng of other reporters and photographers, "Did this woman's advice ruin your livelihood or disrupt your social lives?"

"Well, no," the older woman replied, a bit taken aback, "not in any significant way, no. We suffered occasional financial losses here and there based upon insights she said the spirits provided to her, but our losses were never so horrible..."

"It's the principle of the thing," the woman's husband shot back at the reporter. "We gave this fraud our money for what we assumed was good, sound advice, and instead, she took our money all while lying to us and others. It's the very principle of the thing that boils my blood."

Michelle had no response, no retort, nothing. She could only stand there, surrounded by reporters, her face sore from the slap, and her life in ruins.

"You know, I can relate to how these victims feel," Lord Collier said, "for I, too, do not like to be made a fool of. After all, I did not become the supremely talented and respected illusionist I was before my retirement without demanding of others only absolute honesty and integrity. As a small child, watching the magicians in London, I would grow ever angry at any of these fine men who performed something I could not deduce or figure out on my own. I would hound those men until their secrets could be learned. If they lied to me or tried to trick me in order to hide their techniques, I would see that their careers were taken to a place not unlike where our dear Michelle Whitehall now finds hers."

Collier bowed low for the crowds, sweeping his hand below his chest as he presented himself to be the public servant he saw himself as. Lord Collier stood and continued to address the crowd to the popping of flashbulbs and the scratching of reporters' notes.

"As I grew older and more renowned, I found that while I could tolerate those who tricked an audience with a fun illusion, I could not abide by anyone who did so to ruin the emotional fragility of those suffering or hurting, especially from the loss of a loved one." Collier smiled a sad smile, one of personal loss.

"Is that notion tied into your smoking gun technique?" a squirrelly reporter near the back of the crowd shouted out.

Lord Collier squinted against the sunlight and spotted the gentleman who had asked the question.

"It is indeed," Collier replied. "For those who do not know, once I have deduced that one of these *so-called mediums* or *spiritualists*, is a complete fake based on recognizing techniques and trappings such as those I have shown you all this afternoon, I do indeed hide one last card up my sleeve. As you and your readers may or may not be aware of, I lost my beloved wife on stage some years ago — a tragic accident and one that will haunt me to my grave. Before she succumbed to her injuries, my beloved wife whispered a final sentence to me before leaving this world. The very last thing I do before I am one hundred percent certain of someone's fakery, is to ask them what my wife's final words to me were."

An awkward hush befell the crowd in that moment.

"While I shall never utter her last words to this or any crowd, so long as my crusade continues, I can tell you that no psychic, spiritualist, medium, or the like has ever been able to repeat these simple words to me."

Lord Collier heaved a heavy-hearted sigh while the reporters jotted their notes.

Turning to the constables still surrounding Michelle, Lord Collier gave a slight nod. Michelle Whitehall screamed and kicked and cursed as the bobbies dragged her across the road, past the crowd of reporters, and up into the back of a waiting paddy wagon. Her husband, the one who managed his wife's psychic affairs and helped behind the scenes to run the show, came along as well, much more silent and withdrawn than his wife.

As the police left the scene, many of the reporters and some of the crowd began to follow behind the police wagon as it drove off down the cobbled street. Those reporters that remained began to question the other four guests of the seance. Roger appeared at the older magician's side.

"Shall we call it a day then?" he asked.

"I should think so. Though, I would prefer to call it another rousing success."

Lord Collier and Roger headed to their waiting car and left the scene for the police, the remainder of the reporters, and any other person eager to stay and watch the quiet end to such an explosive career.

Lord Collier's study looked less like a place of quiet reflection and contemplation and more like a twisted museum of the unusual and the macabre. The electric chandelier that crowned the room was made of elk and deer antlers and cast long, dark shadows across the room when the heavy, red curtains were drawn across the windows as they were now. Arranged along the tops of bookshelves sat all manner of pickled oddity or miscarried animal fetus. On the walls hung posters of Lord Collier's various shows, each one proclaiming that the Master of Prestidigitation was to be seen to be believed. The scenes on the various canvases depicted many of his most famous acts — sawing a woman in half, producing fireworks from his hat, a flock of doves, sparrows, and crows erupting from a pie on a simple table, and an image of a young woman waving coquettishly from behind the glass of a locked chamber filled with water.

It was this last image that was the most haunting for Lord Collier. The illusion was a simple one of his own design and was incredibly popular back in his performing days. This was also the very gimmick that his late wife had perished within — trapped in a glass box filled with water and locked tight — her last performance was to be the one that skyrocketed Lord Collier's name into the very heights of morbid curiosity from the public and a reason to finally retire for himself.

Lord Collier sat in a high-backed chair, his pipe smoldering at the end of his mouth, his reading glasses balanced precariously on the end of his nose, as his eyes scanned over a pile of clippings and newspaper articles he had been sifting through for the last hour. A huge wooden grandfather clock in the corner of the room droned the minutes away and provided the only constant sound besides the occasional shuffling of papers. The carved owl atop the clock itself, its wings unfurled as it looked ready to strike at some unsuspecting prey, always intrigued the retired magician. Something about the wooden top piece to the timepiece always struck him as both majestic and eloquently menacing — a personification he himself preferred to offer to the world at large. Long ago he had stopped signing autographs or giving interviews. After Maddy, his wife, had passed away, he had become more and more withdrawn from the world of the stage as well as the everyday world of London and English Society.

Maddy had been his young assistant; they had worked together for years before he had popped the question. Her death at the hands of his water-chamber illusion had not only occurred at the height of his popularity and prestige, but it had also paved the way for improving his fortunes. Like all his past assistants, Lord Collier had taken out an extensive life insurance policy should the unthinkable ever occur. While part of such an act was always meant to help stir controversy and improve his image as a magician's magician and someone willing to conjure the unthinkable and deadly, it had never been needed until Maddy's accident. In an effort to prove to the public that Maddy's death had not been his fault and an attempt to cash in on such a tragedy to bolster his own coffers, Lord Collier had donated the majority of the payout to various charities around London, catching the attention of the Royal Family and directly contributing to his eventual Knighthood.

Now, a decade retired and driven to prove that he was still relevant and not one to be so easily duped, Lord Collier's study was a nest of exploration into anything and everything unusual, unexplainable, and uncanny. It was here, his sacred headquarters, his inner sanctum, where he could read up on and study not only the tricks of the spiritualists and psychics, but where he could research all those who would claim to have such extraordinary gifts. In Lord Collier's mind, the study was his war room, and he was the valiant general leading the battle against such flagrant poppycock.

The gears, cogs, and sprockets inside of the clock whirred and spun, and the time tolled one in the afternoon. Lord Collier, still eyeing the clippings spread out before him atop his grand and cluttered desk, considered his next target. This was never an easy task. A lot had to be taken into consideration, and at the end of the day, whomever he targeted to bring down had to be popular enough to give him the media exposure he needed to help drive the smaller operations into the open and out of business.

In the month that followed his operation to end the Whitehall charade, he had learned of three other rather prestigious spiritualists in the greater metropolitan area who had decided to close up shop for fear of being his next target. No press, it seemed, was better than bad press for anyone not looking to have their tricks exposed.

The door to the study crept slowly open, groaning in protest. A head popped into the room, and an expression that was a mixture of curiosity and concern danced across Roger's face. Without saying anything, the Bostonian's head withdrew, and a moment later the door opened in full and the portly man stepped into the chamber, a silver tray in his hands and a thick packet of mail under his arm. Steam rose from the teapot in the center of the tray, trailing behind Roger like the smoke of a train as it traveled down the line. The white and blue China cups and sugar spoon tinkled as the man stepped up to the desk and placed the tray squarely in the middle of the pile.

"Not now, Roger," Lord Collier grumbled.

"If not now, sir, then when?" Lord Collier looked up at his old show manager and current partner and gave a stiff smile. "You've been in here since five this morning, and I know for a fact that you have not yet eaten." Roger reached down and picked up the teapot, then poured himself and Lord Collier a cup each. Without hesitation, he plucked one lump of sugar for the retired magician and dropped it into his cup, then took three lumps for himself. Next came a small amount of milk followed by the revealing of a plate of small finger sandwiches. Roger passed Lord Collier his cup and a plate of the sandwiches before taking his own plate and tea and sitting in a battered and well-worn armchair across from the desk.

Lord Collier sighed as he took the offered food and drink and placed them on the desk beside the clippings. "You know, Roger, you are worse than a nanny or my old mum," Lord Collier said with a playful grin before biting into a fish paste sandwich.

"You know as well as I do, old friend," Roger said playfully, "that if Maddy were still alive, she would have let you starve ages ago."

"I'll drink to that," Lord Collier said, raising his steaming teacup in Roger's direction. Roger, remembering about the mail, pulled out the pile still tucked under his arm, reached over, and placed it on the desk before the old magician. "Anything good?" Collier asked, putting his cup down and wiping his fingers on a cloth before picking up the pile of letters.

Part of Roger's job was to open and read any and all correspondences Lord Collier received. After reading over each letter, Roger would then set about putting them into Lord Collier's preferred reading order: correspondence from family and friends first, letters and clippings related to his work next, bills and society invitations third, and finally, fan letters and requests for appearances. Lord Collier loved having fans; he just dreaded having any sort of dialogue with them, even if it was one-sided. He instead found more comfort in paying his bills and setting about monitoring the ins and outs of his estate.

"Nothing much," Roger said before taking a bite of his own sandwich. "The usual mixture of fan letters, gala invitations, and other such nonsense." Lord Collier nodded as he leafed through the letters. With everything in order, he placed the mail aside next to his clippings and articles. "What have you managed to find for us next?" Roger asked, motioning to the desk.

"Nothing as of yet," Lord Collier said before going in for another bite of sandwich and another sip of tea. The two men sat in silence for a time, breaking bread and letting the unspoken words of their friendship remain unsaid.

The minutes passed and then Roger spoke. "So, what is the plan after all of this?"

"What do you mean?"

"What is the great Lord Collier to do once all the fakers and charlatans have been driven out of town and the mobs have had their day? What's the next great frontier to be explored, old friend?" Lord Collier regarded Roger with the scrutinizing eyes of an old college professor, studying and analyzing.

"Perhaps I'll go into painting or interior decorating. I really can't say, old friend," Lord Collier said with a playful grin. "Honestly, I don't know. There are only so many charlatans in the world, but we all know the hydra-like nature of them; you remove one head and many more sprout in its place." Collier sighed again, leaned back in his chair, and removed his glasses. "I suppose I will have to stop this idealistic crusade at some point. I mean, I'm only one man — two if we count you — and people will always be gullible and easily manipulated into having that one last conversation with those they have lost or to gain a glimpse into the great beyond and know that it will all be fine.

"I spent nearly half my life entertaining people, doing what I could to be the best of the best, and now I spend my time exposing those who claim to be the best of the best at what they do. The difference is, when I tricked an audience, there was a contract. You know that there is no such thing as magic, but you are going to allow me to pretend that there is and you will be entertained by it. With these people, it's different. It's more painful. The contract stipulates that you are in pain or need and that the other party is going to convince you or lead you with the sole goal of making money all based on a series of lies," Lord Collier said. "There are no lies between a magician and his audience; there is only the truth — I will deceive you and you will be fine with the deception."

Roger nodded, sipping his tea. "It's a tough and thankless task, but someone has to do it, I suppose," Roger replied. Lord Collier nodded back. The two men raised their nearly empty teacups in a gesture of agreement and respect, then allowed the silence between them to reappear. With the clock behind him ticking away, Roger reached out for his napkin and instead accidentally dropped the cloth on the ground before him. As he reached over to pick it up off the floor, something fell out of the man's inner jacket pocket and landed on the ground beside the napkin.

Snatching up the item, a look of realization passed over Roger's face, and he shot up from the ground. Lord Collier noticed the look and watched as Roger quickly tried to stuff the envelope back into his coat pocket. While the human hand was in no way faster than the human eye, Lord Collier was still able to snatch the letter and envelope from his associate.

"What is this?" Lord Collier asked, thumbing past the torn-open top of the envelope and reaching inside for the contents. A look of worry began to form on the Bostonian's face as Lord Collier, the contents in one hand and the envelope in the other, read over the address scrawled across the surface. "It's addressed to you, my good fellow."

"It most certainly is," Roger said, reaching out in vain to try to take back what now sat firmly in the clutches of the old magician.

"Betting on the pups again? Is this one of those old collection notices, come back to haunt you for skipped payments to some rather nefarious bookie or such?" Lord Collier said in a playful yet painfully sincere tone.

"Nothing of the sort," Roger stammered, taken aback by the accusations being bandied about. The man had not bet on a sporting event or race in years. Still, shame flushed his round red cheeks all the same.

Lord Collier gingerly placed the envelope upon the desk before him, looking less like an old man in his study and more like a scientist, preparing to dissect some helpless animal. Unfolding the letter, Lord Collier's eyes darted over the scribbled note.

"I am writing to inform you that I have made a most incredible discovery — a young woman, a "spiritualist" for lack of a better word, who seems to be as far from fakery as one can be. This young woman, possessed by the summoned spirits, knew intimate details and facts about not only my life but the lives of those brought forth from beyond the veil. I witnessed things I dare not wish to witness again in this life or the next — things to defy explanation and the very laws of nature herself. I do not seek reward or compensation, though I know many debunkers have presented a purse for proof in the past. I am simply writing to you, dear cousin, because what happened to me tonight, I think, has fundamentally changed my life forever," Lord Collier read aloud before sitting back in his armchair and silently rereading and looking over the letter.

"It's my cousin Lilly. She believes in the great beyond and those who seek to breech that realm and bring back news. She is not one to make up anything fanciful or false," Roger said meekly, perhaps more meekly than he had intended to sound.

"Why did she send this to you? Why did you not intend to tell me about this? What are you hiding, old friend?"

"My cousin sent the letter with the intent of informing you of someone you might wish to visit and debunk. I called her upon receiving this note yesterday, and she told me that what she saw was without a doubt true and incredible."

"But then why keep this from me," Lord Collier asked. "If she thinks what she saw was real, we must go and visit this person and prove them wrong."

"But that is just it. This person," Roger said, looking crestfallen, "is a young girl. This is not someone claiming to be capable of such feats and then charging people a good fortune for advice from beyond the grave." Lord Collier looked skeptically at both his associate and the letter and envelope, both of which he had in his hands once more. "This is a young woman who does what she does for small trades of food and services or meager amounts of coin. She is not seeking fame and fortune or wealth; she is simply a young girl trying to make ends meet."

"You know as well as I do that something like this cannot stand. The world must know of the forgery these people are creating and the lies they are perpetuating. It does not concern me if this child is not seeking to make a tidy profit from this venture. But know this: she never will once I am through with her."

Roger nodded solemnly. He in no way disagreed with Lord Collier's position, but he was very concerned that an innocent young woman would have her life and livelihood ruined by this man, and all because he had forgotten to take Cousin Lilly's letter out of his coat pocket before bringing in the tea. Lord Collier handed the note and envelope back to Roger. As Roger set about replacing the letter into the envelope, Lord Collier stood.

"I need to use the phone, my good sir," he said in a booming tone of voice. "I will notify the press immediately. In the meantime, find out all you can about this young woman and report back to me."

Roger stood, stuffed the note back into his coat pocket, gave a slight nod, and left to fetch his phone book from his room that contained all the necessary press contacts. Lord Collier pulled out from a nearby desk drawer a notepad with a series of questions and answers written out. As always, when facing an audience or the press, Lord Collier wanted to be as prepared as possible.

* * *

The process of weeding out the fakers and so-called spiritualists occurred thusly — Lord Collier would send Roger to visit said spiritualist and ascertain as much information as possible. Next, Lord Collier himself would visit a day or two later, dressed in a full disguise, in an effort to do his own investigations. Finally, he and Roger would attend together in altogether different disguises, playing their parts until the big reveal and press conference.

Usually, Roger loved step one. In all the years he had worked with the world-renowned magician, he had learned a great deal not only in how most illusions worked but in lighting techniques, rigging, and countless other little ins and outs of stagecraft. He now possessed nearly as keen an eye as Collier's for how lighting could be manipulated to hide or enhance certain effects. He was also quite adept at knowing what to listen for. Outside of the most audacious cacophony, he could hear strings being pulled and cards being shuffled underneath a table.

While Roger reveled in the chance to hone his skills and present Collier with his assessment, something about this felt off. The feeling of unease grew deeper as he stepped through the London fog and the dingy flats where the purported medium lived. In the gray light of late morning, the world around Roger was filled with shadowy figures as other Londoners went about their day, appearing like apparitions behind the ever-flowing curtain of soot and fog.

Consulting a slip of paper with the address written out upon it, Roger spotted the door he was looking for. The building was squat and decaying. This place was a far cry from how all of Lord Collier's other marks lived; there were no fancy statues or landscaping to be found, just the dirty street bumping up against a peeling brown front door. The windows to the flat were caked in a layer of grime — to say that the rotting building had seen better days was an understatement.

There were no signs — no advertisements — nothing hinting to the public at what lay behind the door. Consulting his pocket watch, Roger was pleased to see that he had arrived earlier than he had anticipated. Pocketing the watch, the portly man cleared his throat politely before giving a short rap upon the door with his knuckles.

A moment passed and then another. The feeling of unease wound around his insides like a constrictor preparing its meal. Just as he began to think no one might be at home or that he had arrived at the wrong residence, the door opened a crack.

"Hello?" a mouse-like voice squeaked.

"Oh, hello. My name is Peters. John Peters," Roger said, using his alias and trying to peer inside through the crack in the doorway. Aside from one glassy-looking green eye, he could make out nothing else beyond the doorframe. "Sorry to bother you, but I have an eleven o'clock appointment with Ester Allen."

"Oh, Mr. Peters," the mousy voice said, "we've been expecting you. Please, do come in."

The door opened to reveal an older woman. She wore a simple cream-colored dress and wore her gray hair in a bob.

"Thank you..." Roger replied as the woman beckoned him inside.

"Abigail. Abigail Allen. Ester is my daughter."

Stepping into the house, Abigail closed the door behind her guest. Inside, Roger found the place to be small but cozy. The parlor and kitchen were one and the same and very well furnished. A small bookshelf stood on one wall while a modest grandfather clock stood opposite, ticking away. The interior walls were painted a dark oak brown, and a pair of small electric lamps dimly lit the room. There was a loveseat and a rather well-worn and comfy-looking armchair, and in the middle of the parlor sat a stained, round wooden table and four chairs set about it. There were no props or anything that appeared to betray the hint of any hidden illusions or contraptions.

"Please, Mr. Peters, do have a seat while we wait for Ester. Tea?" Abigail asked as she moved deftly from the front door to pulling out the nearest chair at the table, and then into the kitchen to get the kettle filled and on the stove.

"Thank you," Roger replied as he slipped into the offered seat. "That's very kind of you."

"Oh, it's nothing. Think of it as part of the service. Sugar? Milk?"

"Three lumps and just a dash." The smile on Abigail's face was one of genuine warmth as she busied herself with the hot drinks. Roger could not help but wonder if the household played host to many unaccompanied male callers at this time of day. While his host placed the teapot and cups upon a small, dented, and slightly tarnished tray, Roger took one more quick glance around the parlor, scrutinizing every detail he could in the hopes of catching some part of the trickery to come.

As Abigail placed the tray on the dining room table, something behind the Bostonian groaned ever so slightly. "Ah, dear. Come down and say hello to Mr. Peters," Abigail said with a big smile and a sense of weariness in her eyes. Roger turned to see a pale young woman, no more than fourteen or fifteen years old, her skin almost translucent and her expression one of pure exhaustion. The young woman stood at the bottom of the stairs that led from the parlor up into the bedrooms above.

"Hello. You must be Ester," Roger said with a grin as he stood to meet the young woman. Ester nodded ever so slightly, averting his gaze. The poor creature was rail thin and looked as though a slight breeze might snap her in two. Ester clumsily made her way across the room and took her place at the table. Abigail handed Roger his steaming cup of tea before pouring another for her daughter. As she handed the cup to Ester, Abigail placed the back of her hand against the child's forehead. "I don't mean to pry, but tell me, are you ill, my child?"

Ester looked up from her cup, her mouth slightly open, her eyes sunken. Abigail took her seat across from Roger and next to her daughter. "She's alright. Her gift—"

"Curse," Ester pushed back meekly with an undeniable hint of annoyance.

"Her gift," Abigail went on, patting Ester's tiny, pale hand, "has a toll. It takes a lot out of her. Last night we had a rather, how shall I put this?" Abigail asked, as she seemed to search the air around her for the right words from behind the veil of steam rising from her cup, "interesting session with one of Ester's regular clients."

"I must be honest with you," Roger said. "I feel terrible having called on you today while you are in this particular state. I can always come back once you've had some time to recuperate."

"It's no bother," Ester said before taking a long sip of her no doubt scalding tea. Roger could hardly put his lips to the liquid, and yet Ester was drinking heavily from her cup.

"Ester's right. We'll get you sorted out shortly, Mr. Peters," Abigail said.

"Is this your only means of income?" Roger asked. "I mean, I don't mean to offend or pry, but I can't help but wonder?"

"After Father passed away and after Mother's accident at the office she worked in, we found it difficult to find work what on account of my *condition*." Ester said that last word with a hefty amount of acid in her tone.

"I'm so sorry to hear that. I hope everything is well with you," Roger said, lifting his cup to Abigail.

"Oh, I'm fine. I used to work in an insurance office, but after the building caught fire from some faulty wiring, I sustained some injuries while trying to rescue some rather important documents."

Abigail held up her hands, and for the first time, Roger noticed the scarring along the palms and fingers. "I can't type anymore. I can barely feel anything I hold, so of course I'm rather undesirable to any employers at the moment."

"So, as you can see, this is the easiest way for us to put food on the table," Ester replied before taking one last swig of tea. A silence fell across the room that nearly drowned out the ticking of the clock as the seconds passed by. "Next," Ester said, breaking the silence, "you're going to ask me how long I've had my gift."

Roger, who had finally managed to get in a sip from his still piping hot tea, placed the cup down before him and looked Ester straight into her dark, hazel eyes. "I supposes I was," he managed to stammer.

"I've had this gift, as my mother likes to call it, all my life. Ever since I was little, I've been visited by these things."

"Things?" Roger asked.

"Spirits, ghosts, call them what you like — *things*," Ester said icily, her gaze still locked upon Roger's. "They come to me like a nail to a magnet. I don't know why me, but I can tell you that it hurts, but for the right price, Mr. Peters, I'm willing to put up with the pain so that you can see what I can do." In spite of how frail and tired the young woman looked, Roger could feel the fire burning within her — hotter than the tea before him and just as dark. "I hate doing this. I hate what it does to me. But more than anything, I hate not knowing if we will be able to eat tomorrow."

"I see," Roger said, not really knowing how or if he should reply. The young woman's conviction was so staggeringly strong. Roger, a man who almost always knew the right words to say in nearly any situation, found himself flustered and sweating profusely as a result. There was a conviction here that struck him — all the other so-called psychics, mediums, spiritualists, conduits, and the like all had a haughty nature to them — they knew that they peddled in, for lack of a better word, bullshit, and it showed. Ester's complete honesty, from what Roger could ascertain, was either the best acting performance he had ever seen or the poor, young thing, while not necessarily telling the truth, thought that she was — thought that what she could do was the real thing. This, Roger quickly realized, was something new. The levels of honesty, the modest abode, and the clear pain the family was in was either the most incredible fabrication to date or there was a simple honesty to it. Could these two truly be doing this to stave off the cold and hunger of the streets for one more day? Roger had to know. "Tell me, while I spoke with your mother about today's appointment, she did not mention pricing—"

"Two pounds and three shillings," Abigail said. The revelation hit Roger like a wrecking ball. Most everyone he and Lord Collier had exposed, from the big time to the smaller scale fakers, had charged many times that modest amount. Roger wondered if maybe they were on to him or that perhaps it was a starting rate. "That's our going rate. Most of the folks in the neighborhood have little pocket money, so we usually charge three shillings or trade for my services, but since you are from the other side of town, we have to charge you the higher rate."

Roger nodded, fished around in his pocket, and produced a five-pound note, which he slid across the table to his hosts. Abigail daintily picked up the note in her scarred hands. "No need to break that," Roger said. "It's all yours. We'll just consider it an advance on the next session."

Abigail nodded and gave Roger a slight smile in thanks. Roger returned the nod, raised his cup, and sipped his tea.

A few minutes later, with the tea drunk, Abigail set about clearing the table and pulling the curtains and closing the shutters — the time had come. Roger watched, anxiously, as the two women turned off the lights in the house one by one and then slowly lit candles placed all around the room. A stick of incense was lit in the center of the table, its heavy aroma sweet and relaxing. No doubt, Roger thought, this was more for Ester's benefit than for the guest's. Finally, Ester took her seat at the table and Abigail took hers, placing a large, open, and empty mason jar before her. The women joined hands with Roger, forming a triangle of arms.

As the clock in the room ticked away the seconds, Ester sat in her seat, slowly appearing to grow drowsy, falling ever closer to sleep with each tick of the clock. While still holding her mother's and Roger's hands, her body began to slump forward, and her head began to bow lower to her chest. The young woman remained in this state for what seemed to Roger to be several minutes. Eventually, his ears perked, and he began to hear a sound that he thought might be the girl's snoring. The room, now bathed in soft, orange candlelight and filled with flickering, dancing shadows felt quaint and almost relaxing. Yet in spite of the room's calming appearance, Roger could feel a creeping sense of disappointment begin to form in his gut. Was that all this was, just another sham built upon a strong story? Deep down, Roger realized that he had hoped this time would be different — he hoped that these two women with their modest lives and home were telling the truth.

In the midst of these thoughts, he began to realize that what he mistook for snoring was in fact the girl's breathing. Her breath was coming and going in deep, painful, ragged fits. Watching the young medium, Roger's stomach tightened and sweat formed on his brow as shock took hold of all his senses — Ester, right before his very eyes, was physically changing.

Never, in all his years helping to debunk psychics and spiritualists, had Roger ever seen such a transformation. Abigail watched with sadness in her eyes as Ester's body began to twitch and spasm. While her grip remained steadfast on both hands, Ester's body began to contort violently. Roger could hear the unmistakable sounds of bones popping and tendons snapping out of place, wincing with each crack as Ester's body began to take on a taller, lankier form. While her skin remained the same pasty, pale tone overall, it grew more taut and thin as her skeletal structure underneath adjusted. The young woman slowly rose from her seat. Eyes agape, Roger watched in awe as a glowing, viscous substance began to dribble out of Ester's mouth and ooze out of her nose, ears, and eyes.

Across from him, Roger watched as Abigail released her daughter's hand and, picking up the jar, held it under the young woman's chin. Roger watched, half believing and half disbelieving, as the slick, pearlescent mucus gradually coalesced on her chin before falling into the jar with a sickening plop. Abigail slapped a lid on quickly. Ester's eyes flashed open. Her breathing was deep, pained, and echoed all around the room. Roger noticed that her eyes were milky white. For a moment he thought that she had simply rolled them up into her head, but then he spotted her pupils, practically hidden beneath what he thought of as a milky, white layer of flesh.

Ester's lips moved. "Who has summoned me?" a voice that was clearly not the young woman's own asked. The breathing continued. The voice, Roger noted, sounded as though it was coming from Ester, from a million miles away, and as if it was being spoken directly into his ear all at once. It was a deep voice, ancient and commanding.

"We have, Ferryman," Abigail said, clutching the jar of glowing mucus to her chest as though it was a baby.

"What would you ask of me?" the Ferryman's voice asked from Ester's lips. The young woman's body was now nearly six feet tall, the arms and legs long and spindly, and the neck bent and longer than anything natural.

"We have a request," Abigail said with confidence.

"A request? Does the one who makes this request know of the toll?" Roger could feel the Ferryman's voice piercing his very soul as it bounced off his bones and echoed endlessly inside of his head.

"He does," Abigail said, looking straight at Roger. Panic set in; aside from the fee he had paid before the session, no other fee had been mentioned. While this kind of scam would not normally worry him and usually helped to strengthen his resolve that who he was dealing with was a complete fraud, something about this situation felt very different.

Ester turned to face Roger. Swallowing, his throat caught as he found himself gazing into the gaunt, hollow face and pale eyes of the Ferryman — Ester was truly nowhere to be found; even if what was before him still retained some of the young girl's features, he was staring down something or someone truly alien. Her simple dress hung off the new, gaunt frame as though it was on a wire hanger in a closet.

"You seek my services?" the voice passing through Ester's lips asked, growling and curling through the air like angry smoke. Roger nodded. Ester cocked her head, regarding him like a curious dog might at the utterance of the word "treat." There was nothing of a puppy before him now — there was only the grave and what unknowingly lay beyond. "Who would you have the Ferryman fetch for you, little man?"

"My mother," Roger managed to stammer with Ester's face in his. The Ferryman regarded him, sniffing the air around his sweaty, balding head — the cold, white eyes scanning him, boring deep into his soul. The head cocked once more.

"I shall fetch her, forthwith," the Ferryman said through Ester without a shred of emotion in either its words or face. Ester withdrew from where she had been hovering above Roger due to her added height. Sitting back in her chair, she looked dead ahead, eyes slowly closing, body slouching, and breathing growing more and more shallow.

The scent of the incense was more intense, and the shadows grew longer and darker as the candles slowly burned down, sweating wax as per their nature. Abigail nodded to Roger, an indication that what was happening was what should be happening. Ester's bones and joints began to crack and creak once again as her body rearranged itself internally. At first, the Bostonian thought that the young girl's body was returning to its previous state, but instead, he could see that she was once again going through what he assumed must surely be a painfully excruciating metamorphosis.

He watched in awe as the bones beneath that pale skin reassembled and fit themselves into their next configuration. Ester's eyes opened and her new face — same thin pale skin — turned to meet Roger's gaze. While the eyes were still that eerie, veinless, milky white, the face that looked to him with that knowing smile caused his heart to skip a beat. The face before him with its high, round cheeks, arched eyebrows, and slender nose was unmistakable. It was a face he had not seen in many years, not since his mother had passed away back in the States, before he and his sister had moved to London.

"Hello, Tottie," his mother's voice said, clear, pitch perfect — uncanny. His mother smiled beneath Ester's taut skin. "How have you been, my boy?"

"Fine, mother. I've been fine," Roger said, tears streaming down his face.

"You look good, Tottie," she said, using the pet name she had given him as a small boy. He had been Tottie and his sister had been Missy — names only she used. "How is Missy?" she asked, placing a surprisingly warm hand atop his clammy, clasped fists.

"She's doing wonderful. She married and has two little boys now. I wish you could see them, Mother," Roger said, tears still streaming down his red cheeks.

"Oh, that makes me so proud," she said, tears now flowing down Ester's pale cheeks. "I miss the two of you something terrible. Both your father and I miss you. He says hello, as does the rest of the family." Roger nodded. A look of longing love passed across her face only to shift to one of deep sadness, like clouds drifting across the face of the moon.

"Mother?"

"I must go. I'm being called back by him."

"But I never got to say goodbye," he stammered.

"No one ever really does, Tottie. Say it now."

"Goodbye..."

A smile lit across his mother's face one instant, and then a look of pure pain and agony twisted up her expression. The candles in the room began to flicker and shudder as though a breeze was passing through the still room. Roger watched in horror as Ester's body began to twist and reshape itself once again. The snapping and cracking of her transformation was almost too much for him to take. A scream passed her lips, long, deep, and primal.

Suddenly the candles snuffed in unison and the scream ended.

"Payment must be collected for this crossing," the voice of the Ferryman growled through the darkness, slowly transitioning back to Ester's meek voice as the sound of her body collapsing to the ground in a soft thud brought the candles back to life.

In the half-light of the room, Roger watched as Abigail, the mason jar of softly glowing, pearlescent fluid, was poured slowly into the unconscious girl's open mouth. As the last of it touched her lips, Abigail produced a single penny and dropped it into her daughter's mouth. Slowly, she closed her mouth and began to massage her child's face. From what Roger could see in the darkness, the young girl's body and face had returned to what he had been introduced to before the session. Abigail forced open her daughter's eyes one at a time, and Roger could instantly see that the milky whiteness was gone.

It took him a few moments to realize how heavily he was breathing. "Is she...?" he began to ask as the girl on the floor slowly groaned and forced her small body into a fetal position in her mother's lap.

"She'll be fine in a day or two," Abigail said somberly.

"Can I help?" Roger asked.

"We can manage," Abigail said, a sadness in her voice that pained him to the heart. Roger nodded, collected his things, and turned to leave.

"I'll see myself out. Thank you for your time and for your daughter's gift," he said as he reached for the front door. Abigail nodded, tears glistening on her cheeks. Roger left them, knowing what was expected of him but not quite knowing if he could do it after what he had just seen and heard and experienced. Wiping away the last of his tears, he slowly made his way back to Lord Collier's estate, his mind still trying to wrap itself around what he had just been through and with whom he had just spoken.

This, he knew, was going to be a long walk home.

A shiny Duesenberg came to a squealing halt in front of the Allen family's humble abode. Lord Collier sat in the back of the purring car, his false beard in place. Roger sat behind the wheel — the whole of the drive, the Bostonian had been trying his damndest to convince Lord Collier to let Ester and Abigail be or to at least go in with an open mind.

Reginald had never been so disappointed in his long-time companion and business partner. Here was a man, he reasoned, who was as dedicated to the mission as he was, and now, somehow after one session with a "poor widow" and her "sickly" child, he was convinced that this was the real thing. Roger had come home from his exploratory trip to the Allen household covered in sweat and babbling almost incoherently about what he had just witnessed. Lord Collier listened patiently, letting the man get off his chest what he could. Everything the man had told him; he knew he could easily reveal for the fakery behind the sham. Roger had discussed actual ectoplasm, but Reginald knew, as Roger should, that no matter how good wet cheesecloth looked, it was nothing more than that. Then he had discussed the transformation of the child's eyes — simple; she was rolling them into the back of her head. Even her new, guttural voice was easy to fake, and clearly, she was able to, if not produce the sounds herself, mouth along to something pre-recorded and hidden.

Finally, there had been the claims of the young woman's physical transformation not only into this so-called Ferryman but into his late mother's spitting image. As with any of these charlatans, Reginald reminded his companion about puppetry, contortionists, lighting, and even cautioned that some kind of narcotic might have been slipped into his tea or even some combination of these could easily account for what he perceived as an actual, physical transformation. Still, in spite of Lord Collier's reassurances to the Bostonian, the man was still convinced. He said it had to do with the name his "mother" had called him — a pet name only she had used in life. For that, Lord Collier suspected that a member of the Allen family or an accomplice had managed to obtain this bit of information prior to the seance. How else, he reasoned, could they have seen through his disguise like that?

Lord Collier was convinced, now more than ever, that a fraud this good had to be stopped. While he still planned to return next week with Roger in tow and the press waiting outside, the old, retired magician still felt it prudent to visit the Allen family on his own, to truly assess what his partner no longer seemed capable of figuring out on his own. "I beg you once more," Roger said, his head hanging down over the steering wheel, "leave this one alone or at least, if you, too, are not convinced, don't bring the hammer down on this family."

"I must admit, once more," Lord Collier said, slipping on a pair of mink gloves, "the biggest mystery of this little charade seems to be how someone like you could have fallen for such an obvious story as the one painted for you by these thieving tricksters." Roger turned around in his driver's seat and gazed into Reginald's eyes — his gaze was steady, unwavering — determined.

"You know I am a damn good judge of character, and what I saw in there the other day with those two was no performance. It was real. As real as you and I talking to one another in this very moment." His gloves on, Lord Collier picked up his cane with its silver knobby top.

"If you insist on playing along with these ridiculous games this family is obviously playing, you and I will have a fair amount to discuss about your employment when we get back."

Lord Collier was always the final word on things — his late wife had learned that — everyone in his sphere knew that. Roger should have known that. It was as obvious to the old magician as the idea of snow in the winter. Without saying another word, Reginald slipped out of the back seat of the car and took his place on the street next to the chugging red vehicle. "Pull around to the alley on the side of the flats and wait for me there," Lord Collier finally said after a long, drawn-out silence. Roger nodded his acknowledgement glumly before pulling away and around the corner. Lord Collier turned and looked the grimy old home over with a sincere scowl on his face.

Behind him, he could hear Roger pulling the Duesenberg away and down the street to the alley they had agreed upon for hiding the car. The scowl on Reginald's face hardened as he cast his gaze over the filthy neighborhood. In the half-light of early evening, the place looked downright disgusting — stray cats darted in and out of the nearby alleys and up to high windowsills to watch the world below them with curiously predatory eyes. Trash and other bits of crumpled, stained, and discarded bits of lower-class detritus spilled out from rusty waste cans and onto the sidewalks and into the wet street.

Lord Collier, nose held high and features obscured by his fedora, leisurely walked toward the door. As Roger had noted in his assessment of the so-called reading, the Allen family did not advertise their services using a shop sign or even a window display. For all intents and purposes, this was a residential neighborhood, and any business dealings were done in living rooms and kitchens and not at front counters.

Pulling down the front of his white coat, Lord Collier made sure that he appeared immaculate. While Roger had visited the family in a modest disguise, Reginald had decided to try something of the upper-class variety to see if that either put the fraud off her game or pushed her to charge him more for what was sure to be a rather amusing but ultimately pointless display.

Clearing his throat, Lord Collier raised his cane and gave a few quick raps upon the door with the silver knob. He waited, checked his breath before holding it in anticipation of the performance to come. A moment passed. Somewhere in the distance, a dog barked and a couple down the road a ways could be heard arguing over some trivial matter or such.

The sound of approaching footsteps behind the door, the sliding of a lock, and then the door opened before Lord Collier — a small woman stood in the doorway. Her features hinted at the kind of added age stress can bring on. "Hello. You must be Mr. Crux," the woman said with a sad hint of a smile.

"Archibald Crux," Reginald said, tipping his hat. "And you, my dear?"

"Abigail Allen. I'm Ester's mother," the woman said. "Please, Mr.—"

"Archibald," Reginald said with his warmest smile. "You may call me Archibald. No need for this Mr. business." Abigail gave a polite nod — the kind of modest response that could be seen echoed in her modest slip dress and simple bob haircut.

"Please, Archibald," Abigail said, motioning behind her, "won't you come in?" Lord Collier tipped his hat once again before stepping through the doorway, past the woman whose hands, he noticed, seemed a bit off, and into the darkness of the house itself. Abigail closed the door behind her, offered to take his hat, coat, and cane, then led him into the house proper. "Tea?" she asked as she hung his hat and coat upon a coat rack by the door and slipped his cane into an empty umbrella holder.

"Oh, no, thank you," Lord Collier said, declining the polite offer. If the woman did put something in the tea to alter the perception of their guests, he would be damn sure to keep that out of his system. Roger's first mistake, he reasoned, was taking the offered drink in the first place.

Looking around at the modest furnishings and decor of the Allen household, Reginald was struck by how much it reminded him of his own simple abode from his days before his fortunes were made and his fame established; before his wife, before Roger, and before his name had been splashed across countless marquees the world over. Now, he looked at the gathered dust and well-worn furniture and felt a shudder run through his soul. Never, he thought, would he in a million years ever long to return to such squalor and classless surroundings. No, his life had changed for the better, and with his investments, Knighthood, and endorsements, he would never have to worry about living the life of some pauper scum ever again.

Abigail headed into the kitchen half of the parlor to serve herself a cup of tea. "Please, Archibald, do sit down. Ester will be with us shortly." Taking his cue, Lord Collier strode across the room and took his seat at the small, round kitchen table.

"Is this where your child performs her readings?" Lord Collier asked, pulling off his gloves, folding them, and slipping them into an inner pocket of his tweed suit jacket.

"They are not so much readings," Abigail said, taking a seat across from Lord Collier, a steaming cup of tea in her deformed hands. "They're more like visits."

"Visits, you say," Lord Collier purred. "I look forward to seeing what these visits entail." Without another word, Lord Collier began to look around the room, sweeping his gaze into every nook and cranny, atop and below the bookshelves, the portraits, and the furniture. If Roger had failed to spot anything, he was damn well sure he would spot something right off. Usually, it was not too difficult to spot the pulleys or strings used in these so-called seances. Before he could find anything of note, a sound at the base of the stairs snapped his attention away from the hunt.

The waif of a young woman stood before them at the foot of the stairs leading up to the second story. The poor soul, Lord Collier thought, looked like a true, living specter. Her frame was small and frail, and her skin was sallow and pale. Her eyes, sunken and sad, looked older than her young years. Lord Collier marveled at the makeup and prosthetic work he saw before him. There were no discernible lines where the fake portions of her face met the real. The makeup had been spread professionally and was not thin in any spots he could make out. A master performance, he knew, was about to be put on display. A giddiness inside him began to grow

— he would revel in how humiliated these people would be once he and Roger came back with the press in a few days' time.

"Ester," Abigail said, standing and walking over to help her daughter to her place at the table. The child sat down, her head hanging limply upon her neck and shoulders and her thin, dark hair draped over her face like a greasy curtain, waiting to part. The girl heaved a sigh. *Bravo*, Lord Collier thought as he stood and bowed to the young miss whose performance was as amazing as Roger had hinted in his ramblings. "This," Abigail said, holding her daughter's small shoulders, "is Mr. Archibald Crux."

"You may call me Archibald," Lord Collier said, sitting back down. The young woman swung her head to look at their guest, and something in her sunken eyes seemed to almost recognize him. A small bit of panic overtook him, and he worried that perhaps the child had recognized him despite his brilliant disguise.

"Mother, I don't feel like doing this today," Ester said, her face growing more and more flush. Abigail nodded in agreement with the child.

"Archibald, would it be possible for you to return another day? The act of using my daughter's gift takes a toll on her physically and emotionally." Lord Collier reached into his pocket and produced a billfold. He knew what they were doing, and he intended to play along. He was adept at the old nickel-and-dime routine; the more money he put down, he was certain, the more willing the "sickly" child would be to use her *gift*.

"Here; I am desperate to reach someone special to me. How would twenty pounds sound in doing this here and now?"

"Mother?" Ester pled with Abigail. "I don't feel up to doing this today…"

"Fifty? Fifty pounds?" Lord Collier asked, slamming the bills upon the table before them.

"That would buy a fair amount of meals," Abigail said, holding her daughter's face in her hand, tears trickling down both mother's and daughter's cheeks. *Oh, how magnificent*, Lord Collier thought. This was a performance to outdo all performances. Slowly, Ester nodded her approval to proceed.

With the money collected, Abigail went about the house, closing the windows, shutters, and curtains. The soft glow of the electric lights inside the house was soon replaced by the flickering glow of candlelight. Lord Collier was especially impressed with the candles placed around the living room adjacent to the kitchen table. All of this, in his mind, was one of the most subtle performances and setups he had ever encountered. He began to wonder if these two were even mother and daughter and not just a pair of hard-on-their-luck actors in it for the pay and payoff.

Her tasks completed, Abigail brought a large mason jar with an open top, placed it before her on the table, and took Ester's hand. Ester reached out for Lord Collier to take her other hand while Abigail completed the triangle and took his open hand. Time passed slowly amongst the flickering shadows and the scent of burning incense somewhere in the kitchen. Lord Collier watched with rapt awe as Ester's head began to droop until her chin was to her chest, her hair spilling out upon the table before her like a pool of blood. Time passed and nothing happened aside from the slowly rising and falling chest of the child. Her grip did not slacken as a deep gurgling sound seemed to be coming from her chest.

Slowly, Ester's head rose, her hair seeming to flow off the table. Her eyes were white, as though a film had settled over her pupils. Lord Collier thought for a moment that the young woman was merely rolling her eyes into the back of her head as he had suggested to Roger, but soon it dawned on him that she must have placed something over them. How she did such a trick with her hands engaged both impressed and frustrated Lord Collier — no trick to him was unknown, but this was something new.

He watched as Abigail released her hold on both Ester's and his hands, picked up the mason jar, and placed it below the young woman's face. Another impressive and confounding trick as a glowing, pearlescent residue began to ooze from not only her mouth but her ears, nose, and eyes. Now he was more impressed than he had imagined he would ever be. The act was the best he had ever seen. Slowly, the giddiness he had been feeling at revealing these two as frauds was being replaced by a sadness that such amazing trickery would have to be spoiled. As the last of what he could only assume was the standard ectoplasm of these charades was collected, Abigail sealed the jar and sat back down with the glowing glass container before her.

Ester's body began to shake and convulse violently. The sound of snapping and cracking filled the air as the small, pale child began to change physically before the mother and guest. Lord Collier had to do all he could to keep himself from jumping up and shouting "bravo" at the top of his lungs as the child's features shifted under her skin like a puzzle being built and rebuilt under a bedsheet. The skin on her face grew taut as the bones beneath appeared more skull-like with prominent cheekbones and hauntingly sunken eyes. Her limbs appeared even longer and she, herself, seemed taller. It pained him to do so, but deep down, Lord Collier had to admit that what he was watching now was perhaps the greatest magic show and performance he had ever encountered. A small pang of guilt fell across his thoughts, and he realized that Roger had indeed been duped but duped by something new — something extraordinary.

"Who has summoned me?" a voice demanded in a low rumble. The supposed transformation complete, Ester now loomed over her mother and the guest, her willowy body moving more like a marionette on strings than an actual human. The voice sounded as though it was directly in Lord Collier's ears and yet it echoed and rebounded around the small house. Truly, a fantastic feat of audio engineering, he thought.

"We have, Ferryman," Abigail said.

"What would you ask of me?" the Ferryman asked, coming low and guttural from Ester's lips or at least appearing to do so.

"We have a request," Abigail said with sadness in her voice.

"A request? Does the one who makes the request know about the toll?" the Ferryman asked.

"He does," Abigail replied, looking from her daughter to Lord Collier. Ester turned to look the retired magician over. A sneer began to form on her lips.

"You seek my services?"

"I do," Reginald said with all the confidence of a fellow performer.

"Who would you have the Ferryman fetch for you, rich man?"

"My late wife. I am to be remarried on the morrow and would dearly love her blessing of my new union," Lord Collier said, giving his scripted answer. Now, he waited for the charade to continue. Ester nodded.

The air filled once more with the sounds of snapping tendons and cracking bones as the form of the Ferryman slowly shifted to something new. Lord Collier watched the transformation, his mind dead set on figuring out the trick when his concentration was broken. Before him, wearing the simple clothes and pale skin of the gifted child, a face both familiar and haunting greeted him.

"Hello, Reginald," his wife said through Ester's lips. There was no mistaking his late wife's features or voice. When she had been alive, she had been an enviable beauty amongst beauties. Now, here, staring her husband down not with the soft blue eyes she had possessed in life but with the pupil-less, milky white of death's eyes, all the moments of their tumultuous marriage came spilling back into his mind. She had been gone for years, but now, unbelievably, here she was.

"Maddy?" Lord Collier asked, instantly forgetting that this was all a sham.

"Reginald," she replied, holding her hand out to stroke his face. Lord Collier's eyes closed as he remembered that touch; soft and gentle. The moment passed and his eyes shot open as the false beard he had been wearing was painfully ripped from his face, the spirit gum refusing to give up its purchase upon his skin. Searing pain pulled him from his reverie and into the painful present. Maddy gazed at him, fury and anger boring into his soul.

"What is this?" Lord Collier screamed, his hands to his face. Abigail came from behind and tried to take her daughter away.

"Fuck off, woman," Maddy hissed as she turned to address the panicked mother. "I'll give you your brat back after I say hello to my husband." At these words, the frightened Abigail slowly stepped back, one hand to her mouth in shock and the other groping the table for the mason jar. "I think it's time the Ferryman got his toll from you," Maddy snarled, pinning Reginald to his chair.

"What do you want with me?" Lord Collier screamed. Maddy's lips grew twisted as her smile grew wider.

"I want revenge."

"Revenge for what?"

"My life, you piece of shit!" Maddy screamed in his face. "Have you been enjoying your life without my nagging?" she asked. Lord Collier struggled to find the words. "Oh, don't think I forgot about my last performance with you," she continued with all the venom of a cobra in her words. "As soon as you locked me in that water tank that night, I knew something was amiss then, but I should have figured it out sooner. I should have known that there was no making a fool of the Great Collier!"

"But…" He trailed off. She was right. When he had discovered her infidelity, her days had become numbered. Like the magicians of his youth who had failed to teach him their tricks, Lord Collier had sought to teach his cheating wife the lesson so many had learned in one form or another — no one makes a fool of Reginald Collier.

Murder was a new way to teach the lesson, but it was one that came easily in the dangerous world of stage magic. While Collier had fired the stagehand, he had discovered his wife had been fucking for months now, her actions required something more drastic. The stagehand had been paid off, as had the roustabouts who did the dirty work down by the London docks — the stagehand would never be a problem again. But with Maddy, he simply refused to suffer fools gladly and be the talk of the town, the famous magician with the finagling wife. No, his reputation would survive, as would he.

So, he did what he knew had to be done.

"The audience may not have noticed my panic, but when I found that you had removed the catch to the trapdoor, I knew exactly what was going on," Maddy snarled.

"I'm so sorry—" Lord Collier managed to stammer.

"Sorry?" Maddy screamed as she slammed into her husband, sending him and his chair toppling backwards. Lord Collier hit the floor hard, his head bouncing. Maddy pounced. "You are the worst kind of fraud," she said. "You cheated me of my life. You cheated me of a family."

"Family? We did not have any children," Reginald wailed, tears streaming down his face more from the physical pain than emotional pain.

"Oh, but we did," Maddy snapped. "That night you drowned me in front of a packed house, you killed your unborn child." Lord Collier turned his head and retched. The memory of that night flooded his mind. The idea of killing Maddy had been simple. He had been resolute in that. He knew it would be messy, but it would also prove to be an airtight alibi. It was brilliant.

Was she telling the truth? He could only guess that she was, and as such, the thought of a child, unborn and nestled comfortably in Maddy's womb as she drowned before him in the tank, sickened him to his very core. Whatever lack of regret he had at the killing of Maddy was instantly replaced by the guilt of what he had done to something so small and innocent. "I'm sorry…" He sobbed, sick running down the side of his mouth as he looked into Maddy's rage-filled face.

"Not sorry enough," she replied, pushing off and standing over him. A look of sickening glee filled Maddy's face upon Ester's skin. "I think it's time you met your child."

Ester stood back while Abigail sobbed in the corner of the kitchen, still clutching the mason jar and its glowing contents. The young woman with Maddy's face, features, voice, and build stood now, her legs spread apart. Lord Collier watched as in the flickering candlelight; dark drops began to appear on the floor beneath her. In the half-light, and with the scent of incense strong in the air, he watched as something slowly descended from between her legs. Like a wet spider, a form slowly dropped from an umbilical string of flesh, landing on the ground beside him with a sickening squelch.

"I know you haven't forgotten them, but I want you to die hearing my last words once more, the words I screamed as I was trapped and drowning," Maddy said. In that moment, water, black as bile, poured out of her mouth and nose as she mouthed something. While Maddy had banged on the glass that night and cried "Let me out!" again and again, only Lord Collier could see the words on her blue lips. Now, with water rushing out of her mouth, he heard her gurgle those words once more, "Let me out!"

His eyes grew wide with fear as the form on the ground beneath Maddy unfolded and began to slowly drag itself across the floor toward him. Gurgling, cooing, and leaving a slimy and bloody amniotic trail in its wake, the child drew ever closer. Faster than he could have ever anticipated something like that to move, the baby was upon his chest, drawing closer to his face with every sickening second. Coming into view, the features of its face were obscured by thick globs of mucus, but the mouth opened wide as its tiny hands and arms found their way around Collier's neck. He never would have imagined that something so small could possess such strength. It was the last thing he would wonder as the small baby's grip on his neck closed in like a vice. Lord Collier, the baby, and Maddy all cried out in pain, hunger, and ecstasy as the small child choked the life out of the old magician.

* * *

Roger had heard the scream from where he sat in the car down the street. While he had never heard his friend and associate cry out like that before, not even the night when Maddy had died, he knew it was Lord Collier just the same. Leaving the car in the alley, Roger ran out onto the street and up to the Allen residence's door. With all his might, he heaved himself at the door. It took a few tries, but before he knew it, the door flew open and the Bostonian found himself tumbling into the residence.

As with his earlier visit, the scent of incense hung on the air and the flickering light of candles illuminated the small world of Ester and Abigail's home. The uncanny feelings he had experienced upon seeing his mother in such a setting were quickly replaced by confusion and fear. He watched as something small and slimy pulled itself away from the frozen, gawking body of Lord Collier and then began to pull itself up what looked like a fleshy rope and up into Ester's dress and between her legs. But it wasn't Ester.

Roger had grown close to Maddy in life, and the two had struck up a strong friendship that had lasted until the day she had died. Upon seeing him, Maddy in Ester's skin walked over her dead husband's body and approached her old friend and confidant. "It's been too long, Roger," she said, hugging him as he stood there, shocked, unable to move. Maddy disengaged the hug and looked into his eyes with the milky white of hers. "Goodbye," she said.

"Goodbye," Roger replied automatically.

192

Maddy nodded, and then her body began to shake. Just as the other day, Roger watched in awe as Ester's body crumpled to the floor and the bones and muscle beneath her thin, pale skin began to snap and morph back into the small young woman's form. As the transformation neared its end, Ester's eyes closed. Turning her head up to gaze at the ceiling, the voice of the Ferryman spoke. "The toll has been paid."

As Ester lay there at Roger's feet, unmoving, Abigail rushed over, crying, and began to pour the glowing fluid back into her daughter's mouth. Her work completed, Abigail sat back against the nearest wall, her legs pulled up to her chin, her body wracked with heavy sobs. After a while, Roger watched as Ester's eyes fluttered open. Painfully, the young woman began to stand and approach her mother. The two held each other, crying softly. Roger turned to look at Lord Collier's body where it lay on the floor — unmoving — the man's neck visibly broken and his throat crushed.

Roger could think of nothing he could say or do in that moment. Like a man possessed, he walked into the kitchen proper, picked up the ceramic teapot he had been served from earlier, and with shaking hands poured himself a cup. It would be a long time before he would stop shaking and longer still before, he could come to terms with everything that had happened that night.

Vacancy

At 1933 South Winchester Avenue stood a modest two-story house built in the Craftsman style so popular throughout California in the early 20th century. A swing hung from the porch ceiling, creaking gently. While there was no breeze that night, the swing groaned as it moved ever so slightly, back and forth. A small tawny cat, its eyes wide and yellow, stood up from its perch on the porch roof, stretched with its arched back in the air and its jaws wide in a yawn, flexed its claws, and then leapt from the roof to a nearby tree and from there, down the trunk and off into the night.

Small snails, determined and slow, made their way across the wet pavement of the path that ran down from the porch to a small gravelly parking lot that rested right off the main road. At the entrance to the parking lot stood a small sign affixed to a pole and illuminated with a single spotlight — Coveting Corner, the sign read in a simple, loopy font painted red on green. Above the painted sign, neon letters reading 'No Vacancy' flickered ever so slightly, humming all the while.

Up at the house, no lights were on save for the porch light beside the front door. Crickets chirped their endless droning chorus — somewhere nearby an owl hooted and then something small screeched in terror. In the house, a light, dim and lonely, grew slowly in the basement windows and then snuffed out in a flash. A man's scream, muted and primal, escaped into the night. The crickets grew silent. The air, already still, grew more so in that moment.

Out by the road, the neon sign continued to flicker and buzz. A moment passed and the word "No" flickered out — "Vacancy" remained bright and inviting.

The crickets began their chorus once more.

* * *

Pat sat in silence behind the counter at the Cup of Joy Cafe. Glancing down at his watch, he grumbled with dismay — if his lunch didn't arrive soon, he was ready as ever to raise hell. A jukebox built in a classic style, complete with bubble lights and a music library going no further than 1979 belted out the last few chords of Buddy Holly's "Peggy Sue Got Married" before marching headlong into Patsy Cline's rendition of "Crazy."

Pat picked up his mug and looked inside it at the cracked enamel and coffee dregs at the bottom. He wasn't usually one for coffee so late in the day, but he was working on less than four hours of sleep in the last forty-eight hours. He couldn't remember the last time he had made the drive from Los Angeles to San Francisco and back on such short notice and in such a short amount of time. When word at the office had come down that they might lose the Aikens account, Pat knew that he would be the one tasked with making the trip and convincing the board to keep the small but powerful legal firm.

As instructed, the bosses had told him to negotiate and keep them on board by any means necessary. Now here he was, halfway to what he guessed was going to be an unholy mess of a meeting and needing some serious sleep.

The door to the quaint diner opened behind Pat, and he found himself drawn from his thoughts as he turned to watch a family, tourists no doubt, stumble in through the door. A husband, wife, and two little boys, all dressed in shorts, polo shirts, and flip flops, passed behind Pat and took a seat at the nearest booth.

Pat looked absentmindedly down at his watch again — it had occurred to him that every time he'd checked his watch recently, he'd failed to let the time sink in. Looking back up, he was about to call for the waitress when the young woman herself, dressed in a stained and faded classic server outfit with an apron and cap, appeared with Pat's order — steak and fries. Sliding the steaming plate toward him, across the counter, she asked him if he needed anything while refilling his coffee cup.

Pat waved her away. He was never the kind of person to use condiments or salt or pepper — he liked his food plain, and dry — simple as that. He surgically cut off every last bit of fat from his steak, sliding the unwanted bits onto a napkin away from his plate. Chewing on a steak fry between sips of coffee, Pat mulled over his plans for the night. He thought about the drive — he hated the drive. Normally everything would have been sorted out via a conference call, but the Aikens account was so critical it required something more delicate than a faceless one-on-one with the head of the board. Pat looked over his shoulder at the family of tourists — a map was spread out on the table, and the husband and wife were excitedly pointing out locations of interest, their kids looking bored and tired there in the booth. Pat sympathized with the kids and their level of not giving a shit, but he also found himself sympathizing with the parents, travelers in a strange land just as he was.

Spotting the server as she stacked glasses behind the counter, Pat waved her over.

"Excuse me," he asked the young woman. "You wouldn't be able to recommend any hotels or motels in the area, would you?"

"I can toss a few names and numbers your way, but I wouldn't hold my breath on anything being available," the young woman said, pulling out her notepad and beginning to jot some information down. "Here," she said, ripping off a piece of notepad paper and sliding it across the counter. Pat looked the four names over. "Like I said, good luck — with the gun show in town, you'll be lucky to book anything within a twenty-mile radius."

"Thanks," Pat grumbled as the server walked away, back to her stacks of cups, while he removed his phone and began to make calls. Just as the young woman had predicted, everything was booked up solid through the weekend. Pat cursed under his breath after each call ended. Between bits of steak, though, he began to form a plan. He looked back at the tourist family and then he turned his attention to the far end of the diner — *bingo*, he thought.

Pat picked up another steak fry, stood up, and walked over to the far wall of the diner. There he glanced over the colorful mosaic of pamphlets and fliers for various tourist traps all along the Pacific Coast. Maybe, he reasoned, his salvation for the night lay amongst the images of rock climbers and wax museums. Combing through the attention-grabbing quotes and exciting images, he finally found what he was looking for nestled near the back of the pamphlet stand. The flyer was old and nothing more than a faded black and white printout of a two-story Arts and Crafts-style house; Coveting Corner, it read with the address below. There was no phone number, just a single line that read: Good clean rooms at modest rates with a fine continental breakfast served until 11:00 a.m.

Pat returned to the counter, the pamphlet in hand. Searching on his phone, he was unable to find any reviews about the place or a phone number. "Hey," he said, waving the pamphlet in the server's direction in the hopes of getting her attention, "do you think this place might have any openings?"

The server took the pamphlet and looked it over. "Possibly," she said, her voice laced with curiosity. "I didn't think this place was still around, but it's been a while since I've been out to that part of the county."

"Is it far from here?"

"No," she replied, handing the pamphlet back. "It's about a mile, mile and a half from here up near the reservoir."

"Thanks," Pat replied as he took his phone out and added the address to his map. The server walked back into the kitchen, leaving him alone with his meal while the family nearby squabbled over their own map and menus.

* * *

Pat pulled up as the sun began to set slowly behind the grassy, rolling hills. The dirt crunched under his car tires as he stopped at the foot of the gravel path leading up to Coveting Corner. He had passed the sign out front on the main road two times before he finally managed to locate the house and the practically overgrown and unpaved road that led onto the grounds. Having unplugged his phone from the car charger when he had arrived, Pat noted that his battery was nearly drained. He cursed himself under his breath upon noticing that he had failed to plug the other end of the charger into the car's cigarette lighter.

Now, here he was, just as low on his own battery, and hoping against hope that this place had an opening so that he could recharge.

Crickets softly chirped from the grassy fields around the house. A smattering of caws cried out into the night as a murder of crows launched from the branches of a nearby tree and took to the evening sky. The place was tranquil and, being out of the way, Pat allowed himself to hope a little that there might actually be a room for rent — after all, he reasoned, the vacancy sign was lit up when he pulled into the drive, and there were no other vehicles in the lot besides his clunker. The house was dark save for the porch light. A slow creaking pulled Pat's attention away from the front door and to a porch swing, swaying back and forth ever so slightly — it reminded him of a dog's tail, wagging back and forth in excited anticipation before receiving a treat.

It took him a moment, but as he approached the swing, he realized that there wasn't any breeze, not even the smallest stirring of the oncoming night air. Reaching out a hand, he placed his palm lightly on the armrest and watched as the swing came to a dead stop. Crickets continued their melodic exchange as Pat slowly lifted his hand from the swing — the whole thing sat motionless now, not an iota of moment left to shudder through the chains connecting it to the porch's overhanging roof.

Strange, he thought as he backed away from the swing and tightened his grip on the handle of his suitcase, a feeling of unease forming in his gut. Pat was never one to be easily spooked, but something was gnawing at the back of his thoughts — he felt less like he was being watched and more like he was being stalked. Out of the corner of his eye he spotted a small glint — on the opposite end of the porch, the end facing the rapidly setting sun, Pat was taken in by the large spiderweb spanning the front end of the porch all the way to the wall of the house itself.

Curiosity took hold, and he quickly found himself drawn to such natural beauty. While the web had no breeze in which to waft, it sparkled nonetheless as the sun moved farther down to the horizon. Pat drew nearer, and as he did, he slowly noticed the large, dark form in the middle of the web — the garden spider was at least the size of a child's fist. There it sat, its legs tucked in, its copper and red body glinting along with the web in the sunset. Pat stared, transfixed by what he saw. He noticed the tiny reflection of himself in the spider's seemingly countless black eyes.

The web moved ever so slightly. Pat jumped back in surprise as the arachnid sprang into action, shooting up the web with a feverish speed. Looking where the spider had landed in the corner of the web, he watched as the eight-legged creature quickly began to wrap a large green grasshopper like a mummy. The interloper was swaddled deftly, and Pat was both impressed and creeped out. Moments, later, the creature extended its fangs, dashed them right into the web package it held before it, and began to feed.

Pat's stomach unleashed a harsh growl. Part of him felt hungry since his cold steak had been almost entirely left untouched, and part of him felt queasy at the sight of such natural brutality on display before him. The weight of the briefcase in his hand pulled him out of his reverie and reminded him why he was at such a lonely abode in the first place. Taking one last look back down the walkway at his little white sedan and then taking in the fields, porch, and spider, Pat felt as if the house itself had not been built by careful planning and construction but had instead sprung from the earth like a toadstool.

He turned to the front door, placed his hand on the handle, found it turned easily, pushed the door open, and stepped inside. The front door swung inward with little more than a slight creak. The ticking of a grandfather clock rebounded through the entrance of the house. Stepping inside, Pat drank in the details — the place was dimly lit by wall-mounted lights decorated in stained glass pastoral scenes of birds and pinecones and dragonflies. The walls were pained in muted oranges and greens, and a deep brown wainscoting seemed to snake from room to room. A small table by the door held a fern that spilled out onto the redwood floor. A staircase stood across from the front door, ending at a landing with a softly glowing array of windows, no doubt looking out on the fields and sunset.

To the right of the stairs, he spotted a modest reception desk festooned with a green office lamp and a large guest ledger bound in red leather. Pat approached the desk and peeked behind it to find no one there. A desk bell caught Pat's notice, and he gleefully tapped the top of it, allowing its peal to ring out.

As he waited, he began to drum his fingers on the oak countertop. After a few moments, he pulled out his phone to check the time and saw that his battery was even lower than before. Without thinking, Pat allowed his hand to wander over to the bell and ring it once more. This time, he heard a shuffling as someone approached from the back room. The man making his way to the counter did not so much walk as he seemed to slither. To Pat, he looked less like a man and more like a crude facsimile of a man —

his pale, almost translucent skin seemed to hang off his skeleton in odd places while the corners of his mouth had a bulldog droop to them. Even his tiny black eyes seemed to be gazing at something far away. Pat, never one to shy away from anyone so physically different than himself, nonetheless felt a strange sense of shameful revulsion that made his skin crawl. In the back of his mind, he cursed himself for feeling the way he did about the gaunt man and his meat-puppet appearance, but it was hard to fight the instinctual bells and whistles warning him that this lumpy, asymmetrical man before him was something to be feared.

"Hello, young man. Welcome to Coveting Corner. How can I help you?"

"Hi there," Pat said, fighting every urge in his body to flee from the unusual man whose mouth seemed to wobble as he spoke. "I'm looking for a room for the night — do you have anything available? I noticed that the vacancy sign is lit out front."

"We have rooms, young man," the man behind the counter said, his voice hollow and emotionless. "How many rooms do you need?"

"Just one for myself and no additional luggage, just the one suitcase," Pat replied. This song and dance was one he was quite intimate with.

"One room? We can do that. Please, sign the guest ledger, young man," the man behind the counter said, his jaw still quivering with each word rather than working open and closed. Pat jumped back a few inches as the man slammed his hand upon the counter, sliding it toward the leather-bound ledger he then proceeded to push in Pat's direction. "Just your name and address will do," the man said.

"No phone number or email?" Pat asked as he opened and book and began to flip through the pages.

"Just your name and address will do," the man repeated like a skipping record. Pat nodded, casting a cautionary glance at his host. Flipping through the pages, Pat noticed that the addresses were from all over the country and even a handful from outside of the United States. Finally landing on a blank page and grabbing a nearby pen, he signed his name and wrote down his address in Los Angeles.

"How much for the one night?" Pat asked as he finished with the ledger.

"Forty dollars," the man said, slamming the ledger shut, sending dust flying and causing Pat to jump back another few inches.

Pat rummaged around in his wallet and pulled out his credit card. "You take American Express?" he asked, preparing to hand the piece of plastic over to the man behind the counter.

"Cash only, young man."

Pat flashed what he hoped was a friendly smile at the old man, but it was hard to tell where the man was looking, and Pat wasn't so sure about the man's state of mind. Listening to him speak, he seemed as if he was miles away, simply hitting his marks and not bothering to deviate from a script. Maybe, he began to wonder, the poor fellow had suffered a stroke recently. Awkwardly smiling at the man behind the counter, Pat slipped his credit card back into his wallet and pulled out two twenty-dollar bills.

As he slid the bills across the counter, Pat noticed that there did not seem to be a register or till anywhere in sight.

"What's the WiFi password?" Pat asked.

"We don't have WiFi," the man behind the counter said, seemingly straining to say the word "WiFi."

"No WiFi, huh?" Pat said while checking the lack of bars on his phone. While he dreaded the thought of being without the internet, he quickly figured that one night of boredom wouldn't kill him. "How quaint," he replied, as he watched the man behind the counter seemingly ignore the cash on the countertop before him.

"Your room," he said, "is right up the stairs — third door on the right." Pat turned to look around at the staircase next to the front desk. Something slammed upon the oaken counter, causing him to jump once more. Turning back to the counter, he watched as the man's hand slithered away from the countertop, revealing the set of room keys he had just placed there. "Your room keys," the man went on, his face still ridged — now he was convinced that the man had indeed suffered a stroke at some point and had not yet fully recovered — what else could explain his odd look and behavior, he pondered?

Pat picked up the keys attached to an unfinished cabinet knob with a key-loop. "Third door on the right," Pat echoed as he hefted the weight of the keys in his one palm and his suitcase in the other hand.

"Third door on the right," the man said, reminding Pat of a trained parrot. Shooting the odd man behind the counter another awkward grin, Pat took his leave and ascended the creaking, groaning staircase, one step at a time.

At the top of the stairs, he came to a stop and cast his gaze down the short stretch of a hall. Three doors lined either side of the wood-paneled hallway. At the end of the hall was a big, bay window looking out upon the sunset. Pat slowly began to make his way down toward the window, noting every creak and groan that resounded as he walked down the dusty, red carpet and on to his room.

In the low light cast by the ceiling lamps positioned above each set of corresponding doors, he noticed the photographs and paintings of native flora and fauna. Reaching his room at last, Pat slid the first key on the chain into the lock and turned the doorknob. The door opened inward without a sound. Considering how noisy the rest of the house was, he was surprised at how quiet the door to his room was.

Stepping into the darkened room lit only by the rapidly fading rays of light from outside, he closed the door silently behind him. Running his hand against the wall, Pat found the light switch and pressed the button. The room was modest, and in the light from the lamps, it was not, he noted, without its charms. Like the rest of the house, the walls were a deep-red wood paneling as was the bed frame, nightstand, and dresser. He smiled as he looked around the room; not bad considering he wouldn't be able to communicate much, if at all, with the outside world.

Stepping into the room fully, Pat noticed a bookshelf on the far wall, filled with tomes — at least, he reasoned, he could easily find something to read. As he lay his suitcase on the end of the bed, he noticed the pictures hanging on the room's walls — just as in the hallway outside of his room, the walls inside were adorned with photos and paintings — these, however, all featured fish. Looking closer at the images, Pat began to see just how ugly the creatures on the wall were; most were angler fish, but some were of deep-sea fish, the kind with massive open mouths filled with hundreds of needle-sharp teeth and glowing eyes, and bioluminescent head frills meant to lure in prey.

Pat gave a tiny shudder. He recalled seeing such monsters of the deep at an aquarium once, and the thought of watching them feed bubbled up to the surface of his memories — a bad dream he did not really care to revisit.

Turning away from the wall art and its alien-like subjects, Pat explored the bathroom and then searched for a wall outlet. Following the cords from the nightstand lamp and alarm clock, he eventually found what he was looking for. With the clock unplugged, Pat jammed his phone charger into the wall and plugged his phone into the other end of the thin, white cable. The phone gave a pleasant chirp as juice began to flow into it. The lack of WiFi still bothered him, but, he figured, at least his phone wouldn't die. He set his morning alarm, placed the phone on the nightstand atop the deactivated alarm clock, and then headed over to the bookcase.

In his youth, Pat had been fortunate to have parents that took him to the library on a regular basis. His father, a bookbinder by trade, had even taught him from an early age how to handle and care for books — the proper way to handle the spine and to turn the pages. All that taken into consideration, Pat was used to not only the odds and ends of a well-maintained tome, but the odds and ends of a unique book collection — to say that the collection before Pat was odd was something of an understatement. For starters, all the books appeared to be new, spines unbroken, pages crisp and perfect between unsullied covers. Glancing at the titles on the spines, he spotted trashy romance novels next to books on animal husbandry, collections of short stories by Mark Twain, books in an array of foreign languages, and even a book on watchmaking.

It was all so eclectic and a bit overwhelming. His finger running along the spines on each shelf, one shelf at a time, Pat finally stopped at one book in particular, *Monsters of the Deep* by Deepak Suresh. Slipping the book off the shelf, he glanced once more over at the peculiar paintings of the even more peculiar-looking fish. Kicking off his shoes with the carefully selected book in hand, he made his way to the bed and spread out atop the tucked in sheets. Grudgingly, the book opened with the same kind of creak as the front door downstairs. Within moments Pat found himself greeted by the ugliest hagfish he had ever seen. Startled, he scoffed at how silly he felt, jumping at the sight of a stupid but hideous fish.

Thumbing through the book, he spotted all manner of aquatic beast from sharks and squid to jellyfish and angler fish. With the hour growing late, Pat began to read the introduction. After a relatively short amount of time, the droning rhythm of Doctor Suresh's writings on the deep sea began to lull him to sleep. The last thing Pat saw before succumbing to the spell of Orpheus was the painting on the far wall of the grotesque fishy monstrosity, vile smile, glowing, and ready to eat.

* * *

Pat groaned as he turned over. The bed had felt so comfortable earlier but now felt as hard as a rock. Groggily, he tossed aside the book that had fallen flat on his chest as he'd fallen asleep. The lights in the room were off, and the only illumination came from a single nightlight in the bathroom. Grumbling to himself, he flopped over on his belly, hoping that moving might make the bed more hospitable. After a few minutes, he turned back over and sat up — the bed, he sleepily thought, felt even harder now; it was almost as if the bed wanted him off it. Instinctively, he reached over for his phone on the nightstand. Groping in the dark, his eyes half-closed, his fingers brushed the surface of the device. Pulling his phone over, he tapped the screen, squinting against the assault of light from the display — 3:42, it read.

Pat started to put the phone back when something caught his eye; the battery was down to ten percent. Perplexed, he unplugged the phone from the charging cable, then plugged it back in. Nothing. No indication of a recharge beginning. Irritation amplified by a need for sleep began to well up within him. "What the fucking fuck...?" he griped.

Reaching down, he checked that the end of the cable was snug in the wall outlet. Feeling that it was secure, he waited for the signature chirp of a charging phone — the sound did not come, nor did the accompanying vibration. Unplugging the phone from the wall, he felt around for the nightstand light's plug. Finding the dangling plug with its two fang-like prongs, he shoved them into the wall and watched as the light lit up. Repeating what he had done upon entering his room, he unplugged the lamp, then shoved his charger back into the wall. Nothing. Slipping from the stone-like bed, he crossed the room, his charger in hand, and tried every outlet in the bedroom and bathroom with no luck. Searching and smoothing his charging wire for any kinks or bumps or frays, he was dismayed to find not a single tell-tale sign of damage.

Looking at the screen once again, Pat's heart sank to see the phone's battery now down to nine percent. Slipping his phone into his pocket, he sat on the edge of the bed. As he sat, covering his face as though he was grieving the loss of a dear friend, a strange rattling and gurgling sound echoed from behind the room's far wall, drawing his attention away from his phone issues. Pat knew that it was nothing more than the house's plumbing and yet it almost sounded alive, like the hunger pangs of a great beast. Sitting still, he listened to the sounds for a while, noting the sound of what he assumed must be gases moving through the house. After some time of sitting and listening, an idea came to him.

Leaving his room, Pat closed the door quietly behind him. While he had not seen other cars in the driveway, he did not wish to disturb anyone who might have shown up after he had. In the hallway, the groaning of the pipes and the creaking of the settling house seemed louder than in his room. Behind the walls leading down the long, dark hallway, his ears followed the groaning and gurgling of gases and liquids moving lazily through the pipes. The churning of fluids flowing from one end of the house to the other pulled along by gravity tugged at Pat the same way — curiosity dangling before him like a cat toy on a string.

The moonlight coming in through the window at the end of the hall was stunted and scattered as it passed through the curtains, giving the walls and ceiling a strange, jagged pattern. Behind the walls, the pipes continued to hiss and complain, like a massive, hungry stomach. In his mind's eye, he saw the pipes churning and squeezing — intestines pushing bile through at a slow, steady pace — the very notion sent a chill down his spine. The floor creaked and groaned lightly as he made his way from one end of the hallway toward the other. The farther he moved away from the bay window that took up the wall at the other end of the hall, by his room, the more distorted the shadows grew. Just as he reached the stairs, he knew that he couldn't go any farther without light. Glancing to his left, he spotted the sheen of a light-switch plate, reflecting in the pale moonlight. Holding his breath, hoping that no one would complain about the illumination, Pat reached out and flipped the switch.

Nothing.

He flipped it up and down, hearing the clicks but not believing his luck. "Son-of-a..." he muttered under his breath as he flicked the switch up and down one last time. Heaving a defeated sigh, he produced his phone and activated the screen — battery life now down to seven percent. The tight beam of light that issued from his phone was not the most intense, but it sufficed. Casting the beam down and ahead, he watched as the darkness leading down the staircase seemed to almost swallow the light whole.

Step by creaking step, he made his way down from the landing, his ears perking at the slightest sound from behind the walls. Funny, he thought, it almost seemed as if the intensity of noises in the pipes was following him. Glancing at his phone's screen at the foot of the stairs, he noted that he had lost yet another percentage point of power. "Low Power Mode" the screen flashed. Pat swiped the warning away and pressed on, coming to the foot of the stairs. Even in the lobby and front of the house, all the lights were out.

Another light switch and more disappointment as it clicked up and down but without any results. A thought struck him, one he was surprised he hadn't thought to entertain until that moment: the power, he surmised, must be out. Creaking and groaning his way across to the front door, it took him a moment to realize that the sounds of the pipes had been replaced by the ticking of the grandfather clock. Moving his foot with each tick and tock, and not realizing it until he came to the door, Pat switched off the flashlight and pocketed his phone. Reaching out and wrapping his fingers around the doorknob, he found that unlike the inactive light switches, the door would not budge. He jiggled the handle, lightly at first and then with a growing intensity and frustration.

Stopping for a moment, he peered out of the right flanking window beside the front door — his car was still there, all alone. He could also see the flickering neon sign that had greeted him upon his arrival. *Why is that still on?* he wondered. Was it getting its juice from off the highway and not from the house? Watching for a moment, he noted the slight flicker of the word "No" before the "Vacancy" neon. "No vacancy," Pat muttered under his breath. "I don't think there's anyone else here."

His mind still reeling at the puzzle of the sign, he tried the door again. This time, after a few hard attempts at turning the unyielding handle, he pulled his phone back out of his pocket and examined the handle by the light. To his astonishment, there wasn't a deadbolt or any other lock on the door. Even the handle did not have a keyhole or a knob to lock or unlock it. Dejectedly, he tried the handle one last time before throwing his arms up in defeat and stepping away from the door.

The frustration left a bitter taste in his mouth. Sweeping his flashlight around the entrance to the house behind him, Pat spotted the front counter. Walking over, another piece of the puzzle fell into place — while the strange, sickly proprietor of the place was nowhere to be seen, Pat's money was still on the top of the counter, untouched. He picked the bills up and looked them over in the flashlight's beam — they were just as he'd left them. Pocketing the bills, he figured he would hand them back to the old man once he saw him again. As he turned to leave, settling on finding a nice comfy chair in the living room until he could decide what to do next, the gurgling of the pipes behind him pulled his attention back to the front counter.

What the hell is all that noise in the walls about? he wondered. Something about the frequency of the noises and the odd nature of them to begin with puzzled him more than anything else. From where he stood on the other side of the front desk, he could hear the sounds moving toward the back of the house and downwards. Perhaps a basement entrance was back behind the counter, he pondered. Needing to sate his morbid curiosity and get some answers, Pat slunk around to the other side of the front desk and stopped dead in his tracks. "Mother fucking..." He trailed off, his hand thrown up to his mouth in shock. Lying sprawled out on the floor behind the counter was what appeared to be the old, sickly man who had greeted him upon his arrival, only now he looked less like a human and more like a deflated sack of flesh.

Pat dropped to his knees and reached out to turn the old man over as he was lying face down. "Are you alright? Can you hear me, sir?" Pat asked, grabbing hold of a cold, thin shoulder and turning over the husk of the man only to find that the face was frozen, twisted, and lifeless. Pat shook the man, panic rising through him like smoke from a chimney. "Sir, can you hear me?" Pat continued to shake the man, and the more he did, the more he began to realize that the man he was cradling and shaking was far less flesh and bone and more or less just flesh.

Pat stood up, allowing the man's body to slip and fall back to the floor with a hollow, sickening slap. "What the fuck is going on?" he said louder than he had intended. Casting his light around the scene, he noticed that where the man's legs should have been below the torso, there was nothing but a strange, pale, fleshy umbilicus running from the pinched-off torso, across the floor, and then into the next room — blue veins throbbed slowly underneath the pale skin. Hands shaking from nerves, Pat followed the flesh-cord from the back of the front desk, and into a small, empty room. The fleshy tube of skin ended in the middle of the room where it met the floor.

Pat looked all around at the spot and noticed that the cord appeared to go into the floor itself. Casting his light around the empty, featureless room, he spotted a door on the other side of the room, a sliver of light seeping out meekly from underneath. Rushing over, he placed his ear against the door itself, hearing the churning and hissing of the pipes on the other side. Standing back, he took a deep breath, reached out with his free hand, and found that the doorknob, unlike the one at the front of the house, moved easily. Glancing at his phone's screen, he noticed that he still had no signal and his battery was down to two percent.

Swallowing hard, Pat turned the knob and opened the door to darkness. Whatever light had been on when he had approached the door had apparently been shut off. The darkness of this new room was deep, deeper than Pat imaged darkness could be. Stepping forward gingerly, he found that there was nothing under his foot, no steps, no railing to grab hold, just air. His balance shifting, he felt himself tumble head over ass into the darkness. His phone spun, the light with it, and all he could see was the darkness around him, and the spinning of his phone. In one instant, he was falling, and in the next he was landing on something soft and tender. Pat pushed himself up from where he had landed and spotted the muted glow of his phone a few feet away. His hands and fingers felt the floor, and it felt like flesh. Getting unsteadily to his feet, he took a few unsure steps and found that the ground, while difficult to navigate, was not impossible. A sense of revulsion swept over him as he struggled to pull and push himself across the floor, the sounds of pained pipes and gases echoing all around him.

As he reached the phone, a smell began to fill his nose. At first, he thought it was coming from him, but as he drew nearer to the phone, he could smell it more and more all around. His hand reaching out, he brushed against something abrasive. In the half-light, Pat picked up his phone and cast the beam around the room. Everywhere he looked, the walls and ceiling were the same glistening, pale, fleshy surface. Casting his beam around, he spotted the door he had fallen through, now closed and far too high to reach. A sense of panic began to rise in him, becoming more and more uncontrollable. While fear locked his legs in place, it still allowed him to look down. In the dying light of his phone, he spotted what it was he had brushed against — all along the floor, strewn about haphazardly, lay dozens of skeletons, bones bleached and smoothed while others were red and raw, still covered in bits of flesh, tufts of hair, and shreds of clothing.

They all appeared to belong to people.

Pat vomited before dropping his phone into a gathering pool of strong, foul-smelling liquid at his feet. In that moment, realization dawned on him — like a fish who had been attracted to the soft, pulsing glow of a deep-sea predator, Pat had been lured by the same, soft, welcoming glow of the "Vacancy" sign out front.

Pain began to take hold of his feet, and all thoughts, worries, cares, and feelings passed from the world. The stinging sensation grew stronger and stronger. Suddenly, the sounds of hunger pangs were all too real as the fleshy walls began to close in. Within moments, the light on his phone went out, and in those moments Pat's dark world was nothing more than the burning all around him and the smothering embrace of the closing walls. As he let out a last muffled, agonizing scream, the "No" on the sign out front of 1933 South Winchester Avenue winked off, leaving the night to the chirping of insects and buzzing of the lone neon word, "Vacancy."

The Snipe Hunt

The sound of cicadas rebounded across the forest, and sunlight filtered through leaves, dancing as a light breeze passed through the tree's boughs. A woodpecker echoed through the valley, the cacophony of its efforts bouncing around the trees and cliffsides. A river, gurgling and cold, ran through the forest valley, splitting off into countless streams and branching tributaries. A few small fish darted in and out of the shadows between rocks as the cool, clear waters moved downward from the mountains, ever downward. Overhead, a hawk circled, searching for its next meal while a small finch, unaware of the danger above, hopped playfully along a fallen tree branch hanging low over the tumbling waters, its beady, black eyes set on a small dragonfly also hunting for small river bugs.

The forest and the river sang a song; it was a primordial melody, written and composed long before man appeared on the Earth. But now, a new song, something less pleasantly discordant in its unique way, could be heard above nature's din.

From out of the woods, a man appeared, burdened with a pack, taking swigs from a canteen, and keeping his eyes to the sky. From behind the man emerged four youths, all boys, all about thirteen years of age and all singing at the top of their lungs — "On top of Old Faithful, all covered in blood, I killed my poor teacher with a forty-four slug."

From behind the boys emerged a teenager, his face a constellation map of acne and red splotches. All six of them wore matching caps that sported a golden maple leaf with three red feathers jutting out of the leaf's top — the symbol of the Wilderness Trekkers. The song continued — "I went to her funeral; I went to her grave. Instead of throwing flowers, I threw hand grenades..."

All four of the young boys and the teenager wore bulging packs of dull forest green, adorned with swinging lanterns, small shovels, sleeping bags, and other such odds and ends of camping. The group resembled a line of turtles slowly traipsing the uneven terrain, more so than a group of campers. While their caps and packs all matched, nothing else of their ensemble was the same between the boys — some wore jeans while others wore shirts; one carried a walking stick while the others did not — even their builds were as varied as the trees they hiked past and around.

"Alright, boys, I think that's about enough of that song," the man at the head of the pack said, stopping to consult his compass. The four boys and the teenager behind him stopped as well, adjusting their burdens and giggling. "Amos, can you bring me the map?" the man asked. The teenager at the back of the group carefully maneuvered himself past the four boys to join the man at the front. Rummaging in his pocket, the teenager produced a folded piece of paper, which he handed to the man. "Thanks, Amos. Boys, let's take fifteen."

In one voice, the four boys unstrapped their backpacks and let them slip off their shoulders and waists and onto the rocky shore of the river. One of the boys, broad of shoulder with dark hair and thin lips, pulled open the top flap of his backpack and produced a six-pack of cola.

"You lugged that all the way out here?" another of the boys asked. He was a tall thin kid with wire-framed glasses and a hawkish look to his face.

"You bet your ass I did," the broad-shouldered boy said, removing a length of rope from the pack and tying one end of it to the plastic of the six-pack. "Trust me, Gil, it'll be worth it. You ever had soda so cold it hurts your teeth?" Gil shook his head. "Well, if Amos and my dad don't give a shit about this bit of contraband, then you will be chattering your fucking brains out in a few minutes."

"You didn't bring diet?" the third boy asked. He was dark skinned, short, and had a round face.

"Why would I bring diet, Darrel?"

"Dunno, just thought you could stand to lose a few pounds, Lance," Darrel said with a chuckle.

"Fuck you," Lance retorted. The three boys laughed, slugging each other in the arm.

"I like regular," the last boy said as he stepped up to the trio. This boy was the smallest of the group, lanky and pale with thick glasses and freckles smeared across his face, all underneath a mop of thick, curly red hair.

"No one asked you, Toad," Gil snapped with a sneer.

"Yeah, newbies don't get to give their opinion," Lance snapped.

"Look at Toad; he thinks he has what it takes," Darrel joined in. The three boys laughed again, a mocking chorus.

"Listen up, Toad," Lance growled. "This soda is gonna be so fucking cold by the time we reach camp, it's gonna turn your guts to ice. We'll see if you have what it takes, pussy." The small boy shrank back and away from the three other boys. "Besides, I don't even know why this Jew-Toad is in our group — the Wilderness Trekkers is for Jesus-loving Christian boys."

"I'm not a Jew-Toad," the small boy said in a timid voice — a tiny act of defiance. In a flash, Lance was on top of him, his pocket-knife out and pressed against the child's cheek. The other two boys stood back, knowing that if the adults spotted the exchange, they could get away with it using their child-like form of plausible deniability.

"I don't care what you say, Shylock," Lance growled, a red fury behind his brown eyes. "You're a fucking Jew-Toad, and you know you don't belong."

"Hansel," the small boy said in a squeaky voice. Hansel was a small boy for his age and as such was easily intimidated both psychologically and physically.

"You don't get to have that name, you Jew-Toad faggot," Lance hissed, the blade of his pocket-knife digging deeper into Hansel's cheek. A single drop of velvet red began to appear where the tip of the knife was digging into the flesh. "I swear to my God, I will fucking kill you if you so much as breathe your toxic Jew-Toad, faggot breath anywhere near me, understand?"

Hansel, still paralyzed by fear and the pain of the blade on his face, nodded as best he could. All the color had drained from his already pale face, and his body had begun to tremble where Lance was pinning it down with his free arm and legs.

"Lance, everything alright?" the man asked from where he still stood with Amos, map and compass in hand.

"Yes, sir," Lance said, standing up, quickly pocketing his knife, and pulling Hansel up in one, swift motion. "Hansel here slipped on the rocks and I was just helping him up."

"Good job, son," the man said. "I tell ya, sport, one day, you will make an excellent Troop Master, just like your old man."

"I hope so, Dad," Lance said with an insincere smile and a quick salute before turning back to Hansel and wiping the boy down. Out of the corner of his eye, Lance watched as his father turned back to consult the map with his older brother Amos. "You've got some of your tainted Jew-Toad blood on your face, faggot..." Lance pushed Hansel away and returned to the other two boys, who praised him with pats on the back and punches to the shoulder. A moment later, all three boys turned as one and spat on the ground at Hansel's feet before turning back to their packs.

Hansel wiped away tears along with the teardrop bit of blood the knife had drawn from his cheek — the blood and the salty tears mingling on the back of his hand.

While the boys egged each other on in their huddle and the adults continued to look the map over, Hansel noticed a small finch out on a branch, directly across from where he stood on the other side of the river. A small smile touched the boy's lips as he watched the bird hopping about on the end of the branch, its head cocked one way and then the other as it hunted. His face still stained with tears, Hansel pulled a small set of binoculars out of a case on his belt and focused on the bird. He watched as it hopped and flittered about for a few minutes. Hansel loved nature, and he especially loved seeing animals in their natural habitat. Satisfied with what he had seen, he replaced the binoculars, jotted down his findings in his nature journal, and slipped his bulky and extremely heavy pack back up and onto his shoulders and hips along with everyone else.

In front of the pack of four boys, Lance tossed his six-pack into the river. The other end of the rope was lashed to his belt. As the group began to move out once more, the cans of soda followed in their wake as they continued up the river.

* * *

Back on the shore where the group had stopped, no one took any notice as the circling hawk, seeing its opportunity, swooped in and snatched up the finch. The small bird was taken so quickly it was unable to even utter a chirp in surprise as it was carried away. The buzzing of the cicadas continued in its ever rising and falling staccato — the white noise of the forest. The dragonfly, unaware that it was no longer being hunted, darted across the surface of the water, continuing to hunt small water bugs, also on the hunt for their own small prey. High overhead, the hawk screeched before vanishing into the tree line.

* * *

While the other boys reveled in their use of the word *Jew* as a slur, the reality was that Hansel was Jewish only in family and not in practice — practicing or not, the taunt hurt the boy deeply. While his parents had been raised in traditional families, they had not attended the synagogue since before their only son had been born. Wanting their boy to experience nature and the great outdoors, Hansel's parents had signed him up for the summer with the local Wilderness Trekkers pack. If his parents had done a little more research on the group, they would have found that in the last few years, the once agnostic group dedicated to camping, community service, and helping to shape young men into model citizens for tomorrow had been slowly infiltrated by a strong, Christian organization with an agenda to make the group, in their terms, "the moral compass of a young man's Christian life."

Hansel, like his parents, had not been aware of this when he joined at his mom and dad's behest. He did not find a warm welcome in the slightest; the name *Toad* by the other three boys was part of his initiation into the group. The idea, as they had presented it to him, had been to give him the demeaning name until he earned his first Achievement Badge in demonstrating his knowledge of safety with his pocket-knife. Once accomplished, he would be given his name back.

This never happened. With his first badge and many more in hand, he was still called *Toad*. Maybe, he thought, this was a

218

common practice for anyone new in the group to endure, but still, he remained their *Toad*, and that did not seem likely to change.

Since Hansel never spoke of his family or their background, the idea that he was of Jewish heritage never struck him as something he would have to fear. Then one night, as fate would have it, Lance and the other boys overheard his parents while picking him up from a meeting — they had been discussing plans for his cousin Kittie's Bat mitzvah that weekend. From that point on, whenever the Trekker leaders were out of earshot, the boys would sneer and call Hansel Jew-Toad.

The title of *Faggot* had been a rather recent addition to the nastiness the trio excelled at.

Hansel was meek; he knew that he was small for his age and easily outspoken and intimidated. Every night he would go to bed crying, but every day, he was far too afraid to say anything to his parents or the Trekker leaders about what was going on. Silently he suffered, hoping that maybe, just maybe, the boys would eventually like him. After all, that was all he really wanted in the end, just to be liked and accepted.

Trailing at the rear of the pack, Hansel did not join in with the chorus as the other three boys sang crudely rhyming songs about women's naked bodies or violent acts against teachers. Silently he marched on, struggling against the weight of his pack and the loose rocks of the river's shore as he followed along.

The heat of the day grew exponentially as late afternoon came on. Soon, the small bits of reprieve as the pack passed into the shade of the oaks, elms, and pine trees was not enough to stave off thirst and the unending sweat dribbling down their faces. Rests became more frequent as the group drank greedily from their canteens, reapplied sunscreen, or snacked on trail mix and jerky. Hansel watched as the three boys cracked open their cans of cola while he collected river water in his canteen. Popping in a couple of water purification tablets, he closed the cap and gave the bottle a few shakes. Hansel could not help but lick his lips at the sight of the other boys downing their ice-cold soda on the edge of the river. The taste of something sugary and cold was more than appealing. The boy winced as the bitter taste of purified water passed his lips and over his tongue as he gulped thirstily from his canteen. The other boys laughed and licked the condensation from their cans while Hansel downed more of the bitter water, he knew he needed but really hated to drink.

The drone of the cicadas rose and fell, rose and fell, over and over as the day and the hike dragged on. Sweat crept into every crack and crevice of Hansel's body, both cooling him off and irritating him at the same time. He was a clean, young man — someone who preferred to shower daily — he knew that at the end of this trip, he would be pining for his parents' detachable shower head like he had never pinned for it before, ready to indulge in the message settings to put him at ease.

The boys hiked on with Amos at the rear once more and Lance's father at the head of the troop. In his private journal tucked into the bottom of his pack, Hansel had written about his hopes that this first ever hike and camping trip would be a turning point between him and the rest of the boys. He had written about how he was both excited and terrified to take this journey and do what the settlers of old had done so long ago; to traverse that final frontier of America's untamed lands. All hope of things going better was rapidly draining away. While Lance and the others had not said so much as another word to him after the knife incident, they still proceeded to ignore his presence entirely, with the occasional middle finger being flashed at him when the older folks weren't looking. Hansel began to wonder how much of his sweat was due to heat and strain and how much was due to the undue stress and duress he was going through at the hands of his peers.

The troop followed the river as it bent and twisted through rocky canyons and sprawling forests. Eventually, their path took them ever so slightly uphill. Hiking became harder, and the packs strapped to their shoulders and hips became increasingly heavier. The noonday sun slowly continued its agonizing journey across the blue, unending skies. At one point, during a rest, Lance and his compadres took off into the woods only to return with gleeful sneers upon their faces as they struggled not to look Hansel's way. While he hoped and prayed that they were simply answering nature's call, deep down in his gut, he knew that, as always, they were up to something nasty toward him.

The afternoon heat finally broke while the group rested under the shade provided by some alders. The sun was beginning to set behind the mountains, and the air was slowly cooling as a result. With their bodies replenished and their whistles whetted, they carried on. Pack Leader Jim Carrel, Lance and Amos's father, reminded the boys to stop singing their wretched songs about violence and hatred but as usual, he gave them only the lightest of warnings, letting the boys return to their revelry a few moments later. He also reminded them every few minutes that they were close to the campsite. With each passing reminder of their progress along the river trail, Hansel's spirits lifted ever so slightly.

As the first stars began to appear above them, and with the deep crimson of the setting sun still lighting their way, they finally came to a clearing next to the river — their destination had been reached. In the waning light of the long afternoon into evening, the boys unpacked and set up their tents by lantern light. The heavy echo of stakes being hammered into the soft forest ground rebounded through the trees and across the river. Amos and Leader Carrel set up the fire pit, and in no time at all, with their tents pitched and the river babbling beside them, they all sat around the fire and cooked their meal of beans, toast, and eggs.

While the beans in the pot simmered above the flames, Amos poked at the logs with a long stick to stir the fire and keep it going. "Alright, boys," Jim said as he sat next to his oldest son on one of the logs, they had dragged over for sitting on around the campfire, "I need you to all look around the camp area and bring back any kindling or fuel you can find for the fire. Whatever we don't burn tonight, we'll burn tomorrow."

The four boys stood up from their log seats, collected their lanterns and flashlights, and set out. As always, Lance and the others stuck together, casting acidic glances every few seconds at Hansel. Traipsing through the underbrush, they used sticks and their lanterns to move aside bushes and undergrowth. Hansel, not being a fan of bugs and creepy crawlers, was glad that he had used the bug spray left for him in his tent. The night was warm, and the sound of mosquitos buzzing filled his ears. After some time, his arms loaded with bundles of dry leaves and dead sticks and branches, Hansel noticed that the sounds of the night insects were growing louder; the buzz was nearly deafening. On top of the sounds, he was beginning to get itchy, all over.

Returning to the camp, his arms overloaded and the handle to his lantern securely in his mouth, Hansel deposited his bounty on the pile. Lance and company had already returned, their meager pile now larger and more impressive with Hansel's contribution. His hands free, Hansel began to swat at the swarming insects all around him. His skin was beginning to prickle and burn from the sensation of them.

"Something the matter, son?" Jim asked as he and Amos looked up from the beans bubbling in their pot above the fire.

"Yeah, I used the bug spray I brought but it's not working. I'm getting attacked."

"Let me see that bug spray," Jim asked. Hansel dashed into his tent, scooped up the bottle where he had left it atop his sleeping bag, and dashed back outside. Jim took the spray and gave a quick squirt to his wrist. He sniffed at the spot a moment, rubbed it, then took his tongue to it. "Son," he said in a condescending manner that said *you are not my son*, "You've been had; this is sugar-water." Lance and the others began to laugh uproariously. Even Amos and Jim gave a slight chuckle — it was their *boys-will-be-boys* kind of response, non-aggressive but still painful. "I suggest you put on your trunks and go wash yourself in the river post-haste."

"Yes, sir," Hansel said with a quick nod. The young boy dashed once more into his tent and by lantern light managed to slip into his water shoes and trunks. Opening the flap to his tent, Hansel found himself face to face with Lance; Darrel and Gil were behind their leader and off to the side, leaning casually and "innocently" against a nearby tree.

"I hope those poor bugs don't get sick drinking your tainted Jew-blood." Lance sneered. "I'd hate for them to die from AIDS or whatever shit you carry in your blood." Hansel did not know what to say or do except stand there, towel in hand, his body burning and the river, glistening so beckoningly, just a few feet away.

"Can I please go," Hansel mumbled, casting his gaze down to the ground.

"Yeah, you can go, but nothing you do will wash the Jew-Toad, faggot stink off of you." Lance scoffed as he stood back, allowing Hansel to pass. Without even looking back, he dashed past the trio of boys, past the crackling fire, and straight into the cold, refreshing waters. His body no longer burned. Instead, he felt a sweet relief from both the hungry insects and the other boys. He sat in the cold river water for some time. Listening to the rushing waters and the chittering of night insects, the young boy watched the stars overhead, drinking in the sight of the backbone of the night as it spread before him in all its celestial glory. Like all good things, though, Hansel's time in the water came to an end as Leader Carrel called him back for dinner.

Hansel toweled off as he got out of the water and headed back to his tent to change. Passing by the campfire, he watched as everyone else ate their meals and laughed and joked around with one another. A pit in the boy's stomach began to grow. What, he wondered with a looming dread, would they do to his dinner? Dressed and coated in a thick layer of the bug spray his mother had packed for him, which he found tossed to the side of his tent, Hansel rejoined the others, who had already finished their meal. Amos handed him a plate with a meager helping of what little was left of the beans, eggs, and toast. While Hansel knew that the small meal would leave him hungry, he was thankful that nothing seemed to have been done to taint or ruin his tiny dinner.

After they ate, the group cleaned their dishes in the river and then set about hanging their bear bags in nearby trees. Once the work had been done and with the fire slowly crackling to a cold death, everyone sat around on their logs to tell ghost stories. In spite of the heat of the summer night and the crackling of the still-hot fire, Hansel sat with a blanket wrapped around him. The small boy had never enjoyed scary stories or movies. When his friends at school had thrown a slumber party and put on a slasher film, they all loved, Hansel wet himself from fear and spent the whole night sobbing to himself in the bathroom.

Now, here he was, miles from home and his parents, surrounded by nature, darkness, and a group of hostile peers — a shudder traveled up his spine, sending shivers throughout his body. Hansel could not tell if this reaction was due to his scenario, or the story

Amos was relating slowly to the boys. As the assistant leader of the group told his macabre tale of ghosts, revenge, and bloody death, Hansel's wide eyes glanced at every dancing shadow and flickering ash that passed through his periphery. The sounds of night birds and insects took on ominous tones, and every tree branch was a pair of skeletal arms, reaching down to snatch him away.

Hansel fought back the urge to scream. He knew that such an act would only add fuel to the fire that was already raging out of control between Lance and the other boys and himself. Unlike most of the boys in his grade, Hansel's voice had yet to change and his scream sounded particularly feminine, at least according to the boys at school. The story concluded with a murderous ending that left Lance in stitches and the other boys joining in. Hansel sat there and continued to shiver and glance nervously all about.

"Alright, boys, time to pack it in — we've got a whole day of fun activities tomorrow," Jim said, standing and stretching his legs and arms. "Thanks for the story, son," he said to Amos. "Darrel, why don't you and Gil fill the bucket and douse the fire."

Lance's two cronies jumped up with a quick salute, Gil snatching the nearby metal bucket before Darrel could. In the darkness, Hansel watched them scurry off to the river to fill the bucket. Moments later, they poured the cold water atop the hot flames, and Hansel watched the dancing, undulating shapes that rose with the thick, white smoke of the doused fire. His imagination took flight and suddenly, the pitch-black woods all around him seemed to be filled with all manner of ghastly creature and vengeful spirit.

Making a beeline to his tent, Hansel did not want to risk drawing Lance's attention and further threats. Without incident, the young boy practically dove into his tent, headfirst. His sleeping bag lay unrolled on the ground and his unpacked backpack stood against the far, opposite wall. The tent was small, green canvas, army surplus, and for the next few days, it was home. Hansel undressed by the light of the lantern he had hung at the back of the prism-shaped tarp. The boy's body ached, his skin itched, his belly was empty, but he was ready for sleep and the reprieve that came with such acts.

Dressed in his nightshirt and night shorts, Hansel slipped into his sleeping bag and then immediately shot out of it, screaming at the top of his lungs. As he had slipped into the bag, his legs and feet had brushed up against something prickly that scratched at his limbs. Tossing open his sleeping bag, Hansel found it to be filled with pine needles and leaves — leaves that upon further inspection turned out to be from a poison oak plant. Hansel thought back to one of their stops along the river trail when Lance and company had ducked into the woods briefly, and the tears began to flow warm and salty down his face. In the next tents over, Lance, Gil, and Darrel were laughing long and audibly.

Hansel brushed out the contents of the sleeping bag into the woods behind his tent, then tried to fall asleep on top of the bag itself.

He continued to cry to himself all through the night, finally falling asleep just before the break of dawn.

* * *

"How did you sleep, *Jew*?" Gil asked in a hushed tone the next morning as the boys sat around the newly resurrected campfire. Amos was busying himself with breakfast — leftover beans, toast, and eggs. Darrel walked past and shoved Hansel forward. Lance sat across from Hansel and stared long and hard at him, his sneer coming and going like waves on a shore.

"You know, I think I'd like some bacon," Lance announced. "How about you boys?" he asked Gil and Darrel, now finding seats beside their leader.

"I could go for some," Darrel agreed.

"Same!" Gil replied.

"Bacon it is," Amos said with a nod as he took out some strips from the small cooler they had brought with them. Without thinking, he slipped the bacon into the pan with the eggs. While Hansel was not a practicing Jew, he had still been raised on a pork-free diet. Knowing that his stomach would not be able to cope with such a thing, he hoped and prayed that eating the eggs cooked in the meat's juices would not give him the runs.

"Nice legs," Lance said without even looking at Hansel. Hansel looked down at the thick, red rashes that had formed overnight on his legs, feet, and hands. The inside of his sleeping bag was a no-go zone until it could be properly washed when they returned to civilization. Jim had given Hansel the usual, the *boys-will-be-boys* song and dance when he had spotted Hansel as he emerged from his tent, bleary eyed and exhausted. The only comfort he was able to take was that the troop leader had handed him a bottle of calamine lotion he had brought for such occasions. Now, slathered in soothing ointment, Hansel watched breakfast cooking, his nose filling with the scents of a promising meal and his weariness abating with the cooling lotion.

Thankfully, breakfast went without any incident. When offered some of the sizzling strips of fried pork fat, Hansel had turned them down and Amos had graciously accepted the decline, apologizing for forgetting about Hansel's dietary restrictions. After breakfast and a trip to the woods with a hand shovel and toilet paper, the boys slipped into their trunks and took to the river. Hansel sat on the shore for a while, watching the other boys splashing and wrestling with one another as the sunlight caused the water to shimmer and sparkle like a million fairy lights on a dark night. Fearful of the currents, he instead decided to just wade in a little, allowing his feet and legs to get wet. The cold water washed away the soothing lotion, but that mattered little as the water felt even better against his skin. As the coolness of the morning air shifted to the rising warmth of afternoon, Hansel finally decided to allow his whole body to slip into the gently flowing waters.

Overhead, insects darted about, and birds hunted with cunning. Hansel found a smooth but stable rocky outcropping just under the water — planting his back against it, he was grateful that he could sit back and relax, allowing the calm waters to flow and churn all around his aching and itching body. While he had never been to a day spa, Hansel wondered if this is what such an experience felt like.

The bliss, however, was short lived. With his eyes closed, Hansel could feel the sun being blocked out as the shadows of Lance, Gil, and Darrel fell over him.

"Enjoying yourself?" Gil asked. Hansel opened his eyes to find the boy's forms back-lit, casting their faces and features in complete darkness while the sun shone brightly overhead, behind them — an ominous eclipse.

"Wakey wakey, faggot," Darrel added with a sharp kick to Hansel's pelvis.

"Ow," Hansel replied, fighting back the oncoming tears he knew were developing. Even before the kick and the crude name-calling, knowing that he was back to being the plaything of the trio set his heart and emotions into free-fall.

"Shut up, *Jew*," Gil snapped. "Jew-Toads can't feel pain; it's a scientific fact." All three boys began to snicker at this. While the kick had not been very hard and his response was more out of an instinctual reaction to the possibility of physical pain, Hansel did not dare to speak any more than he already had unless forced to.

"Listen, Jew-Fag," Lance said, lowering himself so that he could shove his face into Hansel's, "we're gonna be heading out on a snipe hunt tonight, and you're going to come with us." Hansel nodded.

"Okay," he said meekly. "What's a snipe hunt?" The three boys returned to their laughing.

"Of course you don't know what a snipe hunt is. Big fucking surprise there," Darrel said, rolling his eyes and crossing his arms. "A snipe," he added, "is a big, black bird."

"It's got a razor-sharp beak and glowing red eyes," Gil added with that nasty sneer of his.

"This is a real thing?" Hansel dared to ask.

"Of course it is," Lance said, leaning even lower and pressing his face even closer to Hansel's. If it hadn't been for the rock behind his back, the boy would have pushed himself away. "It's as real as the Holocaust is fake, and you're gonna help us catch the fucking thing." Hansel knew that the boys were full of it; he could see it all over their faces and in their body language. What he did not get and what he utterly dreaded was their game — whatever that might be.

"We're not using the guns your dad brought, are we?"

"We're not using the guns..." Gil mocked in a baby voice.

"Of course, we are. What the fuck else are we going to use to bag something like that?" Lance said, finally standing up and giving Hansel back some personal space. The pit in his stomach dropped out like a free-falling elevator. More than anything else about this trek into the wilderness, Hansel had been petrified not only by the prospect of guns being brought on a camping trip, but he was mortified about Lance and company getting their hands on them. Like a condemned man, Hansel could do nothing but acquiesce to their request and hope and pray that his worst fears were truly unfounded.

"We leave at dusk," Darrel said with another kick to Hansel's hip. This time the force behind it was stronger and the act was rather painful. Hansel bit his lip, suppressing his reaction as much as possible. Satisfied with their work, Lance and his boys left Hansel alone with his back to the rock, his aching pelvis, and his tears.

An hour later, the boys were all dressed, sporting utility belts laden with compasses, water bottles, trail-mix-filled pouches, pocket-knives, and flashlights. Each stood in front of their tent, their hiking boots laced up and their bodies slathered in sunscreen. Each of the boys held their walking sticks except for Hansel who had leaned his against his tent while he busied himself with a fresh layer of soothing lotion over his sore legs. All four of the young men wore wide-brimmed sun hats and a white streak of sunscreen on the top of their noses.

As they stood ready for inspection, Jim and Amos emerged from their more modern tent and approached the four kids. Both adults wore similar attire as the boys, with the addition of hunting rifles slung over both men's shoulders. "Alright, boys, we're going to take this nature hike seriously. We're not going to screw around with any animals or plants, and we are going to respect nature. I want you all to follow these orders or I will make you scrub dishes tonight. Is that understood?"

"Yes sir," the four boys said in near unison.

"Good! Let's head out then. Amos, why don't you take the lead." Amos nodded, pulled out the folded map of the area he had been consulting since the group had originally set out on this little camping expedition, and pointed at the edge of the forest a few yards away from the camp and river. Lance, Gil, and Darrel all fell into line like a well-oiled machine while Hansel struggled to rub in the last of the lotion he had applied to his still red and blistered-looking legs. Jim took up the rear and waited for the straggler to finish and follow along.

"Pace yourself," he reminded Hansel as the boy tried to sprint in an effort to catch up with his fellow campers. Hansel took the advice and slowed and matched his pace — there would be plenty of time to catch up once the terrain got a little rougher. *Besides*, he thought to himself, *why do I want to catch up to them? They're just going to torment me anyway.*

The afternoon heat was oppressive, more so now than on their journey into the mountains. The chorus of cicadas, as it had the day before, rose and fell, and with those peaks and valleys of their tune, the temperature seemed to follow suit — rising ever higher. As the group hiked into the shade of the woods, somewhere overhead, an eagle cried out and somewhere else, a woodpecker pounded away. More than fearing a bear or cougar attack, Hansel was infinitely more worried about spider and snake bites or getting ticks and chiggers under his skin. The boy cautiously, and much to the chagrin of the rest of the party, delicately moved aside any plant in his path, stepping around it as if it had the plague.

The deeper into the woods they traversed, the more the small, thin trees seemed to space out and the thicker the trunks grew in circumference — now they were in the realm of giants. The shade grew darker and the ground noisier with each step upon dry and brittle leaves and pinecones or needles. The group hiked for an hour or so. All the while, Hansel, knowing that the idea of the snipe was utterly ridiculous, nevertheless kept a weathered eye out for the fabled beast. Eventually, they came to a clearing where the group sat in the shade and ate their packed lunches, listening to the sounds of nature all around them. After a bit, though, nature became far too boring and Lance, Gil, and Darrel began to converse. It was at that time that Jim came over to Hansel.

Standing over the boy and looking at him down his nose from behind his mirror-like aviator sunglasses, the troop leader looked more like a cop than a camper. "How you holding up, son?" Jim asked, no hint of a smile or warmth in his question.

"Alight," Hansel replied after swallowing the bit of sandwich he had been busy masticating. Jim squatted down, still hovering above the small boy — still infinitely intimidating. His neck muscles twitched and his brow furrowed as he looked the camper up and down, assessing him in that way only adults can that comes off as much more intimidating and terrifying than they might realize it is.

"Son," Jim said in a lowered voice, not even bothering to make sure that neither of his sons or the other boys were listening in, "I think it's about time you and I had a little chat."

"About what?"

"About you." Jim removed his sunglasses, slipping them into a pouch on his belt. "Listen up, kid, I don't know if your old man has ever told you this, but it's time you manned up." Hansel did not reply but he knew instantly that his father, a kind, quiet, and gentle soul, had never once uttered that phrase to his only child. Hansel, in all honesty, did not even fully understand the idea behind the phrase he had heard from other men on many other occasions.

"What do you mean, sir?"

"What do I mean?" Jim asked, seemingly taken aback by the notion that the small boy in front of him did not understand what he assumed he did already understand. "You know. Quit being such a pussy. Take that target off your back and be a man. Watch sports and wrestling. Piss standing up. You know, the kind of stuff real men do." Hansel did not know that that was the stuff of "real men." "Maybe if you quit being such a weak pansy, kids like my son wouldn't pick on you so much. You ever take karate lessons?" Hansel shook his head. "Well, do it. Put some meat on those skinny bones and a violent fire in those eyes. A man sees that fire, like the one John Wayne had behind his eyes, and a man will back down and back away out of fear and respect. No fire, no fear."

"Yes, sir," was all the boy could find in his small collection of answers. Jim stood up, replaced his sunglasses, and nodded.

"Alright then," he said with all the emotional weight of a brick wall. "Man up." Jim walked away, leaving Hansel with half his lunch still uneaten in his hands and his mind reeling in confusion and sadness. Hansel had always thought that he was going to be a man someday, like his father. His dad didn't drink beer or watch sports, but Hansel felt like that was the kind of man he thought he ought to be. Was he wrong, he wondered — was he meant to be something more — something primal?

Hansel pondered about this while he lackadaisically finished the remainder of his lunch. The conflicting ideas and emotions were still being sorted and processed when, after eating and a few more miles of hiking, the group came to a stop in a field at the edge of the forest. The grass was a deep green and rippled like waves as a warm breeze played along the tips of the tall blades. In the distance, the mountain range with its white-tipped peaks loomed like guardians. The field was surrounded by forests along three of its sides while the river ran as the border on the last side.

Jim and Amos shushed the boys, who had been chattering practically non-stop since they had set out once again. Now they quieted down. Jim motioned for everyone to get low to the ground, hiding themselves as much as they could behind the tall, waving blades of grass. Sitting in the dirt, Hansel's small frame meant that he could sit cross-legged and still not have his head popping above the cover of the grass. Everyone else had to get on their hands and knees.

Silently and slowly, Amos slid the rifle off his shoulder and handed it to his father. "Alright," Jim whispered, "here's what is going to happen." The boys leaned in closer to hear more clearly. "We're going to hunt some rabbits for dinner and see if we can't earn you that hunting chit for your records. Now, Lance, I know that we've gone out a few times, so why don't you take point and help the others."

"Okay, Dad," Lance said in an excited whisper.

"Amos and I will get the first few and then the rest will be up to you four." Jim cocked and primed the rifle after switching off the safety — checking the scope, he slowly brought the gun up and to the top of the grass. He swept the barrel of the hunting rifle back and forth like a pivoting security camera. "Cover your ears, boys," Jim said in a whisper as he stopped his sweep and drew a bead on something unseen in the distance.

Hands flew to ears and the gun shot off. The sound was louder than Hansel had expected. It took him a moment to remember that all the other times he had used a rifle, he had been on the shooting range with ear protection.

"Did you get it?" Amos asked, peeking out from behind the grass.

"Yep," Jim said triumphantly.

Over the next few minutes, Amos and Jim passed the rifle between the two of them as they fired upon unseen targets. Finally, the adults passed the rifle to Gil. "Alright," Amos said, helping Gil get into position. "You see anything yet?" Gil had the scope plastered to his eye, his other eye squinted closed. The sweep of the rifle ended abruptly as he quickly whispered to the rest of the group.

"I see something." He breathed in, breathlessly. Time passed slowly and then the crack of the rifle. "I got it," Gil nearly shouted.

The rifle was handed to Darrel, who took it greedily, ready, it seemed, to shed animal blood. Darrel spotted something in the scope faster than Gil, and before anyone could toss their hands up to their ears, he fired. "Ah crap," he groaned. "I think I just shot Gil's rabbit."

Having wasted his turn, Darrel handed the rifle to Lance, who took it, checked it with an eye for careful consideration, then aimed not into the field but into the blue sky. A flock of ducks was passing nearby, their light quacking sounding farther off than they really were. "Ears," Lance whispered before letting off his shot. Everyone watched as the lead duck in the formation tumbled lazily, head over tail to the ground. If the shot had not killed him, the fall certainly must have finished the trick, Hansel thought.

Lance's grin of triumph morphed seamlessly into a scowl of disgust as he handed the rifle to Hansel. Hansel took the gun, his hands sweating and shaking — unlike Darrel, though, his reaction was out of fear and nervous agitation as opposed to the other boy's bloodlust. As always, the rifle felt alien in Hansel's hands. His family was not keen on guns, and they made it known on many occasions. For Hansel, this felt like flirting with the enemy.

Hefting the weapon, Hansel felt lost. The rest of the flock flew overhead and away from where their comrade had fallen. As far as he could see, no other rabbits remained. The boy's body began to shake from adrenaline and anxiety. "What am I supposed to do?" Hansel managed to stammer out.

"Find something and shoot it. Whatever you hit, we'll take back and strip and clean it for dinner, tonight," Jim said sternly. Hansel swallowed, trying his best to calm himself. As each moment passed, the gun felt heavier and heavier in his hands. Hefting the rifle up and onto his shoulder, the small boy put an eye to the scope and looked at the magnified world behind the targeting reticule.

Hansel's breathing came in big, strained gulps as he fought back the fear of holding something so deadly — the decision to take a life now resting in his trembling hands and rapidly beating heart. The boy spotted an old oak on the other end of the field; it was far but that hardly mattered. Squeezing the trigger, his body flew back from the force of the shot going off. The gun flew and the bullet with it, not across the field but up and at an angle, landing somewhere not too far away — a puff of dirt hinting at the point of impact.

Everyone burst out laughing while Hansel burst out in tears.

"I think you missed the tree," Gil cried out.

"The mighty hunter has come," Darrel managed to choke out between bouts of laughter.

Even Jim and Amos were chuckling. The only one not laughing was Lance; the boy instead shot daggers from his gaze at the boy sitting where he had landed, still crying, holding his knees to his chest. In one quick motion, Lance snatched up the rifle and passed by Hansel. "You are so god-damned pathetic, you fucking *fag*," the boy sneered his words, raking across Hansel's soul like claws on skin.

The rest of the afternoon, the other three boys, along with Amos, took turns shooting at anything alive that unfortunately passed through their scope — squirrels, rabbits, chipmunks, even a skunk — clearly the others had no issue with killing. Hansel sat by himself, watching the boys gleefully murder and congratulate one another on their manliness. Now, more than ever, Hansel just wanted to go home, get away from these bullies, and never see them again.

Their kills gathered, save for the skunk, the party hiked back from the field and into the forest. The trio gabbed about their trophies while Hansel hung back, sniffling and wiping fresh tears away from his dirty face. Distracted by his emotions, Hansel had not heard Jim tell them that they were taking a different path back to camp than the one that had led them to the killing field — so when they came upon the waterfall, the sight came as quite the surprise.

Deep in the woods, where the green canopy provided thick, dark shade, they had come to a rocky area. The ground was broken and cracked wide like a shattered window. Through the cracks, water ran from on high to down far below. Eventually, they came to a precipice, overlooking a heavy and rapidly moving stream. The stream came to the edge and fell farther down into the thick, dark forest below. Several meters below that, the waters crashed upon jagged and moss-covered rocks. Cautiously, the group made their way down from the overlook and toward where the waters pooled at the base of the falls.

Overhead, crows cawed and woodpeckers pecked, but the closer they drew to the base of the falls, the quieter nature seemed to get. While Hansel had at first thought that the sounds were drowned out by the cascading falls, he soon began to realize that the absence was less of a thing and more of a feeling. At one point in their slippery descent, the point when the vacuum of sound felt more complete, Hansel thought that he spotted something dark and deep behind the waterfall — a cave, perhaps, he pondered. Whatever it was, for Hansel, it felt as though something was watching him. No one else seemed bothered, but the hairs on Hansel's neck and arms stood at attention, like soldiers ready for inspection as they passed the place where the cave lay. Hansel pushed these feelings out of his head — the primordial sensation of being stalked was just that, he reasoned, and nothing more.

Once the group reached the base of the waterfall, they stopped, set their kills down, took off their clothes, and dove into the cold, dark waters of the pond that had formed from the waters above. A natural barrier of rocks formed a kind of sluice that kept the boys in the pond but allowed the waters to continue on their journey down the stream, through the forest, and on to meet the river.

Not wanting to get naked in front of people he did not know or trust and knowing that the other boys would look at his penis without its foreskin and ask questions or poke fun at it, Hansel opted instead to investigate the area, see if he could reach the cave hidden behind the falls.

Jim and Amos sat on mossy rocks at the base of the falls, chatting amongst themselves while the other three boys punched each other and shoved their friends' heads under the cold waters — no one paid any attention to Hansel as he slipped away and worked his way up and around the falls. The rocks were wet and slippery, caked in layers of dull moss and bright fungus and molds. The going wasn't easy, but the distraction helped take his thoughts away from what kind of punishment the others might dole out tonight once Jim and Amos weren't around.

Curiosity was something Hansel loved to give in to, much to the chagrin of others. On more than one occasion, the boy had poked his head into places or situations it ought not to have been poked into. Still, he was never one to suppress the need to explore, especially when no one else was looking. And yet something, something primal, seemed to call to him from the dank darkness of the cave. As he climbed the narrow shelf of rock leading behind the fast-falling waters, he noticed that the absence of natural sounds was not something in his head — the feeling he had experienced on the way down to the waterfall's basin was real. The feeling was tangible, like déjà vu, something real but hard to grasp and yet not quite real at the same time.

As he drew nearer to the back of the waterfall, Hansel shielded his eyes with one hand from the misting spray and covered his left ear with the other. He pressed his right ear into his shoulder to stave off the loud sound of rushing water as best he could. His back firmly against the cold, wet rock wall, Hansel finally managed to push himself off the thin rock shelf and onto a smaller rock shelf just below the cave. Lowering his hands, he could no longer hear the roar of the waterfall. The world seemed to melt away as he looked up into the small, pitch-black opening of the cave. The entrance was no more than five feet tall, but the cave's depths were impossible to tell from where he stood — it could go for miles, or it could be a shallow indentation in the rock wall.

Time seemed to slow down. The only sounds now were Hansel's shallow breathing and something else, something deep and heavy. It took him a moment to realize that what he was listening to was breathing, just not his own. As he gazed into the darkness of the cave entrance, as the rattling breaths of something heaved in and out, Hansel felt a sense of awe and wonder. Reaching up, into the cave, Hansel could feel the warm, welcoming air, warmer than he would have expected for something behind a cool, flowing waterfall.

A gunshot rang out, breaking the hypnotic spell of the breathing and returning Hansel to the moment. The sound of the waterfall almost drowned out the sound of shouting. Straining to hear against the endless rush of endless gallons of water, Hansel could hear Jim and Amos calling his name. Turning away from the cave, Hansel slipped and slid his way along the narrow lip and emerged from behind the falls to the angry faces of his fellow campers below.

"What the hell do you think you're doing up there?" Jim called out; his hands cupped around his mouth. Amos stood beside his father, the rifle cocked and in hand. Hansel put up a hand, signaling that he was on his way down. Slowly, he began his descent. The last, golden rays of afternoon sunlight were struggling to break through the canopy by the time he rejoined the party.

"Sorry," the boy mumbled his apology. The look Jim fixed him with was full of as much hatred and malice as anything Lance had ever said or done to him. In a way, Hansel almost felt like the troop leader would prefer if he had never come back.

"Sorry? Sorry?" Jim mocked. "Jesus, I thought you'd run off or gotten yourself killed. You can thank Amos for firing that shot to get your attention. At this point, I'd just as soon leave you in these woods, food for the bears." There it was the hammer falling swiftly upon the head of the nail. "At least a bear would know how to properly hunt," Jim spat out. "Now come on, grab your stuff; we're heading back to camp to make dinner, and you're scrubbing the dishes."

The rest of the hike back from the waterfall to camp, Hansel kept his eyes cast down, anything to keep himself from having to see the obscene and rude gestures being thrown his way by Lance, Gil, and Darrel. Hansel did not cry; he had wept all his tears.

Back at camp, the boys set about helping the adults prep the fire and the kills. The afternoon heat hung over the camp like a suffocating blanket as the four young men prepared the fire and fetched buckets of water from the river for boiling. Armed with hunting knives that were substantially larger than their pocket-knives, the boys cut into their kills, skinned them, and removed the meat. Soon, with the fire roaring and the water boiling, the bloody chunks of meat went into the pot along with various vegetables. Everyone's mouths began to water as soon as the scent of their efforts hit their noses.

While nightfall was still a way off, the long shadows of the oncoming summer evening stretched and spread out, reaching from tree to tree. As he sat on a log beside the fire, slowly stirring the stew, Hansel's mind kept wandering back to the cave behind the waterfall. He knew that there was nothing there, just a hollow spot in the rocks, and yet, his senses kept telling him otherwise. In the back of his thoughts, he kept a small piece of his fears in check, dreading the snipe hunt he was expected to go on later that night, but that seemed to pale in comparison to what he was still feeling from his time with the cave.

Suddenly, nothing else seemed to matter.

Hansel was broken out of his train of thought by Amos approaching and looking into the pot, his glasses fogging over from the rising steam. He held out a hand to Hansel, asking for the stirring spoon with his body language and not his voice. Hansel handed it over and sat back as the older boy slipped his glasses atop his head and glanced into the pot. He smelled the concoction, took a timid taste from the spoon, then walked away, leaving the long, wooden spoon slowly spinning in the broth. Amos walked into the tent he and his father had been sharing and popped back out a moment later, a metal triangle in hand. "Come and get it!" he shouted as he rang the triangle loudly.

A small flock of birds shot up from the bush they had been occupying at the edge of the camp at the sound of the ruckus. The other boys appeared from where they had been sitting together at the edge of the river. Hansel knew that they were no doubt plotting how best to get him on the snipe hunt. The boys torturing or harassing him, he knew, was as inevitable as the rising sun.

No one spoke a word to Hansel as they collected their spoons and bowls and gathered around the campfire. Jim used a large, dented ladle to fill each of their bowls, save for Hansel's. The troop leader would not even look his way. Hansel took the ladle and poured himself some broth. As per the troop tradition, Jim said a prayer on their behalf before allowing them to indulge in their simmering supper, and as usual, Hansel merely waited to eat, not participating in a practice that was not a part of his life.

Everyone ate in silence, letting the crackle of the campfire, the gurgling of the river, and the creaking of the trees speak for them. As the meal continued into the slowly encroaching darkness, the warm, light wind that had been sweeping through the valley slowly began to grow in intensity. It was obvious that there would be no ghost stories tonight. It was also painfully obvious to Hansel that he was the sole source of everyone else's anger and frustration — a young boy who had no interest in the ways of a man — this simply could not and should not be.

With most of his stew eaten, Hansel excused himself, washed his dishes in the river, dried them, and headed into his tent, all under the stern, angry gaze of the others.

The heat inside the tent was stale and oppressive, but Hansel did not want to be outside, not while the others clearly did not want him out there with them. Opening the back flap to the forest behind his tent, Hansel sat cross-legged on his sleeping bag. Removing the bottle of calamine lotion from his pack, he set about rubbing more of the light pink salve onto his red, itching legs. As he massaged and rubbed the lotion into his skin, he closed his eyes, leaned back against the tent's upwardly angled wall, and listened to the world.

Birds chirped to one another, the sound of leaves shaking and branches creaking with their hopping and flittering. Something crunched some leaves underfoot as it moved through the undergrowth. Even the sound of the river, bubbling and flowing, could be heard from where his tent sat. A cool breeze passed through the creaking boughs of the trees and into his tent. The breeze mingling with the scent of the lotion began to lull Hansel to sleep, his head filling with the golden beams of sunlight lancing through green leaves.

Hansel did not notice when the sounds of nature had vanished, but he woke with a start upon hearing the snap of a twig. Sitting up, he did not hear the river or the breeze or even the cacophony of the birds overhead. Instead, he heard nothing, save for the same, ragged breathing sound he had heard deeper in the woods at the waterfall cave. Another twig snapped and Hansel found his eyes drawn to a face peeking out from behind the trees. The deer was tall, taller than Hansel would have expected. The antlers on its head were a mighty display. The animal turned and gazed at Hansel, and Hansel gazed back. For a long time, neither blinked nor moved, locked in their gaze.

After several long minutes, the deer turned and fled into the forest, leaving behind the cries and chirps of the birds, the rushing of the river, and the creaking of the boughs in its wake. Hansel was once again all alone with his itchy legs and the forest before him. The sun was nearly behind the mountains now and darkness was slowly creeping across the land. As he checked himself for ticks and other burrowing bugs that might have hitched a ride during the day's hike, the boy failed to notice that someone had slipped into his tent.

As he turned on the spot, checking his underarms, Hansel's voice caught in his throat upon seeing Lance looming before him. The look on the boy's face said it all. "Nice dancing, *fagtard*," Lance sneered. Hansel did not answer as he had no response. "You better get ready for the snipe hunt, you little bitch. I'm gonna give you ten minutes and then you better be prepared. Meet us outside when you're done." Lance stormed out, leaving Hansel dazed from the encounter.

Not wanting to upset the boys any more than he already had, he quickly changed his outfit, swapping his shorts for long pants and tossing a light hoodie over his t-shirt. He strapped on his utility belt with its flashlight and pocket-knife and compass just before slipping out of his tent and into the cool, night air. The campfire was still crackling, the flames licking greedily at the logs, but no one else was around. From what he could tell, Amos and Jim were in their own tent, talking in hushed tones, but Lance, Darrel, and Gil were nowhere to be found.

A twig snapped behind Hansel, and he spun like a top to find the three boys emerging from the woods behind the row of tents. All three wore black, their faces smudged in camouflage makeup. On Lance's shoulder, like a tower, stood the end of the rifle. Hansel swallowed upon seeing the gun. His heart began to beat faster and sweat began to stream down his face and back. "Alright, Jew-Fag," Lance said, slipping the rifle form his shoulder and holding it in front of him like a soldier ready to present arms. "The hunt begins."

Hansel slowly reached for the gun only to have Darrel and Gil slap his hand away at almost the same time. "This isn't for you, Jew-Toad, this is for us. You've got to hunt the snipe with your knife and two hands. I don't have much faith in a pussy like you," Lance added, pulling the rifle back and up against Hansel's chest. Lance cocked the rifle, the sound of it sending chills down Hansel's spine. Something told him that he wasn't going to be looking for a snipe so much as he was about to become the snipe.

The air grew warm as the sweat continued to drip from Hansel's every pore. "You better run, little faggot," Gil hissed.

"Run like your life depends on it," Darrel added.

As always, Hansel did not know what to say or do. His mind told him to run, it was screaming the command like an air-raid siren, but his body refused to move — his legs were locked, his breathing shallow. Lance leveled the rifle at Hansel's chest, his finger hovering over the trigger. Tears began to stream down Hansel's cheeks, commingling with the salty sweat. "Time to run, snipe..." Lance growled in a low, menacing voice. In that moment, staring down the barrel of a gun and looking into the eyes of Lance, eyes glazed over and filled with unbridled rage, Hansel began to wet himself. A moment later and the end of the barrel was pressed against his forehead. "Run, Jew-Toad," Lance whispered with a sick smile.

As the last of Hansel's bladder drained, it felt as though a great weight had been lifted from him and replaced with wings. Hansel turned from the gun and ran. He ran as fast and as hard as he could, straight past his tent and straight into the darkening woods. He could hear his heartbeat drumming constantly in his ears — the thumping was loud enough to cover up the sounds of him crashing through the underbrush. Tears streamed down his face and sweat ran down his back.

The woods closed in on him, their darkness all enveloping, all encompassing. With his chest pounding and his breathing deep, Hansel could not tell if the boys were following him. Blindly he ran until his foot caught on something, most likely an exposed root, and the boy found the ground rising up to meet him, face to face. He hit the dirt hard. He could feel the air leave his lungs in a great rush. Pushing himself up, off the ground, he was relieved to find that nothing hurt too badly, save for his burning chest. Gasping for breath, he slid his way over to the tree whose roots had tripped him up and pressed his back to the thick trunk as quickly as he could.

The adrenaline was flowing freely now, and combined with the lack of air, his head was swimming. Soon enough, Hansel's gulps for air turned to regular breathing and the pain in his chest slowly began to subside. He sat alone in the darkness with nothing but the creaking of the boughs all around him and the warbling of night-birds. The tears still flowed, and while he wanted more than anything to sob long and loudly, he knew that the slightest sound would give away his location. The minutes dragged on, and slowly, Hansel began to feel better. This was just another one of the boy's cruel pranks. No doubt they were all sitting around the campfire, laughing about how stupid he was — calling him any number of degrading names.

As he was preparing to stand, he heard the snap of a twig somewhere behind him. Hansel threw his hands to his mouth and nose, stifling any sounds of surprise he was worried he might make, and strained to listen. Maybe, he hoped and prayed, it was a skunk or deer or mouse moving about. Another twig snapped. Hansel held his still-struggling breath. Sweat poured, practically cascading down his forehead.

"He's got to be somewhere around here," he heard Darrel gripe. "I mean, he's a tiny little pussy. How much stamina can someone like him have anyway?"

"Hopefully, if we don't get him, a bear will," Gil snarled.

"I don't care what ends up killing that little Jew-Toad fag; as long as it's meant to look accidental, I think we'll be okay," Lance said.

"Won't your dad and Amos wonder about the gun?" Gil asked.

"Like my dad wouldn't be doing this too if he could. You know he'll back us. I mean, he hates Jews and faggots as much as us. Did I ever show you his collection of memorabilia my grandpa snuck out of Austria?"

Hansel did not hear the rest of the conversation. The boys were drawing closer to where he was hiding. He knew that he had to move, and he had to do it quietly. Removing his hand from his mouth and nose, he glanced around the trunk where he could see three flashlight beams playing over the undergrowth and occasionally sweeping up into the trees. The trio seemed far away enough for him to slip out, but still, they had a rifle and the range that came with such a killing device.

Giving himself a moment to breathe, Hansel slowly began to move away from the tree. With the other three boys hunting for him in the opposite direction, Hansel slipped off his flashlight from the utility belt. He placed the emitter next to his eye and activated the device. His world lit up, a perfectly round tunnel of light revealing the dark green of shrubs and the thick gray and browns of tree trunks. Moving toward the light he was casting; Hansel slowly took his first steps. As he moved, he cautiously, little by little, began to pick up momentum, looking for any opportunity to bound over roots and branches as he gained speed and distance.

He was well away from his hiding place when he realized the mistake he'd made. A commotion behind him, far behind him, finally reached his ears. "I can see the fucker's flashlight!" Lance cried out. A heartbeat later and there was the sound of the rifle going off, the crack echoing all through the forest. Something hit a tree near him as he ran — he knew what that something was and who it was meant for.

Turning off the flashlight, Hansel decided to just run. Darkness be damned, he needed to get away. Maybe, he thought, he would encounter a Park Ranger station sooner rather than later. He hoped and prayed that someone was hearing the gunshots. As he ran, Hansel noticed that the foliage had begun to thin out a little and the moonlight above was now guiding him through the forest. Eventually, the trees thinned out enough that he realized where he was. Before him, bubbling and babbling, was the stream that came from the waterfall and fed into the main river. Hansel knew that if he followed the stream to his right, it would take him to the river and back to camp — a no-go at this point. To his left was the waterfall and the cave. An uneasy feeling swept over him as he thought about that cave. Oddly enough, it was the same unease he'd felt upon seeing the deer earlier. And yet, the uneasy feeling of the cave was far more comforting in that moment than his thoughts of either returning to camp, knowing what Lance had said about his dad and older brother, or being caught by the boys themselves.

His mind made up; Hansel began his trek. Moving upstream was far more difficult than it had been heading away from the falls earlier in the afternoon; the darkness and the fact that he was literally being hunted did not make the trip any easier. As the boy made his way over the rough, uneven terrain, he thought about everything he had experienced at the hands of Lance, the other boys, and even Lance and Amos's father. Hansel had always been a quiet soul, never one to rock the boat. So often, adults would complement his behavior and say that he was a well-behaved young man. Never in his life, until joining the troop, had he ever heard the words that spewed out of Lance's mouth. He knew that there was hatred in the world — such things had nearly destroyed his family back in Europe not so long ago — but to see it and feel it firsthand was more disconcerting than he could have possibly imagined it to be.

Hansel hoped and prayed that Lance was simply playing a dangerous game with him, but something deep down told him that such thoughts were folly; the boy and his friends were out for blood and had been for some time now. As painful as it was to admit, he knew that they were coming to collect. It wasn't a dream or a nightmare, but still, Hansel dearly hoped that he would wake up at some point to find himself asleep in his tent, atop his ruined sleeping bag or, better yet, back home in his own bed in his own room. The constant itching of his red and raw legs was a steady, unflinching reminder that he was awake and living through something horrifyingly real.

Hansel was grateful as he made his way that the trees were thin enough on either side of the stream to allow him to see by the moon's soft, misty glow. The air grew thick with moisture despite the summer season. As he drew closer to the falls, Hansel could see his breath misting before his eyes. The sounds of the night, hoots, squeaks, and scurrying made him feel safe. Perhaps, he reasoned, those same sounds hid him from the others.

Finally, at long last, the scent of trees and dirt slowly transitioned into the thick odors of moss and overgrowth. The trees began to thicken both around the boy and above his head, hiding the moon once more and throwing his world back into darkness. By now, he could hear the falls up ahead. Cupping his hand to his ear, Hansel angled away from his destination and listened for any sign of Lance and company. He stood still for a long time, how long, he did not take any note, but it was a long time indeed. Nothing. Unless Lance was ready to pounce on him from a hiding spot in the shadows, Hansel decided that he was safe for the moment.

Producing his flashlight, he once again placed it against his temple next to his eyes and switched it on, using the trick once more to see in the dark without throwing off his vision. With each step forward, the ground grew wetter and rockier, and the sounds of the cascading waters ahead grew louder and louder still. Following the porthole of light he cast, Hansel located the wide stream and followed it — soon he found himself at the edge of the pool the other boys had taken a dip in while he had explored behind the falls earlier that day. Hansel cast his light into the churning waters below and watched as small creatures scattered and rebounded under the water's surface, kicked up by the waterfall.

Slowly, putting one foot in front of the other, Hansel made his way up the side of the falls, following the same narrow, slippery path he had found that afternoon. Sidling along the rock wall, he managed to make his way, inch by inch. He had reached the halfway point when he heard a noise, louder than the waterfall — it was the echoing crack of the rifle. Hansel could feel his pulse pounding, his heartbeat ringing in his ears like the drums of war. A moment later he spotted the dancing beam of an approaching flashlight. At first, Hansel thought that he had been spotted, but once he realized that the beam was simply following the path he had taken, he knew that he was still in the clear. Still, they were drawing closer, and he had a ways to go to get to the back side of the falls.

Shutting off his flashlight and shuffling with less care than before, Hansel pushed his small body, using every ounce of borrowed strength the still flowing adrenaline was giving him. His hands groped the rock wall behind him blindly while he alternated from watching the approaching flashlights to spotting how far from the top of the rock shelf he was. Another echoing gunshot and Hansel froze for a moment.

"You fucking moron," he heard Lance yell over the rush of water. "Give me back the gun. That's the second owl you've shot."

"I thought it was him," he heard Gil scream.

"Well, it's the last time," Lance yelled back. There was the sound of a scuffle and then flesh slapping flesh and all went quiet.

"Sorry, Lance," Gil replied.

Hansel could not see the boys, but they were close enough to be heard clearly over the sound of the falls. His heart racing and his head throbbing, Hansel pushed himself harder and faster. For a moment there, his left foot slipped out from underneath him, and he was convinced that he would fall forward onto the rocks below at any moment. The moment never came. He regained his balance and managed to push himself behind the waterfall faster than he could have imagined possible. A moment later, he could see the distorted forms of his pursuers from behind the shimmering curtain of the waters. Hansel pressed himself against the rock wall next to the cave and waited with bated breath.

In that moment, all sounds in his world vanished — the waterfall, the cries of the boys, everything. The only sound that came through the auditory void was that of the heavy raspy breathing he had heard earlier, the same breathing that had drawn him to the cave behind the falls in the first place. Pulling himself up, Hansel slipped into the small cave entrance and immediately sat against the rounded, wet walls of what seemed to be a tunnel.

Sapped of his strength by the effort of fleeing and drained of all adrenalin; Hansel soon began to doze.

He did not sleep long, for something awoke the boy — a scratching. Hansel snapped awake, his mind reeling from the last bits of adrenaline that still laced his blood. For a brief moment, the boy thought that his situation was nothing more than a dream, but in a heartbeat, he knew that it was simply his reality. Peering out of the rounded cave entrance, he spotted a shadow dancing off the back side of the waterfall. He held his breath. The shadow jumped. A moment later, the form of a large, black crow appeared, fluttering into view and perching on the edge of the cave's entrance. The bird scratched at the stone ground before cocking its head and cawing loudly. The sound echoed and rebounded throughout the cave. Hansel had no idea how far back the tunnel went, but the sound seemed to finally die away after a few moments.

Slowly pulling out his flashlight, Hansel switched it on and aimed the beam with a shaking hand in the direction of the large bird. The creature's big, black eyes regarded Hansel curiously. At first, he wondered if he was attributing such actions to the animal from a place of desire, but it soon became very apparent that the bird was genuinely looking him over. The bird cawed once more before hopping into the cave and toward Hansel. Hansel had never been afraid of birds, not even the time as a little child when a wild goose had chased him, honking around a park — the incident had scared him at the time, but it had not scarred him. The crow hopped closer, pushing its feathers out in an attempt to look larger. It opened its wings. Hansel got the impression that it was trying to force him farther back into the cave.

As he slid back, away from the crow and the cave entrance, he could see through the shimmering waterfall that the moonlight was obscured — had clouds rolled in, he wondered? A long, low roll of thunder that threatened to crack the very foundations of the earth he was hiding in answered Hansel's query. The bird, undeterred, continued to caw and hop, drawing closer to him, pushing him out of the entrance and into the cave proper. Standing up, Hansel ran his beam around the chamber — the ceiling was at least ten feet above him, and resplendent in stalactites. This far from the entrance, with the rushing of the waterfall softly muted, the constant sound of dripping water from above called out. The floor, he noticed, was relatively even and littered with pools of water and the occasional stalagmite.

The crow, seemingly satisfied that the boy was fully in the small cave, hopped up onto a nearby stalagmite and found perch upon its flattened tip. Hansel looked closely and noticed in his flashlight beam that the perch was well worn, as if the bird used it regularly. The rest of the chamber was not all that large, maybe a couple of dozen feet all around with no other way in or out. As he played the beam of light over his surroundings, he passed by a low shadow, which caused the crow behind him to explode into a fit of cawing and jumping up and down on the perch. As Hansel brought his beam back to the spot with the shadow, he found that it was no longer there. It took him a moment to realize that the bird had grown silent, and above the sound of the drip, drip, dripping, there was a heavy, raspy breathing behind him.

Slowly turning around, Hansel feared the worst. He knew it would not be Lance and his gang — they would have said something nasty upon finding him. Instead, he hoped and prayed that he had not been led into the den of a cougar or a bear or something worse. Hansel's flashlight swept pass the bird's now empty perch. As he came around to where the cave entrance had been, he found himself face to face with a yellowed skull. The breathing came from behind it. Hansel cautiously stepped backwards, away from the skull that seemed to be floating in the darkness before him. The skull rose as he backed away. His attention turned to what lay before him, Hansel tripped on a small depression in the ground and landed on his back, looking up at a truly horrifying sight.

The yellow, sun-bleached skull was that of a bear. A pair of stag horns, long, sharp, and gnarled, seemed to be growing out the top of the jawless skull. The skull itself appeared to be the head of a hulking mound of animal hides, bound and draped around a large, unseen form underneath. Vines and rotted pieces of rope held the hides in place. Two large hands made with fingers of long, sharpened rib bones clicked on the cave floor. The feet were small and cloven and shuffled as the beast rose to its full height before the small, scared boy.

The raspy breathing grew deeper. Hansel's breathing grew quicker. He felt about to faint until he heard the voice that echoed all around him. It came from everywhere and no single place. It was low, cracked, and deep, as though it had not spoken in eons. Hansel imagined a mouth full of dirt opening and speaking through the tumbling detritus.

The creature smelled of summer heat and winter snow, it smelled of spring rains and fall winds — the scent of death and decay — moss and fungus and wood rot and sap mingled with the scent of birth and growth — pollen and wildflowers and clear breezes and crisp waters. The odors conjured up images of lichen and beetles and fish and hawks and fires and time. It was a smell of ages. It was a smell of time. It smelled as deep and dank as the wet earth and as dry and arid as the highest peaks. It was the smell of the woods. It was the smell of nature itself.

"Don't be afraid, little one," the beast croaked. Hansel gazed at the hulking creature with no eyes and a body made entirely of the woods all around them. "I have been watching you, boy," the voice said.

Hansel was amazed that he could find his voice under such circumstances, but he also found his curiosity slowly winning out over his fears. "You've been watching me?" he managed to stammer. He watched as the crow reappeared upon one of the creature's antlers, cocked its head, and gazed at him with a beady, black eye. Hansel could feel his fear of this thing before him leaving like a breath on the wind. He did not know why something that looked so nightmarish, something cobbled together with the death and decay of the forest, gave him a sense of calm and ease.

"My helpers have been keeping an eye on you and the others of your pack," the creature rumbled. Hansel thought back to the hawk on the hike, the birds shot down in the field as well as the rabbits, and the deer and the crow watching him in his tent. Hansel nodded at this. With his hands no longer shaking from shock and fear, he laid the flashlight down, aiming the beam up at the low cave ceiling, and slowly sat up. In the half-light, he watched the creature shuffle about and then sit across from him, its eyeless bear-skull head regarding him like the crow had.

"Who or what are you?" Hansel asked. "Are you the snipe?" Hansel immediately regretted asking such a ridiculous question, one he knew to be untrue, but still, here was something unreal and supernatural sitting right before him, speaking with him without *talking to him.*

"I have had many names," it said in a low voice. "Sprite, Lashen, Sprigan, Shepard of the Wood, Nymph, Watcher, and from time to time, Snipe." The creature clicked its rib-claws on the ground, making a sound like a swarm of beetles. "I am as old as these woods and mountains and older still. I was here long before man arrived, and I suppose I will be here long after. I came from the old world on ships made of timber and was here to greet the settlers when they faced the dark and unknowing forests primeval."

"Why am I here?" Hansel asked.

"A good question," the Snipe said with a rumbling sigh. "You are not like the others of your ilk — those three boys and the two men, they came here to my realm to cause harm. They have killed my creatures in cold blood and desecrated my soil. They did all this with no love for the land. You, boy, did not kill, and if you had, it would have been from a place of survival. You are gentle and curious. They all seek to harm you for these things, and this I cannot abide!" The Snipe's voice boomed and echoed all around. "I led you here with my guides so that I may protect you from those who would harm us both."

"Thank you," Hansel said.

"And thank you," the Snipe replied.

"What am I going to do?"

"You are going to go back to camp. You are going to take me with you."

"You know where the camp is, and you know what Lance and the others will do to me if I go back—"

"Indeed," the Snipe replied, still clawing at the hard ground. To Hansel, it seemed like the Snipe was sharpening its claw-like bone fingers on the solid, stone floor. "I cannot enter the realm of man unless invited. If you were to take me along, willingly, I would gladly help you in stopping the boys and men from further harming you or me."

Hansel thought on it a moment. Without this thing, he had no real plan of escaping or even surviving his situation. His notion to find some rangers seemed lofty at best. He was without food or proper clothing; what else could he possibly do? The answer seemed simple, and there it was, right before him, dragging its claws across the ground, watching him while the crow hopped about from antler to antler.

"Okay. I'll lead the way then," Hansel said. The Snipe bowed its head in thanks. Standing up, he snatched his flashlight from the floor, walked past the Snipe, and headed for the cave entrance. Behind him, he could hear the creature stand and begin to follow, the long rib-fingers dragging on the ground as it allowed the boy to lead the way.

Hansel crawled out of the cave, slipped down onto the rock shelf behind the waterfall, and slowly made his way back out and down to the pool at the base of the falls. While it was not yet raining, the scent of rain was on the air. Overhead, the sky lit up with flashes of lightning followed by the low, angry rumbling of thunder. As Hansel reached the bottom, he turned to see the Snipe burst through the falls from behind and land in the pond amidst the strobing of lightning and the deafening roll of thunder. Slowly, the Snipe rose from the pool, water dripping from it in rivers of silver against a black, furry backdrop.

"Lead the way," the Snipe urged, the voice booming like the thunder high above. Hansel nodded and then set off down the path. He watched in the beam of his flashlight as the crow flew on ahead, cawing madly as it soared high above the treetops.

The night air was warm and full of the electricity of promise. While Hansel did not look over his shoulder as he hiked back down the wide stream, he could hear the Snipe walking behind him. Flashes of lightning threw the world into a bright, oversaturated light-scape only to return to a darkness that seemed more like a void than a world without sunlight. Hansel's flashlight led the way through the bursts of electricity above him and through the darkness that threatened to engulf the world.

While he could smell the coming rain in the air and taste it on his lips, Hansel was thankful that the storm had not yet broken over him. After some time, breathing heavily from the effort of hiking so carefully in the dark, Hansel could see where the stream that flowed from the falls met the river the camp sat beside.

The boy pressed on.

As he neared the river's edge, he felt the first warm drops of summer rain. Thick and heavy with moisture, the drops fell in a blitz slowly at first, then gaining in speed and intensity. Within seconds, he found himself soaked through. Hansel did not care, though; he was close to camp, and the sense of comfort he had felt in the cave when conversing with the Snipe remained. At last, he reached the edge of the campsite. The tents sat dark and lonely. The campfire snuffed, smoking in the downpour. Thunder rolled. Hansel turned around to find that he was alone, and the Snipe was gone.

Had the Snipe been completely in his head, he began to wonder as he gazed into the sheets of rain falling behind him and seeing only the river and the forest in the darkness and flashes of lightening.

"And where the fuck have you been, you piece of shit?" Hansel heard a voice call out over the rain, snapping him out of his thoughts. Turning back around, Hansel found himself once again staring straight down the barrel of the hunting rifle. This time, however, it was being held by Lance's father, Jim. Hansel looked past the scouting Pack Leader and spotted Lance, Gil, Darrel, and Amos, all standing behind the adult, anger flaring in their faces and smoldering behind their eyes. Even with their rain slicks on and hoods over their heads, Hansel could feel and see the gazes they gave him. Amos held a lantern aloft, illuminating the scene.

"Lance and the others tried to kill me," Hansel stammered over the downpour.

"Lance and the others tried to kill me," Jim mocked. "A likely story, you little shit-bag."

"But it's true," Hansel said defiantly, feeling the anger finally beginning to swell within him. Hansel had always been so proud to not have a temper or to get angry unless it was warranted — this situation felt wrong, and he felt wronged.

"He's a lying fucking Jew-Toad faggot," Lance shot back.

"Yeah," Gil and Darrel said in unison.

Jim lowered his rifle and stepped up to Hansel, grabbed him by the collar, and began to squeeze, his teeth clenching and the veins on his neck popping. "I don't appreciate little lying Jew scumbags like you, trying to make good, honest, Christian boys look bad. I knew it was a fucking mistake to let a lying little punk like you into the Pack." Hansel tried to swallow but found his throat dry — water all around and he was in need of it just to say something.

"What are we going to do with this Jew-Traitor?" Amos asked, stepping up with the lantern.

"Well, we'll make it look like an accident, won't we, son?" Jim hissed. Amos nodded.

"That's what Lance tried to do," Hansel managed to choke out.

"Well, you circumcised degenerate, that's one thing you got right." Jim sneered. "He tried. He tried and he failed. Lance, get over here."

Lance stepped through the rain. Jim held out his arm with the rifle. Lance took the weapon, cocked it, and aimed it at Hansel all in one quick, smooth, disturbing motion. Hansel struggled against the adult's grip, but it was no use; he was too weak and the older man was too strong. Lance brought the gun level to Hansel's head and pressed the barrel to his temple. The metal felt cold and lifeless against his wet, dripping skin. Hansel swallowed, fighting the dryness of his throat, his eyes glazed in terror. Lance's face broke into a smile, the same sickly smile he always wore when torturing Hansel, but this time there was something else to it, a disturbing sense of victory. Hansel shut his eyes tight, feeling his warm tears mingling with the warm summer rain. The boy sniffled and then heard the crack — not of the gun but of wood.

Hansel's eyes flew open in time to see the look on Amos's face. Everyone turned to the young man and watched as his features grew slack and his arms fell to his sides. The lantern fell to the ground and rolled to a stop nearby. In the pale glow of the artificial light, Hansel could see that something was sticking out of the man's chest. It was a branch, pointed at one end and dripping with copious amounts of blood. Everyone watched in silence as the branch slowly slid back and out of Amos's chest with a sickening squelch and snapping. As the branch vanished through the hole in the young man's chest, his body crumbled to the ground, oozing out sticky, dark red.

Where Amos had stood but a moment before now stood the Snipe, its rib-bone fingers shoved into the ground and a series of gnarled, pointy roots slithering back into the earth in front of it. Without hesitation, Lance moved his rifle from Hansel's head and fired at the beast. The bullets left puffs of dust in their wake as they seemed to pass right through the matted fur hide of the creature's body. The bear skull turned its eyeless sockets to Lance. In one quick, smooth motion, it pulled its fingers from the ground and rammed them into Lance's face, sending blood and teeth in all directions. Lance's jaw hung by the thinnest strands of sinew while all the Snipe's fingers had been rammed into the boy's mouth and out the back of his head. The body twitched as it hung there in the air on the end of the claws. As the rifle fell to the soaked ground with a splash and as Lance's body slid slowly off the claws and onto the ground next to his brother's body, Jim let out a terrible cry, which the Snipe answered back in kind in its own low and horrifying, primal scream.

Gil and Darrel, blood splatters running in rivulets with the falling rain, began to scream — seemingly frozen to the spot. Jim, still holding on to Hansel's collar, slightly loosened his grip but not entirely. The Snipe, standing tall, gazed down at Jim, the empty sockets of its bear skull face boring into the man below him, still grasping the struggling child with a fury.

Hansel watched as Gil and Darrel, finally seeming to find themselves able to move once more, turned and headed straight for the woods behind the camp. As the two boys reached the tree line, the undergrowth burst open like a piñata as hundreds of cawing, flapping crows emerged and encircled the pair. Their screams were quickly drowned out by the cacophony of the angry, black birds. Through the churning mass of feathers and beaks, Hansel could see the other two boys, countless slashes across their faces and bodies, clothes shredding as the birds pecked and clawed at them. The cyclone of avian fury abated, and the birds flew off, leaving Gil and Darrel nothing more than a bloody, pulpy mess. Their bodies lay atop one another, blood oozing from gashes that had started small but had been made larger and larger as the birds continued their attack.

Hansel could see where the very flesh had been rent from their bones, leaving red-stained patches of their exposed inner structures. A moment later and the crow from the cave reappeared and found a perch atop Darrel's head. Without hesitation, the bird began to peck and pick at one of the boy's eyes, open and glazed over, frozen in unending terror. Within a moment's time, the crow had managed to pick the eye clean out of the socket and swallow the round mass whole.

Jim was breathing heavily, his face a mixture of rage and confusion and angst, while all around him the ground was littered with the bloody remains of those he had led out into this wilderness. His two sons, their bodies torn and broken like toys, and the other two boys in his charge, both dead — Hansel could feel the man's rage like a heat, radiating through the rain. Slowly, the Pack Leader's grip slipped, and Hansel found himself falling to the muddy earth. Lying at the feet of the Pack Leader, he dared not move. He knew that he was in no danger, but he did not want to draw the attention of the adult who had, until a few moments ago, sought to have him killed simply for who he was.

"What...what the fuck are you?" Jim managed to croak. His face looked strained as he fought to keep himself from crying. Hansel knew the man well enough based on his little "man up" speech that he dared not show any signs of what he considered weakness. Even with so much familial death and carnage all around, he fought his very nature to the bitter end.

"I am," the Snipe snarled, "nature at her most brutal. You took from me without honor, and you sought to kill without reason. For these transgressions, there is a price you must pay."

At these words, the Pack Leader spat, shooting a wad of spit at the Snipe. Hansel watched in what seemed like slow motion as the tumbling wad of bubbly, stringy liquid passed through and between the raindrops only to splatter harmlessly against the Snipe's skull. The spittle slowly crept down from the right eye socket like a thick teardrop. The Snipe remained unmoving. Jim took that moment to bend over and snatch up the rifle where it lay on the ground beside the body of his son. Before he could stand, roots, sharp and barbed, erupted from the muddy ground with a sickening rumble. The roots ensnared the man's body, shooting through muscle and bone with reckless abandon. As Jim's body rose from the ground, lifted as the spiked roots knotted and wound around one another and his twitching form, the Snipe reached out and, with a quick motion, took both hands to the man's stomach and sliced him in two. Dark red blood and intestines spilled out upon the ground, slithering from Jim's upper torso and staining all they touched.

The Snipe stood back, its claws bloody and dripping both rain and red. Slowly, the roots slithered back into the ground from where they had emerged, leaving no trace of their existence in the wet, muddy mess. Hansel watched in silence as the Snipe raised its bloody bone fingers to the air. The lightning flashed and a bolt struck Jim's remains. Another bolt and another and another — soon all five bodies were no more than burning, smoldering lumps upon the ground, steaming as the rain struck them.

The Snipe turned and faced Hansel. The crow, cawing, fluttered and took perch upon the antlers.

"It is time for you to go."

"How will I get back?" Hansel asked.

"My friend will guide you," the Snipe said, the voice calm and booming. Reaching up with one finger, the crow hopped onto the Snipe's claw. Lowering the bird to Hansel's eye-level, the Snipe spoke once more, "Follow this one; he will take you back to the world of men."

"Did you have to do this to them?" Hansel asked more out of curiosity than of surprise or anger. He found that he was neither shocked nor saddened.

"It is the price men must pay — all men who dare to disturb my realm. Judgement has been passed, and these five were found wanting."

"But you didn't have to help me," Hansel said.

"Oh, but I did, child, I did. For you see, I can read men like books. I can see their destinies and desires. You are pure and innocent; you ask for nothing and expect nothing in return. You harm no one, but so many harm you. This is what I must suffer. With you, I leave a message for the world of men," the Snipe spoke deeply and sincerely. "Tell others that the woods are sacred and not to be feared. Instead, they are to be respected and loved, and in turn I will offer love and respect to all who come here."

Hansel nodded in understanding.

"Thank you," he said.

The Snipe nodded back. The crow flew from its finger and landed on Hansel's shoulder.

"Go now," the Snipe commanded. The crow took off and flew to a nearby branch, cawing and calling to Hansel. Dutifully, Hansel followed. The boy and bird were a good few miles from the campgrounds, the beam of his flashlight illuminating the path as he walked through the trees and undergrowth following the river. Suddenly, the night sky lit up and a massive bolt of lightning struck where the camp had been. A few moments later, as the thunder rolled overhead, Hansel could see the smoke slowly rising from the spot by the river.

The forest had begun the cleansing process.

As he marched on through the thinning rain, his eyes on the bird guiding him and the path below him, Hansel felt as though he was coming out of a very peculiar dream. In a day's time, with a small forest fire caused by the sudden storm, now dissipating in the mountains, Hansel was found by rescuers. Upon seeing his bloodied and torn clothing, they asked him what had happened, but the boy remained mute.

Hansel did not speak after that. He spent several days in a hospital in the nearest city to where he had been found by the rescuers. Eventually, it was discovered that a whole Pack of Wilderness Trekkers had vanished in the mountains and that the found child had belonged to that group. Reunited with his parents, Hansel seemed unable to recognize them. Once back home, the boy simply sat in his back yard, his hands deep in the grass and dirt, his gaze far off and distant.

Unable to get any information from the boy, the police and investigators eventually found the remains of the campsite and five charred bodies. They deduced that the fire had started at the camp, killing all but Hansel, before spreading and eventually coming under containment by local firefighters. Hansel, they figured, had been so traumatized by his experiences with the fire that he had been severely affected.

Months turned to years as the boy grew older, and still, he did not speak. Therapy sessions, doctors' visits, guidance from specialists — none of it mattered, and nothing seemed to get through to the young man. Not knowing what else to do with the boy, Hansel's parents decided that some sort of long-term care might be best for their ailing son.

* * *

It was a sunny day when the adult center packed up several of their residents and took them on a day trip to a local state park to walk some trails. When the van pulled up the dirt path and came to the visitor center parking lot, no one noticed that Hansel, a young man who always seemed to have a glazed, far-off look, was slowly gaining a sense of focus after so many years.

The van parked and the two care workers opened the side door, helping their charges out and into the noonday sunshine and heat. Slowly, as if coming out of a long slumber, Hansel stepped from the van, past the care workers, and across the parking lot. Everyone followed at a distance, stopping at the edge of the asphalt while Hansel approached the nearest tree, a tall sequoia with a thick, brown trunk, wrapped his arms around the tree, closed his eyes tight, and hugged it.

"Hansel?" one of the care workers said. "Do you want to come into the visitor center with us?" Admittedly, the young woman had no idea what to do in this moment. As far as she or anyone else at the care center knew, Hansel was pretty much cut off from the rest of the world — what she was witnessing now was something entirely new.

"I will speak for you. I will let them know what must be known," he whispered to the tree. "The time has come."

Everyone watched as the young man let go of the tree, turned around, and then squatted amongst the roots. Dipping his hand into the dirt, nothing happened for the longest time. Looking up at the care workers and his fellow patients, Hansel drank in their looks of awe and shock as small roots began to rise from the earth where his fingers had been plunged into the brown soil.

Slowly, the small roots grew and twisted into one another, and slower still, Hansel came out of the dream. "The time has come…" he said in a steady voice as he looked from those he had arrived with and shifted his gaze to the woods and mountains beyond.

Overhead a large, oily black crow circled the lot, cawing its approval. The pleasant smile on Hansel's face grew as his lungs filled with the mountain air and the scent of growth all around.

Danse Macabre

Clouds passed before the crescent moon, painting the hanging sickle in the sky a glowing jack-o'-lantern grin. It was dark, and the hour was growing late.

The night was just beginning.

A wind, dry and hollow, leapt through the bare branches of the trees and skirted playfully along empty, littered streets. Orange and black candy wrappers bounded down the abandoned streets like tiny tumbleweeds, bouncing through the gutters and mingling with the dead, cracked leaves. Front porches, dark and uninviting, held court, a panel of jack-o'-lanterns, their faces glowing dimly as they gazed out upon one another from across the street, wordlessly judging each other's morbid grins. Like an army of golems brought to life, the candles each carved pumpkin contained within gave them a life — brief but beautiful and terrifying all at once.

Front lawns, festooned with cardboard headstones and strung up webs now collected the flotsam and jetsam of the night as the wind blew tattered bits of costumes and ruined masks — driftwood on a sea of gold, orange, and red leaves — into their waiting embrace. An owl swooped low over the street and took up a perch in an ancient oak at the end of a row of houses. No lights could be seen from behind drawn curtains, no hint of anyone left alive or awake to witness the festivities of the Witching Hour.

The owl, her great horned head and round, glowing eyes, looked this way and that way from below and above and behind. She puffed out her chest, hooted long and low, and then began to preen herself — there was company due to arrive any moment now, and she wanted to look her best.

Farther down the street, a small black cat stepped out of the shadows, her fur as dark as pitch, her eyes two saucers bobbing and weaving as she darted through the shadows and toward the old oak tree at the end of the street. Stopping at the foot of the tree, the panther-like mouser looked up at a gnarled and dark knot in the tree's trunk. She gave a low hiss and a mew before going about the task of cleaning herself. The cat, too, wished to look presentable for the guests now beginning to gather from places near and far. The owl's call had summoned them, giving them the assurance that the night was theirs. Spreading her back paw wide, she licked between her toes and claws, passing the time until the moment arrived.

A sound carried on the wind, distant and haunting, then slowly growing in pitch as it carried onward to the tree at the end of the street. From down the avenue came a small man, a man made of straw and burlap and thread. His eyes were crosses of black yarn looped through large, yellow buttons, and his mouth was a zigzag of brown twine, and his head leaned ever so slightly against the fiddle that rested upon his sagging shoulder. The body bounded and hobbled down the street as a body with no bones is want to do. As it bounced, it continued to play its tune — the Danse Macabre had begun.

From her perch in the oak's branches and from her place at its roots, the owl and cat watched as something dark slithered out of the knot in the wood. The dark, formless mist poured out like a serpent, splitting as it hit the base of the tree, following along the roots and out into the night. The scarecrow played his tune, his head and body lolling from side to side as the black mist reached out like a dark hand, its fingers reaching across every lawn and up to every stoop.

The wind vanished, and yet the tattered costumes and torn masks began to stir as though the breeze was still present. Wide eyed, the cat and owl watched as one by one, the costumes touched by the black mist sprang to life — costumes devoid of children but filled with a gleeful, child-like soul. The jack-o'-lanterns on the porches glowed brighter and more intensely than their small candles were ever meant to, casting grinning shadows across the lawns.

From down the street, a rattling sound could be heard. The scarecrow stopped and stood at a wobbly attention, his fiddle at his side as the Danse Macabre continued. The costumes swooped down from the lawns and sidewalks, bowing to one another before taking their place, giggling with ghoulish glee as they lined the street. The owl, her preening now complete, and the black cat, her fur soft, velvety, and clean, watched with their eyes wide in anticipation. Around the corner, where the street curved away, a cloud of red and gold and orange leaves burst forth accompanied by shambling, rattling skeletons, their bleached bones picked clean long ago, their faces eyeless and their mouths perpetually grinning. They shambled right down the middle of the road, dozens of them, reaching up and tipping unseen hats to all those giggling costumes they passed — gleaming white bones seeming to sparkle in the orange moonlight.

At the oak tree, the skeletons stopped in two long rows, several dozen each. They bowed to the cat and to the owl and to the scarecrow, who bowed low to them in return, his fiddle in one arm and his hat in the other. Slowly, like a zipper, the skeletons parted, and from down the street came a figure robed in black, its face unseen. Around its waist it wore a belt of black rope to keep its midnight-black robes closed. An hourglass, its sands perpetually falling from top to bottom and then from bottom to top hung from the rope belt. A skeletal hand peeked out from one of the sleeves and held fast to a large scythe, its infinitely sharp blade gleaming in the half-light of the grinning moon. The hooded figure took up his place next to the scarecrow, at the head of the column of skeletons, their eyeless sockets following along as the figure passed by and stopped beneath the tree.

The scarecrow presented his bow and fiddle to the hooded figure and in exchange, the hooded figure handed the scarecrow the scythe. Watching with a permanent grin stitched upon his face, the scarecrow leaned against the tall tool of the harvest as the hooded figure's bony fingers gripped the bow and pulled it across the strings with such elegance and grace.

Nodding, the scarecrow reached into his chest, rummaged about in the packed straw, and produced another bow and fiddle, tucked the instrument under his chin, and took up the tune the hooded figure was now playing. The scarecrow's body swayed to the melody while the hooded figure's bony toes tapped on the paved road. The skeletons turned with an abruptness that surprised both the black cat and owl, bowed to the giggling costumes across from each, reached out their hands, and began to dance in time with their partners to the twin fiddles.

Devils and goblins, werewolves and dragons, all danced in time with the dry bones of the dead. Slowly, the air began to grow chilly, and the leaves began to swirl and dance around the revelers.

Haunting wailing and moaning joined the fiddles as the translucent, glowing forms of ghosts and specters began to materialize and dance with one another — men and women, children and the inferred, all glowing white in the pale moonlight, joined in gleefully and silently.

The old tree began to quiver and shake more and more violently as the scarecrow and hooded figure began to play more intensely, increasing the tempo. The owl fluttered to a nearby roof, and the black cat took up residence under an awning. The pair watched in wide-eyed wonderment as the branches of the oak burst into flames, casting long, deep shadows across the yards and the houses all up and down the street. The pair of fiddle players picked up in intensity, their bows working faster and faster and all in time with one another.

Eventually, many of the skeletons broke away from the dancing and took up the tune played on the fiddles. They blew into hollowed out leg-bone flutes and fifes while others took up drums of tanned flesh slung round their necks and xylophones made up of their fellow skeletons' ribs while the bodies still danced in the street.

The scent of burning cinnamon filled the air as the fires crackled and hissed in the oak tree's branches. Soon the dancing, undulating flames began to glow a deep purple before shifting to an emerald green. The colors shifted every few moments, and with every change of the flame's colors, so too did the scents in the air. There was the scent of nightshade, then foxglove, followed very closely by the strong alluring scent of tannis root. While the smokeless flames of the oak bathed the streets in the colors of autumn, the skeletons danced, their bones clattering and rattling, and the costumes fluttered, animated by the very spirit of the night, and all while the ghosts waltzed, their spectral bodies and pale flesh rippling and shimmering in the cool night air.

The night filled with the music of the Danse and the winds carried the scents of leaves and spirits and pumpkins. The reverie carried on for some time. Things would have carried on longer, but such things as magic and seasons must all pass like the hours of the day. So, as the great clock of the town began to strike the chimes of the oncoming new day out into the haunted night, the flames in the tree vanished with a puff of oily, black smoke.

The second toll of the bell and the jack-o'-lanterns began to snuff out one by one, their faces now rotting and collapsing, withering away as pools of foul-smelling juice collected at their base. When the third toll sounded, the ghosts, resplendent in all their splendor of forgotten eras, quickly dissipated, returning to the dark and foreboding places the living dared not venture into. The fourth toll saw the skeletons turn to their hooded leader, who now lowered his bow and fiddle. In a single gasp, their jaws hung open, and then one by one, they turned from the tree and the hooded figure and ran back off into the night, returning to the graves they now called home.

The fifth toll saw the winds die down — the heaps of dead leaves and candy wrappers settled where they could and lay still, ready to be collected in the morning by a world that had moved on from thoughts of the night and all its ancient demons. The sixth toll rang out and the costumes collapsed where they stood. The owl and the cat watched from their respective roof and porch as the snake-like black fog coalesced and slithered across the ground, over the oak tree's roots, up the trunk, and back into the womb of the tree through the open and pulsing knot.

The seventh toll sent the cat rushing off into the night. Without looking back, she bounded down the street and back toward the house she called home and the children inside who would be happy to see their furry friend returned from her nightly escapades, safe and sound. The eighth toll resounded, and the owl spread her wings wide and took off into the night to search for field mice and voles.

The ninth toll echoed slowly and mournfully across the town. The hooded figure handed the fiddle and bow back to the scarecrow, who handed back the scythe before slipping the borrowed instrument back into his straw-filled body.

The tenth toll was like a hammer hitting a nail into a piece of soft, yielding wood. The scarecrow bowed once more, tipping his hat and exposing his mantle of straw before replacing the hat, tossing the other fiddle and bow over its shoulder, and skipping off down the street, the rictus grin forever sewn onto his misshapen face.

The eleventh toll was the hardest of all for the night to accept. The lone hooded figure stood before the great oak and with the tenderness of a mother stroking her belly with child, the skeletal hand beneath the black robe ran over the uneven surface of the tree.

At long last, midnight struck. Spreading its long, raven-like wings, Death turned to regard the street, the scene of the festivities not moments before now empty and of the very spirit of the season — there was no more laughter, no more music, and no more merriment. Death heaved a sigh that contained no breath and, like the owl before it, took to the air silently on crow's wings wide and dark. All that remained where the hooded figure had stood at the base of the oak were a few black feathers.

All Hallows' Eve, like all living things, had come to its natural end — the world was a little less magical, a little less scary, and a little less fantastical. The ancient ritual of the Danse Macabre had come and gone, the spirits of the thirty-first of October had joined in their celebrations and joy and returned from whence they came only to wait and wile away the hours and days and months until they could take to the night and dance their Danse and sing their haunting songs and revel in the very nature of their being.

Eventually, dawn came and with it a new day as the cycle continued on its endless journey.

Acknowledgments

First and foremost, I want to thank you, the reader, for taking a chance and picking up this collection. To say that these 13 stories were a labor of love is underselling how long and hard I worked on these pieces for you all to enjoy. An extra-special thanks to those of you who chose to read this part of the book as well; I have a sneaky suspicion that you, like me, enjoy sitting through the credits of movies to acknowledge all those hard-working, creative folks behind the scenes.

I could not have completed this collection without the constant love and support of my wife, Rachel. She may not be a fan of the horror genre overall, but her encouragement and insight helped me see this passion-project through to the end. She truly challenged me in some very necessary ways to focus on retooling some of the horror tropes and clichés in the initial drafts of these stories, ultimately shaping them into what you just finished reading. In summary, she makes me want to be a better writer through and through.

Thanks also goes to my dog Wash. Taking him on daily walks around the neighborhood and to the park. This grumbly pooch gave me ample time away from any screens to think and ponder and concoct some of these collected tales. Also, he's a very good boy and his snoring as he slept next to me while I wrote let me know that he supported me in this endeavor.

A huge thanks goes to my editors, Kerry Cullen and Sara Kelly for being a couple of the best damn editors a writer could ask for. Both of you challenged me as a writer in ways I never thought I needed to be challenged and I thank you so much for that. In addition, your keen eyes and knowledge of the written word help to add focus to these pieces and to make them the best they could possibly be.

Thanks of course goes out to my father-in-law Hugh Dunnahoe for his incredible artwork not only on the covers of this tome you hold in your hands but for all the horrifyingly lovely pieces that accompany each and every story. Hugh's talents know no bound

ACKNOWLEDGMENTS

and I am so honored and thankful to have been able to at last collaborate with him on something like this.

Thanks, must also got to my family and friends who helped to read these stories as I was in the process of putting this collection together. Chad and Timmy, I am forever in your debt when it comes to your opinions not only on some of the stories themselves but on their order in this collection. Matt, here's to making these tales come alive in new and exciting ways now and down the road.

As odd as it may seem, I cannot close this out without acknowledging and in a way, thanking the anxieties and fears I have had growing up and even now as a full-grown adult. If it wasn't for my mental struggles with my severe anxiety disorder and finding unique ways to treat and challenge it, I wouldn't have been able to pour myself into these tales the way I did. Each of these stories delves, in some small way, into the uncertainties I face on a daily basis and putting those fears of the unknown on the blank page has become one of the best therapies ever — in addition to medication and meeting with an actual therapist of course. I don't hide from my mental illness and I have no shame of it, instead I use it to help me write and now, like the keyboard and laptop producing these very words, it has become a very powerful and useful tool. In a way, I have gazed into the abyss within and found the abyss winking right back at me.

Finally, I want to thank my son, Julian. I wrote this collection in the years before he came into my life. Julian is everything to me — my whole world wrapped up in a 2T t-shirt and toddler babble. I hope you grow up less anxious than your dear pop but I also hope you enjoy some level of scary so that one day you too can read these tales and imagine your own scary stories to tell others on nights when the clouds roll in early, the rain begins to fall heavily, and the spirits come out in need of a good spooky tale.

Colin Walker
September 2024

About the Author

Colin Walker has been many things; a mascot at a popular local theme-park, a movie theater usher, and an arcade game repairman. He has also lived in Swansea Wales, a place no one except those in Swansea seem to know exists. *Forgotten Places* is his first collected work of short stories. Colin has written for short films, podcasts, and is currently plugging away on a second volume of tales from places long forgotten. He also really, really hates pickles.

About the Artist

Cover and story illustrations by Hugh Dunnahoe. Find more of Hugh's work at www.dunnahoe.com.